Acclaim for Terry Devane's
UNCOMMON JUSTICE

"Terry Devane has written a wonderful legal thriller in *Uncommon Justice*."
—Janet Evanovich

"A book for every beach blanket . . . gripping." —*Boston Herald*

"It's rare that a legal thriller captivates its readers on so many levels as does this powerful novel from newcomer Terry Devane. A page-turning suspense tale, a sly and brilliant look at the legal world in Bean Town, and a heartfelt story about a compelling, complex heroine."
—Jeffery Deaver,
author of *The Empty Chair*

"For authoritative courtroom wrangling, sinister plots, and an inspired cast of unpredictable characters, do not miss Terry Devane's *Uncommon Justice*."
—Perri O'Shaughnessy,
author of *Move to Strike*

"A bang-up courtroom revelation." —*Houston Chronicle*

"Mairead O'Clare is as sharp and intelligent as any lawyer you could hope to find. This book is a top-notch thriller. You'll be glad you met Mairead O'Clare."
—Michael Palmer,
author of *The Patient*

"*Uncommon Justice* is uncommonly good . . . The courtroom scenes are compelling. And the case isn't simple."
—The Associated Press

"Terry Devane thrills the reader with twists and turns galore and a wonderfully appealing heroine."
—Tess Gerritsen,
author of *Gravity* and *Harvest*

"Savvy, suspenseful, and fast-paced, *Uncommon Justice* is an impressive series debut."
—William Bernhardt,
author of *Murder One*

"A fast-paced legal thriller with a heroine you can root for, a good mystery, and a satisfying courtroom finale."
—Philip

"Unpredictable and entertaining

"This is an excellent legal thrill
dialogue, and irreverent humor
in a long series."

Titles by Terry Devane

UNCOMMON JUSTICE
JUROR NUMBER ELEVEN

juror number 11 eleven

terry devane

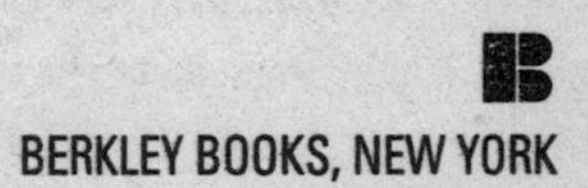
BERKLEY BOOKS, NEW YORK

This is a work of fiction. Names, characters, places, and incidents either are the product of the author's imagination or are used fictitiously, and any resemblance to actual persons, living or dead, business establishments, events, or locales is entirely coincidental.

JUROR NUMBER ELEVEN

A Berkley Book / published by arrangement with
the author

PRINTING HISTORY
G. P. Putnam's Sons hardcover edition / June 2002
Berkley mass-market edition / June 2003

Cover design by Marc Cohen.

For information address: The Berkley Publishing Group,
a division of Penguin Group (USA) Inc.,
375 Hudson Street, New York, New York 10014.

ISBN: 0-425-19066-8

BERKLEY®
Berkley Books are published by The Berkley Publishing Group,
a division of Penguin Group (USA) Inc.,
375 Hudson Street, New York, New York 10014.
BERKLEY and the "B" design
are trademarks belonging to Penguin Group (USA) Inc.

PRINTED IN THE UNITED STATES OF AMERICA

10 9 8 7 6 5 4 3 2 1

To Natalee Rosenstein,

with thanks for providing Mairead a good home

juror number **eleven**

1

Attorney Mairead O'Clare heard Judge Keith Maynard say, "Mr. Gold, your closing argument?"

At the defense table, Mairead looked up from her notepad toward the bench. Maynard was a slim African-American with stern features, reading spectacles, and a voice like James Earl Jones in the telephone company commercials.

Then Mairead felt more than saw Sheldon A. Gold rise from his chair to the right of hers. The fifty-something lawyer with short, sandy hair moved in a relaxed, shambling walk to a spot in front of the jury box not quite within touching distance of the people comprising the first row.

Into her left ear, Benjamin Friedman whispered, "Our Golden Boy, he's a natural, isn't he?"

Mairead turned toward their client. Even though he'd learned to pronounce her name properly—"Muh-*raid*"—she didn't like Friedman's quasi-intimacy. Or his obvious hair transplant, or his reputation as a gangster, for that matter. But, in addition to being on trial for first-degree murder, the man was Shel Gold's boyhood friend. So Mairead gave "Big Ben," his preferred nickname, as reassuring a smile as her nine months in the practice of law could muster.

And quite a nine months it had been: the first five spent as a lowly "drone" associate at the large, prestigious Boston firm of Jaynes & Ward, the past four as a criminal defense attorney in Shel's otherwise solo practice on Beacon Hill.

With the last being by far the best, young lady, said Sister Bernadette's voice in Mairead's head with a different kind of intimacy that she didn't mind at all.

Mairead's eyes strayed to the tall windows of old federal courtroom number 10 on the second floor of the building now leased by Suffolk County's Superior Court. A bright sun finally began taking the chill off an early May morning inside, throwing light onto the court reporter with the "gas mask" over her face, dictating into a tape recorder what each participant in the trial said. The sunlight also caused the network-affiliate television camera operator to shield the lens now focused on Shel. But if the trappings of modern technology were removed, the combination of mauve walls, fluted columns, and six brass chandeliers could have been the arena in which innocent women were tried by the Puritans for witchcraft.

When Mairead came back to the jury box, however, she noticed a woman in its second row was staring at her.

Shit, these people have been sequestered in a motel for seven days now. How can I expect them to pay attention if I don't? And, sensing that Shel was reaching the meat of his argument, Mairead again concentrated on him.

"Through testimony, you've heard the Commonwealth's version of what supposedly happened in this tragic situation." Shel now moved only a few feet parallel to the jury box in an informal version of a palace guard shifting to a new post. "My client Benjamin Friedman stands accused of murdering nine-year-old Yuri Vukonov, the only child in an immigrant Russian family. You heard the boy's father, Vadim, testify that he opened his new butcher shop in early December. A few months later, on February third, Mr. Vukonov was approached by Ben Friedman, who supposedly 'shook him down' for protection money."

Mairead wrote on her pad, *Always use "supposedly," not "allegedly," in front of a jury.*

Shel Gold shifted a little more. "Vadim Vukonov says he refused to pay, and three days later, on February sixth, his son was struck on his bicycle and killed by a 'hit-and-run' driver in the narrow, icy street behind their shop."

Mairead could hear the boy's mother begin to cry again in the gallery of cherry-wood benches. To Mairead's ear, the woman seemed almost theatrical, but the young lawyer instead watched Shel struggle with something, clearing his throat, blinking his cocker-spaniel eyes. Mairead knew, as the jury didn't, that he'd lost his own son many years before.

"A tragedy, to be sure," Shel managed. "But not one that Ben had anything to do with."

On her pad, Mairead wrote, *Personalize the client for the jury: "Benjamin Friedman" to "Ben Friedman" to...*

Shel turned and began walking slowly the other way, always parallel to the jury box. "You heard Ben's driver, Edsel Crow, testify that his boss wanted only to visit this new Russian butcher shop. You heard my client's friend, Tiffany Bomberg, testify that, while in the shop, the only discussion between Ben and Mr. Vukonov centered on cuts of meat. You heard her say that Ben was with her at his house in Brookline at the time three days later when poor Yuri was struck and killed, all of which was confirmed by Mr. Crow, who was outside the Friedman home that afternoon. You heard Ben's accountant, Dario Calcagni, testify that Ben Friedman is a man of considerable wealth, with many business enterprises that surely don't require any cash flow from a small, even struggling, butcher shop."

Mairead watched Shel pause. He'd told her that he preferred to just sketch out a closing rather than try to write and memorize a speech for the jury, and she wondered if Shel was now trying to create a dramatic effect or was just deciding what to say next.

Or perhaps, young lady, a little bit of both?

Mairead nodded her head, then noticed that the same female juror in the second row was staring at her again. Mairead reached over to Shel's side of the defense table and checked the diagram he'd made. Seat number eleven was juror "Balaguer, Conchita." The juror questionnaires had to be returned to the clerk after impaneling was completed. However, Mairead's own stapled notes from the questionnaires listed Balaguer's age as twenty-nine, her occupation as "insurance administrator," and her residence as Roslindale, a neighborhood of Boston to the southwest of downtown with a lot of modest, single-family housing. However, the information meant no more to Mairead now than it had during the voir dire process of "yes" and "no" answers conducted by Judge Maynard toward impaneling the jury, Massachusetts courts generally *not* allowing attorney-conducted voir dires, even in capital cases.

Then Mairead looked down at her own hands, the purple birthmark of hemangioma covering both and extending, under the sleeves of her blouse and blazer, up past her elbows. During her twenty-six years, she'd certainly had her share of people stare at the port-wine stain, but Mairead also had conducted the examination of several witnesses during this trial, so maybe that was why juror Balaguer was—

Shel broke the silence in the courtroom. "I respect tremendously the attention and sympathy you all obviously displayed toward the true victims in this case. Vadim Vukonov and his wife, Tanya Vukonova, have been through the kind of hell no one should have to suffer. But the prosecution hasn't shown any connection between Ben Friedman and the car that struck and killed poor Yuri. Not a single witness can identify the driver of that never-found vehicle. Not a shred of evidence links my client in any way to a 'murder,' especially since the 'incident' here could have been an 'accident.' There's not even a believable motive why my client would have approached Mr. Vukonov to 'shake him down' in the first place."

Mairead said a silent prayer of thanks that Judge Maynard had ruled inadmissible before trial any mention of Friedman's criminal enterprises—which fortunately had never included extortion. Then she saw Shel turn to the first row of the gallery behind the district attorney's table. "And compounding the tragedy here by convicting an innocent man will in no way bring back the son these poor people lost."

Another pause, and Mairead thought of the cliché, "You could hear a pin drop."

Then Shel Gold looked up to the bench. "Thank you, Your Honor."

walking back to the defense table, Sheldon A. Gold saw his old friend—the poster boy for "Tough Jew"—looking a little more smug than advanced the appearance of innocence before a jury. But the man's attitude did unravel a knot in the pit of Shel's stomach.

Admit it: If Big Ben had really commissioned the crime, he'd be more intent on acting as though he hadn't.

Only his client's demeanor wasn't what occupied Shel the most as he sank down beside Mairead O'Clare. Struck—every time, to tell the truth—by the way her auburn hair framed a freckled face and blue, laserlike eyes, he leaned toward her with, "Why was juror number eleven staring at you?"

Mairead used opposing index fingers to tap each birthmarked hand, then shrugged.

Shel felt a different knot tighten deep inside as Judge Maynard spoke again. "Mr. Seagraves, your argument now?"

"Thank you, Your Honor."

Shel watched James Seagraves—early forties, brown hair, solid jaw—uncurl out of his chair with the body precision of a disciplined gymnast. An assistant district attorney in Boston's Suffolk County for more than a decade, Seagraves had resisted the siren song of the large firms who'd love to have someone of his experience—not to mention rugged good looks and bearing—for their white-collar defense practices. Shel had heard the "bearing" part came from Seagraves' serving as a navy officer before the Gulf War. While never having been drafted during Vietnam, Shel found himself thinking that, if he'd had to receive orders from someone, he could do a lot worse than Jim Seagraves.

Problem was, jurors tended to agree with that assessment. And to convict accordingly.

Since the rules of court permitted the Commonwealth to close last in a criminal case, Shel couldn't do much now beyond listening closely, to monitor whether his opponent argued facts not in evidence or committed some other breach requiring an objection to the judge. But Shel also knew that Seagraves hadn't gotten as far as he had by making those kinds of errors very often.

"Mr. Gold just told you that convicting an 'innocent' man would do nothing to reverse the tragedy inflicted upon the parents of Yuri Vukonov."

Shel heard the crying from the front row of the gallery grow louder, several jurors turning that way. Mrs. Tanya Vukonova, a short, stolid woman with listless brown hair, had shown up every day, gripping her barrel-chested, bear-like husband's arm as though it were a lifeline. Her eyes seemed red enough to have been sprayed by ammonia outside the courthouse.

With which Shel could empathize, from a similar time in his own life.

Seagraves now wheeled on Big Ben Friedman. "But Mr. Gold's argument assumes that the defendant is innocent, while the evidence shows otherwise."

Shel thought he sensed Mairead's breathing quicken beside him. But when Shel looked up at juror number eleven, the woman—"Conchita Balaguer" according to his diagram—was staring at Seagraves this time.

Well, the man *is* like a movie star. Only when Shel turned to mention this to Mairead, he noticed she was staring at Seagraves as much as Balaguer had been. Shel felt a little twinge then that had nothing to do with any knot in his stomach, and he decided to listen instead to an impressive, if pretty predictable, litany of facts gleaned from different prosecution witnesses.

Seagraves hit the assistant medical examiner's testimony ("...face and skull crushed, teeth shattered, bicycle kickstand driven through the groin and..."), holding up crime-scene and autopsy photos of the brown-haired, too-young corpse like an elementary school teacher would flash cards. Then the crime-lab technician's analysis ("...and the paint flecks embedded in the decedent's flesh and clothing are consistent with a late-model Pontiac, color turquoise"). Finally, Tanya Vukonova's matching description of the vehicle ("Around the corner like a missile it comes at my Yuri, and I scream as he looks at me for the last time, this child I bore in Russia and swore would grow up free in America").

Now more of a low moan from the gallery, some words in Russian spoken by a male voice nearby.

Shel watched Seagraves stop a moment. Shel could have scripted Big Ben's reaction, which was why he'd had Mairead sit between them. So Shel *wouldn't* have to hear, "Sanctimonious bastard's laying it on pretty thick, Golden Boy."

Seagraves fixed the jury. "And why did this child, whom we *know* to be innocent, have to die?"

The prosecutor then ticked off for the jury what Shel himself had hoped to defuse by mentioning: the visit to the butcher shop and the claimed attempt at extortion, the adamant refusal and the short time lag to the killing.

Now Seagraves wheeled toward the section of the gallery behind the defense table. "And who does the defendant call as witnesses in his own behalf? His 'chauffeur,' Edsel Crow, who on cross-examination admitted he was more bodyguard than driver, and a soldier who, during the Persian Gulf War, was credited with over twenty 'confirmed kills' as a sniper. Tiffany Bomberg, who on cross-examination admitted she and the defendant had been intimate for over a year and who receives no financial support beyond what the defendant shares with her. And Dario Calcagni, who on cross-examination admitted that even as an accountant he didn't know where many of the 'receipts' the defendant gave him to deposit and manage actually came from."

Shel half-smiled and shook his head slightly. It was the only thing to do when the opponent shot an arrow through your heart. But while masking for the jury, Shel also noticed that juror number eleven, the Balaguer woman, was staring again at Mairead, and then he saw Seagraves noticing it, too, and frowning.

The silver lining: Whatever's going on, at least it's distracting a decider of Big Ben's fate—and even the prosecutor himself—from the Commonwealth's closing argument.

Then Seagraves seemed to regain his concentration and turned to his own side of the gallery. "There is innocence involved in this case, all right. The innocence of youth, of a nine-year-old boy, riding his bicycle in apparent 'safety' behind the shop his parents operated in their adopted country, a land of freedom and opportunity. Only to have their son die before his time beneath the wheels of an American car." Seagraves now turned back to the jury as he walked toward his chair, aiming, Shel thought, at juror number eleven. "To have the light of life seep from Yuri's broken body, as his mother cradled him in her arms. On a cold, wintry street, and for the last time."

Assistant District Attorney James Seagraves looked up at the bench. "Your Honor, I'm . . . finished."

As Shel Gold silently complimented the prosecutor's deft pause, the defense attorney heard Benjamin Friedman mutter, "And I'm . . . fucked."

pontifico Murizzi stood from his seat on a gallery bench as the judge, having instructed the jury and designated which twelve of the fourteen would decide the case, left the courtroom. When Maynard's clerk came down the aisle, she said to him, "Pope, I hope you don't work for scum like Friedman very often."

Murizzi didn't answer her. He wasn't insulted by the

play on his first name—truth be told, he kind of preferred it to his real one. But he didn't like the clerk's innuendo. Ever since "retiring early" from the Boston Homicide Unit, the Pope had worked for criminal defense lawyers like Shel Gold, but only when the former detective cum private investigator believed the accused to be innocent.

And while Big Ben Friedman might be a racketeer, Murizzi couldn't see him taking out the little Russian kid. Not with a car, and for sure not when he had that walking ghost Edsel Crow on his payroll.

The Pope watched the "chauffeur" move to the rail of the bar enclosure, probably waiting for his boss to tell him what to do. About six feet tall and maybe one-eighty, Crow wasn't all that impressive physically. But the prosecutor had hit the nail on the head about the sniper stuff, even if the bodyguard's high cheekbones, craggy brow, and coppery skin made you expect to see him using a bow and arrow instead of a scoped rifle. Get close enough, though, and Crow's eyes had the hollow fucking look of a stone-killer, the man seeing other human beings as just targets to be zeroed.

Friedman must have said something to Crow, because the bodyguard came down the aisle, pausing only to say, "Mr. Murizzi, Mr. Friedman would like you to join him for lunch."

The Pope held those button eyes with his own stare. "Tell Big Ben that I think it's one thing to help an innocent defendant, and another to break bread with a fucking mobster."

Edsel Crow didn't say anything, didn't even nod. He just swung his face toward the rear of the courtroom and kept walking, probably to scare the shit out of all the reporters clustered beyond the doors.

look *at it this way, young lady: At least the man has excellent taste in restaurants.*

Mairead O'Clare found herself agreeing with Sister Bernadette's comment, the way Mairead usually had back when she was growing up in the order's orphanage, and the gentle nun was the closest thing to a surrogate mother the little girl with the strangely marked arms ever knew.

They were in Locke-Ober's, an old and very fancy restaurant in downtown Boston. Instead of seating their party in the loud and clattery first floor, the maître d' led them up a narrow staircase to a private room. Big Ben Friedman took the head of the table, which didn't surprise Mairead. Tiffany Bomberg—blonde, lithe, and mid-twenties, dressed like a suburban wife in town for a shopping spree—sat to his left and Shel Gold to his right, with Mairead next to her boss and Dario Calcagni across from her. The poor accountant, doughy and balding in an otherwise nice suit and tie, fidgeted constantly, using his napkin to wipe beads of sweat from the creases in his forehead.

Guy must go through a case of deodorant every month, though, because he always smells like a cachet of potpourri.

Before releasing the maître d', Friedman reeled off three different wine choices. Once the door was closed, Shel said, "Mr. Crow going to join us?"

Friedman seemed shocked. "Golden Boy, you think I'm gonna leave a Bentley alone in a downtown garage? What, you got rocks in your head?"

Mairead wondered who their client thought had been watching the car during closing arguments. She also noticed Tiffany smiling like an automaton, maybe as a practiced defensive reaction to just such remarks.

Then Friedman patted the blond woman's hand. "Bad enough the fucking 'conditions of bail' made me lose all these snowbirding weeks with Tiff down in Boca. I mean, I'm a Jew gangster successful enough to have a Wop accountant instead of the other way around, and this trial's fucking up my business *and* my life."

Mairead noticed Calcagni cower a bit at the ethnic slur, but then Friedman changed his tone. "Golden Boy, I wasn't nuts about that DA's closing there."

Shel said, "Jim Seagraves spins a nice web of evidence."

"Yeah, well, maybe you and your Wild Irish Rose here should spend a little less of my time and money admiring his technique, and a little more tearing his fucking heart out."

Remember, young lady: It will certainly be a fine meal.

"Ben," said Shel, "the Commonwealth's whole case is circumstantial, and it depends on the jury believing outright the Vukonovs' version of what you said in their shop that afternoon."

"It isn't a fucking 'version'! Tiff, you were there. You told it straight, right?"

"Absolutely, Ben," said Bomberg, still in automaton mode.

"So, Golden Boy, the jury's gonna take the word of two immigrants just off the boat, who stand to hit the jackpot if I'm found guilty on the criminal charge and their shark of a lawyer brings a wrongful-death suit?"

As a waiter came into the room with three bottles of wine and three glasses, Mairead pictured the Vukonov family's lawyer, a Russian immigrant herself named Gallina Ekarevskaya, hovering around them in the gallery during trial. Whenever Mairead stole a look that way, Ekarevskaya was eyeing Big Ben Friedman like he was the Christmas goose.

The waiter uncorked each wine and poured small samples in respective glasses for Friedman to approve. Then menus were passed out and specials of the day recited.

I'd choose the duck l'orange, young lady. With a glass—or two—of that Pinot Noir.

"Ben," said Shel once the waiter had left the room, "as I explained to you before, the parents could still sue you civilly even if we *win* this criminal case, because they wouldn't be bound by the prosecution's loss."

Mairead was a little surprised that Shel would give client advice with Bomberg and Calcagni present, but figured what he'd said so far was pretty basic law.

"Calculator, will you listen to this guy?"

Mairead saw Calcagni cower at the nickname, too, but he replied, "I'm listening to him, Ben."

"I mean, Golden Boy, you and me go back to the dawn of time together, but I'll be goddamned before I'll see money I sweated blood to get go into the pockets of foreigners I never—my hand to God!—even touched."

Mairead always thought of that "my hand" expression being more an Irish-Catholic saying, but over the course of the case Friedman had often borrowed idioms from other demographic groups.

Now the man turned to his accountant again. "Calculator, you know I've never been into extortion. It's too messy. Christ, you've got to go after the marks, then you've got to apply the pressure, then you've got to break a kneecap or some ribs, be sure they get the message. That's a fuck of a lot of work for a few bucks a week."

Calcagni nodded, looking, Mairead thought, a little more toward Bomberg than Friedman as the gangster turned back to Shel. "I mean, it's not like I didn't feel for these Russkies. When I read in the paper about their kid getting squashed there, I remember saying to Tiff, 'Hey, what a fucking shame,' though I'd never have let any son of mine ride his fucking bike in a back street where some asshole—probably drunk or cracked out of his head—could smack him when his bitch of a mother should have been keeping her eye—"

At which point, Mairead's cellular phone mercifully began vibrating in her handbag. Hoping it wasn't a friend calling, she drew the Nokia out, even Big Ben Friedman stopping his tirade.

"Hello?" she said.

"Ms. O'Clare?"

"Yes?"

"Dan Corcoran, calling from Judge Maynard's lobby."

Mairead pictured the sturdy court officer, standing in what most other jurisdictions would call "chambers." "I'll let you speak with Mr. Gold."

"No need. Just tell him your jury's coming in."

Mairead glanced at her watch. "They have a question for—"

"Uh-uh. They have a verdict."

Well, said Sister Bernadette's voice, *so much for the fine lunch.*

admit it: the part that's always the hardest.

Shel Gold couldn't remember being present for a single return of verdict without butter churning in his stomach. Oh, he knew it wasn't butter, but butter*flies,* and more of them when a capital case was involved, even if Massachusetts hadn't reinstituted the death penalty for Murder One. That didn't make it easier for him, though, especially since Shel believed that a sentence of life to contemplate what you'd done was far higher punishment than simply—almost kindly—being put out of your misery.

The kind of misery he'd borne over the twenty years since his wife, Natalie, and his son, Richie, had been outside that—

"Courrrrrt!" from bailiff Dan Corcoran.

Everyone stood as the Honorable Keith Maynard ascended the bench and a quartet of other court officers positioned themselves immediately behind the defense table. Partly to restrain Ben, Shel knew, should the verdict go against him, but also to control the crowd, if the verdict went the other way.

As the jurors filed into the box, Shel watched them, more to gauge how they'd come through the relatively quick deliberation and less to guess their decision, which he'd never found a good way of predicting.

Shel did notice one thing, though: That Balaguer woman, juror number eleven, was staring their way again, smiling and almost nodding at Mairead. He stole a quick glance at Big Ben, but the man had his head down, eyes closed, almost in a prayer stance, like when they were little kids and their mothers bobby-pinned yarmulkes in—

"You may be seated," said Judge Maynard's clerk to the

lawyers and spectators. Then she addressed the box. "Ladies and gentlemen of the jury, have you reached a verdict?"

The foreman, a tall and gangly man, stood and extended a piece of white paper. "We have."

Shel watched Dan Corcoran take the verdict slip from the foreman's hand and carry it to the clerk, who gave it directly to the judge. Maynard looked at the slip, poker-faced, then returned it to his clerk.

To vent his nerves, Shel mentally chanted the clerk's next question along with her. "What say you to the indictment charging the defendant with murder in the first degree? Is he guilty or not guilty?"

The foreman's words were, "*Not* guilty."

Shel heard his client whoop and felt the butterflies in his stomach take wing. But even the judge's stern gaze and gavel couldn't squelch what happened next. Shel caught James Seagraves half-turning toward the defense table, glaring at Shel with a disgusted expression on his face before a guttural roar erupted from the gallery. Shel half-turned himself to see Vadim Vukonov vault over the bar enclosure and crash two pretty burly court officers into Mairead as the enraged father clawed his way toward their client.

Shel grabbed one of Vukonov's arms, and—God bless—Mairead clamped on the other, which slowed the man, now bellowing in Russian, just enough for all four court officers to take over and subdue him by holding him down against the table. Papers and writing implements were scattered before Gallina Ekarevskaya, her lawyer voice using Russian and cutting through the pandemonium, calmed Vukonov enough that the officers let him back up. Even then, the man grabbed a sheaf of papers and threw them back past his wife and into the aisle. The court officers escorted Vadim Vukonov toward the doors, the father now just blubbering and kicking the sheaf of papers like a mutilated soccer ball toward the corridor.

"Christ, Golden Boy," said Big Ben Friedman. "I wonder what that asshole would have tried if I'd really *done* it?"

As the clerk somewhat belatedly polled the jury, though, all Sheldon A. Gold could think about was whether Big Ben Friedman's assurance referred only to the killing of the little Vukonov boy and not some influencing of juror Conchita Balaguer.

four hours later, Mairead O'Clare took her fourth aspirin and tried to concentrate on the file in front of her. Big Ben Friedman had insisted they all go back to Locke-Ober's and finish what they'd started, this time as a celebration and including "chauffeur" Edsel Crow ("Fuck the Bentley, Golden Boy: I can always buy another one"). As the lunch evolved into a banquet, Mairead thought it would be insulting to decline the wine that Friedman insisted on circling the table to pour, only Crow not taking any. But, as a result, by the time Mairead and Shel got back to their office suite in the old building on the crest of Beacon Hill, she could barely hold her head up. Only thing was, Mairead had another trial in a larceny case in the Boston Municipal Court the following day. So she had accepted a batch of pink phone messages from Billie Sunday, their secretary/receptionist in the hexagonal foyer off which the law offices radiated like leaves on a clover, and stayed at her own desk to work.

Mairead was about halfway through preparing her cross-examination of the arresting officers when Billie stuck her head in the young lawyer's doorway, the honey-colored dreadlocks—and matching, wide-spaced eyes—contrasting with the darker features they framed.

"Shel's long gone, and I'm leaving. You plan on staying the night, child?"

"A little while longer, Billie. So I don't have to get up too early tomorrow."

The middle-aged mother of three began shrugging into

her raincoat. "Next time, maybe you'll remember what I told you about celebrating with clients."

"I didn't see that it was my decision to make."

"And Shel's Mr. Friedman might be an exception, anyway. But take it as a lesson learned."

"Yes, Mom."

Which got half a smile before the office phone rang behind Billie, and she crossed the reception area to answer it.

Mairead heard only disjointed syllables.

The head reappeared. "Woman for you. Says she's a 'prospective client,' but didn't want to give me her name."

Mairead looked down at the file, then back up at Billie. "I'll take it, but you can go home."

Billie Sunday huffed out a laugh this time, then mimicked her with, "Thanks, Mom."

Mairead's phone rang once as she heard the office suite's door close. "Mairead O'Clare."

"Do you know who this is?" a measured voice, slight accent of some kind, but not the Russian one she'd been hearing for the past week at the courthouse.

"Look," replied Mairead, "whoever you are, it's a little late in a long day to be playing games."

"My name's Conchita Balaguer. Register now?"

Mairead sat up straight in her chair, immediately going into "professional responsibility" mode. She knew that, as a matter of ethics, an attorney could be disciplined—suspended, maybe even disbarred—for contacting a juror in a case. Mairead didn't know if the same rules applied when the juror was the one making the initial—

"Hello?" in a "duh" tone.

"I'm still here, Ms. Balaguer."

"Good. I'd like to talk with you on a legal matter."

"Now?"

"It's pretty urgent."

Think, think. "Does it have anything to do with the trial?"

"Only kind of. I was impressed by how you handled

yourself questioning the witnesses, and I thought maybe you could help me, too."

Don't let it slide, young lady. "But does your matter have anything to do with Mr. Friedman's case?"

"No, it doesn't."

Okay? "Well, I have another trial in the morning, but you could come in afterward?"

"No way. I'm sorry, but my bosses are already pretty mad at me for being out so long for jury duty. They'd never go for another day—or even afternoon—off so soon. And I want your advice tonight, anyway. How about you come here, to my house in Rozzie?"

The nickname for Roslindale, but Mairead had already remembered that from her notes on the woman's juror questionnaire. "Can you tell me what's so urgent about this?"

"Not over the phone, but there's a lot of money involved."

Mairead turned it around in her mind. On the one hand, seeing a juror from a case you just finished seemed iffy. On the other hand, the trial didn't result in a conviction, so it's not like there would be an appeal to perfect—and to protect from the appearance of impropriety.

Also, young lady, this would be the first client you brought in all on your own because of your performance in a courtroom, and you still have bills to pay without any substantial paychecks from Jaynes & Ward being direct-deposited into—

Another duh "hello" from the other end of the line.

Mairead said, "I'd need to take a taxi."

"That's fine. Why don't we say seven-thirty? Here's the address, and the nearest cross street."

As Mairead O'Clare wrote down the directions, she felt a genuine tingle of pride.

Look at me: a rainmaker.

* * *

shel Gold sat on a stool at the Kinsale Pub in Center Plaza. The delayed Locke-Ober's lunch had featured great food, but he'd exceeded the amount of wine he allowed himself, against doctor's orders, as kind of a reward for religiously taking his Zoloft, an impotence-inducing antidepressant that proved necessary after Shel lost both Richie and Natalie. However, Shel also liked to unwind after a trial in the anonymous noise a bar provides, so he sipped his club soda with a twist of lime, and figured to leave the bartender a silly-generous tip to compensate for the space Shel was taking up as the pub got busier.

Then a hand lit on his right shoulder for just a heartbeat as Gallina Ekarevskaya took the stool to that side.

She said, "A Jewish lawyer and a Russian one in an Irish pub. There should be a bad joke from that, don't you think?"

What Shel thought was that Ekarevskaya should spend her time in front of movie cameras, not court benches. He guessed her to be about thirty-five and five-six, with slim, shapely legs. Ekarevskaya's black hair was worn long, nearly to her waist, the eyes violet in color but tipping up a little at the corners, making her seem just a bit exotic.

And, admit it: a bit like Natalie as well.

"You come looking for me, Gallina?"

A laugh as she ordered a pint of Boddington's ale from the bartender. "Do you often flatter yourself so, Sheldon?"

When he'd gotten word that Ekarevskaya had taken on the Vukonovs toward a civil case against Ben Friedman, Shel had done the usual checking on a lawyer he didn't know. The words "sharp," "tough," and "beautiful" had come back, though their sequencing tended to change depending on whether Shel had asked a male or female lawyer.

"Sheldon?"

"Sorry. I was just wondering how you found me, since I didn't leave word at my office."

"I could say, 'We have our ways,'" a sidelong glance as

her ale arrived with a creamy head on it, "but the truth is that I have developed a fondness for Irish pubs, and this is the closest to my own office. And, I suppose, to yours."

Ekarevskaya clinked her pint glass against Shel's smaller one. "To an impressive victory for you today."

"Your client didn't seem quite as pleased."

"Can you blame the man?" She drew deeply on the ale, the head leaving a little milk mustache, which she must have known it would, because she used her tongue to clean her upper lip like a cat licking its chops. "Vadim has lost his son, and he believed the trial was corrupted, as it could easily have been in our home country these last ten years."

Expecting he knew the answer, Shel decided to ask anyway. "Why does he think it was 'corrupted'?"

Ekarevskaya gave another sidelong glance. "A blind person could have seen the way that juror number eleven stared—and even smiled—at your client."

Shel didn't see any advantage in correcting her about Mairead seeming, from his angle, to be the object of Conchita Balaguer's attentions. "Jurors are just people. They do funny things."

"Funny?" Ekarevskaya shook her head. "Before I came to this country, I read the books and speeches by your 'Founding Fathers.' They were 'just people,' too, but they seemed to believe in doing things 'justly.' And, I must say to you, until this trial, I do not believe I or one of my clients has been the victim of corruption in your court system."

"I wouldn't tamper with a juror, Gallina."

Now a full-bore look, the violet eyes jumping a little, though the emotion—anger, maybe disgust?—didn't appear in the voice. "Sheldon, I made inquiries about you, as I am certain you would have about me. Given who you represent, I was surprised to hear characterizations like 'honest' and 'fair' used to describe you. But I tell you this: I believe ADA Seagraves thinks as I do, and I would expect him to do something about it."

"As could you, by simply filing a wrongful-death suit."

"Which I shall do, Sheldon. In my own time."

Meaning, you expected a criminal conviction today, and you would have ridden that horse by filing civilly tomorrow, seeking attachments of real estate, trustee process against bank accounts, probably even a restraining order against Ben selling his Bentley.

Then Ekarevskaya laid a ten-dollar bill on the bar, causing Shel to realize that her Boddington's ale was nearly gone.

Ekarevskaya stood up, the dress clinging a little to her thighs before she shook it down gracefully, almost . . . sensually. "I will buy you this drink, Sheldon, which from the size of glass I can tell is only a soda one. But the next time you speak to your client, ask him if you can accept service of process on my eventual civil action. And perhaps, in the near future, you will be buying me a drink, yes?"

Gallina Ekarevskaya turned and strode toward the door, Shel and half a dozen other male patrons in his line of vision watching her exit with due admiration.

mairead O'Clare said, "I think that was the cross street she mentioned."

The cabbie twisted his head around to speak through the small opening in the Plexiglas shield dividing him from Mairead. "Hey, girlie, I been driving these neighborhoods since before you were puking up Gerber baby food. Now, you got some immigrant behind the wheel, I can see where you'd be worried. But you don't, so just sit back and enjoy the ride, huh?"

And enjoy your tip, too. But Mairead noticed they'd turned onto the road in Roslindale that Balaguer had mentioned as her own. A moment later, the driver slewed to the curb before a small ranch house, a light on over the front door.

"Fourteen fifty-five."

Mairead looked down at her note. "I said the address was seven-twenty."

"Girlie, I'm talking the fare on the meter."

Mairead dipped into her handbag. "Here's fifteen dollars. Please wait for me till I'm sure she's home."

"Oh, gimme a break, huh? Why didn't you just call her on your cellular before this?"

Good question, and an even better suggestion, but Mairead suddenly realized that in her weariness after Ben Friedman's "celebration," she'd forgotten to ask Balaguer for her telephone number.

Mairead said, "Just wait two minutes, okay? I'll come back out and settle with you then."

"Well, make it quick, all right? We're talking Stanley Cup second round from Denver tonight on the cable."

An ice-hockey player herself through high school and college, Mairead actually could empathize with the driver on that, but instead she got out of his cab and walked up the path to the front door, hearing salsa music blaring inside. Tempted to just wave the taxi off and leave the rude man with his forty-five-cent tip, Mairead nevertheless pushed the bell button. Hearing nothing but the same music, she first knocked, then pounded on the wood. Still no response.

Mairead decided to try the handle. Unlocked. The salsa beat louder now as she swung the door open.

It's possible Ms. Balaguer couldn't hear you over her stereo.

Mairead stepped into a tiny entry hall, calling out "Hello?" twice and "Ms. Balaguer?" once. There was a small, neat living room to the right, but the salsa seemed to be coming from the back of the house, so Mairead gravitated toward the sound.

Around a corner was a large room, probably an addition, because it sported a cathedral ceiling with exposed beams. The only problem was that Conchita Balaguer was hanging from one of them, the rope constricting her neck causing her eyes to bug out and her tongue to swell grotesquely from the blue-cast features on the rest of her face.

Mairead closed her own eyes, then shook her head to

clear it of the dizziness she felt. Fighting a gag reflex from the sewer smell in the air, she walked as steadily as she could manage back to the front door and outside, waving wildly at the cabdriver.

Who, giving her the finger over the roof of his taxi, left rubber peeling away from the curb, Mairead O'Clare sprinting down the street, screaming for him to stop.

2

Mairead sat in the backseat of a Boston Police cruiser blocking the driveway to Conchita Balaguer's house. The shorter of the two uniformed officers who arrived after Mairead's 911 call approached and opened the car door.

He said, "Homicide's here to talk with you."

She nodded and stepped out of the cruiser. While waiting, Mairead had watched the rubber-necking neighbors mill around on the opposite sidewalk, held back by the taller uniformed officer. She'd also tried both Shel Gold and Pontifico Murizzi on her cell phone, but got only tape machine announcements on each, and neither had gotten back to her.

Well, young lady, I guess you're on your own.

Nothing new there, thought the birthmarked young woman whose parents had abandoned their infant girl at the orphanage because of her "stigmata."

When the officer led Mairead back through the front door of the house, hushed voices and mechanical sounds were coming down the short hall from the "play room" where she'd found Balaguer's body. And in the living room, a woman wearing blue jeans and a black leather jacket sat on the couch. She held a journalist's notepad, but Mairead didn't think she looked like a reporter. The woman had brown, frosted hair layer-cut to curl at the shoulder and full cheeks, but haunting, almost colorless eyes. Standing up and rolling her shoulders under the jacket, she gave the impression of a wolf masquerading as a chipmunk.

"Ms. O'Clare?"

"Yes?"

"Marjorie Tully, though I prefer 'J-O-R-I-E' for short. I'm a detective on the Homicide Unit. I think you already know ADA Seagraves?"

Mairead jumped a little as the prosecutor entered the room. He was dressed in corduroy slacks and a beige J.Press sweater with two red horizontal stripes that Mairead had thought about buying for herself until she saw the price tag. The sweater broadened his shoulders, and when he smiled, the cleft in his chin seemed to wink vertically at her.

Steady, young lady. This isn't a cocktail party.

Mairead nodded at Sister Bernadette's comment, but said, "Mr. Seagraves."

"Jim, please. If I can use 'Mairead'?"

Uh-oh, both "Jorie" and "Jim." I must be in truly deep weeds.

Tully sat back down, patting the couch cushion next to her. Seagraves waited until Mairead took the hint, then pulled over a large easy chair like it was a light folding one. While his strength came as no surprise, his and Tully's positioning made Mairead feel hemmed into a corner.

The impression they want to create, young lady. Don't let it rattle you.

Mairead said, "I've never been interviewed like this before."

Seagraves reached over, closing his hand briefly on Mairead's wrist. "Nothing to worry about."

When he released his grip, Mairead realized it had felt less like a reassurance and more like a handcuff, which somehow calmed her. This was the real thing, and Seagraves was trying to use his attractiveness to lull her into cooperating.

But why?

Tully said, "I'm Irish through and through, but I'd have

to say you're the first 'Mairead' I've ever met. Named after a grandmother?"

Mairead turned. The detective, too, trying to play some "Old Girls' Club" card, make me feel part of the group. "I don't know, Jorie. I was raised in an orphanage."

Tully glanced at Seagraves, who said, "The officer responding told us you found the body of Ms. Balaguer?"

Mairead turned back to the prosecutor. "That's right."

"Did you touch anything in this house?"

"No. Well, the front door. I saw her . . . I saw her hanging there, and I could see she was dead, so I came right back out again and ran down the street to hold the taxi that brought me here."

"And then you dialed nine-one-one from your cellular?"

"Right."

"Smart, Mairead," said Seagraves. "By using a landline in here, you might have disturbed potential evidence."

Mairead nodded, though in fact she'd never even thought of that.

Tully now. "Between the time you called the emergency number, and the time the uniformed officers responded to the scene, did anyone else come into the house?"

"No."

"So, there couldn't have been anyone else here then?"

Mairead felt a shiver ripple through her. Given how dead Conchita Balaguer had looked, it hadn't occurred to Mairead that anybody else—like a killer—would still have been in the house.

Tully said, "Maircad?"

Mairead looked into the wolf eyes. "I didn't see or hear anybody, but I wasn't in here that long, and I sure didn't search the place."

Tully glanced at Seagraves again, but kept talking herself. "Can you tell us how you happened to be here?"

Mairead went through the telephone conversation at her office, the taxi ride, and coming into the house.

"You didn't think to get Ms. Balaguer's number from her when she called you earlier?"

"Right."

"Is that your usual practice?"

"She was the first client who was coming to me as . . . as a 'rainmaker,' you know? I just didn't think to ask for it."

Tully nodded. "There a reason you didn't call *four*-one-one, ask Directory Assistance instead?"

Mairead couldn't sense where this was going. "By the time I realized I didn't have Ms. Balaguer's number, the cab was almost to her house."

Tully glanced at Seagraves a third time as Mairead continued with, "I didn't see the point, since I'd be knocking on her door in a minute anyway."

The prosecutor said, "But if the appointment had been arranged at Ms. Balaguer's request, why did you ask the cabdriver to wait for you?"

"Because I'd never met the woman before, and I wanted to make sure she was here before he took off and left me stranded."

"But you could have been 'sure' by simply calling Directory Assistance and trying to reach her from your cellular," said Seagraves, not as a question.

"We checked," from Tully now. "Ms. Balaguer was listed: full name, address, and telephone."

"Look," Mairead feeling an edge creep into her voice, "what difference does any of this make? I walked in here and found the body. It wasn't real pleasant, but why don't you ask me about that?"

"Ms. O'Clare," Tully's voice also growing an edge to it as she shifted back to a "last-name" basis, "don't you find it a bit strange that a juror sitting on a criminal case you were trying contacts you out of the blue the day the verdict comes back in your client's favor?"

"She said—" Mairead ratcheted her tone down a notch and started over. "Ms. Balaguer wanted to see me about some other matter. She said she was 'impressed' by the way I'd handled myself during the Friedman trial."

"Which is understandable," from Seagraves, in a voice

like velvet. "You were extraordinary, Mairead, especially for someone just past the bar."

Young lady?

I know: good cop, bad cop. Or hard cop, seductive ADA. "Mr. Seagraves, I—"

"It's Jim, remember?"

Mairead drew in a breath, then let it out, just like she would before an important face-off in a hockey game. "Jim, I left a large law firm and took a two-thirds cut in salary to go with Sheldon Gold. I have bills to pay, and I thought Ms. Balaguer might be a potential client."

"Who could help pay those bills."

"Yes. She said over the phone that 'a lot of money' was involved."

Tully spoke now, and when Mairead turned to her, the detective was holding up a slip of paper in a plastic bag. "This, maybe?"

Mairead couldn't make out much through the plastic. "What is it?"

"A deposit slip. For almost ten thousand dollars. According to the time stamp on it, Ms. Balaguer put that amount in her checking account this afternoon, within two hours of the not-guilty verdict in your case."

Jesus Mary. They're thinking I *bribed* the woman? "I don't know anything about what she did or why."

Seagraves now changed his tone as well. To the cross-examination one. "Ms. O'Clare, Ms. Balaguer kept staring at you in that courtroom during closing arguments. I saw it, you saw it, anybody paying attention would have seen it."

Mairead didn't reply.

Seagraves said, "If somebody on Benjamin Friedman's side of the case got to a juror through you, I'll have your hide cut, dried, and stretched on my office wall."

One of the many good things about playing hockey: It teaches you how to deal with intimidation. "You done with my taxi driver?"

"What?" said Tully.

"I want to know if you're finished interrogating my cabbie, because if you're not going to ask me questions that could help you figure out what happened here, I'm leaving."

"You'll leave when—"

"I drive her out of here."

Mairead joined Seagraves and Tully in looking up at Pontifico Murizzi, standing in the doorway, arms crossed, hip shot, just like Richard Gere, the actor Mairead had thought of the first time she met the man.

"Pope," said Tully with a warmer tone in her voice, "you able to just walk through walls now?"

Mairead watched Murizzi grin and drift into the living room like it was his own home. "Some of the uniforms remember me, Jore. What've you got?"

Seagraves said, "None of your business anymore."

Despite the circumstances, Mairead thought, this should be an interesting pissing contest.

The Pope grinned a little wider. "Ms. O'Clare here called me, left a message on my tape about a juror from her case being dead from hanging. Mind if I take a look?"

Seagraves was about to say something when Tully stood and said, "Can't hurt, huh?"

As the detective led Murizzi into the other room, Mairead felt Seagraves lean farther into her space and grip her wrist again. "Mairead, you've got one chance here, both to hold on to your law license *and* avoid jail yourself."

Noting the switch back to "first-name" basis, but resisting the instinct to break his grip, she said, "Jim, you ever read *Commonwealth versus Croken?*"

"Croken?"

"The criminal case where because a defense attorney and a prosecutor were having a 'romantic relationship,' a conviction by another prosecutor in the same office got thrown out?"

Seagraves appeared thrown himself. "Of course I remember it. So what?"

"Well, anybody watching you looming over me and

playing touchy-feely on my wrist might think you were hitting on this defense attorney toward a similar understanding."

Seagraves let go as though slapped. "How dare you even suggest—"

"I think you guys got a problem, here."

Mairead and Seagraves both looked up at Murizzi, returning to the living room. Mairead figured the prosecutor was thinking the same thing she was: How much of our exchange did the Pope overhear?

But all Murizzi did was take the last empty seat in the room as Tully went back to the couch.

When everybody was settled, the Pope hiked a thumb toward the rear of the house. "Techies tell me there's no sign of forced entry, and the front door was unlocked when Ms. O'Clare got here. Only thing is, there's also no 'Goodbye, World' note, and that corpse doesn't have any stool or other thing around it handy to stand on and jump off, either. Meaning somebody else lynched the decedent, and the person or persons unknown didn't even try to make it look like suicide."

"So?" said Seagraves, impatiently.

"So," the Pope said, standing casually, "you've got a murder on your hands, and since Ms. O'Clare's cabbie—and probably everybody in her law office—can alibi her for the apparent time of death, I don't see a ground for holding her. Mairead, let's go."

Seagraves leaped to his feet. "You've crossed the line, Murizzi. Ex-cop working for a gangster like Friedman and his crooked lawyers."

Mairead watched the Pope saunter over to him and go eye to eye, though, Murizzi being shorter, it was more eye to jaw. "I think you just crossed a line of your own, Counselor. And, without proof, you'd be better off not saying anything else about Ms. O'Clare *or* Shel Gold." The Pope turned to Tully. "Jore, always a pleasure."

"Likewise," she said, Mairead now catching a whiff of flirtation on the word.

* * *

shel Gold turned the key in the door to his small apartment in Brookline. His one-eyed cat, Moshe—named after Moshe Dayan, the black-patched Israeli war hero—ran out into the hallway and did a celebration dance before using the front of Shel's right shoe as a scratching board.

Admit it: You're as glad to see him as he is to see you.

After a little monologue of small talk—begin to worry when the cat starts answering—Shel set the bag from the good deli containing his sandwich of smoked turkey and Swiss on the TV tray next to the La-Z-Boy recliner he'd bought as a present to himself. Knowing it would be a waste of time to open any cat food until after giving Moshe some scraps from his own modest meal, Shel changed into sweatclothes and decided the messages blinking up at him from the telephone machine could still play back in the morning. Then he shuffled over to the mantel, kissed the tips of the index and middle fingers on his right hand, and touched tenderly first the face in a framed photo of Natalie, and then the same spot on one of Richie, frozen forever nearing age two.

Then, wiping a pesky tear from his eye with the other hand, Sheldon A. Gold settled into his chair and clicked the remote to CNN.

"how you doing, Irish?" said Pontifico Murizzi from behind the wheel of his Ford Explorer.

"Not bad, considering," Mairead replied, doing a gut-check to confirm that it was true and a cellular one to see if Shel had gotten back to her.

"Jorie Tully, she's a sharp one. Can sniff out an inconsistency before the second answer fades from the air. But that Seagraves, I was never nuts about him."

No message from Shel. "Why?"

The Pope shrugged. "Too 'central casting' for the role.

Plus, he believes his own line of patter a little too much. The priest as fanatic, you know?"

Mairead had met a few during her time with the nuns. And more than a few sisters like that as well.

Present company included?

"Never."

"What?" said the Pope.

"Just thinking out loud," Mairead said to herself. Jesus, girl, get a grip. Which reminded her of how Seagraves had held her wrist. In another context, pleasurable, even desirable. But in this one . . . She just shook her head.

"Hey, want me to pull over or something?"

The Pope thinks I'm going to toss my cookies. "No, I'm okay that way. I just don't see how or why I'm in this."

A grin. "Your going out to Roslindale in that taxi'd be part of it."

"I know that. But why would the woman call me? I mean, even with no stool and no suicide note, she sure didn't sound desperate or scared on the phone."

"I think you're mixing apples and oranges. I see at least two scenarios."

Mairead turned to Murizzi, a faint cologne of some kind stronger with her being closer, and she felt now, irrationally, that tug of attraction toward him that had dominated their first meeting months before. "Let's hear your possibles."

"Okay." The Pope shifted his butt on the seat as he turned his car into Kenmore Square. "Scenario number one: There's something screwy in Balaguer's life, pushes her over the edge, and she commits suicide by hanging."

"But—"

"You wanted me to tell you my possibles, let me tell you, okay?"

"Okay," said Mairead.

A nod. "So, our decedent commits suicide, but somebody happens on her and decides to make it *look* like murder. The somebody takes the note—if there was one—and moves whatever Balaguer used as her diving board."

Mairead felt herself about to shudder, but quelled it. "Why would anybody want to do that?"

"I don't know. That's your department. Which leaves scenario number two: Somebody wants Balaguer dead, and kills her by hanging. This is a pretty cold and cruel way to do it, since it didn't look as though her neck was broken, and so she would have strangled, probably while the somebody's still there, watching her, maybe even talking to her."

No quelling this reaction.

Murizzi said, "You still okay?"

"Yeah," Mairead said, swallowing something rising inside her. "But that'd be awfully close timing on the killer's part."

"Meaning?"

"Well, he would have had to murder Balaguer in between her call to me and my arriving there, which was less than two hours."

"Not necessarily," said the Pope, turning his car onto Charles Street toward Mairead's apartment house on Beacon Hill.

"I don't get you."

"Irish, how much of a conversation did you have with the Balaguer woman before you got that phone call this afternoon?"

"None, really."

"And the judge handled the voir dire of the jury?"

"Right."

"So, you maybe got to hear Balaguer say 'yes' or 'no' a few times in response to questions from the bench?"

"If that."

Murizzi nodded. "Well, there you are."

"Where am I?"

The Explorer pulled up in front of Mairead's building. "Home," the Pope said, gesturing.

She looked out her window, then back at Murizzi. "You know what I meant."

The Pope grinned again. "Basically, you never really 'heard' Balaguer's voice before that call to your office this afternoon, so you don't know whether it was actually *her* calling you or not."

Mairead hung her head. "Just what I needed." Then she remembered her municipal-court trial the next day. "I have a larceny case tomorrow first thing, but I'm guessing Shel's going to want all of us in the office right after that."

"I'll be there by ten-thirty."

She reached out her hand, touching him lightly on the forearm. "Pope, thanks for being there for me tonight."

"Hey, friends don't let friends drive home from homicides, right?"

Always his gallows humor, young lady.

Mairead opened her door and stepped out. "Give Jocko my best."

"Uh, you bet."

Even without seeing Murizzi's face, though, she felt something wrong in his voice. And as Mairead O'Clare tracked the Pope driving away toward the harbor and, eventually, his houseboat, she wondered what might be eating away at him, too.

3

Billie Sunday watched that spooky man Pontifico Murizzi come through the suite door of the law offices like he was a wisp of smoke from a stranger's cigarette.

You hadn't been watching, no way you'd ever've heard him.

"Billie, Mairead said Shel would want to see me."

"They've been waiting on you." She inclined her head to the left, toward the new child's open doorway. "Mairead?"

"Coming."

The Pope asked, "How did your larceny thing go?"

Billie heard Mairead say, "We pled out," and Shel from his office with, "Pope, glad you could make it."

Billie clicked the answering machine to take messages and gathered up her notepad before heaving herself out of the swivel chair at reception to follow Mairead and Murizzi into Shel's bookcase-lined office.

As usual, she and Mairead took chairs, while the Pope stayed standing, scratching his back against the old-fashioned Wild West safe like a bear on a tree.

Billie was ready when Shel said, "The Homicide Unit has already been to see Ben Friedman."

Over her right shoulder, Murizzi said, "No surprise there."

Shel pursed his lips, tenting his fingers on top of his desk, the way Billie's youngest, William, would when he was worrying something over in his mind. "Detective

Tully seems to think that the hit-and-run case might have been fixed by Ben getting to one of the jurors."

"So does Seagraves," said Mairead.

Billie tried to keep her mind on her job and away from her own husband's death under the wheels of a drunk driver years before.

Shel closed his eyes. "Big Ben told me, 'If I'd fixed the thing, which—on my mother's grave, Golden Boy—I didn't, then why would I kill the . . . woman.'"

Billie wrote it down, but somehow didn't think that gangster would have used Shel's last word.

Murizzi said, "I'll bet Jorie had a comeback for that."

Shel nodded. "Ben got the impression that the detective thought he'd killed Balaguer—or had her killed—to keep from being blackmailed into the future over the bribing."

Mairead raised her hand. "Shel, Friedman actually talked with Tully?"

"Not exactly. Ben's too smart for that. He just let her lay it out before he denied everything and told Tully she could speak to his lawyer. But the man's worried."

Billie heard the Pope grunt out a laugh. "Anybody who isn't just doesn't understand the situation."

"Here's Ben's 'situation.'" Shel leaned back in his chair. "After the favorable jury verdict, and our late lunch, he put Tiffany Bomberg on a plane for Florida, to get things ready so they could maybe salvage the tail end of the season there. He also told Dario Calcagni he could go visit his mother in Maine."

Murizzi said, "I hear the strains of 'no alibi.'"

Shel nodded again. "Except for Edsel Crow, and a couple of bouncers at Ben's driveway gate who'd say anything their employer wanted with about as much credibility as the wrought-iron they guard."

Billie put down her pen. "Seems to me, a man like your Mr. Friedman would've had the killing done for him anyway."

Shel shrugged. "Ben's point as well. But we've got a bigger problem than that."

Mairead said, "We?"

Shel looked directly at her. "For better or worse, you were the one who found Balaguer's body. If the prosecution can muster an argument that you'd be a witness for the Commonwealth and against Ben Friedman, then . . ."

"We might be disqualified as counsel for him," said Mairead, slumping her shoulders.

Billie saw Shel brighten a little, in a way his professional life let him, despite his personal one. Like the man doted on the new child as the daughter he never had.

The Pope chimed in with, "Mairead and I talked about some possible scenarios last night."

After not taking notes through the "Friedman killed the juror" that Shel had already outlined, Billie listened to Murizzi more carefully on the call to Mairead maybe being from somebody other than Balaguer herself.

Shel closed his eyes again, now looking kind of like Billie's grandfather taking a nap after a family dinner. Then her boss seemed to come awake. "Mairead, 'Conchita Balaguer' sounds Hispanic. I didn't hear Ms. Balaguer speak much during the voir dire, but I don't remember any accent."

"The woman who called me yesterday had just a hint of one, but I couldn't say if it was Spanish or not."

Billie said, "I'd agree with that."

Shel frowned. "Then I'm out of ideas. Anybody else?"

From behind Billie, the Pope said, "How about if I take Balaguer's side of it: family, work, and so on."

Mairead said, "And I can take the jurors, since I got to watch them for the whole trial."

Shel frowned once more. "Have to get the permission of the trial judge first."

Mairead said, "I think we have grounds, don't you?"

The frown didn't go away this time. "You being further involved might give Seagraves more reason to disqualify us as Ben's counsel."

Mairead shook her head. "Either the prosecution already

has enough reason, or they won't. Besides, hopefully I'll find out things that *help* our client."

Billie wrote that down, then waited for Shel to comment. But all the poor man said was, "Well then, I guess that leaves me to explain to a lifelong friend why he might be needing another lawyer."

pontifico Murizzi would just never feel comfortable in the new Boston Police Headquarters, called Shroeder Plaza.

It wasn't so much that he pined away for the dump Homicide used to occupy on the second floor of an old police garage in South Boston. It was more that the Pope had never served in the modern facility, with its facade of granite, soaring interior lobbies, and gleaming, carpeted corridors that projected all the character of an insurance company.

But remember, Pontifico, as his mother would say: You still have friends here.

However, the first plainclothes to pass the reception counter in the Homicide Unit was a woman Murizzi had never seen before, despite the badge clipped on her belt just to the zipper side of a new and holstered Glock .40. When he asked for Sergeant Detective Artie Chin, she called out "Artie?" and kept walking, which at least was the way they'd have done things at the old digs.

"Pope, what's up?"

Murizzi grinned at his friend of—Christ, how many years now? Chin had been the first Asian on the unit and between the stocky physique and brush-cut hair could still pass for the marine he'd been before joining the department. The Pope had been proud of the way Chin had learned from him, the way Murizzi had from Ed McNelly and Paul Barnicle before that.

"Hey, Pope, you zoning out on me or what?"

"Sorry, Artie. You got a couple minutes?"

"Yeah, but I was just going downstairs for some coffee. Want to join me?"

"Why not?"

from the defense table in courtroom number 10, Shel Gold watched the Honorable Keith Maynard reading Mairead's motion and affidavit. Shel could feel his young associate next to him, aglow with an excitement he envied. Shel also could feel ADA James Seagraves, sitting behind the prosecution table, seeming to champ at the bit in the otherwise empty courtroom.

The judge looked up. "Ms. O'Clare, I'll hear you on the motion," in that stentorian voice of his.

"Thank you, Your Honor," she said, rising. "*Commonwealth versus Fidler* holds that attorneys cannot initiate contact with jurors following a verdict. In the present case, however, juror number eleven, Ms. Conchita Balaguer, contacted me, as I've described in my affidavit. After that juror was killed, the police investigation has centered on Mr. Friedman. All we're asking is to be able to contact the other jurors in order to prepare a potential defense for our client should the Commonwealth proceed against him."

Maynard nodded, but more, Shel thought, to close a chapter than to agree with Mairead's argument. "Mr. Seagraves?"

The prosecutor jumped to his feet. "Your Honor, first of all, I protest the virtually nonexistent notice provided me by the defense. I received their—"

"Counsel," said the judge, wearily in Shel's view as the man took off his half-glasses. "There's no jury here, so please, muffle the drums a little?"

"Sorry, Your Honor."

"I'd be more interested in your substantive objections, if any, to Ms. O'Clare's motion."

Shel watched Seagraves steady himself. "First, the Supreme Judicial Court in *Fidler* was deeply concerned about jurors being harassed by counsel following their service to the Commonwealth. Therefore, an attorney in Ms. O'Clare's position must be able to show you as the trial judge at least some information suggesting that contacting a juror would be fruitful. Here, however, her motion is directed open-endedly to *all* jurors, and her affidavit provides no indication suggesting what information related to Ms. Balaguer's death could be provided by *any* juror."

Maynard nodded again, then turned his head as he replaced his glasses. "Ms. O'Clare?"

"Your Honor, the reason behind the rule in *Fidler* is to shield jurors from being harassed about their deliberations or verdict. We have no such intention here, especially since the defense *won* the underlying case. But these jurors were sequestered with Ms. Balaguer for the week before her death, and all that's asked on Mr. Friedman's behalf is—"

Seeing the judge hold up his hand in a stop sign, Shel was glad that Mairead had as well.

"Mr. Seagraves," from the bench, "what about that? It seems to me Ms. O'Clare might be right: While the *Fidler* rule arguably requires a motion here, the reason behind that decision really doesn't seem to apply in this case."

"Your Honor," began the prosecutor, "the Commonwealth's position is that harassment is harassment, regardless of its purpose. The jurors that were drawn into the underlying case should not have to suffer Ms. O'Clare's dragnet investigation."

Shel could see the opening. He wondered if Mairead could as—

"If I may, Your Honor," she said. "Is Mr. Seagraves representing that the Boston Homicide Unit will not be—in fact, has not already *begun*—speaking with the other jurors in the underlying case about Ms. Balaguer's death?"

Shel stifled a grin. She really is a natural.

Seagraves seemed to stifle anything but a grin. "Your Honor, the *Fidler* case applies only to attorneys, not police detectives conducting an independent investigation of a possibly unrelated..."

As Seagraves petered out, Shel closed his eyes as the expression "Gotcha" resonated through his chest.

Judge Maynard said, "Mr. Seagraves, I think you've answered a question I should have asked. If the District Attorney's Office, through the police, can contact jurors in the underlying case about Ms. Balaguer's tragic but perhaps unrelated death, then surely the potential defendant should have a level playing field for doing the same. Motion allowed. My clerk will provide to Ms. O'Clare the list of all jurors serving, with number-and-street addresses."

As everyone stood for the judge to leave the bench, Shel Gold was glad Mairead O'Clare didn't turn to James Seagraves. Not just because a winner shouldn't gloat, but also because nobody should have to see the look of pure malice stamped across the prosecutor's face.

personally, Pontifico Murizzi thought whoever decorated the Headquarters cafeteria ought to be shot.

Oh, the layout itself was nice enough, on the first floor of the north wing, with big doors across from the Hackney Carriage Unit for taxi medallions and the Licensing Unit for gun permits. And there was plenty of light from the high ceiling and the windows on the long west wall. But the burgundy and slate floor tiles were too much for the slate tables, and the kaleidoscopic pattern on the chair backs made the Pope's eyes cross. He couldn't argue, though, with the Roll of Honor listing the sixty-nine officers killed in action, including the Schroeder brothers—Walter and John—who lost their lives in separate incidents during the seventies and gave the Headquarters its name.

Murizzi followed Artie Chin along the line of dispensing machines. When the detective ordered a hazelnut coffee, the Pope went with hot chocolate, joking over the "gourmet" choices. They walked to an empty table, but in short bursts, as a number of people from Ballistics and the Crime Lab recognized Murizzi and said a few words.

Finally settling under a framed aerial photo of the

U.S.S. *Constitution*—"Old Ironsides"—under way in Boston harbor, the Pope said, "How are you liking the new Glock forties?"

Chin glanced down at his holster. "They're okay. The seventeens had more firepower—sixteen in the clip, one in the chamber—but they were only nine mil, so you might have to hit the guy a few times. There was talk about going to the Glock forty-fives, but they were too big and heavy, so unless you've got to bring down a fucking moose with one shot, the forties have plenty enough stopping power and the subject won't look so much like *Friday the Thirteenth—Officer-Involved Shooting.*"

The Pope grinned, thinking back a few years to all the *Officer-Involved Shootings of Lockers* in the first couple weeks of unloading the then-unfamiliar semiautomatics.

"So, Pope, what's on your mind?"

"The hanging Jorie drew last night."

Chin paused with the coffee halfway to his lips. "That juror from the Vukonov trial?"

Another thing Murizzi liked about Chin: As with most cops, he thought of the case as being the victim's, not the defendant's. "That's the one."

Chin sipped some hazelnut. "If Jorie caught the thing, how come you're talking to me and not her?"

"I talked to her. Last night at the crime scene." Murizzi summarized what had happened with Mairead.

Chin listened patiently, then said, "Sounds to me like you know more about it than I do, anyway."

"Artic, I think Seagraves is going to stonewall this one, and that probably means he'll be muzzling Jorie on it as well."

"Can you blame him?"

"Meaning high-profile case?"

"High-profile? Pope, think it through, willya? It's one thing when a mobster like Friedman's on trial for a 'maybe-he-did, maybe-he-didn't' circumstantial case like Vukonov, even if it was a kid got his skull crushed in front of his mother. It's a whole other fucking *level* of high-profile when some poor citizen sucked into the system as a sequestered juror gets killed the night after returning a verdict. It throws everybody into an uproar. I mean, the commissioner is yelling so loud about this one from his suite up on Four South that pretty soon he won't need a telephone for interoffice communications."

Take the opening, anyway. "You're pretty sure, then, that it was a homicide and not a suicide made to look like one?"

Chin surprised Murizzi a little by lowering his voice to an almost kindly tone. "Pope, you been a good friend for a long time, and I can think of a dozen reasons I could give the municipal employees who've seen us sitting here for why we're talking this morning. But on the Balaguer case, I can't give you squat, and you ought to appreciate that."

"I do, Artie, I do. Just one thing: the almost ten thousand the decedent put in her bank account yesterday afternoon. Check or cash?"

Chin rose. "I gotta get back to my own cases. Enjoy your hot chocolate."

As the Pope watched Sergeant Detective Artie Chin move off, he noticed three or four klatches of people look toward him in his chair, then look away. Almost like they were embarrassed for Murizzi, coming around as a private license and trying to hustle some table scraps from the "real" cops.

All except for Jorie Tully, a cola in her hand, who stood up and began walking over to him.

mairead O'Clare lugged the heavy, hinged "sample case" containing their file on the boy's killing—and now the jurors' specific addresses, too—out into the still October-like air of the May day.

Beside her, Shel Gold said, "You know, just because the judge allowed our motion doesn't mean these people have to talk with you."

"I know."

"And there's a really good chance that a team from Homicide will already have beaten you to them."

"Yeah," said Mairead, shifting the sample case to her other hand, "but one of my professors in law school said that the police couldn't order a witness not to talk to the defense."

One of Shel's sage nods, like you'd just revealed the most important bit of lore imaginable. "And that's correct. Only the detectives can use a kind of reverse-*Miranda* warning."

"Reverse . . . ?"

"Yes." The lawyers paused for a delivery truck to pass before crossing the street. "All the officer has to say to the jurors here is, 'You know, I can't stop the defendant's people from contacting you, but there's no obligation for you to cooperate with them.'"

Mairead got it. "They close the back door instead of the front."

"And either way, you don't get into the witness's house."

She changed hands again. "Well then, I guess I catch them on their lawns."

Mairead noticed Shel give her a little smile before offering to carry the sample case for a while.

"**you** know, Pope, I wondered when I'd ever see you again."

"After last night?"

"No," said Detective Jorie Tully, taking the chair Artie Chin had vacated. "After you left the unit."

Which really meant after you left the department. Because a kid you "proved" did a murder killed himself rather than face life in prison as everybody's punk, only to have the kid exonerated a couple weeks later.

"Pope?"

He came back to Tully's lips caressing the edge of her cola cup like it was . . . Murizzi shook his head and remembered something Artie Chin had said. "Sorry, Jore. One of the luxuries of retirement: You can zone out from time to time."

"Zone out or . . . fantasize?"

More lip nips.

Now the Pope cleared his throat. "It looks like I'm gonna be in for Friedman on this Balaguer thing."

"I thought as much at the crime scene." Tully finally gave her cup a rest by setting it down on the table. "That young lawyer's pretty cute."

"She is that."

"I can see why you might want to ride in on your white horse, rescue her from any dragons."

"I've seen her up against a few dragons already. The kid played ice hockey, and she does pretty well."

"Hockey." Tully closed her pale, pale eyes once, then picked up the cola again. "I used to play soccer in high school."

"I didn't know that."

The eyes came back, hard. "You never asked." She dipped the tip of her tongue into the drink. "Fact is, you never asked about a lot of things. I always thought it had to do with both of us being on the job. No 'fraternization,' you know?"

Uh-oh. "Jorie, look—"

"No, you look." Tully banged the cola cup on the table this time. "Maybe you don't find me attractive, that's fine. And maybe you do know Artie Chin a lot longer and a lot better. Also fine. But Balaguer is my case, and if you want something, you come to me about it. And I don't want to hear you using as an excuse for going around me that you *do* find me attractive and don't want to compromise me somehow in the unit."

It took Murizzi a moment to process all that.

Tully chugged the last of her cola. "And then maybe, after you're finished 'zoning out,' and this Friedman is locked away for good, you can show me your houseboat version of 'Old Ironsides' up there, because I'd like a private tour, Pope. I really would."

She stood then. Pontifico Murizzi looked up into her eyes, less color to them than Mairead's Irish blue, but no less blazing.

He said, "Jore?"

"Yeah?"

"Do we know if the deposit Balaguer made yesterday afternoon was a check or straight cash?"

4

At Big Ben Friedman's wrought-iron driveway gate, Sheldon A. Gold patiently allowed one of the two no-necks to frisk him. The guard wore a polyester jacket that clashed with his slacks, but always seemed to Shel the smarter of the pair. Then, the frisker got on a cell phone while the other walked their boss's attorney to the front door of the Greek-Revival mansion in Brookline, the first town west of Boston.

Before Shel could reach for the knocker, the massive six-paneled expanse of wood swung open. Instead of Tiffany Bomberg, though, it was Edsel Crow who had his hand on the knob, the lifeless eyes staring at—no, more like through—the lawyer.

Admit it: This is the scariest guy you've ever seen, including anybody you boxed professionally.

Crow said in that low, emotionless voice, "Mr. Friedman's taking the sun."

Shel just nodded.

The bodyguard led him through the house. Passing the kitchen, Shel got a noseful of takeout Chinese, which reminded him he'd need lunch pretty soon.

When they got to the Florida room, Shel first looked through the slanting glass roof past the pool to a treehouse Big Ben had built for his sons when they were kids. Usually, Shel knew, Edsel Crow sat up there whenever his boss was out here, with a laser-scoped rifle in case any visitors were unwise enough to intend Big Ben any harm. Shel wondered if there was a substitute sniper on duty that day.

"Hey, Golden Boy. This really sucks, you know?"

Shel looked down at his lifelong friend. Big Ben Friedman lay in a woven lounge chair, wearing nothing but a royal purple bikini bottom that wouldn't flatter any male over the age of nineteen. On the side table were a cell phone, a pair of tanning goggles, and a tumbler of amber liquid.

Shel bet the drink was single-malt scotch, a little early even for a gangster. "Ben, you holding up all right?"

"Holding up? You hear that, Edsel? My lawyer wants to know if I'm holding up."

Shel felt Crow staring at him. "That's what I heard, too, Mr. Friedman."

Big Ben sat up and swung his legs over the side of the lounge closest to Shel, the belly and love handles sloughing enough to cover the bikini and make the man look naked. "What did I say to you the second you stepped in here?"

"Ben, I'm not sure I remember."

"Edsel, what did I say?"

"You said, 'Hey, Golden Boy. This really sucks, you know?'"

Something about the way Crow repeated his boss's words was more scary than the bodyguard's eyes.

"So, Golden Boy, how do you think I'm 'holding up'?"

Shel tried to shrug, knew it didn't quite come off. "It's been a rough few months."

Big Ben reached for the tumbler, took a long slug of his drink. "Christ, I've gone through two bottles of this in two fucking days, at a hundred and ten a fifth."

Shel was pretty sure the liquor companies all used liters now, but decided not to mention it.

"First one was to celebrate, Golden Boy, and the second because I can't believe my fucking bad luck's circled around to bite me in the ass." Big Ben hefted the tumbler, but put it back down without taking more scotch. "Sit, sit. You want anything?"

Shel had lost most of his appetite. "Maybe some ice water?"

Big Ben just nodded at Crow, who left the room. As Shel took a woven chair across from the chaise, his friend said, "Not exactly Tiffany, huh?"

"She's one in a million, Ben."

"In a billion, Golden Boy, in a billion. Tits, ass, everything tight as a drum. But she's still down in Boca—I couldn't see dragging her back up here till you tell me what's what. Besides, I'd rather be there myself, instead of flogging my dick in this little fishbowl. I mean, it's not so bad, but I feel like fucking Eichmann in that glass booth, you know? First I'm on trial, and then I'm waiting. I don't like to wait."

Shel was almost glad to see Edsel Crow come back with the water. A tall glass on a saucer, with wedges of lemon and lime around the edges.

Just like Tiffany would have done it.

"Drink your water," said Big Ben, "and then fill me in."

Shel chose the lime and squeezed it into his glass. "I'm afraid Mr. Crow has to leave us."

"Why?"

"Attorney-client privilege doesn't apply if a third party's present to hear what's being said."

"What about your African-Queen secretary or even that arrogant fucking private eye? They've been around when we've talked."

"Billie and the Pope are my assistants and therefore part of the circle of confidentiality."

"The circle of..." A derisive grunt. "Well, Edsel's my 'assistant.' Doesn't that make him part of it, too?"

"Ben, a secretary and a private investigator are necessary to the provision of legal advice from me to you. Your...chauffeur isn't."

Now Big Ben did take another slug of his scotch. "So, who'd be in front of a judge to admit Edsel heard what we said?"

Shel thought that the booze was making his friend even more belligerent than usual. "I would, Ben."

The gangster's eyes got a little wider, then he laughed, his jet-black hair transplant shaking like a bull was stampeding through rows of sooty cornstalks. "I'll give you this, Golden Boy: You're one in a billion, too." Then he looked up. "Edsel, how's about you read through the fucking takeout menus, try to find some kind of food we haven't had yet that won't give me the shits for a week."

"Yes, Mr. Friedman."

On his way out, Crow closed the door to the Florida room, the latch clicking shut like the sound Shel expected the bolt on his rifle would make.

"Okay," said Big Ben, lying back on the lounge again. "Where do we stand?"

Shel told him about what was discussed during the meeting in his office earlier that morning. Shel could tell Big Ben didn't like what he was hearing, but there was no interruption until Shel got to the "alternative counsel" problem.

"The fuck do you mean?" His voice thundered through the glass enclosure. "A court's gonna tell me I can't choose my own lawyer?"

Shel explained about Mairead maybe being targeted by the police as a witness against him, finishing with, "So, no judge would let me try to impeach my own associate by cross-examining her in front of a jury because the people in the box would have to disbelieve her to believe me."

Big Ben seemed to accept the reasoning. "Well, I don't see it coming to that, anyway."

Shel suddenly felt very cold. "Ben, I won't stand for any violence."

The gangster blinked rapidly. "The fuck are you talking about now?"

"We resolve this in the courts, not on the street."

Big Ben sighed, his shoulders sagging, and for a minute Shel saw through the bluff and the hair transplant and even the nose job to an old friend who was tired and worried and . . . well, old enough to feel both down to his bones.

"Golden Boy," Big Ben said, clasping his hands, "I didn't do the little Russian kid, and I didn't do this Spanish juror, either. When I said, 'I don't see it coming to that,' I meant I'm innocent. And it'd be kind of nice if my oldest gumbah and supposedly loyal fucking *lawyer* could believe me for a change."

Shel knew in his own heart that he was hearing the truth, but maybe not yet all of it. "Ben, another question?"

A smug grin. "Yeah, there's a substitute sniper up in that treehouse."

"Different question, I'm afraid."

"What is it?"

"Did you bribe Conchita Balaguer?"

Another sigh. "I gotta tell you, Golden Boy. I thought about it. Especially since I knew I was pure on the Russian kid. I didn't want it to be like that movie."

"What movie?"

"*The Postman Always Rings Twice.* Not the Nicholson remake, but the real thing, with our poor cousin-in-faith John Garfield getting the gas chamber for the babe he didn't murder instead of the husband he did." Big Ben's eyes engaged Shel's. "But I trusted you, Golden Boy. And so I didn't try to put in the fix."

"Could somebody have done it without telling you?"

A bewildered look now. "Who?"

"Dario, Crow, even . . . Tiffany?"

"Christ." Big Ben brought both palms to his face, rubbing like an awakening child trying to banish a bad dream. "The Calculator, he's a genius when it comes to money, but a fucking eunuch when it comes to balls, so not him. Edsel, I don't think it'd occur to him to do anything but kill somebody, only he'd do it with a cannon, not a rope. And Tiff, no. In the year we been together, she's never meddled in what I do. She shops and cooks, fucks like a witch burning at the stake, but putting the touch on a juror in a murder case? I can't see it."

"Ben?"

"Yeah?"

"I can't see any of them offering a bribe, either, but could you do me a favor?"

"What now?"

"Ask each."

Sheldon A. Gold watched Big Ben Friedman make two fists of his hands before resting his chin wearily on them and nodding three times.

mairead was able to get directory assistance to give her telephone numbers for the first two jurors on the court's list, but when she dialed them on her cellular, one didn't answer and the other hung up on her. So Mairead turned the phone from RING to VIBRATE and decided to visit the third juror on the list in person, especially since "Fanton, Lorraine" lived within walking distance of the office.

The address on Beacon Street turned out to be near the intersection of Clarendon in Back Bay. It was a Victorian brownstone, some cracks in the mortar and a lot of scuff marks on the base of the front door.

As though the residents use their shoes to open or close it, young lady.

Among a dozen buttons below the little metal speaker box, Mairead found Fanton's and pushed it. Almost immediately the words "Who is it?" came through in a tinny, female tone.

"Mairead O'Clare. I'm one of the attorneys from the—"

"Oh, yeah. I remember your voice."

Good trick, with this intercom.

Fanton said, "Pull open the door when you hear the buzz, but be sure to yank it shut behind you. I'm the second floor front."

The sound came from the jamb, and Mairead was glad her upper body had been conditioned by all the years of hockey, because the door was a bear to open, and, once inside, "yank" was the right word for closing it.

You'd think somebody would howl to the property manager.

Climbing the threadbare carpet runner up a flight, however, Mairead began to think "landlord" rather than "condo association." Her own studio on Beacon Hill was a rental, but the building owner—residing in a larger unit there—kept everything spruced and shiny. Here, the walls were dingy, and the molded plaster at the intersection of the ceiling had whole chunks missing.

Mairead heard some locks being turned, and then music filled the stairway, a jazz instrumental with piano leading.

Over the music, a clearer version of the intercom voice said, "Come on in."

As Mairead crossed the threshold, the jazz piece dropped a few decibels, and then a saxophone went off like a bullhorn, making her spin around defensively.

"Sorry," said Fanton, taking off the mouthpiece and rubbing it against her thigh. "Didn't mean to scare you."

There was a miniature rocker of what looked like velvet-covered metal, and the slim, tallish woman in her late thirties had to stoop to lay the sax in it. Mairead recognized Fanton as juror number five, mainly from the thick brown hair that contrasted with the small-lensed, silvery glasses. But what caught Mairead's eye were the dozens of framed black-and-white photos of musicians on bandstands. Some were spotlit, others backlit, a few barely silhouettes through a smoky haze.

She said, "Quite a collection."

Fanton smiled. "My brother took them. That's Richard Elliot, Peter White, Najee—my own favorite. Those older ones over there are Grover Washington, Junior and Milt Hinton. They both died in the last few years, though." Fanton twirled herself, more like a ballerina than a musician. "When I'm practicing, it helps to be surrounded by my idols."

"You ever dance, too?"

Fanton stayed smiling, but Mairead thought the expression in her eyes shifted a little. "I took ballet lessons for six years, but then I got to the point that, on my toes, I'd tower over every male dancer in the class." Her head moved yoga-like, making her hair tumble onto a shoulder. "I'm glad I went over to the sax, though. A lot longer career." Fanton gestured toward an old chair as threadbare as the runner on the staircase. "Have a seat. Coffee, soda?"

Sitting, Mairead thought back to her Evidence professor, who always advocated sharing food or drink with witnesses to help "open them up." Mairead said, "Diet-anything would be great."

"For me, too."

The kitchen was separated from the rest of the studio by a breakfast counter, allowing Fanton to continue the conversation as she took a bottle from the refrigerator and poured out two Sprites. "You don't mind me asking, what happened to your hands?"

"Birthmark. It's called hemangioma, because in the old days doctors first thought it was the blood bursting through the vessels."

Fanton brought out their glasses. "Is it painful?"

"No." Mairead tried to keep the edge of resentment out of her voice. "And it doesn't restrict strength or dexterity, even."

Fanton handed Mairead her glass. "Well, that's good, I guess."

She feels sorry for you, young lady. But don't resent her. Use it.

Okay. "Ms. Fanton—"

"No, Lorraine, please." The musician lowered herself into a flower-print love seat that looked more decorative than comfortable.

"Lorraine, you know about Conchita Balaguer's death?"

"Heard about it on the clock radio this morning. Weird, you know? I mean, some of my friends have died in car accidents or hospitals, but I never knew anybody before who got murdered. Which I also told the fuzz."

"The . . . fuzz?"

"The Man, a dick from Homicide who talked to me late last night." Sly smile. "Though she was a woman like us."

Jazz slang, young lady. Use that, too.

"Lorraine, we really need help on this from all of you who served on the jury."

Another head roll, the full hair obviously what Fanton thought was her best feature. "Hey, I already *did* help you."

"I'm sorry?"

"On the 'first-blush' vote, when most everybody except Troy Gallup was leaning toward 'guilty as charged.'"

Mairead remembered the name from the impaneling documents and thought of juror number seven. "Broad shoulders, sandy hair?"

"A dreamboat in tweed."

Dreamboat. But since Fanton was the one who brought up the deliberations, Mairead felt she could push the envelope a little. "And he was one of Mr. Friedman's supporters in the jury room?"

"First vote was eight to four in favor of conviction, just Troy, Chita, me, and an old guy named Phil Quinn against."

Mairead made a mental check mark next to that name on the court's list as well before saying, "'Chita' was . . . ?"

"Her nickname. Actually, it was kind of interesting to watch."

"The voting, you mean?"

"The whole gig, I mean. We're these fourteen strangers, sitting next to each other all day in court, for meals, at the motel. But the only thing we've got in common—the trial—is what the judge says we're *not* supposed to talk about until after he 'instructs' us. It was really weird that way, so you end up talking about what's going on in your own lives."

"And did Ms. Balaguer say much about herself?"

Fanton shrugged. "Some. She had this tiny accent . . ."

Mairead almost interrupted, then realized she'd already gotten what she could on that.

"...and when somebody asked Chita where she was from originally, she said, Cuba, but because she left so young, English was almost her first language." Fanton's eyebrows went up. "You remember that Marielito boat lift?"

"Just the words. I think I was pretty young."

"Back in the early eighties sometime, Castro emptied his jails and nuthouses and sent—no, wait, that happened to Jimmy Carter, not Ronald Reagan, because I remember in high school one of my teachers saying that might have cost the Democrats the election."

Mairead could remember Reagan as president, but Carter was just wide ties in old videos. "And Ms. Balaguer came to the States in the boat lift?"

"Yeah. And don't get me wrong: There were a lot of regular people who left Cuba, too, and I'm guessing our little tomato was one of them."

Like listening to an unregenerate old man, young lady.

"Lorraine, was there anything else Ms. Balaguer talked about?"

Fanton seemed to ponder that. "Her job, but she was pretty vague there. Chita mentioned insurance-something as a title, but I never heard any details, so maybe she was more like a secretary."

Or just somebody who did her job and didn't blab about the details to strangers. "Ms. Balaguer deposited a large sum of money into her bank account after she left the courthouse yesterday and before she was killed."

Fanton's eyebrows jumped this time. "How large are we talking about?"

"Nearly ten thousand dollars."

"Man, oh man! Sure beats what I got for being a juror."

"Assuming the payment didn't come from the court system, any ideas on how she might have gotten it?"

Fanton opened her mouth, then closed it again before finally saying, "You mean like... a bribe?"

Press her, young lady. "Any reason for you to think that?"

"Well, she and Troy were the two who argued the hardest that your guy Friedman didn't kill the little Russian boy."

"Didn't *you* vote not-guilty also before that?"

"Yeah, but I didn't get ten G's."

Mairead wasn't sure whether that was jazz slang or gangster slang. "How about Ms. Balaguer's family life?"

"Divorced, I remember her saying that much. Oh, and no kids." Fanton shook the full mane again. "You have to remember, Mairead. There were fourteen of us before the judge cut us down to twelve for the deliberations, so while we couldn't 'discuss the case,' that still left politics and sports and music and so on. Plus, a lot of the 'personal life' stuff was really more what you maybe *thought* was going on in the real world, since you were 'sequestered' and couldn't really know."

Mairead wanted to follow up on part of that. "The jurors really didn't talk about the case before it was over?"

"I know I didn't, and nobody raised it with me. What the others did in private, now, I couldn't say."

Private? "When would any two of you ever be alone, though?"

The sly smile again. "Across a . . . pillow?"

Tread carefully, young lady. "You think some of the jurors were having affairs?"

"At least two I can think of," sipping her soda. "Even before there were just the twelve of us. From the way they looked at each other, always sat next to each other at lunch and stuff."

"Lorraine, which jurors are we talking about here?"

Smile and head roll both. "Guess."

"Troy Gallup and Conchita Balaguer?"

"The dreamboat and the hot tomato. Or hot tamale."

Mairead took a breath, decided to drive over the slur. "You have any evidence of this?"

"Evidence?" Fanton shifted on the love seat, bending one long leg and drawing it up under her butt. "At the trial, the judge tried to tell us that whatever we 'found persuasive' was 'evidence' so long as he didn't tell us to 'ignore' it, right?"

"Pretty much."

"Well, then, yeah, I've got evidence. The first night, dreamboat is in one room at the motel, then the next night, he's in a different one."

"Nearer Ms. Balaguer's?"

"Next door."

"As in adjacent rooms?"

"As in ad*joining* rooms, Mairead."

"Lorraine?"

"Yes?"

"How do you know they were... adjoining?"

A little flush up the throat and onto the cheeks. "Like I said, Troy's a dreamboat. I tried knocking on his door one night, but he didn't answer. So, the next morning, I stayed right outside it, milling around in the hall with a couple of the other jurors. When Troy came out, I could see the inner door on the sidewall of his room. That one was closed, but Tamale came out into the hallway, too, from the room sharing that sidewall."

"Did you ever see them embrace or kiss or—"

"Hey, Mairead? I'm not some kind of pervert, all right? Did I have the hots for Troy? Any normal woman would. But he seemed to be satisfied with what he was getting already."

"Lorraine, what I meant was, did they ever... give away their relationship where you or anybody else might have seen them?"

Fanton seemed to ponder that, too. "Not where I did. But if you're that interested, look on the bright side."

"The bright side?"

A final, sly smile. "You've got almost a dozen other people to ask."

by the time Billie Sunday set the last bag of groceries down next to the fridge, William—her youngest—was almost over his pouting. The "no candy" register had been packed with shoppers, so Billie had tried one of the shorter lines. Only the space around the conveyor belt was laced with chocolate bars, and William had gone through the names of them like he was reading from a catalog.

"Momma," now from her waist level as she put away the frozen goods first. "I still don't know why I can't have candy like the other kids do."

"I told you already, child. We buy this spring water in the big plastic box because it's better for us than the city stuff out of the tap. But the spring water doesn't have fluoride in it, and I'm not going to have you getting cavities for the dentist from the sugar in candy bars that the toothpaste doesn't catch."

"Did you have fluoride in your water?"

"Yes."

"Did you have cavities anyway?"

What's a mother supposed to do? Encourage the boy to make rational arguments like that aggravating man Sheldon Gold, or try and cut him off with a "Because I said so"? For maybe the thousandth time, Billie thought about how much easier life would have been if that drunk driver hadn't taken Robert Senior away from her, and their joint parenthood, so early in their marriage. But that's not the way things went.

"Momma, did you?"

"Did I what, child?" moving on to the cold stuff like deli meats and milk.

"Did you have cavities anyway even with the fluoride from your water?"

"The idea is for your teeth to be better than mine. And your health otherwise, and your education, and—"

"Momma?"

"Yes?"

"I don't think you're answering my question."

Billie closed her eyes, was grateful for the sound of the front door slamming. She looked up at the clock. Too early for her oldest, Robert Junior, to be home from baseball practice.

She called out, "Matthew?"

"Yeah," the voice of her thirteen-year-old middle son on the staircase to the second floor.

"How was school today?"

"Okay," now muffled. From his bedroom, probably.

Billie said, "I'm gonna start dinner pretty soon."

Something, but worse than muffled.

"Momma," said William, "I don't—"

"Hush, child." Then, raising her voice, "Matthew?"

"Coming," now on the stairs again.

"I want dinner ready when Robert Junior gets in."

"Can't stay," now directly behind her.

Billie turned, looked at her middle son. The one child who just never seemed on the same wavelength as the other two. Maybe not even the same planet. He'd probably grown two inches since the first of the year, though his clothes still fit. If the word "fit" could be used for pants so baggy and shirts so loose—from companies like Phat Farm and Enyce—that a person could shoot bullets a hand's-width inside his outline and not hit anything but fabric.

If only his clothes were the only thing to worry about. "What do you mean, you can't stay for dinner?"

"Told Rondell I'd eat at his house."

Rondell Wickes. Billie had met him, and—Lord forgive me—didn't trust him on sight. Transferred up from Miami to attend Matthew's school and lived with his grandmother, on account of some trouble down in Florida. Billie would have bet on drugs, because the boy had that dreamy look of somebody coasting along on something more powerful than vitamin C.

She said, "Rondell's grandmother know she's having a guest?"

"Guess so."

"How about if I just call and make sure you're not crashing on her when she isn't ready?"

"Don't . . ." Then Matthew seemed to use the same word with a different meaning. "Don't have to. I remember now, Rondell say he tell her."

"Rondell *said* he *told* her."

"Yeah, like that."

Billie looked into her middle son's eyes. Tried to use them as a window into the boy's mind. But the shades were pulled down, and she'd had a long day at the office.

"Matthew, call me when you get there."

"Aw, I—"

"You call, so I can thank Rondell's grandmother for giving me one meal of something like peace and quiet."

Turning before speaking, "Okay."

"Matthew, call."

But he was already closing the back door behind him.

"Momma," said William.

"Yes?"

"I still don't think you answered my question."

Billie Sunday clenched her teeth, but decided that, instead of counting to ten, she'd count to three, including all her children among her blessings.

walking toward the marina where he kept his houseboat, Pontifico Murizzi folded up his cell phone. He'd left word on Shel Gold's tape machine about what Jorie Tully had told him in the cafeteria at Headquarters. That Conchita Balaguer had deposited the nearly ten thousand in cash, the teller remembering because it was the most the poor kid had ever been asked to handle. Also that Balaguer had been married to a guy who liked to use his fists to punctuate their spousal debates, a tendency that continued after the final divorce decree to the point where she had to get a permanent restraining order against him. And that Balaguer's bosses had said there was no way she could have gotten that kind of money through her job at their insurance agency.

After leaving Tully, the Pope had spun his wheels on the telephone, with neither Balaguer boss in the office that afternoon, at least according to the twangy voice on the other end of their business line. The ex-husband didn't answer his home phone, and no machine kicked in after eight rings. So Murizzi put both targets on his calendar for the next day, which ordinarily wouldn't have been so bad, as he would have gotten back to his houseboat early enough to have a glass of wine over sunset.

And to share both with Jocko.

The Pope went down the stairs to the floating dock—called a "camel" by the other live-aboards around him, though Murizzi had no fucking idea why, and neither did any of them. Passing the big schooner berthed next to his THE NORTH END, the Pope glanced over. A bald, heavyset man with bandy legs was inspecting some of the bright work near the mainmast. The guy's name was Fletcher Something-or-other, a guy with an accent like John Cleese on "Monty Python" playing one of the Queen's cabinet ministers.

Which Jocko once mentioned the guy actually had been in real life. Both the minister part and—Murizzi had to laugh, at least internally—the "queen" part as well.

Fletcher glanced back at the Pope as though the former detective were a doorman getting a cab for somebody else, then went below.

Christ, thought Murizzi, then shook his head.

Onboard his houseboat, the Pope popped the cork on an Isole e Olena Chianti classico, which he'd bought mainly because Jocko had said that was one of the wineries he'd visited in Tuscany. Though Italian-American, and even naming his boat after that section of Boston he'd grown up in, Murizzi had never been to the old country, counting it as the first place in Europe he'd visit.

Who knows, this summer maybe.

Taking the bottle and a tulip glass out onto the fantail, the Pope set them down on the little resin table next to the matching white chairs. He poured wine until the tulip was one-third full, then swished it around before raising it to his lips.

"Should have swirled a scosh less in the glass first, then dumped it overboard."

Murizzi stopped before drinking, looking up at the slim guy with the blond-tipped, close-cropped hair and dazzling smile standing hands on hips near the stern of the schooner's starboard side.

"Want to show me how?" said the Pope.

"Sure." Jocko hopped down the levels to the gunwale of the houseboat like a puma descending a rocky hill on a nature show. "If you've got another glass, luv, I've got about ten minutes?"

The Pope tried to keep his voice from sounding bittersweet. "Sure."

When he came back through the sliding glass door with the second tulip, the sitting Jocko took it, poured just an ounce of Chianti into it, then swirled and dumped the contents into the harbor. "The reason you do this is to take any residue—like soap or even just dust—off the inside of the glass before you test the bouquet and eventual taste of the wine."

The Pope sank back into his chair. "You learn that at Isole e Olena?"

"Gian Franco—the winemaker there—gave us a personal tour, since Fletcher buys their product by the case."

The word "us" was the part Murizzi heard the loudest.

Jocko smiled. "It was a lovely day, like this one, but we were inside the tasting room. Fifteenth century, with precious stained-glass windows and a long, rough table. A flight tasting of ten different vintages." Jocko poured himself a few more ounces of Chianti. "Possibly the finest wine experience of my life." He looked up and clinked the rim of his glass against the Pope's. "Till now."

All at once, Murizzi felt both warm and hollow inside. "Fletcher isn't going to miss you?"

"Like I said, luv, not for a bit. He's dialing up one of his investment advisors on the West Coast. Something about a Pacific Rim takeover, though I believe he meant a company, not a country. I told him I'd start in on the brass again." Another look. "However, I can think of something else I'd rather be polishing."

The Pope tried to put that out of his mind, since it wasn't going to happen. Then he sipped his wine. Tasted fine, even without the rinse. "Any more on the . . . travel front?"

A cloud seemed to cross Jocko's face. "Afraid so. His nibs is talking about us leaving next week for the Continent."

Now the Pope tried to keep his voice strong, not wheedly. "Be easier for him to fly over, wouldn't it?"

"Easier, maybe. But that's not why he bought that beautiful vessel, and not why he hired me to sail it."

Among other duties, thought Murizzi.

"Don't be so glum, luv." Jocko's eyes softened, his hand straying to the Pope's nearest knee. "We'll surely be able to grab some time here before Fletcher and I embark for the Mediterranean."

Murizzi drank more wine. "Why there?"

"His nibs loves to sail along the French Riviera, but I think he's really missing his villa in Tuscany."

The Pope tried to nod as a cultivated English accent barked "Jocko!" from inside the cabin on the next craft.

The young man jumped up, chugging his wine. "Got to go, luv. Talk to you tomorrow."

But as Jocko hopped back onto the sailboat and made his way to the hatchway, Pontifico Murizzi somehow grew certain that he himself wouldn't be visiting the old country this summer after all.

5

both male jurors that Lorraine Fanton had mentioned, Troy Gallup and Phil Quinn, lived on streets accessible by subway. However, Mairead O'Clare thought that if Gallup had been romantically involved with Conchita Balaguer, it might be a good idea to start with Quinn to gain more information about the relationship.

So after leaving Fanton's apartment, Mairead took a Green Line train from Arlington Street in Back Bay to Park Street Under, then changed there for a Red Line train that dropped her off at the Broadway station in South Boston across from a bakery and two bars.

Which is just about the ratio I remember for Southie, young lady.

Turning east on Broadway, Mairead nodded with Sister Bernadette's assessment. South Boston had been primarily Irish-American for more than a century, and no matter how proud the nun might have been of her Hibernian heritage, there was no getting around the gene pool's proclivity for distilled spirits.

Mairead remembered that the cross streets in Southie were named after the letters of the alphabet. The farther east she went, the more gentrified the stores, bars, and restaurants became, though a number still showed names in Gaelic. Mairead turned onto H Street and found the juror's address, a wooden three-decker with just two doorbells, the lower one having QUINN handwritten beneath it.

After pushing the button near the screened outer door, Mairead didn't hear any chime or buzzer, so she tried it again. Almost immediately, the wooden inner door opened with a whoosh.

Like an airtight chamber on a spaceship.

Mairead recognized the elderly man staring back at her as juror number four. His shoulders were stooped and his face shriveled, the hair on his head more memory than reality. And, as he welcomed her inside, Phil Quinn's hands shook, reminding her of someone she couldn't quite place.

Quinn brought her into a living room where the furniture looked older than what they'd had at the orphanage. A symphonic piece filled the air, but there was something wrong with the reproductive quality, a kind of scratchiness.

Your day for music of the world, young lady.

"That Homicide woman said somebody might be coming to visit," Quinn said, smiling with what were obviously false, yellowing teeth. "I'm glad it's you."

Mairead smiled back. "I like the music. Shostakovich?"

"No, Prokofiev. But close. You study it in school?"

"Just an appreciation class in college."

Quinn nodded wisely, and Mairead suddenly realized who he resembled: Yoda, the Jedi master from *Star Wars.*

The old man beckoned to her with a shaking hand, Mairead following him to a contraption in a cabinet. He said, "Ever seen one of these?"

"No. What is it?"

"Victrola. Old-fashioned turntable. Devil of a time getting needles for it, but for the thirty-three-and-a-thirds..."

Mairead looked closer. There was an honest-to-God vinyl record rotating somewhat unevenly inside the polished wood. "Like *Out of Africa,* when Meryl Streep and Robert Redford are dancing off her porch."

"Maybe there's hope for your generation yet," said Quinn, motioning her to a doilied armchair. "Joanie and I never had kids ourselves, so what I know about you I get mostly from walking the neighborhood."

Mairead sat down, the plush chair nearly swallowing her. "Is Joanie your wife?"

"Was." He gestured shakily to a framed wedding photo near the cabinet, the colors in the faces and clothes looking a little too vivid, a much younger Quinn just recognizable in a brown and beige military uniform rather than a tux. "Passed on over twenty years ago. Haven't changed anything in here since. Not out of some crazy devotion, though. Just couldn't see the need."

Mairead felt herself empathizing. "I grew up in an orphanage, myself."

"Really? With all the folks wanting kids, nobody adopted you?"

Mairead held out her hands. "This kind of put them off."

Quinn glanced at the stains. "Then that orphanage only showed you to stupid people. I had a similar problem with mine." He looked down at both, shaking even at rest. "It's called Essential Familial Tremor. Came on when I was just eight."

Mairead inclined her head toward the wedding photo. "Didn't seem to keep you out of the service."

"No. I was lucky that way. Doctor at the Army physical diagnosed it right off, wrote a letter that got me into flight school. I was lucky on that, too. Twenty-five missions piloting a Bee-Twenty-Nine, and still I came home safe to Joanie." A grin now. "When I was overseas, though, and we'd get a replacement in, first thing they'd do is send him over to me, telling the poor lad, 'You're flying with "Shakes" Quinn tomorrow, boy. Good luck.'"

Mairead laughed politely with the man.

Then Quinn sat straighter in his chair. "All right. Now that we've kind of 'bonded,' what do you want to know?"

Mairead used the same opening that had worked with Lorraine Fanton. "We're trying to figure out who killed Conchita Balaguer and why."

"That Homicide woman seemed pretty focused on your Mr. Friedman."

Mairead decided to mask what Fanton had told her.

"You're not the first juror I've seen. The others said you were an early not-guilty vote."

Quinn sighed, leaned back in his chair. "Couldn't see an established guy like Big Ben—oh, I read the papers since the trial ended, so I know that's his nickname. But killing a little kid over a penny-ante protection racket thing? No, not even if Big Ben *was* a gangster himself."

"And three other jurors, including Ms. Balaguer, agreed with you."

"That's right."

"And she joined Troy Gallup as an... advocate for Mr. Friedman?"

Quinn regarded Mairead before answering. "What did those 'other jurors' tell you about that?"

Mairead decided now to be honest. "That Ms. Balaguer seemed to be having a relationship with Mr. Gallup."

Quinn nodded, so much like Yoda now that Mairead was surprised the elderly man didn't purse his lips and blink slowly. "I don't like to gossip, but Troy couldn't help bragging. First day we were together, the sheriff's people took us to dinner. I sat down next to Troy, and all through the meal, Chita stared over at us. You know how that can be?"

Remembering the woman's eyes during closing arguments, Mairead thought, Boy, do I, but just said, "Yes."

"Well, it didn't take a rocket scientist to know she probably didn't have a '*grand*father fixation,' so I mentioned it to Troy. You know what he said back to me?"

"No."

"Well, pardon my French, but word for word: 'She looks like the best lay of a bad lot.'"

I don't think we're going to like Mr. Gallup, young lady. "You mentioned 'bragging'?"

"Well, yes, but that was after... afterward. And I wasn't the one brought it up. No, it was Troy himself. Breakfast the next morning. We're on line at the buffet that motel put on, and he leans over and says, 'You called it right, Phil,' and then some other things I'm not about to tell you."

"Mr. Quinn, I really need to know."

The old man blushed like Lorraine Fanton had, then turned his eyes away, but not toward his wedding photo. "Troy said, 'She's a screamer, and she swallows, too.'"

Mairead looked down at her pad. "Thanks for trying to spare me. Did Ms. Balaguer and Mr. Gallup seem to... maintain their relationship throughout the trial?"

"Oh, I'd say so." Quinn came back to Mairead. "And I think she was sure he'd 'maintain' it after the case ended, too."

Mairead thought about the voice on the phone at her office that afternoon, when Balaguer—*maybe Ms. Balaguer, young lady*—had said she wanted to talk with a lawyer about something. "Are you implying that Mr. Gallup didn't feel the same way?"

"Came right out and said so. We were making our goodbyes to each other after the judge told us we could leave, and I mentioned that I hoped things'd work out between him and Chita. Well, Troy gives me this wink and says, 'Phil, I'm not gonna be sequestered anymore.'"

"Meaning, Mr. Gallup might be back to..."

"Playing the field'd be the nicest way of putting it, though he didn't come right out and say so."

"Anything else you recall that might help us find out who killed Ms. Balaguer?"

Quinn squirmed in his chair.

Mairead said, "Please?"

He sighed again, but more deliberately, coming forward a little, his elbows resting on his knees, hands shaking still. "There was one juror, she seemed kind of... incensed that Troy and Conchita were going at it during a 'murder' trial. I don't know that such matters, but she came up to me once, asked if I didn't think we should go to the judge about them."

Expecting to hear Lorraine Fanton's name, Mairead said, "And which juror was this?"

Now Phil Quinn did purse his lips and blink slowly. "That Korean woman, Ruth Kee."

* * *

when the trolley conductor called out the stop, Sheldon Gold pulled the overhead cord to signal that a passenger wanted to get off. Shel wasn't sure that was necessary anymore, but old habits were hard to break, and leaving the trolley eleven blocks before his apartment had itself become one of his oldest.

And one you can't break, no matter how much sense it might make.

Shel walked slowly toward the Estate, not because he really dreaded arriving, but more because it was part of the ritual, too. And the contrast. On the outside, you had the nice neighborhood, the beautiful old building and its manicured grounds behind the high stone walls.

On the inside, you had dreams that became nightmares.

Arriving at the massive entrance door, Shel pressed the button set into the jamb and then looked up to the security camera, mustering a smile for the poor person who had to spend his or her time staring down at people like him. Then Shel heard the familiar sound of a key slipping into a lock on the other side of the door, and the quarter ton of oak swung open.

The attendant was black, saying "Afternoon, Mr. Gold" with a perky Caribbean accent. She stood trim but strong in a powder-blue jumpsuit, the name Angela stitched into a breast pocket. The last time Shel had been met by her was back in February, when the staff was still wearing its winter uniform of lemon-yellow. He'd once asked the director about the seasonal changes and gotten the answer that the brighter colors seemed best for the shorter, darker days.

Shel never bothered to ask, "Best for who?"

Angela chatted politely as she led him along a series of corridors he could have navigated blindfolded. When they reached another strong but inner door, Angela told him she'd be right outside and wished him good luck.

Thanking her, Shel knocked once, heard the voice he expected, and opened the door.

"Finally, the Lord of the Manor comes home to his castle."

Shel stared at the woman standing from a barrel chair next to a circular reading table. Nearly fifty, she still had the lush, chestnut hair and almost oriental eyes that turned up just so at the corners, as though drawing you in for a closer look.

Admit it: Gallina Ekarevskaya really does have those same eyes, just in violet instead of... "Natalie, you know how things are at a law office."

His wife came up to him. She wore a long-sleeved sweater that diplomatically hid the needle marks from—

"Oh, Shel," hugging him, then grinding her pelvis into his. "How about an... appetizer before dinner?"

He managed to keep from shuddering. "Nat, I think that'd be kind of tough, timing-wise."

"What a poop." She took an abrupt step backward, then spun once for him like a fashion model. "Did you even notice this new skirt?"

He knew it to be a decade old, but said, "Nice. How was your day?"

As she began a litany of shopping and cleaning and making phone calls to people neither of them had seen for years, Shel tried to make himself comfortable in the other barrel chair. He never liked the fake leather, but the director had said it was easier to clean than—

Natalie suddenly stopped. "Oh, and I managed to get in some gardening today, too."

Shel didn't take that seriously until he looked at her hands, the fingernails trapping some grime. "Planting?"

"Of course 'planting,'" she said, sinking back into the chair. "It's May, and therefore springtime, despite the cool weather. Or hadn't you noticed?"

"I've been kind of busy, Nat," Shel said, having trouble tearing himself away from the long, delicate hands. "Big Ben Friedman's had some problems."

"The monster-mobster? Shel, even if he does pay our bills, how can you represent that man?"

Shel lapsed into the best part of any visit for him, the chance to share his day and work with someone who could picture at least some of the players.

Ten minutes later, Natalie said, "Shel, Shel. Always off trying to help others instead of being home on time. The Prodigal Husband."

Uh-oh. "Nat, I also wanted to—"

But his wife's head already had twisted. "And speaking of 'prodigals,' what do you suppose could be keeping our wandering son?"

"Nat, I don't—"

"Richie?" in an almost conversational voice.

Shel shook his own head. "Nat, why—"

"Richie?" calling out this time.

"Natalie, please try—"

Then she whipped her face toward Shel. "You. You were the one! Oh, you son of a bitch, people told me. The po*lice* told me." Her hands dug into the sides of the chair at the cushion as she began to shriek. "How you left him there in the stroller, outside the store in the middle of that mall. 'Just for a minute, Nat. Not even thirty seconds!' Oh, you cocksucking liar."

Yelling himself, Shel said, "Angela, I think—"

Natalie came out of the chair, but in her left hand was a three-prong gardening fork, each tine like a curved claw. "You motherfucker, you abandoned our son like an animal."

Shel was up and managed to cross his hands at the wrists, first blocking, then catching her hand as she tried to rake at his face with the tool. The door burst open, and Angela was behind Natalie in two quick strides, clamping firmly on her elbows. Shel, as gently as possible, pried his wife's fingers from the handle of the fork.

"You motherfucking worthless piece of *shit,*" Natalie said, struggling futilely in Angela's secure grip. "How could you do this to us? How could you—"

Angela said, "I think now would be good."

And Sheldon A. Gold, hearing the phrase that every staffer at the Estate eventually had to say to him after each of his visits ended in disaster, kept the garden tool and backed away toward the door. Less in defense and more to steal another look, however painful, at the woman whom he felt condemned to love forever.

okay, said Pontifico Murizzi to himself. You're over it.

If not over him.

The Pope pushed any thoughts of Jocko from his mind as he drove his white Ford Explorer Sport in the evening rush hour up Route 1-A toward Lynn, a city north of Boston. He'd originally gotten the two-door SUV because he needed its roominess for hauling stuff to and from the houseboat. But Murizzi kept it because, amazingly, the vehicle was only a foot longer than a Honda Prelude, and so the Explorer could fit into the smallish parking space the marina allotted him.

Which might remind you again of who lived next door there. At least for a while longer.

Stuck at a traffic light just before Wonderland, the racing track featuring greyhounds chasing a little metal rabbit, the Pope tried to review his relationship objectively, like it was a case he'd been working. When the big schooner had moored next to him that past November, he and Jocko had gotten together almost immediately. Murizzi knew that the sailboat's owner was just visiting investments in the Sunbelt, but figured not to cross a bridge till they came to it.

And now Jocko was saying they had.

The light changed, and the Pope moved slowly around the old racetrack, taking the rotary and continuing northward along the bays of Revere.

It'd been clear to the private investigator from the get-go that Jocko was too young, and footloose, to want a long-term thing, but Murizzi also had begun to hope that maybe the time they were spending together might change that. And the Pope sensed some indecision on Jocko's part. But only now and then, when they'd talk about what it'd be like to have a permanent home, even if it was on a boat. And how they might please each other for the indefinite future. Murizzi had even stopped by the Gay & Lesbian Advocates & Defenders on Washington Street, picked up their "Marriage Fact Sheet," but—

A truck blared its foghorn at the Pope, who cursed until he realized his Explorer was wandering across the dashed-line lane divider.

Christ on a crutch, man. Pay fucking attention here.

Murizzi focused again on the moving traffic in front of him as opposed to the traffic jam in his mind, taking the left by the old General Electric plant and driving into downtown Lynn. Though not that far north, the city was in Essex, not Suffolk, County, and so the Pope hadn't been there much while on Boston's Homicide Unit. But it didn't take long to find the address for Rigoberto Balaguer in a rundown apartment building off the main drag.

Murizzi left his car in a curbside space and went up to the front door, being careful to step around the crumbling parts of the cement stoop. He could hear what sounded like south-of-the-border music coming from the back of the place, so when nobody answered the bell, the Pope walked around the corner.

Getting closer, voices speaking machine-gun Spanish overrode the music, but even without understanding the language, he could hear the effect of alcohol slurring the words. Coming into view of the postage-stamp yard, Murizzi saw brown spots among the weeds and a patio with cracked flagstones. Beside a rusting hibachi with a crudded grill, three guys were in various stages of collapse in lawn chairs, a boombox nearby. They swilled beer from long-neck bottles, more on ice in a ten-gallon cooler, but half a dozen dead soldiers were already lying at their feet.

"Good evening," said the Pope.

One of the guys was fat, one skinny, the third more broad and rangy than most Hispanics Murizzi had encountered. It was the third who said, "The fuck are you?"

"What do I look like, Immigration?"

The Pope didn't know if the other two spoke English,

but they seemed to recognize that last word enough to set down their long-necks and move more quickly than steadily around the other corner of the building.

Murizzi walked over to the boombox and turned it off. "Didn't mean to rain on your party."

Up close, the third guy had kind of aristocratic features, but his hands were callused and scarred. He pushed himself higher in the chair, his palm slipping off the aluminum arm, nearly bringing him crashing to the ground. "What do you want, man?"

A lot less accent now. On the job, the Pope had always tried to avoid as much prejudice and stereotyping as he could, partly because he considered himself a good man, and partly because thinking narrowly could keep a detective from spotting connections important to making a case. And now Murizzi wanted to find out what Conchita Balaguer could have seen in the guy enough to marry him.

Which caused the Pope to realize he was assuming something. "Rigoberto, we have to talk."

"So sit. We'll talk."

Well, that provided identification, at least. Murizzi took one of the vacated chairs.

"That other cop, she already ask me her questions about Chita, though. The one with the good smile and the eyes of a *bruja.*"

Probably Jorie Tully, but no need to disabuse Balaguer of what side of the street the Pope now worked. "What does *'brew-hah'* mean, Rigoberto?"

Balaguer sneered. "What's the matter, man, you never go to college, learn a second language?" A swig of beer. "I went to college." A measured nod now. "Couple years, anyway. That's how come Chita first picked me out, you know it?"

Another question answered. Sort of. "Rigoberto, what does *'brew-hah'* mean in English?"

"*B-R-U-J-A,* a witch who puts curses on people."

Murizzi thought back to Tully in the cafeteria at Headquarters. "She can do worse than that. And so can I, you aren't straight with us."

"Look, Chita was my old lady. She even go for the whole nine yards, change her name to mine when we got married." A wave of the bottle. "But we got divorced, and I got my own life back again."

Push it a little. "According to the court papers, you didn't feel that way a while ago."

Balaguer chugged some more beer. "Chita, she was good in bed, man. Only a *maricón* gonna walk away from something like that."

The Pope was pretty sure "*maricón*" translated as "faggot," and he cleared his throat. "Rigoberto, where were you the night your ex-wife was killed?"

"After we got married, she got these ideas in her head. 'You a piece of shit, Berto. I can do better.' Like that."

"How about answering my question?"

"Chita, she think because she get this job working for insurance agents that she's better than me." A sly smile through the sauce. "What do you think she's thinking now, eh?"

Murizzi was growing tired of this act. Reaching across the space between them, he snatched the bottle out of Balaguer's hand and side-armed it into the foundation of the apartment house. The glass shattered, the remaining beer frothing and hissing on the flagstones.

"Hey, *cholo*," but with no aggressive movement behind it, "the fuck you doing?"

"Trying to improve on a three-second attention span. Now, where were you the night Conchita Balaguer died?"

"Right here, man. Drinking beers."

"With the two upstanding citizens that just bolted on us?"

"Yeah. Getting back in touch with my roots, you know it? And we was drinking all that night. I don't hear about Chita till the foreman at work tell me some police are outside."

The Pope said, "And where is work?"

Balaguer mentioned a company and street a mile or so away. "You go ask your *bruja,* man. She talked with all my friends there."

A dead end if Tully already vetted the alibi. "Your ex-wife ever say anybody but you was bothering her?"

"Man, like she's gonna tell me about that?"

Murizzi said, "How about ten thousand dollars?"

"Ten thousand . . . ?"

The look in Balaguer's eyes was awfully good acting for somebody who seemed this deep in the suds. "Your ex ever say anything about ten thousand dollars coming her way?"

"No, but man, I know we divorced, only maybe some of that come *my* way?"

You're wasting your time.

As Pontifico Murizzi stood up and retraced his steps toward the corner of the building, he heard Rigoberto Balaguer say, "Man, maybe I don't see any of her money, but that Chita, she was good in bed."

Then the sound of another long-neck smashing against something hard.

6

"Law offices," said Billie Sunday reflexively into the phone at her desk around 11 A.M. that next, Wednesday morning while trying to decipher one of Shel Gold's scribbled motions toward typing it reasonably accurately.

"Mrs. Sunday, please?"

Billie's mind rocketed to her boys. Aside from a few neighbors, only the schools had her business number.

"This is Mrs. Sunday," her own words sounding hollow as she said them.

"My name is Clarence Hightower. I'm the assistant headmaster at your son's school."

Billie searched in her mind for the man's face, couldn't find it. "I have three children, Mr. Hightower. Which of my sons?"

"Oh, I'm sorry. Matthew Sunday is the one we need to talk about."

Billie wished he'd get to it. "Is Matthew all right?"

A pause. Oh, Lord God, please not—

"He was involved in a fight, Mrs. Sunday. Would you be able to—"

"Mr. Hightower, is my son hurt?"

"Just some bruises, we think."

Billie felt her heart settle down in her chest. Bruises she could deal with.

Hightower said, "But my question is, can you come to the school this morning?"

"I'm at work now, as you know. When would you want me there?"

The man's voice grew lower. "As soon as possible, if you please."

"I'll be there in an hour," said Billie Sunday, starting to scribble a note herself for Shel and Mairead before the telephone was even back in its cradle.

mairead O'Clare entered the Korean restaurant. From the exterior, all you could see was the name superimposed on a background of what she thought were bamboo blinds. Inside, the bamboo motif continued in the form of screens, separating the front counter from the dining area but not blocking a view of it. There were exotic green plants, some huge, in bamboo containers. Mairead wondered if they were native to Ruth Kee's ancestral homeland.

Mairead approached the Asian woman behind the front counter. And while the now smiling though plain face certainly looked like the juror from seat number eight, Mairead decided something was off about the hairstyle.

"Excuse me," she said. "I'm looking for Ruth Kee?"

But the counter woman was staring at Mairead's hands.

More like a doctor carefully examining than a stranger first noticing.

Then the woman looked up. "You are the lawyer from my sister's trial?"

"One of them. I'd like to speak with her, please."

"She is very busy right now." The woman gestured. "We have many early customers today."

"I can see that, only—"

"Why are you here?" said virtually the same voice behind Mairead.

Turning, it was amazing how similar the two women looked, even dressed, though the second one seemed more sour than plain. "Are you and your sister twins?"

"Yes," said the apparent Ruth Kee. "But I want to know why you have come to our restaurant."

"To talk about the death of Conchita Balaguer."

"I do not wish to spend any more of my time on that... slut."

Well, Phil Quinn wasn't wrong about her attitude. "Please, Ms. Kee. It's very important that we find out who killed Ms. Balaguer and why."

"Not to me."

"It was important for you to do your duty as a juror. Now you might be a witness." Mairead decided to try a bluff. "And it'd be a lot easier for us to explore that here than in front of a stenographer."

Kee frowned. "The police already have talked to me. They said I don't have to talk to you."

In for a penny, young lady. "And you don't. But then we'd have to subpoena you for the trial, and you'd have to wait for hours like you did in the jury box while—"

"Okay, okay." Kee glanced around the restaurant once and spoke to her sister. "Table seven will probably want another bottle of wine if you ask, and table three will need steak knives."

Ruth Kee then said to Mairead, "Our office."

It may be "their" office, young lady, but I have a feeling sister Ruth is the queen bee of this hive.

Nodding, Mairead O'Clare followed juror number eight back through the same door.

shel Gold picked up the note from Billie Sunday that sat anchored by a stapler on the seat of his desk chair. Moving the paper and its anchor so he could sit down, he hoped that her son wasn't in too much trouble. Shel debated leaving a reply note, but Billie's read "gone for a few hours," and he decided that it'd be much easier to offer help in person later.

The "in person" thought brought back an image of Natalie from the evening before, and a deadening sadness. Shel couldn't really blame the Estate staff for missing that garden fork, however dangerous it might be. After all, you don't keep the "residents" restrained like prisoners, they're going to get access to things usable as weapons. No, the sadness was more because every treatment the doctors had tried over twenty years had failed to bring his wife out of her psychosis.

And, admit it: The sadness was also partly because, unlike Billie Sunday, you never had a son in his teens to worry about.

Shel banished that side of his life from his mind. Mairead was really the one he wanted to see, to find out how much progress she was making with the jurors. It seemed to him that, before approaching Jim Seagraves on whether the DA's office was going to pursue Big Ben Friedman, the potential defendant's lawyer ought to know everything he could about Conchita Balaguer.

"Hello? Who is here?" said a familiar, if not friendly, voice from the reception area. Wincing, Shel got up from his chair and went out there.

what Billie Sunday thought was, "Oh, my poor baby," but what she said was, "Matthew, I want to talk with you first."

She'd been led into the headmaster's suite by the big, male uniformed officer at the main entrance of the building. Her son sat alone on a bench outside an inner-office door with a plastic plaque reading CLARENCE HIGHTOWER, ASST. H'MASTER. Black and purplish bruises blotched Matthew's chin, and the flesh of his left cheek puffed up to where it nearly closed that eye. There was some blood on his flannel shirt, too, but whether his or another child's she couldn't—

"Afraid I can't let you do that, ma'am."

Billie turned then to see another uniformed officer—female and Indian, or maybe Pakistani—standing kind of the way Robert Senior used to when he was addressing a captain or major but knew he had the goods on the man.

Billie now found herself not much liking that attitude when she was on the receiving end of it.

"And just how do you plan on stopping me?"

The officer smiled. "Mr. Hightower said no one was to interview the suspect until—"

"Matthew is my son."

The officer shrugged. "Mr. Hightower said no one, ma'am."

Before Billie could work herself into a good fit, the inner door opened and a round, bald man who looked like Al Roker on the *Today* show stuck his head out. "Mrs. Sunday?"

"Yes."

"Could you and Matthew come in, please?"

The officer said, "Mr. Hightower, will you be needing me anymore?"

"No, thank you."

The officer nodded, then said to Billie, "Have a nice day, now."

ruth Kee's office was bright but spare, with none of the nice touches of atmosphere that marked the restaurant outside it. In fact, Mairead was reminded of the way her own office had looked at Jaynes & Ward: strictly utilitarian.

"Sit," said Kee as she eased down into the tall chair behind the generic metal desk.

Mairead took one of the two chairs in front of it. "Can you tell me what you know about Conchita Balaguer?"

"Aside from the fact that she was a slut?"

"Including that," said Mairead, trying to keep a burr from growing in her voice.

"Conchita—or 'Chita,' as she asked us to call her—was just that."

"Just what?"

"A 'cheater.' Or a 'cheetah,' both the Boston pronunciation and the big cat, stalking its prey and pouncing early."

I'm confused, young lady. "And the . . . 'cheating' part?"

"Well, what would you call it? Here we're all supposed to be upstanding protectors of democracy, and she's rolling over for Troy Gallup before we're sworn in. Or almost that soon."

Kee came forward in her chair, planting her hands on the desktop like she was about to rise. "Look—Ms. O'Clare, right?"

"Right."

"My parents brought my sister and me to this country when we were just three. And, yes, they were Christians and taught us to behave a certain way. I worked really hard to be a good student, and then a good citizen. So, when I received my juror notice, I didn't try to avoid it because I have a business to run. I did my duty, just like you said out front. But," Kee now leaned back, "our Chita couldn't handle that without rutting like a pig."

Mairead had always thought "rutting" was what a male animal did. "Granted you didn't approve, what can you tell me about their relationship?"

"Hot and heavy, as the saying goes. But it really did apply to them." Another frown, temporarily twisting Kee's features from sour to ugly. "Troy arranged to have a room adjoining hers. All of us knew about it, but I wasn't going to lodge a protest with the judge on my own, and nobody else cared enough to join me."

"Any indications of trouble between them?"

"Between Chita and Troy?"

"Yes."

Kee nodded slowly. "I overheard her one day saying to another juror that she was having some trouble, but I don't know if Chita meant with Troy. Then again, probably not, since this 'trouble talk' was maybe midway through the trial, and they were still bouncing the headboard off the wall for days afterward."

"The name of this other juror?"

"Hildy Crowell."

As Mairead was trying to picture which juror she'd

been, Kee said, "You know, the one who should have had two chairs?"

There was an obese blond woman in seat number six. It had bothered Mairead to see that woman twisting her thick fingers on the rail of the jury box, and then it bothered Mairead even more that someone else's appearance could make her feel the way she imagined others felt when they saw her own hands.

"Ms. Kee, did Ms. Balaguer ever discuss money issues?"

"Not with me."

"Anything else you can remember?"

"Well..."

I sense a little gossip coming, young lady. "If it would help us, please?"

"I don't like to tell tales on people, but another male juror was panting after Chita, too."

"Who?"

"Our foreman, Ralph Bobransky."

Mairead remembered him. Dark-haired and tall, but kind of sickly. "How do you know this?"

"How? Ms. O'Clare, the fourteen of us lived on the same hallway and ate the same meals for over a week, and then twelve of us sat around the same table for a couple of hours hashing out your Mr. Friedman's fate." Almost a smile. "We were lucky. Nobody screamed and yelled or tried to jump out a window. But Ralph practically drooled every time Chita would get up and leg away from us. You ever notice that about sluts?"

"What?"

"That they have great walks? I wonder if it's the chicken or egg: They have the walk because they're sluts, or they become sluts because they have the walk?"

Mairead O'Clare didn't at all mind saying good-bye to Ms. Ruth Kee.

"**YOU**," said Vadim Vukonov from the office suite's corridor doorway. "You I want to see."

Shel Gold watched as the barrel-chested man padded around Billie Sunday's reception desk like a bear trying to corner its prey. His eyes were wide in a blocky face and his brown hair unkempt, as though he'd maybe drunk his breakfast.

You don't want to hurt this man any more than he has been. "Mr. Vukonov, we can't talk—"

"I don't want talk. For a week in your courtroom, all I hear is talk, talk, talk. But no justice. No justice for my Yuri and me."

Shel didn't know whether Vukonov's omitting his wife, Tanya, from the rant was a good sign or a bad one. "Sir, you are represented by Gallina Ekarevskaya, and as the lawyer for Mr. Friedman, I cannot—"

"Friedman, Friedman. He is nothing but a Jew gangster. These we have in Russia, too, as soon as the Soviet Union goes into the garbage. The gangsters pay bribes to our police, and then they steal from all of us. Only here, the Jew lawyers help them, just like you help Friedman."

Shel tried not to bristle at the slurs, but he also didn't think the situation was getting any better. "Mr. Vukonov, please. Just leave my office, because without your lawyer's permission, I can't speak with you." Try pulling some authority. "The rules of the court."

The man's eyes grew wider, the whites clearly outlining the dark irises. "Rules? Rules, you tell me? I tell you. Our Gallina the lawyer, she say to me, 'This is America, this is fair country. Friedman hurt your Yuri, the law will make him pay for that.'" Vukonov took two menacing steps closer. "But then the gangster and you does something to the jury so he walks away from his crime," another, stalking step, "and he kills yet one of the people from it." Now Vukonov balled his fists. "And you tell me about *rules?*"

As Shel thought, Play your last card, Vukonov lunged forward, swinging a roundhouse right. Shel took it off his left bicep, enough momentum behind the fist thanks to Vukonov's sheer butcher's strength that Shel felt his arm go numb.

Admit it: You don't have a choice anymore.

As Vukonov stepped in to clinch, Shel drove a right uppercut under his chin. Vukonov sagged, his legs now wobbly, and Shel had to grab for the poor man's jacket to retard his fall and ease him down into a sitting position on the floor.

Vukonov's hand went to his jaw, missing connections the first couple of times he tried to rub it. Shel gave him a few moments to refocus.

Okay, play your last card, even if a little late. "Mr. Vukonov, I lost my own son to a kidnapping."

That seemed to rock the Russian nearly as much as the uppercut had. "You . . . you . . . ?"

"He was taken from his stroller when my wife was in a store. We never saw him again."

Vukonov first shook his head, then nodded.

Shel said, "So, if anyone can empathize with you, it's me. But I can*not* talk with you about anything without Ms. Ekarevskaya present. Now, please call her today."

Vukonov wasn't much better at getting to his feet than at rubbing his jaw. But after using the corner of Billie Sunday's desk to steady himself, the man managed to make his way to the door, leaving without another word.

And, checking his own knuckles for damage, Sheldon "Golden Boy" Gold said a prayer for his most recent opponent, who was more a comrade in . . . harms.

assistant Headmaster Clarence Hightower's office struck Billie Sunday as a refuge for the man. It had all kinds of framed photos of him in school baseball uniforms, with other frames holding his diplomas from three different universities. Only thing was, the man himself seemed kind of rabbity, twitching here and freezing there as he began to lay out what had happened.

There were five of them altogether in the office. Billie and Matthew both knew Rondell Wickes, all ska'd out in his hip-hop outfit and grinning despite a plastered-up lower lip to go with the scrapes on his hands. However, Hightower had to introduce Billie to Rondell's grandmother, Lucille Gaffney, a woman staunchly proper in probably the best dress she owned and at most only ten years older than Billie herself.

"So," began Hightower, nervously glancing down at notes on his desktop, "it seems Rondell and Matthew got into a scuffle in the school yard this morning."

That didn't sound right to Billie. "They were fighting each other?"

"Ah, no. Actually they were fighting three other students."

"Two against three?"

"Yes."

Billie looked to her son. "Matthew, who started this?"

Hightower said, "Uh, Mrs. Sunday, I'd like to conduct this meeting, if you don't mind."

Stung, Billie turned to him. "You were there?"

"I beg your pardon?"

"You were there when this 'scuffle' got started?"

"Well, no, I wasn't."

"Then how about we hear from our two boys on the way things happened?"

Rondell's voice piped up with, "Don't have to say nothing without no lawyers here for us."

Billie stiffened at the boy's remark. She knew how a lot of parents handled disciplinary issues now at schools. Bring in the attorneys, blame the teachers, anything but admit that "my poor baby" could have done some—

Hightower said, "Mrs. Sunday, and Mrs. Gaffney, if—"

"That's *Ms.* Gaffney," said Rondell's grandmother.

"Uh, sorry, yes. However, if you two wish to retain counsel, we'll have to postpone this meeting. I must say, though—"

Billie thought she should interrupt. "Mr. Hightower?"

He turned to her, a question in his eyes.

She said, "I work for lawyers. Maybe if we can find out

what really happened here, we can decide better if we need any representation for our boys."

Hightower seemed to like that idea.

Then Rondell said, "I ain't saying shit."

Gaffney snapped at him. "Rondell! This is business at your school, and you don't use that kind of language or tone conducting it."

Billie watched Rondell give his gramma the kind of look that probably made his folks send him up from Miami to live with her. "Matthew, you start, then."

Her middle son glanced at Billie out of his good eye, but more the "Aw, Mom, do I *have* to?" look than the one Rondell gave. "Okay, we be in the 'yard this morning—"

Billie said, "We *were* in the *school* yard this morning . . ."

Another glance before, "We *were* in the *school* yard this morning, and these three dudes started dissing our threads."

With some reason, Billie thought, but instead said, "What are the students' names?"

Her son reeled them off.

Billie engaged Hightower now. "These three, are they white, black . . . ?"

"All three of the victims are white, Mrs. Sunday. However—"

"Victims?" Billie moved her hand, gently, to Matthew's bruised face. "Let's get a look at these 'victims.'"

"Yes," said Lucille Gaffney. "Why aren't they here, too?"

"Well, uh, you see, the teacher who came upon the scuffle identified Rondell and Matthew as the ones doing the beating."

Billie thought back to something Mairead had once told her about hockey games, that the referees always see the *second* player to throw a punch. "Then how is it my son looks like he got trampled in a stampede? You think Matthew and Rondell were hitting themselves?"

Hightower twitched his rabbity nose. "Mrs. Sunday, I can only work with what is reported to me."

"Then let's get your 'reporter' in here with us. Or let Matthew tell you what happened."

"Very well," from behind the desk.

Billie looked down at her middle son. "Go ahead now."

Matthew took a breath, but he fixed his good eye on the assistant headmaster. "We were in the school yard, getting ready for our next class, when one of the dudes throws some dirt at Rondell. Calls him . . ." Billie watched Matthew glance at his friend once before coming back to Hightower. "Calls him a 'raggedy reggae nigger.'"

"Hateful language," said Lucille Gaffney.

Matthew nodded. "Dumb dude don't even know the differences in the music, reggae to ska to hip-hop."

Billie realized she wasn't sure *she* knew those differences, either.

Matthew became more animated. "Well, I grab the dude threw the dirt, and then somebody hits me from the side, so I throw the first dude on the ground, hear all the air go out of him like a 'whump' sound. Only I get hit again before I can, like, defend myself against this second dude. That's when Rondell pokes the third dude, who goes down crying. I'm finishing with the second dude when the teacher comes and pulls me off him."

Billie thought her son had done proudly—and believably—in his own defense. "Matthew brought home some rules and regulations of the school back in September. Seems to me that 'racial slurs' were part of what's prohibited."

Hightower froze this time. "That is correct."

Billie waved at the assistant headmaster's diplomas. "Seems to me also that a man with so much education probably has a pretty good handle on whether black students get disciplined more than whites."

Hightower seemed to speak from memory. "Actually, of all suspensions nationwide, only about thirty-three percent are blacks, while almost fifty percent are whites."

Billie remembered something she once read about statistics like that. "And how many whites are in those schools as opposed to blacks?"

Hightower spoke less quickly. "About sixty-three percent are white, and about seventeen percent are black."

Billie balanced the numbers in her head. "So, the seventeen percent of the students who are black get thirty-three percent of the suspensions?"

Lucille Gaffney said, "Good Lord Almighty!"

Billie leaned forward in her chair. "Then those three white students ought to be getting called in here mighty quick, with *their* parents. And an apology to be issued forthwith."

Billie couldn't recall exactly which of Shel's legal documents that last part was supposed to be in, but it seemed to catch Hightower's ear just right.

He said, "Well, as I'm sure you can appreciate, Mrs. Sunday—and Ms. Gaffney—that's exactly why we have informal meetings like this one. To square away matters that don't need to proceed any further."

"Any further," said Billie, "*after* the apologies."

"Uh, yes. That's what I meant, of course."

Rondell's voice said, "Apologies ain't gonna mean nothing. We still gonna be wearing our threads, and they still gonna be dissing us." Then, in a different, almost mature tone that seemed to include everyone in the room. "Get used to it. I have."

outside the Kee sisters' restaurant, Mairead O'Clare checked her list of jurors. Of the ones she hadn't yet seen, Ralph Bobransky was closer than Hildy Crowell, so Mairead headed toward his address.

At the edge of Bay Village near the theater district, Mairead approached the red-bricked main building of New England School of Law, her alma mater. Walking by the high windows of the first-floor library, she could see clusters of students poring over law books in individual carrels and shared tables.

Just think, young lady. Less than a year ago, you were studying for final exams, and now you're doing "legwork" in a homicide case.

Yeah, but at least I know the latter is better.

Bobransky Hardware was tucked between a barbershop and a dry cleaners. Inside, the place was a bowling alley of tools and paints, with cabinets holding tiny metal drawers of sized nails and screws. When Mairead closed the outer door behind her, a black Labrador retriever heaved itself up from where it was lying under the broom display and wagged its way over to her. As Mairead bent down to scratch between its ears, she heard a man's voice say, "Wait a minute, you're the woman from the trial."

Mairead looked up. "That's right."

Behind the cash register, Ralph Bobransky set down a large carton with an audible thud, as though it were very heavy. He grinned, then began to walk around the counter. Given his hefting of the box, Bobransky didn't seem quite so sickly. He was tall enough that he'd blocked out the red-tipped white cane and dog harness mounted on the wall behind him.

Bobransky tilted his head as though he had a crick in his neck, something Mairead now remembered him doing during the testimony, too. "I used to be blind."

She said, "I'm sorry?"

"Helped me notice your hands right off when we got seated in the jury box. Even asked a doctor about it after the trial. Hemangioma, right?"

"Right."

A satisfied nod. "When you haven't had your sight for a while, you tend to notice things that are different. And that you'd never seen before."

Bobransky seemed to want to talk, so Mairead decided to go with it. "Were you born with your blindness?"

"No. No, I had a head injury from playing basketball. I was ten, and another kid submarined me during a layup on this concrete court. Well, the impact scrambled something in my brain, and the optic nerves started to fail. Took about four years for me not to be able to see at all, and then it was a series of canes and Seeing Eye dogs like Shadow there to get me through."

"And what happened to make you see again?"

"Six years back, I fell in here. Oh, I know what you're thinking: How could a blind man help people in a hardware store in the first place? Well, my father owned this before me, and as I was losing my sight, I worked here till I knew where everything went. And after I went blind, my dad or the other employees would just reorient me to any new stuff. And it's true what they say, about the other senses taking over. Especially the senses of hearing and..."

Bobransky moved both his hands to Mairead's face and deftly touched here and there. She willed herself not to flinch.

"See," he said. "I could have told anybody interested that you were probably attractive, with wide-spaced eyes and a nice nose and jaw, all proportional. I could tell the gauges of screws, nails, even the—"

Mairead said, "But about you regaining your sight?"

"Oh, right. Well, I tripped—blind people are always falling, especially in places they take for granted they know, this time because a new stock boy had left a box in an aisle when a customer asked him for help. I hit my head pretty hard, and since it was late in the day, I went upstairs to bed—my apartment's on the second and third floors here. Well, Shadow wakes me up the next morning—licking my face, a little ritual we still have—only there's something... different." Bobransky's voice stumbled a bit. "There's light in the room, coming through the windows because I never had to pull drapes or curtains. And I can see. For the first time in twenty-four years. I can see Shadow's expression and new cars and how I've... aged."

Mairead tried to turn the conversation back to the reason she was there. "Mr. Bobransky, I—"

"Please. I can't be that much older than you are. Call me Ralph."

"Okay."

"And your name's Mairead, right?"

A little alarm bell went off inside her head. *He's not quite the disarming man he seems, young lady.*

"Mairead O'Clare. Listen, I really need your help regarding Conchita Balaguer."

"Poor Chita. So full of life. Hard to believe she's dead." Bobransky tilted his head differently now. "The newspaper said you found her."

"I did."

"I've never seen anybody hanged before."

Before? "You saw her, too?"

Mairead thought Bobransky reined up pretty abruptly. "I meant I'd never seen anything like that *before* I lost my sight."

The little alarm bell tinkled again. "Can you tell me what you remember about her?"

Bobransky tilted his head a third way, maybe a legacy of so many years of blindness that he constantly redirected for his hearing. "Chita was aggressive, the kind of person who might focus on something. Or somebody."

"Anyone in particular?"

A laugh. "Nice try, Mairead. But another thing from being blind that you never lose is how to detect deception in somebody's voice. In fact, I think probably the best possible jurors—or judges, for that matter—would be people formerly blind, if there were enough of us to go around."

"Did Chita focus on anyone in particular?"

Now a rueful grin. "What I meant about hearing deception in your voice is that you already know the answer to that question."

"Then maybe you can confirm what I've been told."

Another tilt of the head. "All right. Chita and Troy Gallup were an . . . 'item.'"

"They were having an affair."

"Yes."

"Did you find Ms. Balaguer attractive?"

"I think we all did, except for that tight-assed Ruth Kee."

Be subtle, young lady. "Ms. Kee thought . . . ?"

"That Chita was original sin in three-inch heels." Another laugh. "And hell, Ruth was probably right."

"Did you see anybody argue with Ms. Balaguer or otherwise seem to have a grudge against her?"

"No." Now not even a laugh. "Look, I admit that I was interested in Chita, especially after that first day, when I realized we were going to be spending a lot of time together, sequestered. But it was pretty clear she wanted Troy, so I just sat back and enjoyed the scenery."

"Did Ms. Balaguer ever mention a large sum of money to you?"

"No. No talk about money, period."

"Anything else you can tell me that might help determine who killed her?"

"Just that I'd guess your client's off the hook."

"Because?"

"Chita—and Troy—really pushed the rest of us into a 'not guilty.' Why would Friedman kill his fairy godmother?"

"I hope the police feel the same way."

Another of Bobransky's seemingly infinite head tiltings. "Speaking of 'feelings,' I get vibes from you that we both might benefit from pooling our disabilities."

Jesus Mary. "My hands and arms are stained, not disabled."

"Not what I meant, Mairead," Bobransky taking a shuffle step toward her. "I mean that I can understand what it's like to be 'different,' and therefore we might find depths of synchronicity inside us that you never thought could exist."

From bad to worse, young lady. "Look, Mr. Bobransky—"

"Stick to Ralph."

"I'd rather stick to business. I'm just doing my job, and I don't have any 'vibes' that make me think we'd be good together."

Bobransky parted his lips, but all that showed were his clenched teeth. "Listen, honey, I don't know how much you've lost in life because of those blotched hands and arms, but I know what I lost for twenty-four years. And I'm making up for lost time, whether it's with a freak like you or a ball-buster like Chita." Then, suddenly, Ralph Bobransky began to cry, and Shadow to growl ominously. "I could fall again, you know." He waved an arm around his store. "I could fall and lose my sight all over. Or I could just wake up one morning and it's gone. The doctors can't explain why it came back, and they can't guarantee it'll stay forever. So save your 'I'm just doing my job' bullshit for your femi-Nazi friends, okay?"

"Mr. Bobransky, I'm truly sorry to have bothered you."

"Yeah, sure. Apologize after getting what *you* wanted."

As Mairead O'Clare turned to go, she was even sorrier that Shadow continued to growl at her.

7

As soon as Pontifico Murizzi walked through the door of the Stover-Trent Insurance Agency, he thought, Boston had trailer parks, this receptionist'd be living in one.

Sitting alone behind a large desk in the oak-paneled waiting area, she was blond, but more washed-out than dyed, the hair tied back into a ponytail. Her face was bony and drawn, her short arms and small fingers collating some documents as she talked on one of those little "copilot" mikes with what struck the Pope as a hillbilly accent as well, and therefore probably the woman he'd spoken to by telephone the day before.

"Nossir, I don't expect Mr. Trent until two, maybe three? . . . Well, sir, he wasn't exactly positive when he went out to this meeting? . . . Yessir, I sure will leave your message right on his desk, front and center. . . . And you have a nice one, too."

The woman hung up, shoving some of the documents aside so they no longer covered the brass pup tent with the name LURLENE INCH on it. That and her smile, the teeth small and with too much space between them, made Murizzi regret his first take on Ms. Inch, even if it might have been right on the money.

"Can I help you, sir?"

The Pope took out the leather ID case holding a laminated copy of his investigator's license. "I'd like to talk with whoever can help me with Conchita Balaguer's death."

Sometimes, Murizzi had found over the years, you hit people with it, boom, like that, and they're enough shaken to do what you want before thinking too much. The approach had become especially important since the Pope no longer had the authority of the department behind him.

But Lurlene Inch seemed to consider the request without speaking right away, which upped her capacity to be a receptionist in Murizzi's eyes. "Well, sir, I'm afraid there's nobody here who knows anything about poor Chita's passing. The police already talked to all of us?"

Woman ended some of her sentences with that question-mark lilt. "Who was her boss?"

"Mr. Trent and Mr. Stover own the agency, like it says on the sign outside? But Mr. Stover's doing a site assessment, and Mr. Trent's—"

"Out till two, maybe three."

The smile that reminded the Pope of a picket fence. "That's right as rain, sir."

Play her for what she's worth. "How many employees on board, total?"

"Well, there's the two men I just mentioned, then five clericals—like Chita was?—and me out front here."

"No claims people?"

"The girls—the clericals?—handle those, which really means they just batch them up and send them off to the actual *in*surance companies."

"And the companies run their own string of claims adjusters and investigators?"

"Yessir."

"How about if I talk to a couple of these clericals?"

Inch gave him a look like it broke her heart to break the news. "I'm real sorry, but I can't let you do that without Mr. Trent or Mr. Stover giving it the okay?"

The Pope glanced behind him and moved toward one of the two-toned captain's chairs with a Dartmouth College crest on it. "You're talking to me without 'the okay,' right?"

"Yessir, but I'm the receptionist. Talking to people who come through that door is my job."

Murizzi dragged the chair over to conversational distance from Inch's desk. "Then let's talk."

Another picket smile, her left hand going up to pat—no, more . . . primp—her hair where it didn't need any. "I guess I thought that's what we had been doing, sir."

Jeez, you're gay, but you can still feel it. That wave of heat rolling across the desk. The projection of "I really enjoy doing the deed, and I'd love to show you just how much."

The Pope said, "Lurlene, how did Ms. Balaguer get along with everybody else?"

"Well, sir, she never did have very much contact with our *in*sureds. They'd just call in about questions or accidents, and Chita would do her section just like the rest?"

"Her section?"

"Of the alphabet? All the clericals have letter assignments that correspond to the first initial of the last name of the customers."

"And what was Balaguer's section?"

"Chita had the M's through the O's."

Murizzi did the math. "Twenty-six letters in the alphabet, and one of six clericals is responsible for just three letters' worth?"

Something passed over Inch's face. "Yessir. You see, we have lots of Irish people as *in*sureds, and they have just a passel of O and M-C names, like O'Dell and McGraw, for instance?"

The Pope thought the receptionist had done a nice job throwing up that answer, but while it got off the ground, it just didn't fly right. "Balaguer work on that same section the whole time she was here?"

The something stayed on Inch's face this time. "Well, no sir. When Chita first got hired on, she had the L's and the P's, too."

"But then those got tacked on to other clericals' sections, right?"

"Right."

"Lurlene, any reason Balaguer might have gotten a lighter load than anybody else?"

Murizzi could feel Inch looking at him differently now, curiosity maybe winning over the heat reaction. "I think if I ever need a private investigator, Mr. Murizzi, you're the one I ought to be calling."

"Because?"

The elbows came onto the desktop now, and Lurlene arched her small torso forward, like a little girl about to share a secret. "Truth be told, I thought that maybe Chita and—"

"Lurlene," boomed the voice carried in by a draft from the opened front door. "After the police left, didn't I tell you that we'd be having no more conversations about Conchita until *after* her death was resolved?"

juror Hildy Crowell worked in one of the many state office complexes on the Cambridge Street side of Beacon Hill. As Mairead O'Clare climbed the granite steps and went through the metal detector at the visitors' entrance, though, she decided it seemed to be one of the shabbier buildings her tax dollars supported.

Assuming, young lady, that you make enough money at this new job to actually owe *any taxes.*

Mairead took the middle of three elevators to the eighth floor. Acronyms and arrows covered the corridor walls, and it took a moment to decipher which was the one she wanted. Inside that agency's suite, a counter stood like a barricade, and what Mairead took to be bulletproof glass separated her from the skinny man in a too-large dress shirt and shiny tie, both the color of pewter and set off, if you could say that, by three rings in his right ear and a round stud penetrating his bottom lip. He seemed to be reading a magazine.

Through a speaker that would have embarrassed a drive-up hamburger joint, the man said, "Help you?" without even looking up.

"I'd like to see Hildy Crowell, please."

"Inspector Crowell is busy right now."

Mairead was surprised by the "inspector" part. "If she's in, she may want to see me."

The man finally looked up, terminal boredom in his eyes. "And why is that?"

"I'm attorney Mairead O'Clare," making a snap judgment that her Board of Bar Overseers card would have more juice behind it than a simple business one. "It's about the murder case Inspector Crowell's involved in."

The word "murder" banished any boredom from the skinny man's eyes. "Just a minute. I'll try to get her."

He actually hustled a little, moving between the desks behind him before turning a corner and disappearing.

Mairead's watch showed it was only forty seconds before the man came hustling back to his side of the glass. "Please go out into the hall and knock on the first door to your right."

Mairead thanked him and retraced her steps into the corridor. That first door was unmarked but seemed to sport a sturdy lock. Rapping her knuckles on the wood, Mairead felt a little awkward, like an actor in a spy movie who hasn't been shown the script.

She had to knock a second time, but the person now opening the door from the inside was instantly recognizable as juror number six. Again, Mairead was troubled by how much the woman's appearance repelled her.

"Well, as I live and breathe," said Hildy Crowell, the first person in the real world Mairead could ever remember actually speaking that phrase. "Come on in."

The office Mairead entered felt more like an interrogation room. The long table and stolid chairs were wooden, and, like old middle-school furniture, whittled on and gouged.

Crowell waddled—*"walked," young lady*—to the chair at the far end of the table next to the only pad and pencil in sight. The "position of power, the throne," as one of the litigation partners at Jaynes & Ward, heavily into posturing and body language, once impressed upon Mairead. The chair creaked—*I concede you that*—as Crowell dropped into it. Not to be outmaneuvered when she already felt uncomfortable, Mairead pulled a chair from the side of the table and positioned herself at the opposite end, so that she and Crowell sat nearly twelve feet apart.

Mairead was surprised when Crowell smiled warmly. "I saw that in you during the trial."

"Saw what?"

"Independence of spirit. You'd be a tough maid to cow, wouldn't you?"

First "as I live and breathe," and now "a tough maid to cow"? *Maybe the woman's been reading too many historical novels.* "I have a job to do, Ms. Crowell."

"How about Hildy, and, I know it's pronounced 'Muh-*raid*' from the courtroom, but how do you spell that?"

Mairead went through it, and Crowell wrote something on the pad in front of her.

Then the woman looked up. "You're here about Conchita Balaguer, right?"

"That's right. But first, can you tell me what you do here?"

"We inspect."

"And what do you inspect?"

"That's rather confidential, I'm afraid."

Mairead felt her head canting to the side and wondered briefly if she'd picked up Ralph Bobransky's "tilting" tendency. "You can't even tell me the area of responsibility you have?"

"It varies."

"From minor stuff to..." Mairead gestured vaguely down the hall, "...bulletproof-glass stuff?"

"Yes, but it's confidential."

Mairead leaned forward in her chair. "Hildy, I could just look up the acronym of this agency in the legislative statutes and the code of administrative regulations to find out what your office does."

"Give it a try."

Meaning you won't find what you're seeking, young lady.

Mairead nodded with Sister Bernadette's words. "Then why agree to see me at all?"

"Good question. Can you figure it out?"

First her appearance repels, now her secrecy intrigues. "Why are you making this so hard?"

Crowell smiled, with maybe just a curl of cruelty at the corner of her mouth. "You looked at me in the courtroom, and I could see the revulsion in your eyes. You, of all people."

Mairead didn't want to admit the woman was right, so she challenged her second remark. "Me, of all people?"

"Your port-wine stain. Or whatever you call that when it's so widespread. Let me guess now. The other kids at school—maybe even the ones in your family—had nicknames for you, right?"

The child the others called "Stiggie"—short for "stigmata"—could feel that edge creeping into her voice. "I had nicknames, but no family."

For the first time, Crowell seemed to lose her train of thought. "No family?"

"I was raised by the nuns in an orphanage."

"Oh. Oh, I didn't . . ." Crowell now seemed to soften a little. "Well, Mairead, I was obese from the time I was three. They didn't call it 'obese' back then, though. I was 'fat': a fat pig, a fat sow, a fat hippo. The statistics say that we're getting more overweight as a nation because we're ingesting more calories, either bigger meals at home or fattier ones at restaurants, where we eat out twice as often as we did in the seventies. But I was always like this, and if you think grammar-school plays or high-school gym classes were hell for you with those hands, try fending off titty-twisters from ten cheerleaders in the girls' locker room."

The woman wants you to empathize with her, young lady. And you should, but tactfully.

"Things like that happened to me, too, till I took up ice hockey."

Crowell nodded, the smile now softer, too. "The way you moved in the courtroom—and your calves—I thought maybe ballet."

Mairead tried a grin. "Ballet on skates, maybe."

"You're doing a fine job."

"I'm sorry?"

"Of picking up on me. That I wanted you to empathize with the poor beast of considerable tonnage."

Okay, turn it around. "Is that why you became an 'inspector,' then? To get even?"

"To square things. Used to be, an employer would take one look at me and try not to laugh. Only they didn't try very hard. Now obesity's covered as a 'disability' under both . . ."

Crowell leaned back, her chair complaining bitterly. "You're better than I thought, Mairead. You drew me in again without my being aware of it."

And I've about had my fill of this sparring. "Hildy, what can you tell me about Conchita Balaguer?"

"You don't quit, do you?"

"It never seemed to work as well as continuing to try my best."

A deep sigh from Crowell, then a shrewd look. "All right, I'll share what I can of what I know. Ready?"

"Ready," said Mairead, not breaking eye contact to look for a pad of her own.

"Chita was a troubled woman. You've heard that most people see jury duty as a kind of disruption in their lives?"

"Yes."

"Well, she seemed to actually enjoy it. Especially the sequestered part. And I don't just mean rolling in the hay with boy-toy Troy, either. I mean I think your case for Ben Friedman was kind of a . . . time-out for her. A respite from whatever was roiling her personal life."

"And did Ms. Balaguer tell you what that was?"

"No. Chita did imply she was having a problem at work. I didn't—I couldn't—reveal what I do for the state, but I suggested she might want to consult with an attorney."

So, young lady, it seems your phone call might really have *been from Ms. Balaguer, and your version of it is at least partially confirmed by Ms. Crowell.* "Hildy, it might help me if you could repeat exactly what she said to you."

Crowell rubbed her chins—*young lady?*—with the swollen fingers of her left hand. "Chita phrased it like a hypothetical question. 'Hildy, what if a person at work had a problem with another person. Is there some state office she could turn to?' Well, I didn't want to blow my own cover with her—"

Why would Ms. Crowell need *to have a "cover story" for Ms. Balaguer?*

"—so I just replied, 'What kind of problem, Chita?' But she wouldn't be any more specific, so I told her she should contact a good lawyer."

"Did Ms. Balaguer ask you for any . . . recommendations?"

Crowell smiled warmly again. "I told her somebody like you would be who I'd choose."

More confirmation for that telephone call. "You mentioned before about 'blowing your cover story.'"

"Slip of the tongue."

"And even if it wasn't . . . ?"

"Confidential."

Mairead took a mental inventory, couldn't see a category she hadn't covered. "Anything else you can tell me?"

"Off the record?"

A little adrenaline rush. "Of course."

Hildy Crowell hunched forward, and the screeching sound of a nail pulling out of her chair filled the room. "Mairead, you have just the most beautiful eyes."

Ralph Bobransky again, just on a different vector. "Ms. Crowell, nice talking to you."

* * *

"golden Boy, we got problems."

Cradling the receiver from his desk between his chin and shoulder, Shel closed the file he was reviewing. "The police?"

"No," said Big Ben Friedman from the other end of the line. "It's the Calculator."

"I thought you told me yesterday that Dario was going up to see his—"

"Mother in Maine, right. Only thing is, I just tried to call him there—fucking Neanderthal doesn't have a cell phone, can you believe it?—ask about him maybe fixing that juror, like you wanted. But his mother says she hasn't seen him."

Shel pictured the heavyset and florid accountant. "That's not like him, is it?"

"The Calculator? He's like a fucking clock, the whole time he's worked for me." Then Friedman cleared his throat. "Golden Boy, I'm beginning to feel kind of paranoid here, like whoever set me up for that juror's killing got to him."

Shel turned it over a few times. "But why target Dario?"

"The fuck should I know, why him? Maybe he's the only one around me can't take care of himself, and they're trying to fuck with my mind by disappearing the poor shit."

Which made Shel think of something—or someone—else. "Ben, have you heard from Tiffany?"

"Yeah, yeah. I talked to her before I tried the Calculator's mother. She's fine, telling me she's getting great tan lines, the little fox. Oh, and Tiff says she didn't fix that juror, either. But we got to do something about this thing."

"Dario, you mean?"

"Who the fuck we been talking about for the last three minutes? Of course him."

"Can you send Edsel Crow up to Maine?"

"Yeah, and probably scare the shit out of every hick he meets. I was thinking instead maybe you send that arrogant prick dick of yours."

"I don't know, Ben. The Pope's pretty busy checking into Conchita Balaguer's background."

"Look, Golden Boy, the Calculator's mother, she's gonna be Italian, right? So maybe your guy and her can hit it off. But I gotta find out whether somebody's harpooned the poor whale or I'm not gonna be able to sleep at night."

Shel Gold shook his head, but took down the telephone number and address of Dario Calcagni's mother in Maine.

to the booming voice over Pontifico Murizzi's shoulder, Lurlene Inch said, "I'm truly sorry, Mr. Stover, but this gentleman—"

"And just who are you?"

The Pope stood up. "I'd say Lurlene here was about to tell you."

Murizzi could see it in the guy's eyes. The way they returned his practiced, I've-got-you cop look. This half of Stover-Trent Insurance was scared about what had happened to Conchita Balaguer, and even two days after her death, the guy hadn't learned to hide it.

Lurlene said, "Mr. Stover, this is Mr. Murizzi. He's a private investigator?"

The Pope watched the guy make a visible effort to become civilized. "Sorry, but this whole... situation has us all a little jittery."

Murizzi pegged the guy for fifty, give or take a year, his hair reduced to a fringe of gray and brown riding over his ears. Around five-eight, he was about the right build for a pulling guard on a high school football team back when regular human beings still played the game.

The Pope said, "I work for Shel Gold, the defense attorney in the case your Ms. Balaguer sat on."

Scared seemed to turn into resigned. "Look, perhaps we can speak in my office?"

"Fine with me."

Stover said, "Lurlene, please hold my calls, but if Trev comes in, have him join us."

"Yessir."

Stover led Murizzi behind the reception area and through an open office of six cubicles, three on each side of an aisle with computer cables like braided hair rising up into the suspended ceiling. Women of all ages and colors sat in five of the cubicles, causing the Pope to think the empty one must have been Balaguer's. None of the clericals said anything to Stover, and a couple never even looked up.

Passing a closed door, Murizzi read the name TREVOR R. TRENT on a brass plaque, which explained the "Trev" who might be joining them. At the next door, Stover turned the knob without needing to use a key.

So, everybody trusts everybody else, too.

Stover's door had his last name on an identical plaque, preceded by NORRIS N. A victim of his own parents on the name front, the Pope wondered how bad the middle name had to be for the guy to go with "Norris" as the lesser of two evils.

"Please, take a seat."

Murizzi noticed the captain's chairs here were the same as the ones in the reception area, down to the Dartmouth crests. "You go to school up there?"

"The Big Green. Actually, my partner, Trevor Trent, and I were classmates."

"Hanover, New Hampshire, right?"

The Pope could see Stover stoop to condescend as he plopped his bowling ball of a body into the swivel chair behind the desk. "That's right."

"Cold in the winter."

"You attend college around there, too?"

"Uh-uh. UMass, Boston, nights while I was still in uniform."

"Army?"

"The police, before I went on Homicide."

Murizzi liked the reaction that got. A real hard swallow above the perfectly knotted tie.

Stover said, "Well, maybe if you could enlighten me on why you're here?"

"It's like Lurlene and I told you out front. Shel Gold's asked me to dig around your Ms. Balaguer's life, see who might have had it in for her."

"We've already spoken to the police. A female detective."

Jeez, Jorie, when do you fucking sleep? "Any kind of investigation, it's easy to miss something. Lots of times, a second person asking slightly different questions gets more helpful information."

Stover busied himself with shifting some papers aside on his desk, enough like the way Lurlene did it to make the Pope think maybe it was part of the agency's training course. "Mr. Murizzi, I hope you understand this. We're terribly upset about Chita's horrible death, but we just don't know anything about it."

"Sometimes people know things they don't realize they know."

"Well, perhaps. But that female detective also told Trev and me both that we don't have to talk with anyone else."

"And she's right. But you can, and I guess I'm wondering what all the hesitation's about. You're 'terribly upset,' but you don't want to help find out who murdered your employee?"

"That's the police's job, and they also told us the gangster from the trial probably killed Chita. Or had her killed."

"There's a difference of opinion on that."

"I'm sure. But, nevertheless, Chita's death also leaves us one experienced clerical short, and so the other girls just have to work that much harder."

Lurlene Inch had used "girls," too, but it sounded wrong coming out in a "man-to-man" conversation. "To process the insureds your Ms. Balaguer covered."

A small smile again. "Well, in the insurance business, 'covered' is a technical term, and Chita certainly never wrote any policies."

Murizzi wanted to press the point without getting Inch into trouble. "Jorie told me—"

"Jorie . . . ?"

"Tully. 'That female detective'?"

"Oh, sorry."

"Anyway, she told me that Ms. Balaguer didn't have quite the caseload of your other clericals."

That got another hard swallow. "I'm not sure I follow you."

"She carried only a couple letters of the alphabet, the way you divide up the work around here."

"Well, yes."

"Even though she was 'experienced.'"

Stover seemed to be racking his brain for an escape hatch. "True, but only because the number of—"

The Pope heard one tap on the door behind him just about simultaneous with its being opened, then, "Sorry to interrupt, Nub, but Lurlene said you wanted me in?"

Christ, thought Murizzi as he stood up, even the guy's nickname is an embarrassment.

Stover rose from his chair, too. "Trev, this is—I'm sorry, but I've forgotten your first name?"

"Pontifico. Pontifico Murizzi."

"Trent, Trev Trent."

As the new arrival extended his hand, the Pope figured him for the personality guy, his partner for the technical side. And if Stover was the pulling guard, Trent had that quarterback build: only about six-one, but broad shoulders, big hands, firm shake. Most of his hair, kind of nicotine-colored, even a cleft chin, like a "preppy lite" version of Seagraves, the bulldog ADA.

You went for jocks, you could do worse than getting it on with this one. But he and Stover feel more like partner/friends than partner/lovers, and while both are wearing wedding bands on their ring fingers, one's plain gold, the other engraved.

Trent said, "Is that Pontifico as in 'the Pontiff'?"

"That's right."

An easy smile. "I recall reading about you in the *Globe* a while back. You were a police detective on that tragic case of the innocent boy who committed suicide in prison."

A memory that never left, but Murizzi upped his assessment of Trent. A glad-handing rainmaker, maybe, but also sharp and maybe just a little malevolent.

Which suited the Pope just fine. "That was me, yeah."

"Well," said Trent, kind of like Ronald Reagan used to, with that downward glance and upraised brows. "Lurlene told me you're here about Chita?"

Murizzi waited for the quarterback to cross easily to the other captain's chair and gracefully lower himself into it before returning to his own. Even moves like Seagraves, only more aware of himself instead of natural.

Stover said, "I was just informing Mr. Murizzi of how busy we are and that we won't be able to spare him any time."

As Trent was about to speak, the Pope jumped in with, "Actually, we'd just gotten to why Ms. Balaguer seemed to have less of a load than your other clericals."

Trent seemed to change his horse. "How Nub and I run our business is hardly any of yours."

"Is that what you told Jorie Tully?"

"Your Homicide colleague? Or *former* colleague, I guess. Although I don't recall Chita's work assignments being part of our conversation with her."

"Sometimes Jorie finds things out without you realizing it."

Trent crossed one leg over the other, Murizzi noticing for the first time the guy actually had cuffs on the pants of his suit. "And maybe Lurlene overstepped her bounds. But no matter. We'll tolerate one more question from you, then Nub and I return to matters of greater moment that command our attention."

The Pope repressed an urge to backhand the guy across

the mouth. "Okay. Where did your Ms. Balaguer get roughly ten thousand in cash to deposit in her account the afternoon she finished jury duty?"

Trevor R. Trent gave the Pope another of his easy smiles. "I did say one more question, not one more answer." He came up out of his chair like he was going back into the game after his defense had caused a turnover. "And if you aren't off our premises by the time I hang up my jacket, we'll be calling some of your *other* former colleagues."

The Pope offered a smile of his own, clapped his hands silently three times, and said, "Be seeing you again, Trev. You, too, Nub."

Then Pontifico Murizzi rose, did his best copwalk out the office door, and smiled at all the clericals back down the aisle separating their cubicles.

8

Mairead O'Clare sat down with Billie Sunday on the two chairs in front of Shel Gold's desk, Pontifico Murizzi crossing his arms and standing in front of the safe.

Shel was already settled into his padded chair, with some of the white stuffing peeking out from the bustle behind his head. "All right, where are we on Conchita Balaguer?"

The Pope spoke first. "I talked to Artie Chin at Homicide, and again with Jorie Tully. They're treating this one as high-profile, all the way."

Mairead felt herself nodding. "Every juror who'd see me said they'd already been visited by police detectives."

Shel pursed his lips. "How many jurors were willing to talk with you?"

"So far, five of the thirteen survivors." Mairead wanted to hold what she thought of as her "bombshell" till last. "The first one, Lorraine Fanton, is a jazz musician in Back Bay. She told me that Balaguer was one of four initial voters for Ben Friedman during deliberations. The other three were Fanton herself, Troy Gallup, and Phil Quinn, with Quinn—an older man in Southie—confirming that."

Shel said, "Their juror numbers?"

Mairead told him, and her boss closed his eyes, as though he were trying to picture the box in the courtroom.

Then Shel opened his eyes again. "What did Gallup have to say?"

Take your own time, young lady. "I haven't seen him yet.

But Quinn also told me that another juror, Ruth Kee—who runs a Korean restaurant with her twin sister—'disapproved' of Gallup, but more of Balaguer, which Kee confirmed when I spoke to her."

From over her shoulder, Murizzi said, "What do you mean, 'disapproved'?"

"I wanted to be sure, so I spoke to Hildy Crowell—an obese woman who works for the state—and Ralph Bobransky, who was the jury foreman."

"And?" said Shel.

"And Bobransky admitted to finding Balaguer attractive."

Mairead watched Shel's eyebrow go crooked. He said, "Anything come of that?"

Billie and the Pope both stifled laughs, Mairead realizing she was half a beat late on why.

Shel said, "Sorry, but were they . . . ?"

"No," Mairead said, feeling her cheeks blush toward the color of her hands, but more from being slow on the unintended pun than from Shel's real question. "However, according to Fanton, Quinn, Kee, and even Bobransky, jurors Balaguer and Gallup were."

Mairead heard a low whistle from Murizzi's station by the safe, then, "That the reason you held off on seeing Gallup?"

She half-turned. "Yes."

"Smart," said the Pope. "That's how I would have handled it, too."

As Mairead turned back to Shel while trying not to beam unashamedly, she noticed Billie look up from her pad. "If I got the list right, this Hildy Crowell *didn't* confirm the affair?"

Young lady, Ms. Sunday's not just writing, but reading and thinking, too. "Actually, it was more that she didn't confirm much of anything."

Shel's brow twitched again. "I don't follow, Mairead. You said she talked with you."

"Turns out Crowell isn't just a 'state employee.' She's an

'inspector' for some kind of—her words: 'confidential matters.'"

"Uh-oh," said Murizzi.

Shel stared at Mairead. "Hildy Crowell didn't elaborate?"

"No."

Shel's eyes went from Mairead to the Pope. "What do you think?"

"I've got a friend who handles computers in one of the state offices. I pay him a visit, something might pop out."

Shel nodded. "Mairead, you said Crowell didn't confirm much of anything?"

And Mr. Gold isn't just listening, he's hearing as well. "Shel, Ruth Kee said she thought Balaguer was having a problem *not* related to the affair with Gallup, and Crowell told me that Balaguer implied she was having a problem with her job."

Shel looked to the Pope.

"If anything," said Murizzi, "it seemed to me the insurance agency was treating Balaguer *better* than her coworkers."

Mairead continued. "Crowell also said she advised Balaguer to consult with an attorney, using me as an example of a good one to see."

Shel grinned. "Which supports Balaguer's call to you here and punctures the bribe theory."

Billie shook her head. "The prosecutor thinks we somehow bribed Balaguer, then her call to Mairead on Monday might have been for everybody on our end to get a good laugh from this Crowell woman's 'advice.'"

Shel shrugged. "The Lord giveth, huh?"

Mairead said, "I have a more threshold question on that: Before they're impaneled, nobody knows which jurors of a hundred will actually hear the case, right?"

"Right," from Shel.

"And, once they're impaneled, and they're sequestered, how does anybody, Ben Friedman included, get to them *with* a bribe offer?"

The Pope said, "Lots of ways, Irish. Chambermaids at the motel can leave a note under their pillow. Servers at meals can put a note in their napkin. Then there's court employees, cellular phones, et cetera, et cetera."

Shel took back the lead. "Mairead, did you get any sense of whether some of the jurors you've seen already had a motive for killing Balaguer?"

"Honestly, only Ralph Bobransky, the foreman. He used to be blind, and—"

"*Used* to be?" said Billie, now a "skeptical mother" tone in her voice.

"A sports injury as a kid took his sight, and a bad crack on the head restored it."

Mairead didn't feel Billie buying it, but Shel seemed to. "So he's what, a little . . . aggressive in life now?"

I'll say this for you, Shel: You keep surprising me. "Yes, and when he hit on me, too, he didn't take being rejected lightly."

"Anybody else?"

"Nobody else hit on . . ." Mairead stumbled, remembering Hildy Crowell's parting shot.

Shel prompted her with, "Mairead?"

She hesitated, then realized that not mentioning the advance would be using a double standard just because the Pope was in the room. "Crowell made a pass at me, too."

Mairead could feel all eyes on her, but Murizzi broke the tension by saying, "I'll try to check that out, too."

Shel looked up at him. "Pope, anything else from your end?"

"I paid a visit to Stover-Trent, the insurance guys. Both Ivy Leaguers, and what you might call 'emphatic' about me *not* taking up any more of their precious time. The receptionist let slip that our Chita had her workload reduced by the bosses despite everybody agreeing that Balaguer was an 'experienced' clerical."

Shel said, "And that reduction was the 'better treatment' you mentioned earlier?"

"Right."

Mairead thought of something. "Any explanation for where Ms. Balaguer came up with nearly ten thousand dollars?"

The Pope said, "Jorie told me the bosses had said they had no idea, but frankly, I had the feeling both Stover and Trent wanted to know if I had that question, even though they didn't want to answer it."

Mairead watched Shel digest that. "All right. Pope, anything on Balaguer's ex-husband?"

"Rigoberto. A blue-collar guy, some college but not much ambition. He tried to make it seem like he didn't care if Chita was dead, but the moke was just drunk enough to let his anger and injured pride—over her dumping him—shine through. And, my experience, abusers tend to escalate when they don't think they're being respected."

"Alibi?"

"Drinking with his buddies. And I think Rigoberto would be more likely to choke her out with his bare hands than hang her, but I wouldn't eliminate him from our lineup just yet."

"Okay," said Shel. "Good work all around. Unless somebody has a better idea, I'd say Mairead should continue with the remaining jurors, and the Pope to stay on the ex and the insurance agency."

Murizzi said, "Agreed, but a suggestion?"

Mairead half-turned to him again, but the Pope's eyes were on Billie.

He said, "There's an empty cubicle at Stover-Trent now, and both the bosses were moaning about how much work there was to do there. How's about Billie paying them a visit of her own, see if she can get a short-term job."

Billie shifted in her chair, Mairead being reminded briefly of Hildy Crowell straining hers. "I already got a job."

Shel said, "I think it's worth a shot, though. Could be the other . . . 'clericals,' Pope?"

"Right."

Shel came back to Billie. "Could be they'd talk with a

new 'peer' hire about their thoughts on how one of them came to be killed."

Mairead found herself watching Billie, but also feeling something was wrong.

Billie finally looked up from her pad. "Shel, I need a day or so on account of Matthew."

Shel seemed hurt, but—to Mairead—more for Billie than because of the single mother postponing a ploy that he thought made sense.

Shel said, "It can wait a few days."

Billie just nodded.

Then Shel looked around at each of them. "You all should be aware of two problems from my end. First, Vadim Vukonov came by earlier today."

Mairead thought even the Pope sounded confused. "What, the berserk father from Friedman's trial?"

"Yes," Shel said, now rubbing his right hand across the knuckles. "He tried to fight with me."

Murizzi said, "You mean, *fight* fight?"

"I'm afraid so. He seems to believe what I'm sure the police have told him: that Ben Friedman had Conchita Balaguer killed to cover up a rigged trial, and that we might have helped him somehow."

"So," said Mairead, remembering Shel punching out another guy in a prior case and feeling even more sorry for poor Vukonov in this one, "what are you going to do about it?"

"Talk with his lawyer toward keeping that side of things strictly in the courtroom."

"But," said Billie, "I should be watching for the man, he decides to socialize again."

"We all should be careful."

Then Mairead sensed a shift in Shel's focus. "The other problem is, Ben Friedman's accountant seems to be missing."

"What?" from the Pope.

Mairead said, "The guy Friedman calls 'the Calculator'?"

"Right." Shel rubbed his knuckles some more. "Ben told me Calcagni never arrived at his mother's house in Maine."

Murizzi said, "The hell do you think's going on here?"

"I don't know, and I don't believe Ben does either. But I'm wondering, Pope, if you could drive up there, maybe find out."

"Why don't we start at this end, try to track the guy from his home base?"

"Because I'm guessing he'd have driven up there himself, and maybe you can get a sense of what could have happened to him, if anything, on the way."

Mairead felt Murizzi hesitating. "That'd mean I'd have to shelve the insurance people. And this Hildy Crowell, too."

Shel appeared to have decided the question of priorities before the Pope raised it. "I think Calcagni should come first."

"Your call. I'll need an address and telephone."

"Right here."

Mairead watched the older lawyer extend a single sheet of paper toward Murizzi, who came forward to take and read it. Then Shel sagged back into his chair, a little bit of the white stuffing poofing out around his head.

Her boss said, "Anything else?"

Mairead heard all three of them intone the word "no."

Like a quiet prayer, young lady.

Shel Gold nodded one last time. "Let's get on with it, then. But Billie, could you stay a minute?"

With everything else running through her mind, Mairead O'Clare felt relieved to be spared whatever was weighing on Billie Sunday's.

"SO," said Shel, in that quiet voice you'd think was a patronizing "bedside manner" before you knew him long enough to realize it was his *real* one. "What's going on with Matthew?"

Billie Sunday had kept her pad open till that point, then closed it on her lap. "Just something at school."

"Grades?"

Billie felt a little torn: The man was trying to be a friend, not a boss, but it really wasn't any of his business so long as it didn't affect her job.

On the other hand, you can't go to that insurance agency for him, it *is* affecting your job.

"Matthew and a friend of his got into a fight with some other kids."

Billie watched Shel's brows fuss like nervous caterpillars over his eyes. "Anybody hurt?"

"Not bad enough for a hospital, but the school's taking it seriously."

"And you might have to go over there again?"

"Yes."

Billie thought Shel was having some trouble coming up with his next question. Or maybe just trying to phrase it right.

He said, "Do you think my talking with him would help?"

Shel, you are a good man, but you're not his father, or my husband. "Probably not."

That sheepish smile of his, the one that makes it hard for somebody to say no. "I don't know, Billie." He rotated his fists, but without any macho in the motion. "I've had a lot of experience with fights."

"Yes," she replied. "Only this time it was white against black."

A closing of the eyes now. "And I'm one but not the other."

No sense sugarcoating things. "That's right."

A nod with more sadness than agreement in it, Billie thought.

"Okay," said Shel Gold, "but if you change your mind, I'll still be here."

"You always have been. And I appreciate it. Truly."

Another nod, this one more to end the conversation with

the barriers that Billie Sunday felt no lower than they'd been and, to her mind, forever would be.

pontifico Murizzi sat on the fantail of his houseboat. The absence of breeze and chop was actually nice, this month having been pretty cold for May, even in New England. The Pope could appreciate the way the sunset fingerpainted the glass and metal parts of the skyscrapers across the still-elevated Central Artery, but he was really thinking about his look-see outside the Russian butcher shop an hour before.

Murizzi had found a parking space on the opposite side of the street from the Vukonovs' storefront. He'd already been around the back during his investigation of the hit-and-run on their kid months before, but this time the Pope wanted to get a sense of whether the berserk father might be planning more trouble for Shel.

Or Irish.

However, the action Murizzi could see all seemed like normal customer traffic. Guys and women in clothes that looked foreign by design and cut strolled in, strolled out, yakked for a while on the sidewalk. There was just one guy who caught the Pope's eye as an aberration. Not much size to him, more like an albino ferret, with white hair cropped short and white eyebrows even. He wore a black leather jacket and black jeans, and was the only person to carry something *into* the shop rather than out of it. But the package in brown paper was small, and Ferret reappeared within a couple of minutes, empty-handed. The guy did give the street a scan, like he was used to doing security for somebody in the old country, which made some sense to Murizzi.

After all, Vukonov thinks his kid was killed by a gangster with enough clout to buy a juror and then do her, too, stands to reason he might ask one of his Russian pals with experience in the field to help watch the store.

Still, though, the Pope trailed Ferret with his eyes until

the guy was a ways down the street, where he hopped agilely up a stoop and into a small single-family near the end of the second block. After an hour or so, Murizzi didn't see any more of him, or his kind, around the butcher shop, so he decided to head back to the marina.

And sit like this on his fantail, a bottle of red wine and two glasses resting on the white resin table in front of him. Only problem was, one glass—and the other chair—remained empty.

Jocko was fifteen minutes late, some New Age instrumental piece coming from the schooner in the next slip.

No sense in just sitting here. Get something done.

The Pope went through the sliding glass doors and snatched his cordless telephone from its cradle, then came back out on deck. He'd tried the Calcagni woman up in Maine twice already from his cellular while outside the butcher shop, but the line was busy both times.

And this third as well. Long-winded broad, or maybe a computer freak using her only phone line to surf the 'net.

As Murizzi clicked off his cordless, he began to notice the sailboat next door creating little ripples, as though it were being gently rocked. He didn't have to turn around to know the harbor was still flat.

What the fuck, you know this Calcagni woman's home, and probably will be tomorrow, too.

The rocking of the schooner stayed rhythmic, but began to increase in pace. Only one thing the Pope could think of would do that, as he and Jocko had proved on numerous occasions themselves.

I mean, Pontifico Murizzi said to himself, how the fuck many things can there be to do in Maine?

9

Mairead O'Clare thought to herself, Finally, a warm morning.

The wind had died the night before, and it hadn't risen again, at least not by ten that Thursday. So, toward finding juror number nine's apartment on Charles Street near the Red Line stop, Mairead wore only a yellow blouse, linen blazer, and green skirt.

Just like the dress code back when I taught you, young lady.

Yeah, only now none of it's "tartan plaid."

Josephine Arria's building had the usual double-door security, but when Mairead rang the bell over the last name, a woman's voice answered so quickly, it was as though she'd been waiting for the chance.

"Ms. Arria, this is Mairead O'Clare. We spoke by telephone yesterday afternoon?"

"Oh, yes, please come up. Third-floor landing."

The inner door buzzed, and Mairead started climbing the steps of a stairwell that held a faint smell of garlic and other cooking odors, like the sidewalk entrance to a restaurant.

When Mairead reached the third-floor landing, a door swung wide, and more of the spice scent wafted over her.

"Mairead, Josephine Arria, but I prefer just 'Jo.'"

They shook hands, Arria not looking down at the hemangioma.

Young lady, I like her already.

The door gave onto a tiny vestibule, barely room enough for a table itself barely big enough to hold a handbag and key ring. Arria led Mairead past a copper-garnished kitchen that looked awfully professional, while a massive mahogany table dominated the big window of the living/dining area the way a sofa might in most other apartments.

"Can I get you some coffee or tonic?"

The fact that Arria used the old New England expression for soda made Mairead like her even more. "Coffee would be fine."

A proud smile. "I have a cappuccino machine, if you'd . . ."

"Great."

As Arria turned to enter her kitchen, Mairead followed. The juror was about half a head shorter, with lustrous brown hair and large brown eyes, somewhere around fifty. She swooped around the room like a rock drummer playing her kit of instruments.

Mairead said, "Are you a chef?"

A little laugh. "No, but I was born in Rome and raised in Verona, so I grew up around cooking."

Mairead hadn't heard any accent in the voice. "How old were you when you came to the States?"

"Nine. But my father was American, so I learned both English and Italian. If you speak each language from infancy, you're fluent without accent in either, except for maybe somebody from Sicily or Genoa knowing I was from elsewhere in the country."

The cappuccino machine began to gurgle and hiss. "Jo, I really appreciate your seeing me."

"Let me take a wild guess." Arria turned and flashed a warm smile. "The same policewoman who visited me beat you to the punch with the other jurors, and they all clammed up."

"Pretty close."

Arria positioned a flower-print china cup under the spigot. "Tell you a little story. An uncle on my mother's side immigrated when he was eighteen years old. There was some stealing at the first place he worked, and Uncle Sal was the first one suspected. Italian, so he must have been mafioso, right?"

Mairead thought it safest just to nod.

"Only thing was," Arria placed the cup on a matching saucer and handed it to Mairead while positioning an identical cup under the machine, "the real culprit turned out to be the owner's son, 'Chad' or 'Skipper' or some nickname like that. So I kind of identified with your Mr. Friedman being blamed just because the police made him out to be some kind of gangster."

Mairead thanked the Founding Fathers for putting certain criminal-defendant protections in the Constitution's trial clauses.

Arria reached for her own saucer. "Of course, afterward I read in the paper where your Mr. Friedman really *is* 'some kind of gangster,' but it still didn't make any sense to me that he'd kill that poor little Russian boy. And it wouldn't have to my uncle Sal, either, God rest his soul." She turned to Mairead. "Sugar?"

"No, thanks."

Mairead followed the woman back to the dining table. They sat down, and Arria lifted her cup to clink gently against the other, then said something in Italian.

"What does that mean, Jo?"

"Roughly, 'good health and long life.'" A change in Arria's otherwise kind face. "On which Conchita Balaguer certainly got shortchanged."

They sipped their cappuccinos, Mairead thinking it might be the best rendering of the frothy coffee she'd ever tasted. Then, "Did you sense that Ms. Balaguer was in any kind of danger?"

"Sensed during the trial, you mean?"

"Yes."

"Just the opposite," Arria said, going on to confirm the apparent affair between Balaguer and Troy Gallup.

"Jo," said Mairead, "any sense that he was angry with her, or even jealous in some way?"

"No. Again, just the opposite. I had the feeling they were making the best of a bad situation—the sequestering, I mean. However, if I were the kind of person who bets on such things, I wouldn't have guessed they'd be together very long afterward."

Mairead took more of the cappuccino. "Why not?"

Arria set down her cup. "Chita was basically a good kid, but Troy seemed to me a tomcat."

Consistent with everything else we've learned. "So you don't think Mr. Gallup would have had a reason to hurt her?"

"Not that I could see. Or 'sense,' as you asked me earlier."

"How about anybody other than Mr. Gallup?"

That same change of expression on the kind face. "Well, there's a line from Shakespeare—*Othello,* I think—where one of the characters says of another, ''Tis the strumpet's plague, To beguile many and be beguil'd by one.'"

"Somebody other than Mr. Gallup was 'beguiled' by Ms. Balaguer?"

"Ralph Bobransky. Our foreman?"

"I've met him."

"Well, first he tried to cozy up to Chita, and after hitting a stone wall, he tried Lorraine Fanton."

News to me. "You saw this?"

A nod. "And she told me over a lunch to watch out, because I'd be next." A modest smile. "And I was."

"Jo, I'm not sure how to ask this next question."

"Save you the trouble. No, I turned Ralph down, too. But I think it really was Chita he wanted. Or fantasized about. Give him credit, though. He was a good foreman. Fair, let everybody have their say on the evidence, which I've heard isn't always the case. And nobody seemed really . . . incensed over another's views." A little wink. "We did think, however, that you maybe could have done something about Mr. Gold's appearance."

"His . . . appearance?"

"The rumpled suits, kind of like an unmade bed?"

God, what I first noticed, too, but now I've known him long enough that it doesn't even register. "Anything else you can tell me about Ms. Balaguer?"

That turn of expression again. "I'm not sure it's important to you."

"Jo, we won't know that until you tell me."

"I may even be wrong about my—what did the judge call them, when he was instructing us? Oh, yes, about my 'inference from my observations.'"

"Try me anyway?"

"Well, I had the impression—drew the inference—that one of the female jurors was also . . . interested in Chita."

Don't prompt her with a name, young lady. "Which one, Jo?"

A sigh. "Hildy Crowell. The rather overweight woman in the first row?"

Mairead O'Clare took another sip of the cappuccino, wondering how soon the Pope would be back from Maine to check on that aspect of the case.

wondering how soon the Pope would report back from Maine, Sheldon A. Gold saw Billie Sunday knock on the jamb of his almost-closed office door.

"Yes?"

"Gallina Ekarevskaya is here to see you."

Shel stood up, thinking to ask for enough time to put his jacket on, then realizing that Ekarevskaya would know he was doing that just for her. "Show her in."

Billie nodded, Shel checking his cluttered desktop for anything his likely eventual opponent shouldn't be able to read.

Ekarevskaya came through the doorway, wearing a burgundy dress and short black boots with high heels that gave her an even longer, leggier stride. Shel didn't think it was exactly "boots" weather.

But admit it: What you know about women's fashion wouldn't fill a very small thimble.

"Sheldon," said Ekarevskaya, shaking her hair, the long tresses shimmering like an ebony waterfall. "How are you this morning?"

"I'm fine, Gallina. Sit, please."

When they both were settled, Shel said, "What brings you here?"

A sly smile, the corners of her eyes tipping a little more toward her temples. And even more like Natalie's. "Perhaps I did not wish to wait until the bars opened."

Shel thought back on their drink at the Kinsale Pub just after the Friedman jury—no, better think of it as the *first* Friedman jury—came back with its verdict. "I meant more, why have you come to see me this time?"

"To apologize for my client's visit to you."

Shel leaned back in his chair, suddenly aware of a little stuffing floating awkwardly like a feather past his left eye. "It was somewhat"—the only word he could think of—"awkward."

"More so for Vadim, I think. When I confronted him after your telephone message to me, he admitted you had bested him with your fists. This he told me in Russian, so I do not believe he would compliment you such if it was not true."

"He was very angry, and I was very lucky."

The sly smile again. "In America, we seem to make our own luck. Vadim thought you moved like a professional boxer."

"A long time ago."

A nod, but the smile stayed put. "I think there is more to you than the—what is your fairy tale with Baby Bear in it?"

"Goldilocks and the Three Bears."

"Goldilocks, like the hair?" Ekarevskaya tipped her hand toward her own.

"Yes."

"Sheldon Gold and Goldilocks." A small laugh, but not sarcastic. "Except that you are one of the bears, not the innocent."

"Enough years of law practice, Gallina, and none of us is innocent."

The smile grew broader. "I think you and I shall enjoy spending our time together on this case."

Here it comes. "And what case is that?"

A disapproval, the nostrils flaring a little. "Please, Sheldon. After you have received my compliments, do not insult me by playing the fool. You must know I mean the civil case I shall file against your gangster for the wrongful death of poor Yuri. As I asked you in that pub, will you accept service of process on his behalf?"

"To be honest, Gallina, with all that happened right after you spoke with me, I forgot to ask Mr. Friedman about that."

"Try to remember, Sheldon. Soon."

Yes, but maybe try a probe now. "Frankly, I'm surprised you haven't brought suit already."

"I have not yet decided on the best timing."

"Meaning, you're going to wait until the prosecutor tries Ben Friedman for the alleged murder of Conchita Balaguer."

"Alleged?" followed by the small laugh again, now definitely sarcastic.

"But you're going to wait."

"I am going to file when it is the best time for my clients." Now no smile at all. "One other thing Vadim told me in Russian. You lost your own son?"

Shel tried not to show the pain he felt even now. You don't want to make her think it's a current burden or weakness for Big Ben's lawyer. "Like the boxing, a long time ago."

"But like the boxing, something no one can ever forget. I am sorry for you, Sheldon. And I will understand if you must substitute another attorney for your gangster in the Vukonovs' case."

"No," in the strongest tone Shel could muster, "I think you and I will be litigating this together."

Gallina Ekarevskaya stood abruptly, the action once more causing her dress to cling briefly against her thighs, just like in the Kinsale. "I already look forward to that."

Admit it: Despite your professional allegiance to Ben Friedman, and forty-some years of personal friendship, you're looking forward to spending time with this woman, too.

jeez, is this Maine or Alaska you're driving through?

Pontifico Murizzi found himself on Interstate 95 just past Kennebunkport, resisting the urge to drop by President Bush the Elder's summerhouse, see how retirement was treating *him.* The Pope monitored his progress in the Ford Explorer by glancing down at the map of the state he had opened on the passenger's seat. It seemed that, in two hours, he'd barely crawled northward, and so he'd kicked the cruise control up to seventy, make a little better time, despite the CAUTION—WATCH FOR MOOSE IN ROADWAY signs.

Can't complain about the scenery, though. Down in Massachusetts, the trees were just starting to bud, but up here, the evergreens were the only things not stark and bare, which lent a kind of crispness to the view, needles over leaves.

Only that crispness extended to the air, too, so Murizzi had cranked down the moonroof fifty miles before.

After what seemed like an eternity of rolling hills growing into humpy mountains, he finally reached Augusta, the state capital. The Pope headed west from there, not east into the city, but as far as he could see, it was a mishmash of gas stations and fast-food drive-throughs.

Another forty minutes on winding, country roads, and Murizzi found the route that Shel Gold had written on the paper clipped to his map. Great, except that instead of house numbers like any normal street, this one had rural mailbox numbers, like Andy of Mayberry on TV.

Well, at least the boxes were close to the pavement, because a lot of the houses sure as shit weren't. Including, as the Pope blew by it, the old red farmhouse of Ann Calcagni, set kind of picturesquely on a knoll overlooking the main road, and with just its number, no name, on the green box with the tiny flag.

Murizzi had to go another half-mile before finding a driveway toward making a U-ey. Once headed east again, he pulled into Calcagni's, the loose chunks of gravel ricocheting off the undercarriage of his truck.

Christ, how do these people plow their snow? Or maybe they just abandon cars, go with dogsleds all winter.

And sure enough, as the Pope got out of his Explorer, he heard barking from behind the house. A middling-size dog with some coyote in its facial features came bounding toward him. Only no other dogs followed, and even that one was kind of skinny to be pulling a sled.

"Ria?" A female voice around the side of the house somewhere.

"He's okay," Murizzi called back, figuring the woman was worried about the dog maybe running into the road.

"I know *she's* okay. I was concerned that Ria would take a bite out of you."

The Pope looked down at the slavering dog, who kind of backed onto its haunches, like a cat about to pounce on a mouse. "I think maybe she's getting that idea."

"Ria, come," the woman's voice now a command, and the dog obeyed by turning and loping back around the side of the house.

Definitely some coyote in this one, thought Murizzi as he followed behind at an easy walk, the bright blue sky making the country air feel scrubbed clean to his city-boy lungs.

Clearing the corner of the house, the Pope could see a gazebo with a white, domed roof and some fancy fretwork adorning its red pillars. Like a bandstand on a village green, only this example was barely big enough to hold a hot tub.

And to hold the woman watching him from it, her head

and shoulders the only parts visible above the water line with steam rising from the surface. She had dark hair worn up in a bun, even features, and looked a little too young—and, tell the truth, attractive—to be the Calculator's mother.

Murizzi said, "Ann Calcagni?"

"No, but I used to be."

"Sorry?"

"I divorced Mr. Calcagni years ago and went back to my maiden name."

The Pope paused to let her give it. When she didn't, he moved closer to the tub, the coyote dog materializing from around the side of the gazebo, but now looking more friendly than hungry.

Good rule of street stops, though: You don't get the information you want, close in on the subject, make them feel they've got to answer to get you off their backs.

Except that as Murizzi reached the railing of Ann Whatever's gazebo, he realized he might already be too close to this subject. Not because of Ria, whose tail was wagging fast enough to whack weeds, but because the Pope couldn't see any evidence of bathing suit on the dog's owner. And her face, now framed in sections of suds from the tub jets, seemed to be mounted against a background of white, puffy clouds.

"Uh, Ms. . . ."

"Just call me Ann. And you?"

"Pontifico Murizzi. I'm a—"

"Wait a minute. Your parents named you after a . . . pope?"

"After the popes in general."

"Yes, well, tell me about taking Italian names. I married Dario's father thirty-two years ago because he was wildly attractive and I was hopelessly in love. And because, at age sixteen, I *had* to. But once he grew more hair from his ears than his scalp, I decided enough was enough. I found this little sanctuary up here and canonized myself as Saint

Ann." A different look. "You spent much time in Maine, Pontifico?"

Murizzi thought about the endless drive that morning. "Some."

"Well, this part of May is the best time of the year, next to September. The mud season's over, the—"

"Mud season?"

"Yes. During our winters, the frostline goes down about three feet into the ground. Causes the paved roads to heave and crack, but the problem for the dirt ones—actually, gravel ones, like my driveway—is that when the April rains fall, that frost comes right up out of the ground, turns everything to mud."

The Pope said, "Hard to get around then?"

"You bet, but nothing compared to what we'll have in another two weeks."

"And what's that?"

"Black flies, Pontifico."

Again Murizzi waited, but Ann Whatever didn't go on. "You mean some special kind of bug?"

"Oh, they're special, all right. They look like a fruit fly on steroids, but once the females mate, they need mammalian blood to fertilize their eggs. The fly has jaws, but its saliva contains both a local anesthetic—so you don't feel the bite happening—and an anticoagulant—so your blood flows freely. Then the female flies off, leaving droplets of blood running down your neck or arms and a bite mark that, if you scratch at it, produces a welt the size of a dime that lasts for a week. If you listen, you can actually hear the moose plunging blindly through the woods, driven mad by the things going after their eyes."

Mud to your axles, vampire fruit flies, and stampeding moose. No wonder people love Maine.

"Pontifico, do I still have my . . . 'audience' with you?"

The Pope had to smile at that one. "Ann, I'm actually here looking for a certain accountant right now."

A resigned sigh from the woman, the dog settling back

down on the grass next to the gazebo. "I told Dario he'd get into trouble with the police over that Mr. Friedman, and I was sure of it after the horrible man called me this week, demanding to know where my son was." A more critical expression from the eyes. "Or are you *with* the police?"

"Used to be. Now I'm a private investigator in Boston. And we need Dario to help us out on a trial."

"Trial? I thought that was all over with."

Read, it's Thursday, and the lady's talked with her son sometime since the verdict on Monday afternoon. "This is a new trial."

"A series of trials? Actually, that's a pretty good metaphor for my life with Dario." A pause, and another critical look, this time into the water in front of her. "No, that's not really fair. The 'trial' was being married to his father, who, frankly, resembled you in some ways. The hair, the build, that kind of shoulders-forward, hip-cocked way you have of standing."

Great. You remind a woman you need information from of the ex she hates. "Ann, about Dario?"

"Why don't you call him 'the Calculator,' like that horrible Mr. Friedman does?"

"Truth is, I don't know your son that well. And he's not in any trouble himself. We just want him as a witness."

"And you can't find Dario down in Boston?"

"He told people there he was coming up here to see you."

"Well, Pontifico, he didn't tell people up here that."

It took a moment to sink in. "You mean your son didn't even tell you?"

"No. Just called me. Said that with all the hubbub over the trial they'd just gone through, he needed a break."

"Dario say where he was going?"

"No."

"And you didn't ask?"

"My son's an adult. And besides," kind of a languid laying back of the head, "I don't want him butting into my life, so why give him possible cause by butting into his?"

Murizzi shifted his stance a little, conscious that Ann Whatever's eyes followed his hips. "Why do you suppose Dario didn't let you in on his plans?"

"Beats me, Pontifico."

"Any reason he'd tell his boss he was coming here?"

"Probably thought nobody would drive four hours to check on him."

Lady, you're preaching to the choir on that one. "Which still leaves me looking for your son without any way to find him."

"You try plane reservations, car rentals, train tickets?"

"Some of that's confidential."

"Oh, I don't know," said Ann Whatever, shifting herself on the bench under the water. Let that hair fall naturally and rub a little makeup on her, she could pass for striking, depending on the body Murizzi couldn't—and wasn't particularly interested to—see. "I thought ex-cops could get pretty much anything they set their sights on."

The Pope thought back to Lurlene Inch at the insurance agency, but this was a more subtle, sophisticated approach. Not hot and quick, but cool and slow, like the languid rolls of the head. "Doesn't always work that way, Ann."

"Pity."

Murizzi tried a different tack. "You have any reason to think Dario was in any kind of trouble?"

Genuine concern flickered across the mother's face now. "What kind of trouble?"

"Nothing I know of, but did he seem nervous at all on the phone to you?"

"Dario's always nervous. Personally, I think his father was the reason, always yelling at him over the least little thing. You see, as my ex lost his hair, he lost his temper along with it. Not lucky like you, Pontifico, to have had a maternal grandfather who didn't carry the male-pattern baldness gene."

Jeez, this woman's grading your gene pool now? "Ann, I'm not trying to press you on—"

"Come to think of it, though, you do look a bit . . . nervous yourself." Ann Whatever rose slightly in the tub, so that the tops of her bare breasts broke the cloudy surface of the water. "How about some Maine relaxation, Southern California–style?"

The Pope actually thought about it, but the image brought back memories of Jocko playing games with him in warm water, and so Pontifico Murizzi told Dario's mom thanks anyway and made his way back to the truck, the coyote dog bounding along beside him as though about to begin a great adventure.

10

"Mr. Gallup," said Mairead O'Clare from the reception area of the corporation headquartered in Boston near the Prudential Center.

Juror number two, tall in height and broad of shoulder, barely broke stride on his way out the front door, a nicely tailored gray suit draping his frame and a small duffel bag slung over one of those shoulders. "Whatever you're selling, I'm not—wait a minute." He came to a full stop, his sandy hair in the JFK cut Mairead recognized from old news documentaries Sister Bernadette insisted they watch at the orphanage. Gallup had strong, chiseled features and a cleft in his chin like Michael Douglas.

Or Kirk, young lady. But it isn't hard to see why Ms. Balaguer might have found him "a dreamboat," is it?

Gallup said, "You're the lawyer from the trial."

"Yes," Mairead said, extending her hand.

The man looked down at her skin, didn't extend his own.

Thinking, Another one of those, Mairead dropped the hand to her side. "Mr. Gallup, I'd like to speak with you about Conchita Balaguer."

A cold smile, then a leaned, whispered, "On the scale of one to ten, a seven point five."

Phil Quinn's assessment proved right on the money. "Is there somewhere we could—"

"Look, I'm on my way to the gym, doll. If you want to

come with me, we can talk while I work out, and that way I kill two little birdies with one stone, okay?"

Add patronization to the list. How do women fall for somebody like this?

Then Gallup flashed a smile like the hero on the cover of a romance novel, and Mairead had an inkling. The man also reminded her of ADA James Seagraves, but Gallup was a shallower model of the same car, a tad more tinny when you shut the door.

Riding down in the crowded elevator, Mairead didn't speak, since Dreamboat was using his cellular. On the street, Gallup's stride and pace were hard to match, even with him talking into the phone and her strong legs.

It must have been exceedingly frustrating for a man with this level of energy, however misdirected, to have been confined on a sequestered jury.

Mairead agreed, and spent the rest of the time walking to the gym noodling ways to use that insight.

On Boylston Street between Clarendon and Dartmouth, Troy Gallup veered through clumps of people on the sidewalk and entered a glass doorway under a large red-and-white flag. He climbed one flight of stairs and turned right, Mairead close behind.

A counter was staffed by a young woman wearing a placket-collared shirt. She took an orange card from Gallup, pattered on her computer, then returned the card. "Towel, Mr. Gallup?"

"I'll need three, doll."

The young woman gave him a tired look before laying the neatly folded towels on the counter one at a time.

Gallup said to her, "This is a friend of mine who wants to see the club toward joining. I'm going to take her around as I do my routine."

"She really should fill out a—"

"If she likes what she sees, maybe she will." Gallup turned. "Let's go."

As Gallup began climbing some internal stairs, two at a

time, Mairead mouthed the words "I'm sorry" to the young woman, who shrugged back a "What can you do?"

By the time Mairead reached the next level, Gallup was nowhere to be seen. She walked up each of two more flights, settling on the third level, outside the men's locker room.

He'll certainly have to take off that suit to exercise.

Two minutes later, Troy Gallup came around the corner of the locker room and into an area of air-resistance machines, some of which Mairead recognized from the weight room near the hockey rink at her college. The machines, however, weren't what caught her eye.

The man was buff, no argument there.

Gallup wore a strappy track singlet, silk shorts, and white socks with some elaborate, sculpted cross-trainers. His legs were like tree trunks, the triceps in his arms and pectorals in his chest perfectly defined.

"Mairead, I usually do twenty-four minutes on the stationary bike, then twenty on the StairMaster, then twelve on the recline bike," each piece of information delivered in a tone that suggested she'd want to get his program stats right the first time. "But today, I'm a little pressed, so we'll do just the StairMaster, since my quads are solid, but my calves need some toning."

Mairead just nodded, afraid of what might come out if she spoke aloud.

They descended one flight to a cardiovascular area of bikes, cross-country skiing machines, and step systems. Gallup chose the StairMaster closest to a window overlooking Trinity Church. Another machine abutted on the other side, and a mirrored wall rose behind, so Mairead had to sit on the wide sill and speak to him sideways, his head moving from the computer readout to scope other women in the club, walking by or working out.

After Gallup pushed some computer pads on the "dashboard," he started pumping his legs alternately on the treaded shovels, as though climbing steps. "Okay, you've got twenty minutes. Usually I read a magazine on this machine, but for you, doll"—a turn from profile-only to give her the toothpaste smile—"I'll make an exception."

Lucky me. And then Mairead realized she *was* lucky that Dreamboat, unlike some other jurors, would see her at all. "Mr. Gallup, I'd—"

"Oh, come on, Mairead. We're in the new millennium, right? How about Troy?"

This part of the "new millennium" was going to be sickening. "Troy, I understand from other jurors that you and Ms. Balaguer had a relationship during the trial."

"You could call it that, and she probably did, too."

"But you wouldn't?"

"Look, ten minutes into being called for that jury, she was giving me the eye. Talking with her, I find out she has an ex-husband who's a real macho shithead. Then, we're told all fourteen of us are going to be sequestered. It was like *Survivor*, you know?"

Mairead had heard of the television show, but its concept had sounded so awesomely stupid, she'd never watched it. "In what way?"

"Well, on the show, people get voted off the island, one by one, right? In the jury version, we had to stay together, hear the whole case, and then two got 'voted off' by the judge. But before that, all fourteen of us had the same idea: We're stuck together for a while, may as well make the most of it."

Notice, young lady, he said "the most," not "the best." "So, you and Ms. Balaguer decided to become lovers."

"Practically ripped my clothes off the first night. Which nearly *pissed* me off."

"I'm not sure I follow."

"Hey, doll, I didn't come to court dressed like a bum. I was wearing a six-hundred-dollar Bill Blass, like the one you just saw me in, and Chita nearly tore the sleeve from the saddle."

Bummer. "So you had an affair with Ms. Balaguer."

"What else was I supposed to do? The motel they put us

up in had three dinky little bikes and one Universal machine that was probably assembled before you were born. Instead of twiddling my thumbs, I diddled Chita's buns."

Mairead wondered how long it had taken Brain Trust here to come up with that pithy line. "Any problems with the relationship?"

"Not from my end. Chita hadn't had anything like me, at least from the way she moaned and howled. I got the impression that her ex was kind of a pencil dick."

Mairead bit back an urge to scream herself. "So, everything was fine during the trial?"

"No, doll, it was *stultifying*. The boredom, you guys always whispering to the judge over on the other side of the bench. Witnesses who couldn't speak understandable English, those incredibly transparent parents, bawling over a little yard-ape they couldn't be troubled to watch. It was like having to sit through this really bad play for a full week."

It bothered Mairead that Ben Friedman and Troy Gallup had the same take on the Vukonovs, but then from the jury box, Gallup and the others had had a better view of the gallery than the lawyers did. "I understand you were one of the first jurors to vote not guilty."

"Huh," said Gallup, twisting his head around to watch his calf muscles working in the mirror and nodding at what he saw. "So, all that judge talk about us 'not discussing the case' really was just a crock."

"You're not supposed to discuss the case pre-deliberation, but it's okay to talk about it post-verdict."

"Yeah, well, there was certainly some pre-bullshitting, too."

Remembering that Shel and she had won the case, Mairead didn't feel unethical in following up on that. "Jurors discussed the evidence before the trial was finished?"

"I remember saying to Chita—even *before* she tried to swallow my pride—that the whole case was a hoax, that those Russians were probably so stupid they ran over their *own* kid by accident. But since they found themselves in the land of milk and honey, why not fuck the system and some poor guy who made something of himself to get money they don't deserve."

Mairead began to think back to the voir dire of the jurors before they were impaneled. How the judge asked very few questions, yet wouldn't let Shel or even Seagraves ask any. The beauty of that process was that trials didn't bog down early because of jury selection, but if one like Troy Gallup could slip through the screen, imagine some of the attitudes that got "represented" in the box on other kinds of cases.

"Hey, doll, you finished with your questions?"

Mairead shook her head to clear it and help pass the umpteenth "doll" remark. "So you were the one who suggested to Ms. Balaguer that Ben Friedman wasn't guilty."

"Not of killing that kid, and she agreed with me." Another lean-over whisper. "Now I grant you, a Jew who sounds like he has a sixth-grade education and doesn't own a sweatshop or a slum probably didn't make his fortune playing by the rules. But that's true for your Italians and Spics, too, so I didn't hold it against him."

Bear up, young lady. "Had you planned to continue your relationship with Ms. Balaguer after the trial ended?"

"That's what I mean again, about that word 'relationship.' Chita was wet and tight, a great combination in the 'tunnel of love' every night of the trial, so I didn't hit on anybody else from the jury. But once we were free and back in the world, would I have worked her into the starting rotation? Hard to say. Given the other talent I've got going for me, Chita might have been bull pen material, call her to the mound only if one of the starters was on the rag or away for a weekend."

I wonder if they have barf bags at health clubs? "Did Ms. Balaguer ever mention any money she expected to receive?"

"Yeah. Said that after the trial, she'd be getting some bucks, but she wouldn't tell me how much or where from. I figured she was just dangling the bait."

"Bait?"

"Yeah. To keep me interested in her after we weren't going to be sequestered anymore."

End of the line on that, young lady. "Troy, who do you think killed Ms. Balaguer?"

"No idea, doll, past the macho ex-husband. He's a Spic himself, and once their blood gets boiling, they're capable of anything."

Mairead drew in a long breath, held it for a count of five. "Where were you when Ms. Balaguer was killed?"

"That was the night we got off duty, right?"

Odd thing to forget. "Yes."

"Well, I felt so logy from sitting around all day and stuck with the same people all night that I just went for a walk. I stopped at the apartment instead of the office, and then I came over to the club to work out."

"When were you here?"

"Didn't pay too much attention, but before dinner. Like five-thirty to seven?"

Picturing the counter downstairs, Mairead had an idea as Gallup droned on. "It's more crowded then, but Mondays the foxier chicks who didn't get any over the weekend come out to shake their groove things. Remember that song?"

I just want to remember where the exit is. "Troy, thanks for your time."

"Hey, happy to help. Here..." He dragged a card from the pocket of his shorts. "I wrote my home number and address on there, you need anything else."

Vulgar as the guy is, a willingness to help might be his one redeeming virtue. "Thanks again."

Not yet letting go of the card, Gallup said, "Especially if you need it... over a weekend, doll."

Consider that virtue *un*redeemed.

Mairead retraced her steps down to the reception area. The same woman sat by the computer, but no one else was in front of her counter.

"Did you like the place?"

"Yes," said Mairead. "But I really wasn't here to take a tour."

"I didn't think so." The woman glanced upstairs. "That guy's brought half a dozen women through here, all young and attractive like you. None of them has ever joined that I know of."

Sensing some common ground, Mairead said, "A question?"

"Sure."

"When you take a member's orange card, what do you do with it?"

"Oh, I just check the membership number and enter it into the computer here, be sure the person's paid up currently."

"Does the computer also enter the time that person stops in?"

"Well, yeah."

"But not the time he or she leaves."

"No, we wouldn't check on that."

Mairead said, "Could you do me a big favor?"

"If I can."

"Ask the computer whether that guy with me came in on a given date."

The young woman looked around, apparently saw nobody. "He really is an asshole."

"That doesn't begin to cover it."

A shared smile, and the woman tapped the date on her keyboard.

at old Bowdoin Square, Sheldon A. Gold walked past the limbless, headless torso statue in white marble lying on its back that served, for Shel anyway, as a kind of warning about who worked inside the red-bricked building carrying the address One Bulfinch Place. On street level, there were just two anonymous elevators inside the lobby, but Shel knew to take one of them to the third floor, where the door slid open on a small reception area of dull pink walls and purplish carpet, some framed drawings by local public-school students as decoration. Opposite the stand-up display holding brochures on "Rights of Victims" and "Abuse Prevention" in various languages, Shel told the nice woman behind the thick glass whom he'd like to see. In exchange for his driver's license, she gave him a laminated VISITOR badge, which he clipped onto his belt.

Before long, the elevator Shel had used disgorged ADA James Seagraves, who beckoned commandingly.

While riding up to the floor for the district attorney's Homicide Unit, Shel tried an icebreaker. "It ever bother you that your logo is a statue of a mutilated torso?"

"What, the white marble thing?"

"Yes."

"It belongs to the health club next door. And besides, I've always thought it looked like a molar."

And sometimes a cloud is just a cloud, thought Shel as Seagraves, with military briskness, led him down a corridor.

Inside Seagraves's office, the armed-service metaphor really hit home. His file cabinet and desk were olive drab, and a corkboard on the wall had unit shoulder patches pinned to it. Flanking the corkboard was a photo of a younger Seagraves in naval dress uniform and another of some modern warship.

Shel sat down across the desk from Seagraves, who hit a key on his computer before saying, "You're coming to see me near the end of a very long week." The prosecutor reached for a manila case jacket with an Acco clip showing on its front. "I'm assuming this is about Benjamin Friedman?"

After meeting with Gallina Ekarevskaya, Shel had tried calling Big Ben, but got no answer, not even one of his old friend's goons. "I was wondering if you'd come to any decisions about my client."

Seagraves grinned, and not warmly. "I have, actually. The guy's a gangster, a slob, and a murderer."

"Not according to the jury."

"Maybe, but only on the last count."

"And then only, I grant you, on the killing of poor Yuri Vukonov. But the decision I was wondering about was whether you were intending to indict Ben on Conchita Balaguer."

Seagraves settled back in his chair, lacing his fingers behind his neck. "Grand juries indict, Gold. I just present evidence to them."

Shel thought about mentioning that the prosecutor was the *only* lawyer who *did* present evidence to the people in that room, but instead he said, "Do you plan to take the Balaguer incident to a grand jury?"

"Why would I tell you, either way?"

Sugar over vinegar. "Well, I was thinking that if the indictment was handed down, we could all save some aggravation by arranging for my client to surrender himself for arraignment and bail."

Now Seagraves frowned. "You seem awfully cooperative for a defense attorney who's already gotten the guy off on one murder."

"If the hit-and-run of Yuri Vukonov even was a murder, and not just a tragic accident. But I don't see any reason not to handle what, if anything, comes next as gentlemen."

"Or gentlewomen."

"Meaning?"

"Did Ekarevskaya sue the bastard yet?"

"No."

"She's been on me like a pit bull about bringing your guy back into the system, probably hoping for a victory by our office, give her more ammo for the Russians' wrongful death suit."

"Maybe Gallina's just being patient."

"Not from my dealings with her." Seagraves came forward in his chair, all business now. "Look, Gold. The detectives have worked day and night on this Balaguer killing. They've canvassed her neighbors in Roslindale, fellow jurors, coworkers—"

"Suspicious bosses, violent ex-husband."

Seagraves paused. "And that ten thousand dollars in cash."

"Almost ten thousand, which Ms. Balaguer deposited in her bank account. Tell me, you remember any bribe-taker doing that with the proceeds when they were already in currency?"

"I'm not going to try my case in this office, Gold. I think Friedman bribed Balaguer, or had her bribed. And I think she tried to gouge more after the acquittal, using the threat of her coming to us and flipping on the fix."

"Which Ben would have laughed at, telling Balaguer that'd mean she'd have to kick back the money into court and maybe face a criminal conviction herself."

"Or which your client—*not* the most self-composed of citizens—might have gone haywire about, and called for a couple of his thugs with a rope, teach the bitch her ultimate lesson."

Admit it: You don't think your friend did that, but Seagraves's portrait of Ben's not so far off that a new jury wouldn't.

Shel asked, "So, where do we stand?"

"Same place we were before you wasted my time today. But I will give you this: We indict Friedman, and you'll get a courtesy call."

Shel mustered what he'd been told was his "gracious" smile. "Then I haven't wasted my time."

"Just remember, Gold, the call may not be for a surrender opportunity. And tell your client to stay by his phone, too."

As James Seagraves appended that last clause, Shel Gold was taken back to his own futile attempts to reach Ben Friedman and barely kept himself from cringing at what they might mean.

billie Sunday opened the front door of her house to the muffled sounds of hip-hop music coming from the upstairs. It was a little early for Robert Junior to be home from baseball practice, and earlier still for William to be picked up at his after-school straddle care. But Billie had left work just to have this chance to catch Matthew at home without her other two sons around.

To have a genuine "heart-to-heart," as her husband, Robert Senior, would have called it.

Billie carried the tote bag that doubled as handbag and briefcase toward the answering machine on the table near the kitchen. Rewinding the messages, she took out the copy of the *Boston Herald* that she'd intercepted before Shel got a chance to read it. Billie had spotted a follow-up article on the disappearance of a ten-year-old boy in February from a small town forty miles away. There was a grainy photo of the poor child, his dark eyes looking out with happiness and deviltry under darker hair. A second photo showed the parents and their lawyer, holding a press conference, talking about the National Center for Missing and Exploited Children in Virginia, and begging anybody with information on their son to step forward.

Billie had kept the paper from Shel because of that article, not wanting to heap another father's sorrow on top of his own over losing Richie so many years before. But now, Billie admitted to herself, the real reason she'd hooked the *Herald* was because it gave her a booster shot toward confronting Matthew again, not just about what had happened in the fight at his school, but to avoid Billie being photographed holding her own news conference, begging for help in finding her middle son, "last seen in the company of one Rondell Wickes."

Shaking her head, Billie decided the phone messages could wait to be returned, and she climbed the steps to the second floor.

The music—surprise, surprise—was coming through Matthew's closed door. Robert Senior always believed that a heart-to-heart was better held on "neutral ground," but Billie figured that she'd learn more about her middle son's situation and attitude by talking to the young lion in his own den.

Her knuckles rapped lightly on the door, then a little harder before she heard a disinterested "Yeah?" from behind it.

"Matthew, I'd like to talk to you, please."

"Doing homework."

"Now, please. Can I come in?"

"Guess so."

Billie turned the knob. It was an old house, and the bedroom doors had locks and murder-mystery keys, but Matthew's wasn't engaged.

What Billie saw: her son, first and foremost, lying on his bed in a shirt and pants with as much material in their baggy selves as the top sheet under him. He wore a Dallas Cowboys ball cap backward on his head, a notebook open in front of him, and a textbook open in front of that. Billie wasn't sure how good an actor her son was, but she got the feeling that the books weren't just props he'd grabbed for when her knock came at his door.

What Billie heard: Somebody howling lyrics she didn't even think were English until she caught maybe the tenth word.

What Billie smelled: No marijuana, or beer, or anything else except that tang of testosterone you get when entering any room inhabited by a male teenager.

Billie sighed, almost in relief: Laundry stains she could handle.

Without his good eye leaving the books, Matthew said, "Whassup, Momma?"

Instead of answering, she glanced around the room. On his bureau, a portable boombox flanked by jumbles of CDs outside their little plastic cases. On his walls, posters of his music idols. On his desk, another jumble, this one of papers.

"Matthew, can we turn down the music?"

This time he looked up, frowning, the bruises from the day before almost like clown makeup. But the thirteen-year-old rolled off his bed and switched off the box.

"Now, can we sit and talk, please?"

Matthew came back, expressionless, and sat on one side of the bed like an Apache at his campfire.

Billie eased down on an opposite corner. This boy is so strange, even to the mother who knows he's her son.

"Matthew, how was school today?"

A shrug. "All right." Another shrug before she could ask her next question.

Billie said, "Everything okay with those other boys?"

"The ones we whupped?"

"The ones from the fight."

"Yeah. They gave us a wide turn in the yard this morning." Then a hesitation. "Uh, thanks for standing up for Rondell and me with Hightower yesterday."

"The man was only doing his job, and all I did was try to help him see the right way to do it."

A third shrug.

"Matthew, talk to me."

"About what?"

"About what's going on, truly."

"Thought I already did."

"You and Rondell, what do you do together?"

A fourth shrug, what his mother always thought was Matthew's version of a Valley Girl's "like," he used it so often.

Billie said, "Give me some examples, please?"

"We hang out, listen to the music. You know."

"No, but I want to."

Billie sensed her son on the edge of a decision. He said, "Really?"

"Really."

"Okay." A deep breath. "Here's what I been told—"

"What *I've* been told."

Matthew stopped. "Momma, I know you want me to talk like the lawyers you work for, but you want to hear the truth about the music, I got to tell it my own way."

Worth the sacrifice. "Go on."

Another deep breath. "What Rondell tells me is, back in the eighties, the rappers got started, cut some tracks about raping and killing and drugging, so the government people got mad, and MTV made the brothers clean up their acts, wipe them down to PG for the parents, follow?"

Lord, if MTV is PG . . . "I follow you, Matthew."

"Then come a time when the 'gangsta-rap' start to come true in real life, with the drugs and the murders of the MCs—they're the ones do the rapping."

"The singers?"

"Kind of. Hip-hop grew out of that stuff, but the—'mainstream' is what Rondell call it—the mainstream want things they know work, like Hollywood with its car chases and booty babes for the movies. So that's what you see on the TV. Only that ain't what hip-hop is really all about."

Burying the "ain't," Billie said, "What is it all about, Matthew?"

"It's like stories of the street, only kind of poetry about it." Her son became suddenly animated. "The real MCs, the ones don't have no major label burning their disks, they the brothers busting the real rhymes, swears and all. They creating tracks that tell about what it's like, be in a school where the teachers don't teach and the toilets don't flush. Where the white kids get the grades and the scholarships, and the black kids get the 'condescension' and the 'detention.' Just like with Rondell and me against those white boys."

Then Matthew seemed to step back a little. "I'm too young for the eighteen-and-over shows, but I can take a bus, hang with Rondell and the other brothers at this record store that has CDs, yeah, but also EPs and twelve-inchers with a couple of songs on them from the local cats like Mr. Lif or Akrobatik or the Nightcrawlers. It's my way of expressing myself, Momma. The beats, the rhymes," Matthew tugging on his shirt and pants, "even the clothes, like Mecca and Fubu. It's who I am, a son of yours interested in the truth."

"Does Rondell think the same way?"

"Rondell into the music more than me. He's like my mentor."

"So long as he doesn't get you into anything else."

"No sweat, Momma."

"We lost your father to a drunk driver. I don't want to lose you, too."

"Hey, I get high on hip-hop, not drugs or booze."

Billie Sunday stared at her middle child, and then thought again about that *Herald* article on the couple who lost their son, and decided she had enough to be thankful for to embarrass Matthew by reaching across the bed to him and dragging the boy over for a hug.

talk about your long days.

Pontifico Murizzi nearly closed his eyes as he pulled the Explorer into its space on the apron of the marina where he kept his houseboat. After leaving Ann Whatever to stew in her hot tub, he'd thought about having some dinner, staying over at one of the mom-and-pop motels along the main drag near I-95. Only thing was, all the restaurants he passed were low-end chain places, and while he didn't like to think of himself as a food snob, the fact is that, raised in Boston's North End, the Pope didn't believe in wasting calories on inferior fuel. So instead he figured to get back to the city at a reasonable hour, maybe catch Jocko for a glass of wine.

Only Murizzi hadn't accounted for the traffic accident.

North of Portland, some semi driver had rolled his rig pulling two trailers of—fasten your fucking seat belts—cattle. The truck and both trailers blocked the entire road southbound, and the state police, in their infinite wisdom, hadn't the common sense to divert *more* vehicles from getting onto the highway farther north. All of which meant, according to the radio the Pope turned on about half an hour too late, a nine-mile backup.

Like a lot of the people caught in the jam, Murizzi got out of the Explorer and walked forward, trying to figure a way around things. Only after a hundred yards of median strip, with guys cursing and their kids crying and women shushing them, the Pope could see it was hopeless. Dead and dying cows were scattered over the lanes like there'd been a range war, the pop of the staties' sidearms sounding oddly impotent in all the open air as they put the worst hurt of the animals out of their misery.

All told, Murizzi had been stuck for more than four hours while the Mainers dealt with the mess, the eventual drive south still pretty well choked with traffic for the hundred-plus miles back to Boston.

Now, though, at least you're home, safe and sound. And count your blessings, you could have been just behind the semi, and they'd be scraping you off the pavement like those poor fucking cows.

The Pope felt a little lighter in spirit as he hit the camel, a crust of scum at the floating dock's edge bobbing with each step he took on it. Plastic bottles that once contained Gatorade or Cranapple juice, soggy cardboard containers that once held raisins, cigars, and pastel-colored condoms.

Christ, don't people realize they fucking *live* here?

Still walking but shaking his head, Murizzi at first thought the combined movements were causing an optical illusion. But as he got closer to his houseboat, visible—*too* visible—fifty feet ahead, he realized it was no illusion.

The schooner was gone.

Forcing himself not to break into a run, the Pope reached his own stern and vaulted over the gunwale. There was a folded piece of paper, held down by a spare pulley, on his resin cocktail table.

Murizzi opened the paper, which read in blocky handwriting:

Pope,

His nibs decided today was the day, and I have only this minute to write. Any note's a poor way to say thanks for having been a brilliant part of my life, even my "education." But one chapter closes and another opens. For both of us.

Luv,
Jocko

Pontifico Murizzi closed his eyes and ground his teeth, then crumpled the "note" and flung it into the water, not caring what particular pieces of the shit floating around his boat the paper could now call neighbor.

11

Very well, young lady, this is nothing you haven't done before.

Going over the boards and onto the ice surface, Mairead O'Clare tried to believe Sister Bernadette's voice. At the beginning of every hockey season, there had always been a sense of uncertainty. The sense that—no matter how many individual moves and line-mate drills the coach had put Mairead and the other team members through in practice—this was a real game, against real opponents who wanted to beat your brains out, not nurture your development with encouraging words.

Only this wasn't the beginning of a season, this was close to the end of one, even if it was the first time Mairead had skated competitively since turning her left ankle some months before. But she'd taped the ankle and tested it, at first gingerly. Then, with both tape and brace, a little more intensively with cuts and turns, even bashing herself into the boards (as was permitted in the "boys' rules" games she preferred to the no-checking restrictions of "girls' rules"). And the joint had passed all those preliminary tests.

This, however, was the real thing.

Without Mairead, her team in the predawn league had slipped three places in the standings, and it needed to win this game to assure a fourth straight year in the play-offs. Even with the demands of attending law school, Mairead had played with a rotating version of these men and women since college, and she didn't want to let them down by contributing to the end of their streak.

Her first shift on the ice went fine. She received three passes from her center, and Mairead in turn laid the puck on the blades of other teammates, exchanges both crisp and tactically effective. And while none of the plays in which Mairead had been involved resulted in a shot on goal, much less a score, it felt good and right to be back doing this.

While another line of her team's forwards and a pair of defensemen were on the ice, though, an opposing female right wing juked around a defender who spent too much of his time in the brew pubs and not enough skating backward, the wing shooting the puck through the "five-hole" between the kneeling goalie's heavily padded thighs, resulting in a 1–0 lead for the other team.

"Okay," Mairead said, hearing herself pump on the bench, "let's get it back, all right?"

On her next shift, Mairead received a bullet pass at center ice from her right defenseman. Turning on the jets, Mairead spun the opposing winger trying to check her into a three-sixty, the defender losing her balance and going down on her stomach, effectively out of the play.

A male defenseman tried to cover for his teammate by coming over on an intercept angle, to take the body and let the goalie control the puck. But Mairead was able to partially slip his check, the glancing impact torquing her ankle, but no pain from the injured area. As Mairead dug in her skate blades to accelerate toward the goalie, he scudded toward her, to block out more of the net with his body. However, her left leg just wasn't providing much push-off, and when Mairead tried to wrist the puck into the upper corner of the goalmouth, her shot missed the crossbar by two feet.

"Buck fever, bitch," said the goalie, quietly enough so the ref couldn't hear him.

Back on the bench after the shift change, Mairead tried

to catch her breath and assess the situation. Testing her ankle, she still found no pain, but no real strength, either.

Rather like a Novocain shot at the dentist, young lady.

Mairead agreed, then focused on following the flow of the game so she'd have the feel of it when she went back onto the ice.

Fortunately, her next shift change wasn't on the fly but rather prompted by a whistle for an offside play. As Mairead jumped over the boards this time, she landed on the bad ankle, a stinger surging from the heel of her foot to the back of her knee. As the linesman waited for all players to assume their positions around the centers facing off toward the drop of the puck, the pain was there every time Mairead pushed off on her left skate.

No biggie. I've played through pain before.

However, the opposing center controlled the face-off, and the defenseman who came up with the puck feathered a perfect carom pass off the dasher on Mairead's side of the ice. The streaking winger she was to be guarding blew past her before Mairead could fully turn, much less get started after her. The winger finessed the defender on Mairead's team and lifted a beautiful backhand knuckleball over the goalie's stick hand for a second score, making it 2–0.

Back on the bench, Mairead's captain/coach—a nice guy named Bob, an architect in his thirties—shoved over beside her. "Mairead, you okay?"

Be smart, young lady, not brave. "It's the ankle again. No first step when I go to my right."

The captain nodded. "We've all been there. You want to rest it or risk it?"

Which Mairead thought was a pretty diplomatic way to ask the question. "Let's see how I feel between periods."

"Okay, but you untape the thing, you'll never get your skate back on."

Mairead just nodded to herself this time.

Still down 2–0 at the end of the first period, Mairead made her way down the ramp toward the locker room for the short intermission, made shorter by all concerned because of the cost of ice time at the rink, even at 5 A.M. Walking on skates, always a teetering, awkward method of movement, was nearly impossible with the bad ankle.

"Hey," said one of the less capable defenders on her team, a woman who'd played—barely, in Mairead's memory—for Brown, "you really, like, hung us out to dry on their last goal."

"Thanks for noticing."

"If you can't help us, at least don't hurt us, huh?"

"Bob'll decide that," said Mairead, clumping on despite the pain.

In the locker room on the old, scarred bench, Mairead applied a bag of ice to her ankle through the still laced-up skate until the buzzer sounded to return to the rink surface. On the way back, the ankle felt a little better.

Or just a little more numb?

After Bob looked at her, Mairead nodded, and he sent her over the boards for the first shift of the second period.

All right. Let's see what happens if I go full bore.

Anticipating correctly, Mairead intercepted a pass in the neutral zone at center ice and tore down her right-wing side toward the opposing goalie. She'd been able to work up a good head of steam using mainly her sound ankle as the throttle. When a defender closed on her, Mairead scooted the puck forward between his skates, and a skip move left the guy sliding by harmlessly. Mairead sidled around him, gathered the puck, and kept heading toward the net.

Last time, I tried high and missed badly. Get inside the goalie's head and you'd hear, "She won't try that again, so go down butterfly, protect against the low slap shot and smother any rebound."

Mairead swooped in and across the goalmouth, watching for the telltale dip of the goalie's knees that would signal the butterfly drop onto the ice, his lower legs splaying out along the goal line. But then get just under the puck and flick it just . . . so!

The goalie went down, then waved his glove hand futilely at the puck scything its way through the air and into the top corner of the net.

Mairead heard the check as much as felt it, the forgiving glass atop the dasher bending into the empty stands to cushion her impact. The ref whistled just as he stopped pointing into the net, signaling both a goal for Mairead and a penalty for the late hit on her.

Exhilarated, she skated back to her bench, getting blade taps from her teammates as she went down the length of them, even the borderline player from Brown saying, "You go, girl!"

Mairead settled her butt back down on the wood, took a nice deep breath as well. It felt good to be back.

If only lawyering could be as simple, young lady.

Which did take something off the spell of the moment, but not much.

sheldon Gold arrived at the office to find that nobody had gotten in yet, so he checked his watch, which indicated Billie was half an hour behind her usual start time.

There's got to be something more happening in her life than a simple fight her son had at school.

Then Shel checked the answering machine. A message logged the prior night from the Pope said he'd been to Maine but hadn't found Dario Calcagni, the mother thinking the accountant was going someplace after the trial to decompress. The message ended with a promise from Murizzi to start looking into the mysterious "inspector," Hildy Crowell, next. Shel thought the Pope sounded awfully tired, maybe from the long, fruitless drive.

The second message was Mairead, saying she had a hockey game but should be in fairly early. After talking with jurors Josephine Arria and Troy Gallup, though, the young associate didn't think they'd be much help to the cause.

Strike two, thought Shel.

And then he wished he'd counted the number of times he'd tried to reach Ben Friedman the prior day after the meet with ADA James Seagraves. At least seven, which worried Shel. Occasionally, he'd had trouble contacting Ben himself, who was often off somewhere or incommunicado by choice. However, almost always Tiffany Bomberg or Edsel Crow at least would answer the phone, and Ben had sounded pretty interested in hearing what the Pope might have found out regarding his accountant Calcagni.

Which is when the suite door opened, and Billie Sunday stepped through it.

"Shel, sorry I'm late."

"Hey, you're the one who wants to be in early. I'm not such a clock-watcher."

A nice smile on the face that looked as tired to Shel's eyes as the Pope's voice had sounded to his ears. The lawyer said, "Everything okay with Matthew?"

"I think so. We had a good talk yesterday, and, frankly I got the best night's sleep I've had this week."

Shel hoped his smile conveyed how glad he was to hear that. After filling Billie in quickly on what Murizzi and Mairead had reported, he said, "Any chance you could visit that insurance agency this afternoon?"

"If Stover-Trent doesn't hire me on sight, you think I could sue them for discrimination?"

Which made Shel Gold's smile a little broader.

what a way to live your fucking life.

Pontifico Murizzi tried to get comfortable on one of those silly-looking "ergonomic" chairs next to a friend of his from the old neighborhood who now worked computers in a state agency. It was maybe an hour before the office "officially" opened, but the Pope had done what he'd been told the prior night after reaching his friend—Tony—at home and requesting some access here. Now they both stared at a monitor screen, with Tony—gut thick, hair thin—playing the keyboard like a nerdy Liberace. Only, to

Murizzi, the stuff flashing and rolling on the screen seemed more like physics formulas than hard information.

"Talk to me on this, Tone."

"First, I've got to get into the computer banks of Hildy Crowell's agency, and then be sure I can back out again without leaving a trail."

"Like Hansel and Gretel, but in reverse?"

Tony gave the Pope kind of an odd look. "I suppose."

Waiting while his friend picked his way through some kind of computer minefield, Murizzi couldn't keep Jocko's leaving like that from his mind. Granted, the trip to Maine turned out to be poor fucking timing, but Fletcher the former Queen's Minister was going to sail for Europe at some point, regardless of what the Pope wanted.

And Jocko, knowing his bread was spread with British butter, was going to be at the schooner's helm. Not to mention, whenever sailing conditions permitted, probably on Fletcher's "rudder" as well.

So, your own boat of life hits an iceberg, close the watertight compartment on the hole in the hull, spin the wheel till the door's fucking sealed, and plow on.

However, it still took another five minutes of stupefyingly dull clacking before Murizzi heard Tony say, "Okay. We're in."

The Pope didn't see much improvement, screenwise. "Now what?"

"I've got to break through the firewall surrounding the good stuff."

Another five minutes, Murizzi was thinking, No wonder you're turning into Curly of the Three Stooges, Tone, you spend the entire working day exercising just your ten fingers.

"Through the wall," said his friend. "What do you want to know?"

The Pope told him.

More clacking, but now Tony frowned, hit a few more keys, then shook his head.

"What?" said Murizzi.

"Encoded and encripted."

"In English, Tone?"

"Computer records of your Hildy Crowell have been transferred from the data bank—probably onto a diskette or even zip drive—then deleted from the bank itself."

The Pope tried to process that. "Somebody pulled the manila folder on her from the filing cabinet."

"Essentially. With no indication I can see of where or why, other than this code designation."

"Okay, then, what does the code 'designate'?"

"I don't know."

"What do you mean, you don't know? Computers are your life, right?"

"Yes, but let's say I was an auto mechanic for Ford, and you asked me the part number for a Chevy. I wouldn't know it without the catalog."

"And you can't find Crowell's catalog through your computer here?"

"I can't find her *agency's* one."

Christ on a crutch. "Wait a minute. Didn't you tell me once you could raise a deleted computer folder?"

"'File' would be more accurate in this context."

The Pope resisted the urge to slap Tony on the back of his head for splitting hairs he barely had there anymore. "Okay, whatever you call it, can't you bring up a 'file' that's gone the way our police lab can bring back a serial number filed off a gun?"

"Tell the truth, I don't know how your guys do that. But yes, there are software programs that can recover deleted files."

"So, do that on this here."

"I can't."

"Why not?"

"I'd need access to the hard disk of the computer involved."

"The fuck do you have on your screen now?"

"I have remote access. I don't have the actual hardware

in front of me, with a slot to slide in a diskette, or better, a CD with more capacity and—"

"What you're saying is, you'd have to be in the agency itself, sitting in front of their computer physically."

"The light dawns on Marblehead."

The Pope thought about getting mad, but if Tony was telling the truth—and Murizzi couldn't think of anybody better on computers than his friend—then it was time to leave the "twenty-first century" and go back to the old-fashioned way.

Meaning, a face-to-face with somebody who might already know what Tony couldn't find out for him.

12

Billie Sunday heard the woman behind the reception desk at Stover-Trent Insurancc say, "Can I help you?" and—Lord forgive me—the first thing she thought was, This child does *not* like people of color. Then as the woman nicely introduced herself as Lurlene Inch, and added a "thank you, ma'am," when Billie spelled her first name, she thought, Well, maybe I was going too much by the cracker accent.

After Lurlene accepted Billie's résumé, the child said, "Please have a seat," and went back to an office door, knocking before disappearing inside. Billie took one of the wooden captain's chairs—a lot more comfortable than those plastic scoop things Shel insisted on having in their waiting area—and thought about what one of the owners here might ask her.

If he'll see you at all.

Then Lurlene popped back out of the office. "Mr. Trent will interview you now."

Billie rose, went past Lurlene through the open door, and heard it click behind her.

"Ms. Sunday, welcome! I'm Trevor Trent."

Maybe it was the way the man put too much into the "welcome" part, but Billie decided she wouldn't trust this clefted-chin fraternity brother to sew a button back on her coat. "Thank you for seeing me so quickly."

The man shook hands—firmly—and then bade her sit as

he settled back down into his desk chair and held up a piece of paper she assumed was her résumé. "Very impressive credentials, Ms. Sunday."

Lull the man. "Billie, please."

"Billie it is, then."

Nothing reciprocal from him. So both interviewer and applicant know where they stand.

Trent glanced down at the paper again. "However, I don't see anything about insurance work here."

"No sir," replied Billie, kind of the way she thought Lurlene might. The man hired the child as receptionist, maybe he likes deferential. "But I'm a quick learner, and with three boys to mother, I really do need the job."

Billie knew from what Shel once told her about employment law that Trent couldn't ask about things like marriage and family, but she sensed he was the kind who'd want to have the information.

The man nodded. "I've always thought women with responsibilities outside the office made the best workers inside the office."

Guessed right, girl.

"On the other hand, I'm wondering how you thought to apply . . . *here?*"

"Well, I didn't see any ad in the newspaper, but I did read about the tragic death of one of your people, so . . ."

Trent frowned. "That was four days ago. Why did you wait till now?"

"I didn't think it was fitting to come sooner. But one of my other jobs, a lady died in a traffic accident, and I know how hard it was to get by without a good worker when the rest were grieving over her."

Now a nod. "I think you might do just fine, Billie." Trent picked up the telephone and pushed one button. "Lurlene, please come in here and take our new employee around to meet the other clericals, then ask one of them to show her our systems. After that, check back with me on another matter."

As he hung up, the man rose from his chair and extended his hand again. "Welcome to Stover-Trent!"

Those exclamation points, thought Billie Sunday, would take some getting used to.

"**pope,** how you doing?"

"Pretty well, Jorie. You?"

"Can't complain."

She may have answered that way, but as Pontifico Murizzi settled into the swivel chair at an unmanned computer terminal in the Boston Police Homicide Unit, he thought there was something else in her voice.

"So," said Tully, "this still about the Balaguer case?"

"Yeah, but maybe only indirectly."

She took a quick look at her watch. "Better make it more directly."

Could be that "hurry" was in her voice, but Murizzi read it more like "stress."

"Jorie, my lawyers are running into a stone wall on one of the other jurors that sat on Friedman's trial."

"They don't have to talk with anybody on your team."

"I know, but this juror was willing to talk, she just didn't want to say anything."

A poker face from Tully. Which means you hit a nerve, otherwise she'd laugh or joke about it herself.

"Same answer, Pope."

"The woman we're talking about is Crowell, Hildy."

"Just one of fourteen, with thirteen surviving."

"Come on, Jore. This Balaguer thing is high-profile. You trying to tell me you haven't done an A to Z on every warm body in that jury box?"

"I'm not trying to tell you anything."

"Or maybe you're trying *not* to tell me anything."

That did get a small smile. "All right, Pope, you'd have found out from somebody eventually. Crowell is a really self-important bitch."

"I got that impression. What does she do that makes her that way?"

"More what she used to do."

"Which was?"

"She investigated employment discrimination for one of the state agencies, but..."

Murizzi let the pause lengthen into silence.

Tully finally laughed, the pale eyes sparkling. "I'll give you this, Pope. You haven't lost your interrogation touch."

"What's Crowell's skeleton, Jorie?"

"The woman was a little overaggressive. She's more than a little overweight, and she couldn't handle any situation without turning it into a full-court press."

Murizzi had certainly known a few cops like that. They go from patrol to detective, and they can't get the mad-dog, TV version of working a case out of their minds. "So, she came on too strong."

"And not the only way she... came on."

The Pope wanted to walk softly, so he asked a question he already had the answer to. "Gay or straight?"

"It was pretty hush-hush, but apparently our Hildy liked one of her female coworkers a bit too much."

"And Crowell couldn't exactly investigate herself."

"Fortunately, she and the coworker were peer employees, not superior/subordinate, and the agency head didn't want an 'orientation discrimination' countercharge, so Hildy just got transferred."

"To what now?"

"Domestic Abuse."

"Still as an investigator?"

"Yeah. The way I understand it, she acts kind of like a safety net for the cases that slip through the cracks of the regular system."

Murizzi tried to picture that. "Meaning, some husband's too free with his fists, and the court doesn't catch him cold, Crowell digs deeper?"

"Basically." Another glance at the watch. "Pope, I gotta go."

"Maybe some *ex*-husband even. Like Balaguer's?"

She stood up. "Sorry."

As Pontifico Murizzi watched Jorie Tully walk away, he

thought he'd heard something more in her voice on that last word as well.

the smarter of the two no-necks at the gate leading to the driveway of the Brookline mansion said, "Mr. Friedman's not seeing anybody today."

Shel Gold didn't think the guard had changed his clothes since Tuesday, since the guy's jacket still clashed with his pants. "I'm Big Ben's lawyer, and I need to talk with him."

The other no-neck said, "He needed to talk with you, we'da been told."

Shel fought his impatience. "You've passed me through here a dozen times."

The smarter no-neck said, "And every one of those times, we were told in advance to let you in."

The other guard said, "And this time, we was told in advance not to let nobody in."

A terrible possibility flickered across Shel's mind. "By Ben himself?"

The dumber guy looked at the smarter one, which was all the answer Shel thought he needed. Without another word, Shel sucker punched the smarter no-neck with a left cross, the eyes rolling up letting the former prizefighter know the guy was unconscious before he hit the ground. The dumber one seemed almost as jolted by the sight of his partner keeling as he was when Shel's right fist, propelled by an angled shoulder and twisting hip, caught him on the left side of his jaw, causing him to fall back against the gate, Shel waiting for the man to slide down onto his rump before deciding he didn't have to hit him again, either.

Rubbing the knuckles of his right hand—which hurt more than the left—against his chest, Shel rifled the pockets of the smarter guard till he found the key to the gate. Unlocking it, he left it open as he ran up the driveway to the main entrance.

As before, the door opened, but this time, Edsel Crow's

cold eyes weren't the first thing to catch Shel's attention.

Rather, it was the impressive rifle aimed right at Shel's heart.

Crow said, "Barrett Eighty-two Ay-One, fifty-caliber. My personal best in Desert Storm was an Iraqi tank commander at two thousand meters, but this distance, even your grandmother couldn't miss."

Shel tried to swallow, made it on the second try. "I want to see Ben."

"The guys at the gate should have told you he wasn't seeing anybody."

The man's used to terrifying people, so don't act as though you are. "I got the impression from them that it wasn't Ben who gave the order."

"So?"

"So that's why they're sleeping for a while."

Crow didn't look toward the gate. "I saw the whole thing on our closed-circuit video. Mr. Friedman told me you used to be in the ring, but from the way he said it, I got the impression you weren't very good."

"Barely good enough."

Crow grinned, but the muzzle didn't waver. "And exactly why did you punch our guys out?"

"It occurred to me that you might have done something to Ben."

Which provoked a reaction Shel had never thought possible.

Edsel Crow laughed. Loud and long.

"Fuck me," said the sniper as his muzzle did tremble this time. "How did anybody as dumb as you ever get to be a lawyer?"

Shel felt the tension go out of the air between them. "Like I said before, 'barely good enough.'"

Crow let his laughter die down before shaking his head. "Mr. Friedman said you were loyal, and that's one thing I care about, too. And so do you, taking out our guys and then staring down a rifle. So, okay, I'll tell you this much. Mr. Friedman's not here."

And something's definitely not right. "He left without you?"

"Seems that way."

"Well, where is he?"

Crow pointed the gun at the ground. Involuntarily, Shel's eyes followed the muzzle down, a little red dot from what Big Ben had once called the "laser scope" dancing like a crimson moonbeam on the slate stoop beneath his feet.

"Mr. Friedman doesn't want anybody to know."

"Look, I have to speak with him."

"Do me a favor," said Edsel Crow as he stepped backward into the house and began to close the door. "Wake those guys at the gate up as you leave."

mairead O'Clare walked into the office suite trying to hide her slight limp from the ankle, but then realized she was wasting her effort.

The place was empty.

She checked the telephone tape, finding enough messages with times mentioned in them to make her think both Shel and Billie had been gone for a while. Mairead hoped Billie wasn't having more trouble with her son.

Maybe half an hour later, and deep into writing a brief in another case, Mairead heard the phone at the reception desk. She let it go, knowing the tape would kick in shortly.

Except the call might be important, young lady, and you don't have a legion of staff to tell you that as you did at Jaynes & Ward.

So Mairead took a painful step on her bad ankle and managed to reach Billie's desk halfway through the fourth and last ring before the tape's activation. "Law offices."

"Give me Shel Gold."

Mairead recognized James Seagraves's voice and felt that same delicious little shiver go through her that had nothing to do with trial practice. "He's not here right now."

She thought the man on the other end of the telephone made a chuckling sound. "Mairead, right?"

"Right."

"And you know who this is?"

"Yes."

"Well, tell your boss that I gave him his courtesy call."

Maybe, but from the tone of the prosecutor's voice, Mairead thought it was more a "taunting" one. "Can I tell him what it's about?"

"He'll know, but since it seems you don't, I'll spell it out. Our detectives are approaching your client's house right now with an arrest warrant."

Think, young lady. What would Mr. Gold say?

"But I thought Shel told you he'd arrange for Mr. Friedman to surrender instead of—"

"A little late," replied James Seagraves. "Detective Tully is on her cell phone to my other line here, and I can hear the Brookline Police's sledge crashing through your client's front door."

13

"Well, Billie," said Etta, "let's start with the phone system."

Billie Sunday nodded as the woman—the oldest clerical Lurlene had introduced her to before walking back toward Trevor Trent's office—began explaining the buttons on the telephone in Conchita Balaguer's former cubicle. Etta had hair dyed that odd orange Billie always associated with women afraid they were going bald.

Moving on to the computer, Billie sat and Etta stood behind her, saying, "First, press that key at the upper-right corner of the board."

When Billie complied, the screen came to life with a musical chord, kind of like the organ at church.

As the two women waited for all the little icons to pop up on the now buzzing screen, Etta said, "Did you know Chita?"

Billie sensed something behind the question, but just replied, "Only by reading about her."

"Which is how you found out the job was open?"

"Yes, and I felt bad about trying to take advantage of your friend's tragedy. But I'm by myself with three mouths to feed."

"I've been down that road, too," said Etta, warmer on her answer than she'd been on her question.

Billie decided to follow up. "Did Conchita have any children?"

"No, unless you count her husband. Now, use the mouse to open the menu bar at the FILE heading."

Billie did as she was told, seeing a vertical list of options. "I got the impression from the newspaper that she was single."

"Okay, ex-husband, I guess. But not somebody I'd wish on anybody. Okay, now highlight ENTERING CLAIM."

Billie moved the mouse to that option and single-clicked, a detailed form appearing now on the screen. "How do you mean?"

"Chita's ex?" said Etta. "He was just a bastard, stalked the poor girl. She had restraining orders against him, but Berto'd still call her, from pay phones so there wouldn't be any record showing his home or job. A bastard, through and through."

"Cause her any trouble here?"

"Not that you'll have to worry about," replied Etta, pointing toward a line on the claim form.

the first thing Sheldon A. Gold thought as he entered his office suite was, Quite a crowd, but it doesn't feel like a party.

Not surprisingly, Mairead was there, resting a hip on one corner of Billie's reception desk. And rising from two of the scoop chairs were James Seagraves and a woman who looked more police than prosecution, the same being true for the crew-cut man standing against the far wall in a bulky, ill-fitting sports jacket.

Shel said, "I guess I must be late."

Mairead seemed to stifle a laugh, with the other three not showing any appreciation for the joke.

Seagraves motioned toward the reception desk and spoke in a tone that made Shel look for icicles hanging from the perfect teeth. "I called you as I said I would, a courtesy to let you know we were picking up your client Friedman."

"I thought that was supposed to be toward surrend—"

"Only I got your associate instead. And when Detective Tully went through the door out in Brookline, it seems you'd been there, but the defendant wasn't. You tipped him, you son of a bitch."

Chronology. When you're confused, focus on the chronology. "You're saying I was at Ben's house *before* Mairead received your call?"

"That's exactly what..."

As Seagraves trailed off, Shel thought he saw the corners of Tully's mouth twitch up. "Then how could I have tipped my client about something even my office didn't know yet?"

"You were there," said the prosecutor, the chill still in his voice, "and your client booked out somewhere."

"I was there, but not when Detective Tully arrived. And somehow I don't see Edsel Crow welcoming her by reciting a list of the day's visitors. So, how did you know I went out to Brookline?"

When Seagraves just clamped his jaw shut, Shel heard Mairead say what he'd been thinking. "Stakeout."

Big Ben's house had been under surveillance. So Tully or some other officer would have seen your dust-up with the guards at the gate, and then you outside the front door, with Crow's rifle pointed dead-on. Yet they did nothing.

Admit it: Somehow you'd hoped for more from "Protect and Serve."

Seagraves opened his mouth enough to say, "Our enforcement efforts aren't any of your business, but Friedman's whereabouts are. I want to know exactly—"

"Ben spotted your surveillance. And he somehow got away before the grand jury handed down an indictment."

"The fucking pool van," said the male in the sports jacket, speaking for the first time. "It looked right, but—"

"Shut up, Trooper," barked Seagraves, like he was still in the service and giving orders.

Shel now was glad he'd *never* served under him.

Then the prosecutor jabbed an index finger like a spear at both Mairead and her boss. "Your gangster-client got to

Balaguer on that jury, and since this morning, he's under indictment for murdering her. If either of you know what hole Friedman's hiding in, the first one to tell me maybe avoids disbarment."

Shel could sense Mairead getting angry enough to respond, so he jumped in first. "You're a guest in our offices. And it's the Board of Bar Overseers and eventually the Supreme Judicial Court, not the Suffolk County DA's office, that recommends and rules on disbarments. Finally, I have no idea where Ben is, but even if I did, I wouldn't have any obligation to tell you."

Shel noticed a glitter in Tully's eyes, like she was genuinely enjoying watching the attorneys clash antlers. A woman who conveys a lot while saying nothing at all.

Seagraves said, "You hear from Friedman, and we'd better hear from you."

Shel thought it best simply to shake his head over that one.

The prosecutor motioned abruptly to the state trooper and the detective to follow him out the door. Trailing the two men, Tully paused as she passed Shel and said quietly, "Tell the Pope I want to see him."

When the door closed behind the three, Shel heard Mairead say, "Now what?"

"I think you should try talking to another juror."

"I'm running out of them, but okay. Only, how about you?"

Shel Gold moved around the reception desk and toward his office, closing his eyes and massaging the bridge of his nose. "Me, I have to think."

pontifico Murizzi thought the factory where Rigoberto Balaguer worked looked like something out of a Frankenstein movie.

There were big overhead tracks, some kind of engine sliding along them, though the Pope got the idea that the engine was more passenger than locomotive. Some guys wearing outer-space helmets were welding, others pounding sheet metal with mallets, still more moving what looked like machined components onto a dolly calibrated to roll along tracks embedded in the floor.

If you'd ever been in an artillery barrage, this is probably what it would've sounded like.

"Hey," from a potbelly in a hard hat, "you see that sign out front?"

"The one says, 'Private Property, No Trespassing'?"

Hard Hat got as close to Murizzi's face as the belly would allow without actually making contact. "Yeah, that one."

"I'm looking for Balaguer, Rigoberto."

The guy seemed to stand down a little, though he didn't actually move back. "You a cop?"

"What do I look like, his valet? Get him over here, or I'll be back with a couple of uniforms and haul him out."

Hard Hat blinked twice, then did step back, scanning half the floor before cupping his hands and yelling, "Hey, Berto? Berto!"

It always amazed the Pope that citizens in a democracy could be bluffed so easily.

But then again, you had the real authority long enough, it probably takes a while to wear off.

Murizzi saw one of the welders raise his hand. Then the same guy lowered it and turned off his torch before hitching the mask back off his face.

Balaguer all right. But as he walked over, the guy didn't set down his torch.

Hard Hat said, "Officer here wants to talk to you. Take it outside."

Balaguer kind of grinned, but nodded. Given the torch, the Pope motioned him to go first.

Once in the sunlight, the mask came off completely, and Balaguer laid it to the side of a chunk of concrete the size of a BarcaLounger. The welder actually reclined on it, too, his face to the sun. "Want to know why I didn't tell him you aren't a cop anymore?"

Murizzi thought back to seeing Balaguer behind the decrepit apartment house on "beer night" and was fairly sure the moke had taken him for a cop then, but said, "I'll bite."

Balaguer hefted the torch, no threat in the motion. "You ever handle one of these?"

"Not for a living."

"Yeah, well, you did, you know an asshole like that *maricón* gives us fifteen minutes' break in four hours."

The Spanish word for "faggot," again, but Balaguer still seemed to be just talking loosely, so the Pope didn't roust him on it.

The torch returned to the side of the "lounger." "Inside is not so bad compared to July, August, but except for winter, it's always better out in the fresh air."

"Even if you've got to spend it with me."

"Even if." Balaguer folded his arms across his chest. "So, you figure out who did my Chita yet?"

"The smart money still likes you for it."

A grin. "Then you're not any closer to knowing what happened."

"And you're not worried we will?"

"What," said Balaguer, sweeping a hand back toward the factory, his grin growing wider, "and risk losing all of this?"

"I was thinking more that maybe Conchita was tired enough of your act she might go to the authorities."

"She already did that, man. It's called 'divorce.'"

"Problem with divorce, though: It isn't 'final' just because a gavel comes down on a bench somewhere. I'm guessing your ex-wife really didn't like you hanging on after she ended the marriage, Berto."

"What she like don't matter so much."

"But maybe a judge would think otherwise. And maybe you aren't sure just what can happen to you if she made official noise about it."

The Pope was pleased to see Balaguer's grin fade. "Hey, man. I already *know* what the judge gonna do. He make me go to this group."

"Group?"

"Yeah, like on the television, Springer and that Sally Jesse. You know, 'Husbands who abuse their wives, and the consequences.' Well, I got to do this group therapy shit, once a week. Sit around and listen to these other *maricónes* 'share' what they do to their women. Man, I gotta tell you, half the guys, they get off on *telling* us maybe more than they got off on *doing* the real thing." For just a moment, Balaguer looked troubled, the Pope couldn't see why.

Then the guy shrugged on his rock. "But all that don't matter."

"Why not, Berto?"

"For one thing, I was with my beer buds, like I told you the first time. And I'm a college boy, remember? Just because the good office jobs don't want a 'wife-beater' don't mean I can't figure out that I'm in for worse than 'group therapy' if I kill the bitch."

The Pope hated to admit it, but Balaguer's explanation rang true. "So I'll ask you again, Berto. Who do *you* figure lynched Conchita?"

"I don't know," the eyes now closed, but the widest grin of all on Rigoberto Balaguer's face. "Only, you find out, man, let me know, okay? I go see the dude on visiting day, thank him proper."

14

"So, Billie, Mr. Trent wanted me to make sure you're all right with the computers and all?"

From the wheeled, swivel chair in her cubicle—or Conchita Balaguer's—Billie Sunday looked up at the receptionist, Lurlene Inch. "Thank you. Etta did a fine job of telling me how everything works."

Billie watched Inch glance around before saying, more like she was talking to a child in church, "Is that all she told you?"

An alarm bell went off inside Billie's stomach. "Well, Etta said the next thing we're supposed to do is an actual claim."

Inch shook her head, the dishwater-blond ponytail prancing on her neck. "Not what I mean." The woman reached across to a temporarily empty cubicle and scooched its chair over to where she was nearly knee-to-knee with Billie. "I meant, did Etta tell you anything about what was going on around here with Chita?"

The alarm bell grew louder. "The poor woman I'm replacing?"

Inch smiled, but it came off like a female version of that little movie-monster doll, Chuckie. "The poor woman you're in*vestigat*ing's more like the truth."

"I don't know what—"

"Sure you do, and you want to know more. So, let's save the both of us some time, okay? Here's what you want to know. Mr. Stover, he had a thing for Chita." Inch hunched her shoulders even closer. "It's one thing when everything's 'consensual'—which I always thought should be 'consexual,' account of that way, the word would make more sense."

She inclined her head vaguely back toward the offices of the owners of the agency. Billie had the feeling Inch was letting on about a relationship the receptionist was having with Stover or Trent, but Billie couldn't tell which boss she meant.

Inch's eyes got real focused. "Only Chita, she really didn't want any part of Mr. Stover, and when he roamed too far with his hands one day, she went to Mr. Trent and made this big stink."

Billie thought about asking a question then, but decided that she might learn more by just listening to Lurlene vent.

"Well now, Mr. Trent agreed that his partner was doing wrong, and so he told Chita he'd pay her ten thousand dollars in cash, just like that," a snap of the small fingers, "to drop it. And Chita promised she would. I know, because I was there."

Billie thought, Does that mean Lurlene Inch is having an affair with Trent, since he seems to trust her, or with Stover, because Trent wouldn't want to give his own mistress any ideas of *her* own?

The receptionist seemed to read Billie's mind. "Mr. Trent felt like he needed a witness to all this. Then Chita had to go for jury duty, but soon's she got back, he gave her the money, and I was witness to that, too. So, there you have it."

Billie knew what the woman meant, but felt she had to make a show for her. "Lurlene, why are you telling me all this?"

A look of disgust. "Mr. Trent is real smart, but not as much as he thinks he is. When he told me to come back to his office—after I introduced you around?—he'd already figured you for wrong. But I'm just a mite smarter than that, Billie—or whatever your for-true name is. I could figure how and why you were wrong."

Inch suddenly stood up and bent forward, like to scold that same child in church. "Now, why don't you go back to your Mr. Murizzi and tell him we're just one more dead end on Chita's killing?"

And with that, Lurlene Inch turned on her heel like a little tin soldier and marched back toward her reception desk and out of Billie Sunday's sight.

favoring her left ankle, Mairead O'Clare flopped into the one big easy chair that could fit in her small studio apartment on Beacon Hill, only a few blocks from Shel's office. She didn't want to stop back at work without something more to contribute, and she didn't have that something.

Face facts: I don't have *any*thing.

Mairead had tried every last juror, by phone or on foot, including even the several who had turned her down originally. Same answer from each: No thank you, Ms. O'Clare, ranging from polite to abrupt.

I know what's going on here: With Big Ben Friedman indicted but not arrested, ADA James Seagraves would have had the police contact every juror with the chilling news: That gangster—who maybe killed one of you?—is on the loose. And nobody concerned about being next wants to talk with the man's lawyer.

For which you can't really blame them, young lady. Put yourself in their shoes.

Mairead nodded with Sister Bernadette's comment still ringing in her head, but that didn't shed any light on what to do next.

At which point, a different kind of ringing started, one that echoed throughout the one-room apartment, and Mairead reached for her telephone.

* * *

"**SO**, *this* is the thing I've never been invited aboard."

Pontifico Murizzi, sitting alone on the fantail of his houseboat, looked up at Jorie Tully, standing on the camel catwalk at his stern, fists on her hips. But the Pope didn't hear any flirtation in her voice this time around.

Murizzi rose from the resin chair, careful not to bonk into the table holding a half-glass of wine. "Let me give you a hand."

Tully's feet—and fists—stayed where they were, the failing sun reflecting off her features, making the pale eyes more striking. "No, thanks. Your boss didn't tell you I wanted a face-to-face?"

"I don't have a boss anymore, Jore."

"No dodging this one, Pope."

Uh-oh. The shit is rapidly approaching the fan. "Shel Gold left a message on my machine, but—"

"You burned us somehow on Friedman."

Which reminded the Pope of his last face-to-face with Tully. "That why you were in such a rush to leave me at Homicide? You were going out to the guy's manse in Brookline to serve a warrant on him?"

"I already told you: Don't try to dodge this."

"Dodge what? Jorie, Balaguer was a high-profile case, remember? And you're the one had Friedman's place under surveillance there. Only thing is, him or his sniper spotted your stakeout, and then they worked around it."

"Fuck you. The shame of it all is, I think there could have been a future for us, Pope, a real future, especially once you left the unit." Tully swung those pale eyes around the boat basin. "Here, or maybe a nice house somewhere."

Jorie, Jorie.

Her eyes came back to Murizzi now, with anything but affection in them. "Only no more. In God's great fucking scheme for the universe, I don't give a shit about Seagraves and his outrage. You, though, you traded on our relationship as cops to tip Friedman somehow. And for that, I can't forgive you, Pope. But I can forget you."

Tully turned away and began her own version of the copwalk on the camel back toward the stairway that led up to the parking lot, though Murizzi thought she put a little more swing into the hips than he remembered.

Then the Pope sat back down and picked up his wineglass. Looking to the empty slip next to his, he decided maybe it was best for Jorie Tully to come to the right decision—romantically speaking—even if it was for the wrong reason.

On the other hand, Murizzi could almost hear his mother, seeing his long face and sensing his tone of voice, say, "*Some*body's certainly feeling sorry for himself."

And she'd be right, you know?

Okay. So, get off this barge and go out somewhere.

Murizzi set down his glass.

A bar, but not to cruise, not yet anyway. Just a gin mill with some music and the sound of other people. You watch them for a while, you'll start to feel better.

At least, by comparison.

"**SO** that's what happened at the insurance agency, child."

Still in her big easy chair, Mairead O'Clare listened to Billie's voice on the other end of the line, but her right hand was taking notes as fast as the older woman spoke.

Billie added, "I tried Shel, both at the office and his apartment, but didn't get anything but the tapes."

"That's okay. What this Lurlene told you about the money Balaguer deposited gives us what we need to blow the 'bribed juror' theory out of the water."

"Anything more I can do from here at home?"

"Not tonight. But thanks for calling, Billie. You've made me feel a lot better."

"Sleep tight."

As Mairead heard Billie hang up, she was thinking of anything *but* sleep.

The first good news you've had on this case since the original verdict, young lady. I think you're entitled to a little celebration.

Even if I didn't exactly come up with the good news myself.

Mairead thought about calling Shel, but Billie had said she couldn't reach him, so that seemed a waste. And it would take a while to explain to any of her friends from New England School of Law exactly *why* it was that she was celebrating.

Not to mention the ethical problem of disclosing the confidential client information necessary for your explanation to make sense to them.

Still, though, it *was* Friday night, and Mairead had picked up a copy of the *Boston Globe* the day before.

Rummaging through the newspapers on the floor, Mairead found the Calendar section that listed the local entertainment venues, including any with live music.

15

Sheldon Gold looked down at Moshe. The cat was on its haunches under the TV tray, cocking his head this way and that to follow every morsel of food into his master's mouth. Without making a sound, or even begging, technically.

Though cats don't so much beg as . . . hint.

Shel had gotten home after stopping for a corned beef on rye this time, the fresh-baked, thick-slice sour rye with caraway seeds he'd loved since moving into the neighborhood.

After Natalie lost Richie in that mall, and Shel lost Natalie to the Estate.

Once in a while, Shel tried a restaurant for a sit-down meal other than breakfast. Only sitting down generally meant sitting alone, and he didn't like to make the other diners uncomfortable, wondering about the man in the poorly pressed suit eating all by himself.

Shel then had to laugh, at least on the inside. It had been warm enough leaving the office that Friday afternoon, he'd forgotten to put on his suit jacket, so he suddenly found himself riding the Green Line subway wearing just a necktie, shirt, and slacks.

Which puts you head and shoulders above most of the rest of the men—and women, now—on the car, what with "Casual Friday" having overtaken most Boston businesses. Supposedly even some of the banks and major law firms had gone to "Casual Every Day" throughout the year, which Shel couldn't believe until a classmate from Harvard confirmed that it was dress down like the dot.com clients, or lose them to other, less formal attorneys.

Breaking off a little piece of corned beef for Moshe, Shel tried to imagine going to court without a suit on. For a trial, even a motion, he'd always remember the jacket part.

At least, Shel was pretty sure he would.

The cat gobbled down the morsel like it was the first food he'd ever seen and the last he'd ever get. Shel decided to give him one more—just a small treat, what could it hurt?—when the phone rang.

Shel looked from Moshe to the phone across the room, then back again. The cat had already fixed his remaining eye on the bit of corned beef between Shel's thumb and forefinger. And, when at home, Shel generally let the tape machine pick up, especially during his simple dinners, as he'd already done once since getting home that evening.

A second ring, somehow more insistent to Shel's ear, though he knew his reaction to be more psychological than physical.

Then he realized the reason for the reaction: Mairead had needed him before on Big Ben's behalf, when she'd found Conchita Balaguer's body that night the trial ended. Shel was out with Gallina Ekarevskaya at the pub, so he couldn't have gotten Mairead's call anyway. Still, it bothered him enough to—

The phone rang a third time.

Shel set his sandwich down on the TV tray—and, he hoped, out of Moshe's reach—before crossing to a small table. "Hello?"

"Golden Boy, the fuck were you doing, taking a shit?"

"Ben," Shel said, trying to keep a mixture of exasperation and relief out of his voice. "We've got to talk."

"You're telling me?"

"Where are you?"

"Golden Boy, you got to get down here, and I mean *now.*"

"Ben, the police—"

"Fuck the police. This is way past that."

"But you've been indict—"

"Golden Boy, what we're talking about is life and death! Now, you get on the next Delta flight tonight."

"Ben, look—"

"No, you fucking *look.* I'm staring into the muzzle of a fucking gun, understand? And without your African Queen there, I figure you don't have a chance in hell of digging out my Boca address, so get a pencil and do exactly as I tell you."

Shel realized he heard something now in his old friend's voice that he hadn't sensed in forty years. It wasn't hopelessness, or even fatigue.

No, admit it: This is abject fear.

mairead O'Clare walked into Scullers jazz club, allowing her eyes to adjust to the light.

Or lack of it, young lady.

Nodding, Mairead gave the ticket she'd bought three seconds before to the man—read, bouncer—at the door, who had a cocktail waitress take her to a table for two about three rows back from the small, cabaret-style stage. Big windows on the wall behind the stage overlooked the Charles River, and Mairead guessed the club was named after the people who rowed high-performance shells back and forth from the university boathouses on the riverbanks.

Only not at eight-thirty on a Friday night, even in May.

Mairead looked around at the thirty or so other tables in the wood-paneled room, a beautiful venue for listening to music. Then her eyes braked on a man sitting alone at another table for two, a wine bottle in front of him, but only one glass, and that one in his hand.

Mairead's eyes had adjusted enough to be sure. The Pope.

Before her waitress could come back for a drink order, Mairead made a decision. Standing, she sidled between the tables until she reached the one where Pontifico Murizzi sat, sipping his wine and staring at the empty stage as though musicians had just left it and he was somehow hoping for an encore.

"Pope, how you doing?"

Murizzi looked up at her, what she took to be genuine surprise on his face, which kind of tickled her, because it reminded her of the only other time she'd surprised him.

Coming out of his houseboat's cabin naked to welcome the visitor he thought was Jocko.

The Pope stood up, but instead of inviting her to join him, he said, "I didn't know you were into jazz?"

"Sometimes, when I get tired of wearing leather and chains to slam-dance in the mosh pits."

Mairead saw Murizzi grin now, that Richard Gere half-smile that nearly melted her heart the first time she'd met him, before she . . . well, *knew*.

He said, "You here with anybody else?"

"No. You?"

"No." His free hand did an imaginary sweep-off of the other chair at his table. "Join me?"

When Mairead hesitated, the Pope surprised her. "Please?"

"You've got a great view of the stage here," said Mairead, catching the eye of her waitress and motioning in a way that made the server nod and come on over.

shel Gold was never what you'd call nuts about flying.

Oh, he'd done his share, vacations, the occasional out-of-state case where a plane made more sense than a car or even a train. But the first jetliner he'd ever been on blew an engine in midair, and the thing dropped like a shot duck toward the earth. The pilot later explained—they still did that back in the early seventies, before passengers sued for getting mustard instead of mayo on their sandwiches—that he feared their "aircraft" might explode on the descent into a smaller airport, and so he went in steeply to cause as small a "cone of destruction" on the ground as possible.

While Shel had always appreciated the man's candor, it didn't contribute much to his confidence in getting on another plane. But Boca Raton was nearly fifteen hundred miles south of Boston, which pretty much eliminated anything but an airliner.

Or a space shuttle, given Big Ben's anxiety over the phone.

However, Shel couldn't get a flight to the Palm Beach Airport, which was closer to Boca. The airline agent at the counter in Boston's Logan told him there was a middle seat available, though, on the last plane that night to Fort Lauderdale/Hollywood, twenty-some miles farther south.

But only if he hurried.

Sprinting the last fifty yards beyond the security checkpoint, Shel reached the gate just as the jetway door was being closed. He accepted the glares of the passengers on either side of the aisle as he worked his way to row 17, but Shel wasn't completely prepared for the absolutely murderous looks given him by his seatmates, each of whom already had piled magazines, candy bars, and water bottles on 17B toward sublimating the flight of three-plus hours.

Once settled into the seat, Shel tucked his elbows into his hips, yielding the armrests to the early-comers who so clearly resented him. Then he saw a telephone of sorts mounted into the back of row 16. Shel thought about calling somebody—Mairead, Billie, even the Pope—just to let an ally know where he was. But he couldn't remember any of their home numbers off the top of his head, and his calendar/address book was still in the breast pocket of his suit jacket on the coat tree at his law office.

And you call the office phone, nobody's going to pick up a message till Monday A.M. *And what do you have to tell them anyway, until you meet with Big Ben and size up the situation?*

So Shel Gold, still in his work clothes except for the suit jacket, tugged down his tie, folded his hands in his lap, and closed his eyes toward a long, hopefully uneventful flight.

* * *

was it only a few years ago we'd all be together on a Friday night?

Billie Sunday tried to remember the age when Robert Junior first started going out on his own. Oh, she'd drive him here and there, especially when he first started dating, feeling a little like those chaperons in an old novel—translated from the Spanish—that a friend of hers from Venezuela once gave her to read. But now Robert Junior had his own friends, mostly black, a couple white—like Carmine, the car dealer's son—who gave him rides or just walked with him in groups big enough to stare down the few gangs that were still operating since the Boston Police had put most of the leaders into the jails or into the ground.

Which kind of left the streets open to a new crop of free-lancers, a neighbor of Billie's on the force had told her. Younger kids, mostly, and not yet into the violence of the drug trade.

Younger kids like Rondell Wickes, Billie feared. And friends of his like her Matthew.

On the other hand, since the fight at school, Billie couldn't have put her finger on a single incident that she could prove was wrong about Rondell. It was just the boy's attitude, the way he showed in Assistant Headmaster Hightower's office that he'd given up on the system making things right for his ownself, or anyone around him, or even anyone *like* him.

That loss of hope was the real killer, Billie thought. Takes away all the sense of listening to rules and parents who spout them.

And Matthew was out that night, probably with Rondell somewhere. Billie believed in curfews, and in having a general sense of where her older two boys were off to. But she didn't believe in tacking an "s" on the front of "mothering," on account of that'd just make them do worse things than if they thought she trusted their judgment.

So instead of fighting over what was going to be on the

TV that night, Billie sat with William, her youngest, snuggled up against her thigh on the couch, and suggested he read to her from a book she'd gotten at the library. Its title was *Freak the Mighty,* a story about a small, smart, sick boy who becomes friends with a big, slow, healthy one. It didn't have any African-American characters in it so far, but Billie liked the way the back cover talked about how each of the boys helped the other.

She figured that William would get tired of the book and want to go watch TV or play a computer game, but to her mild surprise and greater delight, William instead read for half an hour before falling asleep against her, his soft breath washing regularly across her bare arm like one of those oscillating fans she'd priced at the Kmart a week before.

And Billie Sunday decided to leave the book in his hands rather than chance waking the little man from what she hoped would be good dreams about him helping others, too.

shel Gold was awakened by the abrupt bouncing of his plane's landing gear on the tarmac of the airfield. Blinking, he looked involuntarily to his left and right. The seatmates didn't seem to have warmed up to him during the flight.

Once past the jetway, Shel followed the signs for GROUND TRANSPORTATION, which wasn't hard, the terminal nothing like Logan's labyrinthine monsters. One escalator, and he was down and outside, the humidity oppressive enough even at 11 P.M. to wilt what was left of the structure in his shirt. But as soon as he hit the curb, a taxi honked, and the dispatcher asked Shel where he was going. After Shel told him, the dispatcher waved that taxi over, then leaned into the driver's window of another cab that Shel would have thought had first dibs.

Probably some kind of zone system, he thought.

When Shel got into the taxi's rear seat, the driver turned. Young, light-skinned black, with cropped hair. "Where you going, my friend?"

A Spanish accent. Shel said, "Boca Raton, please."

"Boca? That's twenty-five miles from here, cost you a fortune on the meter. You sure you don't want to rent a car?"

Amazing. You can blow out your candle, Sheldon: You've found an honest man. "I'm in a hurry, and what I *don't* want is to get lost on the way there."

"Your money, but, you don't mind me saying so, you don't look so good tonight, my friend."

"It's been a long day," said Shel, hearing the anxiety and weariness in his own voice.

"No offense, but your clothes and all, can I see some money first?"

Taking out his wallet, Shel knew there was no sense checking it for major cash. "Credit card okay?"

A grin, but more bantering than mean. "Like the man says in that rabbit commercial, you got some ID?"

Admit it: You can't blame him.

And so Sheldon A. Gold wedged out the driver's license that would prove by photo and name that he was, indeed, Sheldon A. Gold.

"**god,**" the Pope heard Mairead say after a tune ended with a sax riff that seemed to take the roof off the club, "this guy is totally phenomenal."

Pontifico Murizzi looked up at the performer, named Warren Hill. He was cute in a tall, grad-student kind of way, but the Pope was pretty sure Mairead was reacting more to the guy's playing. "One of the best of the new 'smooth jazz' people. Got a signature song that'll blow you away."

Just as the Pope finished, Hill said, "I wrote this next number to commemorate an important day in my daughter's life. It's called 'Turn Out the Lights.'"

From behind them, one of three older black women at another table burst out with, "Oh, that's what I came to hear!" By the time Murizzi turned around, though, the poor lady had clamped both her hands over her mouth in obvious embarrassment, her two friends joshing her in the ribs as they rocked back and forth with silent laughter.

The Pope looked up at Hill, wondering how he'd react.

Smiling all the way, the guy came down off the stage, strolled over to the old woman, and hopped his butt up onto the empty table next to her. Then he proceeded to fucking serenade the lady with his sax like he was Romeo to her Juliet, only with Romeo on the balcony and Juliet down in the garden.

It was the last song of the set, but Murizzi thought it the best, even without the showmanship, which would have made any piece better.

As the crowd, including Mairead, gave Hill a standing O, the house lights came up just a little. Some people began leaving their tables.

The Pope glanced down at his—okay, now *their*—second bottle of Merlot, still a good two glasses left in it, and said, "You want to stay awhile longer, Irish?"

Mairead sat back down. "Are you kidding? Of course I do. Pope, that was beyond awesome."

Murizzi had wondered something about Mairead for a while. Until having wine with him at the jazz club, she didn't seem to use any of those "Valley Girl" expressions he couldn't stand. But before the Pope asked, Why now?, he went over with her what he'd learned talking to Rigoberto Balaguer about his ex-wife, Conchita.

Mairead drained the last of the wine in her glass. "Well, I've got some good news about the suspected 'bribe.'"

As he listened to what Billie had found out at the insurance agency, the Pope found himself nodding. "Explains the deposit of cash and the call to you at your office about 'big money.' Probably makes the caller Balaguer, too, and justifies your going out to her house that night. It also means, though, unless I'm missing something, that our killer *did* hang the lady in a pretty short time frame between her call and your finding her at the house. But it all hinges on Lurlene, right?"

"According to Billie. Why, you think that's a problem?"

"You haven't met Lurlene. I have. Let me roll it around awhile, let you know."

"Excellent."

Another Valley-Girlism, and the Pope decided to take the plunge. "So, we got some time before the next set. Tell me, how come you don't sound 'clueless' when you talk at the office? Or anywhere else besides here, for that matter."

"How come?" The blue eyes turned on him like spotlights. "Maybe because I'm smart, and I studied hard, and I listened to the nuns a little more than the movies."

Touch one nerve, may as well touch them all. "What was that like, being an orphan?"

Mairead's face turned from glowy to glower, and the Pope immediately regretted asking her. But then she said, "You told me your story, about that convicted boy who hanged himself before you found out he was innocent. So I guess you're entitled."

Another thing that strikes you right about this Irish. She's like a cop, can see both sides of the situation and bend a little when she should.

Murizzi poured her another glass of Merlot. "I'm listening."

He watched Mairead's face settle, like she was about to recite a poem she'd memorized but didn't especially love. "I was raised in an orphanage, but I wasn't exactly an orphan."

Murizzi sipped his wine. "You weren't?"

"Uh-uh. My mother and father abandoned me there when I was just a few weeks old."

The Pope felt his eyes wandering down toward her hands, willed them not to. "The stain."

"Like it was the Mark of Cain or something, I guess. Anyway, I never really knew any other home than with the nuns. Nobody was much interested in adopting somebody who had hemangioma this bad, and the sisters didn't see much point in rotating me among foster parents."

"Okay. That's how you got there and stayed there. But what was it like?"

Mairead took somewhere between a sip and a gulp of wine, and Murizzi made a mental note that he was driving her home, no questions asked.

"Not so bad, really. I mean, we weren't kept in cages with bread and water under the door. But it was also funny, like school and summer camp were all blended together, with no time at . . . home?"

Murizzi thought he should nod, so he did.

"Another thing," said Mairead. "We *did* watch a lot of television, even though the nuns made us read books, too. But a lot of the books in the library were hand-me-downs from earlier orphans: history, or romance, or even westerns, while what we wanted, what we didn't have, were . . . families. So we'd watch the soaps, or the sitcoms with ridiculous mixes of kids and parents, partly because we could identify with the mix and wondered about the parents."

Murizzi thought back to his neighborhood, his block in the North End. More family than you knew what to do with, but even a hint of "homosexuality," and it'd be your pop or an uncle swinging backhanded and knocking you across the room.

The Pope said, "Any abuse?"

"Some," Mairead said, more measured now. "Some of the older boys, of course. But some of the girls, too. We were curious, and we didn't really have that many things to . . . play with?"

Murizzi knew enough not to laugh, thinking of his own tortured feelings about that kind of . . . "playing." And, based on the glassy look he was now seeing slide over those piercing blue eyes, the Pope decided he wouldn't be pouring Irish any more of the Merlot, either.

"my friend, this is your address."

Shel Gold looked up, feeling dubious because he couldn't

see any number on the skyscraper condo building to the ocean side of the road, any more than the if-not-identical-certainly-similar high-rises his taxi had been passing for the last ten minutes.

"You sure?"

The driver twisted around to face him. "They like to call their buildings here by names, not numbers, but I saw the sign they got for the deliveries, other side of their driveway. Believe me, this is your address."

Shel shrugged and handed over his Visa to cover the astronomical amount on the meter. Then the driver gave him a receipt wrapped around a business card. "Just in case you like another nice ride *back* to the airport sometime."

As the cab pulled away, Shel trudged up the marble steps to a grand front entrance with illuminated fountains feeding one another down a small slope. Inside the lobby, decorated with large canvases of abstract art that Shel found jarring, the woman behind the security desk asked him if she could help.

"Mr. Benjamin Friedman's apartment, please."

"Ah, yes. Ms. Bomberg called down to say there'd be a visitor. But, uh, if you wouldn't mind . . . ?"

For the second time in half an hour, Shel the Disheveled took out his driver's license, the polite woman comparing the photo to his face before returning the laminated card. "Floor twenty-one, Mr. Gold."

"Which apartment?"

"Mr. Friedman's is the only penthouse there. I'll call up to let Ms. Bomberg know you're coming."

"Thank you."

Shel followed the guard's pointed finger to a bank of elevators, the first three of which went only to the eleventh floor. Turning, Shel found the three to the rest. As he stepped back off the car on the top floor, he thought, Ben, Ben, a penthouse on "twenty-one" for luck.

At least until Tiffany Bomberg, a tissue to her eyes, and a nose red without benefit of makeup, tearfully opened the big door. She wore a pair of shorts and a tank top, making her look somehow both younger and less sophisticated than usual. She also virtually yanked Shel into the foyer before forcefully closing the door behind him.

The lawyer saw a magnificent view of the ocean, the water seeming to constantly turn color from the moonlight and waves visible through the floor-to-ceiling windows. He saw white, sculpted carpeting and white leather furniture that could make you snow-blind. And he saw a miserable-looking Benjamin Friedman in one chair, trussed-up in duct tape like a metallic mummy, with a quivering, sweating Dario Calcagni sitting across from him, a large black handgun wavering in the accountant's two hands.

Maybe the twenty-first floor isn't so lucky for Big Ben after all.

Shel thought he saw something that he at first questioned, then began to understand: Bomberg looked to Calcagni, and not to Big Ben, for a signal. When the accountant nodded, she walked over to Friedman and, very gently, peeled off the duct tape covering his mouth.

Before the tape was half gone, though, Shel could hear Big Ben saying, "Golden Boy, it took you long enough."

"I couldn't get a flight into Palm Beach, so I had to—"

"Fuck that shit," said Friedman as Bomberg moved away from him. "Come over here and get me out of this."

Shel looked to Calcagni, who shook his already-shaking head more obviously.

"Ben," said Shel, a trickle of sweat rolling down his spine that could have come from the combination of outdoor humidity and indoor air-conditioning, though he doubted it. "I don't think that'd be a good idea just yet."

"I don't mean take this fucking tape off me," as Bomberg moved toward the accountant's chair. "I mean talk with the fucking Calculator here."

"Talk with him about what, Ben?"

A growl like a grizzly. "Talk to him about how I'm not gonna kill him, he lets me loose."

What in the world . . . ? "Kill him because—"

"For Christ's sake, Golden Boy, stop asking questions and start making promises!"

Shel didn't see Ben tolerating another question, however reasonable it might be, so he turned to Calcagni. "Dario?"

But it was Bomberg who spoke. "Dario came down to see me. We're in love."

Shel literally felt himself teeter. "You and Dario?"

"Her and the Calculator, yeah." Friedman spit onto his white, sculptured carpet, but more, Shel thought, from having had his mouth taped for a while than from anger. "Behind my back, and for months."

Bomberg broke in. "We've felt this way toward each other for a while, that's true. But we didn't do anything about it till Dario came down here to see me."

From the mummy, "Like that makes a world of fucking difference."

Shel didn't think that Ben was improving his hand any. "Dario, Ben said something about . . . 'promises'?"

His boyhood friend couldn't stay out of it. "The Calculator thinks that just because he's shtupping my woman in my own fucking resort condo that I might do something violent to him."

Shel noticed Calcagni's fingers seem to close tighter on the gun and decided that the accountant could probably see through the sarcasm in his boss's voice to the truth draped by it. "Ben, how about I talk with Dario for a while?"

"Why the fuck do you think I called you down here?"

Shel focused on the man with the gun. "Dario, you and Tiffany are serious about your relationship?"

Calcagni stopped shaking left-right long enough to nod his head up and down.

"Tiffany, the same for you?"

"You think I'd risk everything I had with Ben if it wasn't?"

Shel thought there might have been a little warning for Calcagni in that statement as well, if from a different quarter. But first things first. "Okay, then. I think I understand the situation."

"Golden Boy," said Big Ben, "the situation is that the Calculator is so fucking terrified that I'm gonna have him clipped over this that he's gonna clip me first unless you convince him."

"Convince him of what, Ben?"

"That I'm not going to fucking kill him with my bare hands the first chance I get."

Talk about a man who desperately needs somebody else to speak for him. "Dario, what can I say to convince you that Ben won't kill you?"

The muzzle of the gun wavered some more, but at least, to Shel's temporary relief, in a downward direction as Calcagni spoke for the first time. "I know how Mr. Friedman respects you. If you get him to promise you that he won't kill me, then I'll believe it."

Steady here. "You just want him to . . . promise me?"

"Right."

"And then you'll put down the gun, and I can untie him?"

"More like fucking 'untape' me, the way these two have—"

Shel said, "Dario?" then waited for the accountant's eyes and gun to leave Friedman and come back to him before repeating, "Dario, just Ben's promise?"

"To you," said Calcagni. "Mr. Friedman won't go back on that, because he's more scared of losing you than he is of losing Tiff."

"You don't have a fucking *clue* about whether I'm afraid of anything."

Shel turned back to his friend. "I think you should make the promise."

Big Ben fussed, Big Ben fumed, Big Ben inhaled and seemed to be trying to do a Superman, breaking his bonds from the inside out. Then he exhaled, and Shel was reminded of the time a few days before, after suggesting that maybe one of these two people could have tried to fix his trial by bribing Conchita Balaguer.

"All right, Calculator. And Tiff, too. I promise on my

honor, on my sons, to Sheldon A. Gold, Esquire, that I will not kill either one of you for betraying me." A softening that almost produced a tear. "I mean, Jesus Christ, all the trouble I'm in right now, I need you guys with me. You're more family *than* my family."

This time Shel noticed Calcagni glance up to Bomberg for a signal. When she nodded, the accountant let the gun sag, and his new lover took a knife Shel hadn't seen from the back pocket of her shorts and walked over to Big Ben Friedman, cutting the tape in quick, efficient strokes, like she freed people from it ten times an hour.

As Big Ben rose and stretched his legs, Bomberg stepped back toward Calcagni. After laying the gun on the arm of his chair, the heavyset accountant struggled to get up himself.

Friedman shook his shoulders, then smiled at Shel. "Golden Boy, you did real good on that promise. Only I just said I wouldn't kill this Wop prick. I didn't say I wouldn't beat the fucking pasta out of him."

At which point Shel Gold was amazed to see Tiffany Bomberg step between her new lover and her old, brandishing the knife in a way the lawyer didn't think she'd learned in finishing school.

16

For the third time in the five minutes that Saturday morning as she walked gingerly toward the office, Mairead O'Clare said to herself, "I am *never* going to drink red wine again."

It's the tannic acid, young lady, which—

"Please?"

As Mairead chided herself for cutting Sister Bernadette off, the dapper, elderly man approaching on the sidewalk stared, then manifested an intense interest in whatever kind of tree his little mop of a dog was marking.

Great. Now my hangover has me talking out loud in front of strangers.

The night before, she'd helped the Pope kill two bottles of Merlot, actually feeling a bond with him on a personal, if not romantic, level. But after he offered to drive her home, the bad ankle made Mairead stumble in the parking garage, and she also had some trouble hoisting herself into the passenger's side of his Ford Explorer. However, Mairead still enjoyed the evening.

If not the morning after.

She'd popped three aspirin and drank every ounce of spring water in her refrigerator back at the studio apartment, but nevertheless the sun's rays felt like nails being driven through her eyes.

Mairead's head was still throbbing as she got off the elevator and expected to need her key to the office suite door.

It was unlocked, though, Billie Sunday sitting at the reception desk, typing some forms.

Mairead said, "I didn't expect to see you on a Saturday."

"Same. But you'd best listen to this message on the tape machine."

"that's the beauty of red wine," Pontifico Murizzi said to the sun dancing off the light chop in the harbor. "Nice buzz, but you don't pay the piper come morning."

The Pope stood on his fantail, wearing just tennis shorts and boat mocs, thinking back on the jazz club and Mairead the night before. He'd been concerned that she was getting hammered, the amount of wine she put away, but Mairead was a healthy five-seven and maybe one-thirty, so he figured she could hold her own. Only as soon as Irish stood up from the table, she started listing to port, and he'd had to steady her half a dozen times on the walk to the car. During the ride to her place, Mairead nearly passed out twice, him keeping her talking the only thing keeping her awake. He provided escort to her building's entrance, too, helping Irish with the front lock and almost breaking his own rule by going upstairs with her, be sure she was okay. But Mairead insisted in that indignant way all drunks have that she was "fine," and he'd never met a person—straight or gay, male or female—who used that word and thereafter was grateful for anything you did. So, he suggested she down three aspirin and as many glasses of water before hitting the sack.

Murizzi grinned as a motor launch puttered out at no-wake speed. What do you want to bet Irish swan-dived into bed without even taking off her clothes?

When the launch drew even with his bow, the bikinied woman sprawled on its wave deck gave him a nice smile. Then the potbellied guy at the helm noticed where she was looking, and he swung farther away from the Pope's boat. The guy kind of scowled, too, and unfortunately that reminded Murizzi of Fletcher, and therefore of Jocko, and the empty slip next to his.

Christ, get over it already. The thing's history.

The Pope rolled his head to loosen the shoulders and continued with stretching exercises. He'd lifted some of them from joggers he'd watched over the years, others from a yoga book he'd picked up at a bargain table outside a bookstore. Murizzi always believed in what the old-time ballplayers said when interviewed about the newer crop that had replaced them: too much emphasis on the weight room and not enough on being limber.

So the Pope began by bending over to loosen the lower back, too, first just touching his fingertips to the deck, then slowly extending until he could press both palms between his spread feet, the legs unbent at the knees. Feeling the disappointment and—yeah, say it—the sadness flowing down into the boat, he slowly brought the hands to his mocs, stretching now laterally as well as vertically.

Murizzi had just begun to do arm rotations, kind of like a dress-right-dress with both hands, when his phone rang inside the cabin. He went through the open sliding door, then picked up his portable. "Who's talking?"

"Pope, it's Mairead."

"Hey, Irish, how you feeling?"

"Like crawling off into the rocks to die. But Shel called the office last night, and I think you'll want to know what he had to say."

admit it: not exactly one big, happy family.

Shel Gold looked around the dining table set for breakfast in front of the tall windows that showed a couple of sailboats doing a do-si-do in the ocean beyond. The table was big enough to seat eight with plenty of elbow room, but right then there were just the three of them.

In the high-backed "throne" at the head, Big Ben held his head in his hands, supported by his elbows on the table.

He looked badly hungover, which was to be expected, the amount of single-malt scotch the man had downed the night before after being released from the duct tape. But the lavender robe—probably a twin to the one from his Florida room in Brookline—hung unsashed from his shoulders, which slumped like those of a man without hope.

Dario Calcagni sat on one of the long sides, his head up, the eyes never leaving Big Ben. The accountant fidgeted constantly, a bead of sweat sliding at that moment from a crease of skin below his hairline and toward his brow. He wore a billowing polo shirt the color of a tangerine, with some kind of long shorts, their hems nearly touching his knees when he'd been standing.

Shel didn't even want to think about what he looked like, and he could smell himself in his clothes. Tiffany Bomberg made polite, mindless small talk from the kitchen area and, receiving no answer from any of the three men at the table, replied to herself in a voice so sweet it was brittle.

Shel thought back to the "celebration lunch" at Locke-Ober's after the verdict. If that meal was unnaturally cheery, this one was naturally depressing. And with good reason. The cuckolded gangster, the disloyal accountant, the unfaithful mistress.

Although Ben's divorced, so does Bomberg technically count as his "mistress"?

"Does everybody want lox on their bagels?" came her voice from near the toaster.

"Whatever," said Big Ben.

"That'd be great," said Calcagni.

"Thanks," said Shel, grateful for anything to say into the black doom of the beautiful morning and the forced politeness of this little British play they were reenacting.

As Tiffany began serving them, Shel heard Ben Friedman roust his head from his hands with a blubbery sound that was less like a man crying and more like a walrus roaring.

Then Ben said, "What I don't get, for the tenth fucking time, is what you see in this tub of lard."

Shel had hoped for more from his friend by way of diplomacy and grace.

Tiffany said, "And for the tenth time: It . . . just . . . happened." She paused with the food to engage Calcagni across the table, whom Shel had sensed would be the last one served, as though he were the host and Ben the guest. "We looked into each other's eyes, and we saw into each other's souls."

Ben made a noise from inside somewhere that made Shel glad his friend hadn't ingested any food as yet. "Then why the fuck didn't you just *tell* me? Why did you two have to go around behind my back?"

Tiffany returned to the kitchen area, but Shel sensed the boil being lanced as Calcagni spoke. "It's like Tiff said last night. We didn't do anything behind—"

"Was I talking to you?"

Shel watched Calcagni cower.

Then Friedman turned to his lawyer. "Golden Boy, was I talking to this fucking traitor?"

"You could have been interpreted that way, yes."

As Shel sensed Ben ready to roar at him, Tiffany came back into sight with a platter of scrambled eggs in her hands and said, "Ben, you promised."

The gangster turned to her. "I promised I wouldn't kill this fat fuck who betrayed me like one of those guys from Shakespeare."

Shel thought, Not the British play I've been picturing.

Big Ben now looked squarely at Calcagni. "I never promised I wouldn't drag his fucking ass over the coals about what he did to me."

"*He* didn't do anything to you," said Tiffany. "*We* fell in love for us, not to hurt you."

Shel sensed his friend would now turn to him again.

"Golden Boy," Friedman's head swinging like a pendulum in denial. "Explain this to me, would you?"

"I can—"

"Explain to me how I could be sitting here, in a waterfront condo in fucking Boca that set me back two million, hosting a fucking en*gage*ment shower for my trusted accountant and prodigal bimbo—"

"Ben," one of Tiffany's hands going from the platter of eggs to her hip, "that's uncalled for and—"

"—with the only guest my fucking lawyer, who's probably going to charge me by the fucking hour for the pleasure of witnessing this slutting nympho—"

Uh-oh, thought Shel, watching Tiffany begin to tremble.

"—Bobbitize me by letting this putz of a bean counter hide his salami in—"

Shel ducked as the mass of eggs was slung by Tiffany off the platter and onto the face, throat, and shoulders of her now certainly former sugar daddy.

Admit it, though: the one thing other than duct tape that's shut him up.

Dario Calcagni jumped from his chair, surprisingly nimble for such a large man, Shel felt, when suddenly it sounded like a peal of thunder had hit the front door of the condo. Shel turned around to see four or five people in black-visored helmets and body armor burst from the foyer into impressive military stances, machine guns leveled at all around the breakfast table while a jumble of voices yelled "Police! Don't move!" and "Hands in sight!"

Then one of the intruders removed his helmet, and Shel saw the face of his cabdriver from the night before.

The man gestured with his weapon toward Ben Friedman. "The hell happened to him?"

Tiffany Bomberg hefted the platter, only a few yellow gobs remaining on it. "Ben decided he wanted his eggs over hard."

Sheldon A. Gold shrieked out a laugh, then put a lid on it when he realized he was the only one in the room who seemed to think her answer was funny.

17

billie Sunday thought, You can tell from the expression on the child's face what she's going to say.

Mairead looked up at her and not the Pope, but spoke into the receiver cradled between chin and shoulder. "We have *got* to get a speaker phone in this office."

What did I tell you?

Billie had been in the rest room when that aggravating man Shel finally called again from Florida, so it was Mairead who picked up at the reception desk. Now the child was relaying Shel's voice to her and the man who wasn't spooky enough as he was, but had to live on a boat, too.

Mairead said to them, "Shel's persuaded Ben Friedman to waive extradition."

"That ought to speed things up," from the Pope.

"They'll be on the next plane. With a couple of Boston detectives."

"Jorie will be pissed, not getting to spend any quality time in Florida."

Billie shook her head. Who in their right mind would want to be in Florida now that spring had finally come to New England?

Into the phone, Mairead said, "No, Shel, nothing on the other jurors. . . . Hold on, I'll ask." To Murizzi now, "Anything on the ex-husband?"

"Zip."

"Shel says, 'Anything on anybody?'"

"Same."

Billie waited, but when the child began speaking into the phone again, she said, "Tell him you didn't ask me."

The child cuffed herself in the forehead like a character from one of William's cartoons. "Shel, you should talk to Billie about Stover-Trent."

Mairead handed over the receiver, having to uncurl about a yard of twisted line to do it.

"Shel, you using your sunscreen?"

A tired sigh. "I haven't been on the beach much, and there weren't even windows where they took us from Ben's apartment. What have you got?"

Billie summarized for him what Lurlene Inch had told her about the payment to Conchita Balaguer.

"Billie, that's great. Mairead's off the hook."

"You want us here this afternoon when you get back?"

"No. By the time they process Ben—hold a second."

Billie could hear him shouting to somebody.

Shel came back on. "They're calling our flight. Ben should be arraigned first thing Monday morning. I'll need you and Mairead in the office tomorrow to prepare our brief on bail. And ask the Pope if he can meet us there Monday after the hearing."

Billie relayed those commitments and got nods back. "Shel, we're all on board. Anything we should be doing meantime?"

"Probably, but I have no idea what."

mairead O'Clare left the office on Saturday afternoon at about two and began walking down Tremont Street toward Bay Village, her ankle still aching but feeling better for being used. However, after the call from Shel, everybody seemed kind of . . .

"Disheartened" is the word I'd use, young lady.

Captured it, all right. I mean, it's good to know that poor accountant is okay and not lying in a ditch somewhere with three bullets through his head from another gangster's version of Edsel Crow. But Ben Friedman back in custody and facing a second trial? Not exactly how I fancied spending the next few months, especially given how tiring—no, disillusioning—it's been listening to the jurors from his first trial destroy many of my idealistic notions about what goes on during deliberation.

And now I'm going to listen some more, assuming they'll even talk to me again.

Mairead's college hockey coach had once said to her, "If something isn't going right during practice, it's not going to get any better during the game." Well, if the trial was the game, then investigation stuff was like practice. And Mairead had always prided herself on not quitting just because the hockey skill involved was hard to learn.

Once the Pope had left for his boat, and Billie for her house, Mairead had taken out her list of jurors and begun dialing. She started with the sax player, Lorraine Fanton in Back Bay, but got her tape machine. Same with Josephine Arria on Beacon Hill. Phil Quinn in Southie was a simple no-answer. Next closest was Ralph Bobransky, and when Mairead tried his hardware store, she recognized his voice before disconnecting. Then a call to Ruth Kee's restaurant: The co-owner was due in after 3 P.M. Finally, Mairead tried Troy Gallup at the home number he'd written on his business card when they'd gone to the health club, getting his tape, too, but not willing to leave her cellular number.

Which I still think was a good decision, young lady.

No-brainer, really. I don't want Troy-boy being able to reach me whenever he feels like it.

Except that left Ralph Bobransky as the only viable candidate until Ruth Kee arrived at her restaurant. And Mairead was now just turning onto his block.

When she entered the store this time, a male couple was exiting, talking excitedly about refurbishing their bedroom with whatever was in the two bags and one box they were carrying. Inside, she spotted Bobransky immediately, helping a customer sort through a cabinet of screws or nails.

Shadow, the black Labrador, came around a corner and began growling at her.

Good memory, pup.

Bobransky turned toward her at the noise, saying something Mairead couldn't make out as he left the customer to fend for himself at the cabinet.

As Bobransky approached, the dog moved—still growling—to where it stood between Mairead and its formerly blind master. Bobransky hushed Shadow just by using its name, but the dog stayed on guard.

Mairead said, "He's really loyal to you."

"More protective. Shadow can sense when someone wants to waste my time."

"Mr. Bobransky—"

"Ralph, or you can get out now."

Appease him, young lady. "Ralph, Ben Friedman has been arrested for the murder of Conchita Balaguer."

"Couldn't happen to a nicer guy."

"But you thought he was innocent in the death of Yuri Vukonov."

"Mairead, your client is a gangster. I was persuaded he didn't kill the little Russian boy. That doesn't mean he wouldn't kill somebody else."

Okay, that one would give me trouble, too. "Did Ms. Balaguer ever mention to you that she was having difficulties at work?"

"No. After she . . . rebuffed me in favor of Troy Gallup, she did everything she could to avoid being alone together. And Chita certainly didn't confide in me." Bobransky tilted his head in that odd way Mairead remembered from her first visit to the store. "But I told you all this the last time you were here. Why come back?"

"Mr.—sorry, Ralph, I just don't know what else to do. I'm hoping you might have thought of something else that could be helpful."

A smile, but nothing warm behind it. "You're at a dead end, and so now you have to come crawling back even to people you insulted."

Accept it, young lady, if he's willing to keep talking. "You, uh," Mairead noticed the customer walking from the cabinet to the counter, "kind of hit the nail on the head."

Bobransky seemed to hear the sound of shoes behind him. "Well, not that your discomfort isn't enjoyable, but I have a business to run. Unless you've changed your mind about... us?"

"Not during this incarnation."

Ralph Bobransky leaned down. "That skin, you're lucky anybody wants to bother." Then marched toward his cash register.

The bad news is that he'll probably prove the nicest experience of the afternoon.

pontifico Murizzi opened the Coleman cooler next to him and had his first Mountain Dew of the day. Beauty of the stuff was that it tasted to him like it had booze in it when it didn't, and the caffeine level was high enough to keep an elephant awake on stakeout.

Which is where the Pope found himself, sitting in the Ford Explorer outside and down the street from Rigoberto Balaguer's apartment house in Lynn. Murizzi had a map of Massachusetts open on his steering wheel, so anybody going by would think he was just another lost tourist trying to figure out how to get back to the Sumner Tunnel and into Boston. No need to worry about the Lynn police, because he'd stopped by the station first, let the locals know he was surveilling one of their citizens.

Most cops the Pope knew hated stakeout. It wasn't *like* watching grass grow: It *was* watching grass grow. If you were lucky, that is, and had a place with lawns and maybe trees for shade in hot weather. Because you sure as shit couldn't run the engine for eight hours straight to get air-conditioning. And without starting up, the AC never really seemed to work, at least not in any car Murizzi had ever driven. Come winter, the problem didn't go away. It just reversed itself.

Not to mention the dilemma of where to take a leak. The Pope always favored a resealable tonic bottle, like the one in his hand. What the poor female officers had to go through, he didn't even want to think about.

Then Murizzi spotted a guy he was eighty percent sure had been Balaguer's fat drinking buddy from his first visit there. The guy kept coming down the street, but never looked toward the Pope or even his SUV. The guy did go down the driveway and behind the apartment house, though.

Starting early today?

Pontifico Murizzi took a swig of his Mountain Dew, thinking what his first partner in Homicide once told him: Whenever things aren't going right in an investigation, sit on a guy you feel is wrong.

Of course, that didn't make the prospect of spending the evening in a truck seat any more appetizing.

"**but** my sister already talked with you, yes?"

Mairead tried to keep her temper with the Korean woman behind the counter of the restaurant, amazingly full despite it still being afternoon. There were many children scattered among the Asian adults, so maybe the early dinner allowed entire families to eat together.

Or perhaps, young lady, the parents themselves still have to work later on.

Mairead said, "I need to speak with her for only a short while. Please?"

Another Asian couple assisting an elderly man using a cane came through the door. The Kee sister said to Mairead, "Wait, yes?" before greeting the newcomers warmly in what Mairead assumed was Korean. After the sister gathered menus, she slowly led the trio to a table.

From behind, a familiar voice said, "You are here again?"

Mairead turned, Ruth Kee's plain face bearing roughly the same expression the lawyer had seen reserved for the woman's recollections of Conchita Balaguer. "Ms. Kee, I have just a few more questions."

"No." Kee took her sister's position of authority behind the counter. "The police talked to me, and I saw on the television about your Mr. Friedman, arrested in Florida."

"Please, we—"

"I said no! Already you've taken time I don't have, and we are very busy. You can see that."

"Last time you told me that it was your civic duty to serve on a jury, so—"

"Civic duty? Let me tell you about civic duty. My ancestors in Korea were ruled by the Empirc of Japan for thirty years before the Second World War began. Japanese was the required language, and Koreans in their own country had to adopt Japanese names. During the war, Korean 'comfort women' were kidnapped and used by Japanese soldiers, and Korean men were slaves in Japanese mines. Yet the children of these people cannot become citizens in Japan—or vote there—unless they take a Japanese name again. And finally, after fifty years, some of the families torn apart by the 'police action' that separated North Korea from South are being reunited, but only one hundred people at a time, and then only for a short 'visit.'" Kee leaned stiffly forward, her small hands flat on the counter now. "That is the 'civic duty' I know. I answered your questions once. No more. Now, leave my restaurant or I will call the police on you."

Dead end, young lady.

all his years as a criminal defense attorney, and Sheldon A. Gold had never ridden back from another state with a client-in-custody.

And you could have donc without the experience this first time.

Benjamin Friedman had to sit boxed into a window seat at the back of the aircraft, the burly state trooper on the aisle in his row. Detective Jorie Tully sat across from them.

Shel was near the front of the plane, seeing Big Ben only as the attorney needed to walk by to use the bathroom, which he did twice, even though they served no meal on the lunchtime flight.

Shel ate all the little foiled snacks the flight attendant could spare. When he thought about it, though, he kind of sympathized with the woman. After all the years of complaining about airline food, maybe passengers shouldn't be so surprised the companies decided to stop offering it.

When they landed at Logan and arrived at the jetway, Shel noticed that the detectives made no effort to leave. It was only after every other passenger had filed out that they got Ben up and into the aisle, Tully in front of him, the trooper behind. As the threesome drew even with Shel's row, his client said, "Can I talk to my lawyer a minute?"

The trooper shook his head. "You had ten hours with him down in Florida."

Tully said, "Let me check the seat pockets in this next row. Then we'll give you exactly sixty seconds, watching from up by the cockpit door."

Shel thought he should thank her, and he did.

When the two detectives shuttled Ben into the cleared row and took up their stations at the front of the plane, Shel hunkered down in his seat. "So they can't hear us."

"I don't give a fuck if they can, Golden Boy." Ben rattled the shackles now back on his wrists. "I don't like this shit, and I *really* don't like jailing."

"I'll ask that you're put in a segregation unit."

"Hey, Golden Boy, let me tell you something, all right? You're in a jail, and you got nobody to watch your back, it doesn't fucking matter where they put you. I want out, and I want it fast."

Shel was about to explain the long odds on bail being approved when Tully's voice said, "Thirty seconds."

"Ben, I'll do what I can, but it may have to be extreme."

"Extreme? Golden Boy, we're not talking snowboarding here, or that screwy bicycle acrobatics the kids do nowadays. We're talking me rotting in a cell when I didn't do a fucking thing, to that kid or that juror."

"No judge is going to overlook your going to Florida like that."

"Like what? It's a free country, for Christ's sake. And besides—"

"Time's up," said Tully, she and the burly trooper moving back down the aisle.

Shel didn't like the look in his client's eye now. This was raw, naked fear, harder to see than to hear. And Shel remembered suddenly from the ring how you could sometimes smell it, coming off the other fighter.

Like it was coming off his old friend in the reconditioned and warming air of the plane.

As Shel stood and stepped back to let Ben be led back into the aisle, the man said, "Just do what you have to do, Golden Boy. Whatever you have to do."

Shel knew that remark was completely innocuous in context, but he still wished the two detectives hadn't been there to hear it.

However, the best was yet to come.

When the four of them entered the now nearly empty departure lounge, an African-American woman began walking toward them.

You know you've met her, but where?

Speaking to the burly detective, the woman said, "Is this Benjamin Friedman?"

"No interviews," said Big Ben. "No comment."

"I'm not a reporter, sir." The woman reached into her handbag, and Shel noticed Tully tense. But all that came out was a packet of papers.

Now Shel remembered where he knew the woman from. A constable, she'd once successfully served civil process for him on a recalcitrant defendant.

The woman said, "These are for you, Mr. Friedman," handing them to the man with the shackled wrists. "The complaint and summons in the case of *Vukonov versus Friedman* for the wrongful death of one Yuri Vukonov."

As the woman left them, Big Ben Friedman turned to Shel and said, "When God shits on you, Golden Boy, it's like he has diarrhea."

waiting in the hallway outside the apartment door, Mairead second-guessed herself for the third time since entering the lobby downstairs.

No choice, young lady. You couldn't reach jurors Fanton or Quinn, and two others effectively refused to speak with you. You're lucky to have caught this one finally at home.

Sister Bernadette, I hope so.

The door swung open, Troy Gallup in just a pair of workout shorts. "You found the place all right, doll."

Doll. "Yes, but I'll stay out here till you can get fully dressed."

A macho laugh from deep within "abs of steel." "I'm trapped in a suit five days a week. The less clothes, the more... natural, don't you think?"

Gallup stepped back, and Mairead forced herself to go by him into the apartment.

Which was surprisingly civilized. When she'd tried Gallup again from her cell phone, and he'd said he'd see her, but only at "his place," Mairead had expected *Playboy* posters and fishnets hanging on the walls, kind of an Austin Powers obviousness to the guy's physical dwelling consistent with his character. But the framed photos and prints were tasteful, and the furniture warm and well matched: nubby, oatmeal color on the sectionals, contrasting dark wood on the accompanying tables. Plus a killer view of the Charles River out one of the windows.

"Nice place," she said, meaning it.

"Yeah," Gallup said, moving to one of the sectionals, then patting the seat part of the next one with his hand, "I was shacked up with this interior designer for about six months. Pain in the ass toward the end, but she had taste."

At least in furnishings, thought Mairead, as she perched

on the edge of the adjoining sectional at the farthest point from Gallup.

He leaned forward, inching toward her in the process. "Some wine, doll? Or beer?"

Make an exception here to the "bond with a witness" advice. "No, thanks."

"I have stronger, too. And not all of it comes from a... bottle?"

A druggie on top of everything else. Just better and better. "No. What I'd like is to ask you some more questions about Conchita Balaguer."

"Well, I can tell you the answer to the first one is 'No, she wasn't as lucky as you.'"

I don't get it either, young lady.

"Mr. Gallup—"

"Oh, come on," another six inches toward her with his butt. "You know it's Troy, and I know it's Mairead. And the question was, 'Did Chita get to see this place?'"

Luck runs a lot of different ways. "Troy, remember the money Ms. Balaguer told you she'd be receiving after the trial?"

"The pipe dream? Yeah, I remember."

"Well, we think Ms. Balaguer got a large sum from her employers the very day you finished jury duty with her."

Suddenly, a different look in his eyes, concern maybe? "How large?"

"About ten thousand dollars."

Relief now, and a grunted laugh. "Doll, you had me going there for a while. I thought maybe I kissed Chita off a little too soon."

Mairead braced herself to get through the questions and get out of this man's company for good. "She never spoke with you about her job?"

"Well, yeah, kind of. That it was boring. But so was the trial, like I told you at the health club. Chita was a woman with needs, like every woman has. She just... acknowledged them a little more directly than you."

Ignore it, young lady. "Did she mention any other lovers?"

Gallup edged closer still, now within forearm reach of Mairead's nearer leg. "Only that some guy had the hots for her, but it wasn't mutual. So she did him every couple of weeks, make life easier for her. Problem for Chita was," the hand now strayed to Mairead's knee, "the guy left her . . . unsatisfied."

One more try. "The name of this guy?"

"Don't remember her saying. In fact, maybe she just forgot," Gallup's hand now sliding up Mairead's thigh, "the way she'd scream when I brought her to the top, over and over and . . ."

As Troy Gallup brought his lips in for a landing on Mairead's, she balled her left fist, then swung that elbow into his right cheekbone, as though she wanted to knock it across the room.

Gallup slid down off the couch and onto his knees, both the free hand and the wandering one clamped on the right side of his face. "The fuck you doing?"

Mairead stood up, assuming a position of good balance despite the ankle. "Saying no."

"You didn't say a fucking thing!"

"I was talking, you weren't paying attention. Sometimes actions really do speak louder than words."

Gallup dropped his hands and lunged forward, from his knees and toward her shins, as if to tackle her. She sidestepped away from the sectional furniture and placed the toe of her right and fairly sensible shoe in his left rib cage, digging deeper until she felt some cartilage separate.

Gallup roared, but then folded up on the floor, his left hand now going to his ribs while the other stayed on his cheek. "I asked you . . . if you wanted to come . . . see me on a 'weekend.' . . . And then you called . . . and it's Saturday. . . . What am I supposed to think?"

Mairead said, "I'm leaving now, Troy. Let's have this be our last conference before we see each other in the courtroom, okay?"

As she moved to the apartment door, trying not to put

too much of the adrenaline she felt into her stride, Mairead O'Clare could hear about six different variations on the word "bitch" being flung at her back.

On the whole, young lady, I think you're right to prefer even that to... "doll."

18

As "Friedman, Benjamin D." and the indictment number were called out by the clerk in the kangaroo pouch in front of the judge's bench on Monday morning, Shel Gold looked over Mairead O'Clare's auburn hair to the dock where his client was getting shakily to his feet. Shel tried to give Big Ben a shielded thumbs-up, but given appearances, the lawyer decided his old friend's stay in jail since Saturday afternoon hadn't gone any better than predicted.

Shel himself had spent most of Sunday in the office with Mairead, preparing for this bail hearing and writing a short brief—typed by Billie on her sons' computer at home and then Xeroxed by Shel at a Copy Cop shop. The brief dealt with the Massachusetts statute on the factors to be weighed in deciding whether to allow an accused to be released before trial by posting a bond. But frankly, the law wouldn't be quite as important as the facts in this second consecutive "high-profile" case. And "high" enough that the bail hearing was being held in the First Session (which occupied the old federal Court of Appeals' wood-paneled, red-carpeted cavern on the fifteenth floor) rather than in the Clerk/Magistrate Session downstairs.

Your one piece of luck: Today's judge is the Honorable Mary Frances O'Brien. The woman looks like a librarian, but served as a public defender in the federal trial courts.

And she really believes a defendant is innocent until proven guilty.

"I've reviewed both sides' briefs," O'Brien said from the bench. "Mr. Seagraves, I'll hear you first on whether bail should be set in this capital case."

"Thank you, Your Honor," said the prosecutor, rising without notes at his table, Detective Jorie Tully sitting on the far side of him. "The Commonwealth believes, based upon the statutory grounds, that bail should be denied in this matter. First, if released, the defendant poses a significant threat to the community, in that this heinous crime of hanging a juror from his *first* trial may be only the initial deadly consequence of that earlier case. Second, the defendant has demonstrated more than a significant risk of flight before trial, in that he already fled the jurisdiction for South Florida and had to be captured there and brought back here by detectives from the Boston Homicide Unit."

"Enough for now, Counselor. Mr. Gold?"

Shel rose from his chair of brass-tacked blue leather, thinking for the tenth time how much nicer the session's furniture was than his own. He also sensed more than saw Tanya and Vadim Vukonov in the gallery behind him, though today without their lawyer, Gallina Ekarevskaya, which disappointed Shel more than he would have guessed.

"Your Honor, to begin with, Ben Friedman was released on bail prior to that first trial Mr. Seagraves mentioned, yet my client appeared faithfully each day of it to face the charges against him. Also, Mr. Friedman was found *not* guilty by the jury in that case, and therefore he had no motive to later kill Ms. Balaguer, one of the members who argued strenuously for his innocence during deliberations."

"Wait a minute," from O'Brien. "How do we know that fact?"

"Judge Maynard allowed our motion to contact the remaining jurors after this decedent's death. My associate, Ms. O'Clare," Shel said, nodding toward her, "interviewed seven of those thirteen jurors, with all seven confirming Ms. Balaguer's position during deliberations. And none of them expressed any fear of Mr. Friedman to Ms. O'Clare, thus refuting the prosecution's 'deadly consequences' argument."

Seagraves said, "Your Honor, I'm informed by Detective Tully, seated to my right, that six jurors—a near majority—refused to speak with Ms. O'Clare, perhaps because of *just* such a fear of Mr. Friedman."

Shel shrugged. "Or perhaps because the Homicide Unit spoke with them first, implying Ben Friedman was a danger to them."

"That's enough byplay, gentlemen," said O'Brien. "Have any of the 'remaining thirteen' suffered any kind of assault or 'accident' since the first trial?"

Shel figured to let Seagraves answer that one.

The prosecutor looked down at a stone-faced Tully, then said, "Not to our knowledge, Your Honor."

"And Mr. Friedman was discharged from any form of custody after that first trial?"

Shel decided to score a point. "Except for round-the-clock surveillance of his home in Brookline by the police following Ms. Balaguer's death."

"Surveillance, Your Honor, justified by the very fact that Ms. Balaguer was killed only hours after that trial *and* only hours after depositing almost ten thousand dollars *cash* into her personal bank account."

"A deposit, Your Honor," said Shel, "which represented the de facto settlement of a civil claim Ms. Balaguer had raised."

Shel relied on his peripheral vision to see Detective Jorie Tully lean back far enough in her chair to stare at him around Seagraves.

Good: They don't know about any sexual harassment at the insurance agency.

The prosecutor said, "Or, given the timing, that money could have represented a bribe to that juror from the very defendant charged now with killing her, perhaps to—"

"'Could have' and 'perhaps' don't cut it, Counselor." The judge turned to Shel. "How about the 'risk of flight' aspect?"

"Your Honor, Ben Friedman appeared faithfully each day of that earlier—"

"As you've already told me, Counselor. I'm more troubled by the trip to Florida."

Shel didn't want to lose the momentum he felt he'd built with O'Brien. "My client merely went down to his condominium in Boca Raton, where his friend, a Ms. Bomberg, already awaited him. The existence of this condo was virtually common knowledge, it having been brought up at that first trial. And the defendant didn't have any restraints on him, aside from that surveillance I mentioned earlier."

Seagraves seemed to reach a boiling point. "The same defendant who smuggled himself out of his own house in the back of a pool-service van, and whose whereabouts would not have been known without the Boston police following Mr. Gold, and the Florida authorities cooperating, one of their officers even impersonating a cabdriver to take Mr. Gold to his client's hideout."

Judge O'Brien had begun staring at the prosecutor. "You were surveilling defense *counsel* as well?"

Seagraves glanced over toward Shel. "Only after the indictment was handed down, and the defendant had fled the jurisdiction."

Shel raised his hand, like a child in a classroom, which he'd always found to be a good way to show implicit respect for a judge—now looking his way again—deep into any court argument. "Your Honor, the defendant did not 'flee the jurisdiction.' As indicated twice before, the police had him under surveil—"

"Counselor, your hitting the stakeout point three times is *not* exactly a charm."

"Sorry, Your Honor," said Shel, sensing he was now losing momentum. "But Ben Friedman just wanted to go down to be with his friend at an oceanfront condo in a nicer climate—"

"Florida in May?" from the bench.

"—and he didn't even *know* that the indictment *had* been handed down when he left his Brookline home."

Seagraves said, "Left it hiding in a service van, when Mr. Gold himself had visited that same home just hours before."

Judge O'Brien narrowed her eyes at Shel.

Accept it: She's gone over to the Commonwealth.

"Is that true, Counselor?"

"Your Honor, I did visit Ben Friedman's house that day, but *after* he had left it and *before* Mr. Seagraves called my law office and indicated to Ms. O'Clare that our client's arrest was imminent."

"Your Honor," said Seagraves in a low, confidential tone that unfortunately felt just right even to Shel at that moment. "The defendant has the financial resources and... 'business flexibility' to leave the Commonwealth again at any time. The fact is, Benjamin Friedman correctly anticipated that the police were going to pounce upon him, and he evaded them by secretly fleeing nearly fifteen hundred miles away. Both *Commonwealth versus Booker* and *Commonwealth versus Toney* make that 'trip' admissible at trial toward establishing a defendant's state of mind on guilt, and it should persuade you to deny any bail here. Put simply, how far will the defendant run if he's released once more?"

"I've heard enough." O'Brien now peered down at her clerk. "Bail is denied."

From the dock, Shel heard a clear, almost pitiful, "Golden Boy, I can't do it."

As the judge turned toward the source of the words, Shel said, "Your Honor, in that case, I respectfully request a short trial date."

O'Brien turned back to him. "How short?"

"One week from today."

"That's ridiculous!" stormed Seagraves. "I'd have virtually no time to prepare the Commonwealth's case."

Shel glanced over at him before addressing the bench. "If the prosecution was ready to 'pounce' on Ben Friedman in Florida, they should be ready to try him back here as well."

"I agree," said the former public defender.

"But, Your Honor—"

"Mr. Seagraves, you get half a loaf. Defendant is remanded to the custody of the Suffolk County Sheriff's Office, and the trial of this matter will begin next Monday before... Judge Keith Maynard, who my calendar reads will be available then. Anything else?"

The prosecutor seemed to recover. "An oral motion for reciprocal discovery under Rule Fourteen, including any and all documents relating to the decedent's alleged 'civil claim' involving that cash deposit."

"No objection," said Shel, not wanting to risk *his* half of the loaf by arguing any further.

"Should other matters arise, take them up with Judge Maynard." The Honorable Mary Frances O'Brien turned a page in front of her. "Mr. Clerk, next case, please?"

pontifico Murizzi looked at his nearly filled bottle of Mountain Dew. Roughly the same color as the original contents it held Saturday evening, but a lot warmer and less appealing.

He also watched the probable drinking buddy of Señor Balaguer stumble around from the back of the house, looking more tired and hungover than drunk. No sign of the guy himself, though, either the day before or that Monday morning, unless he bugged out during the half hour between 3 and 3:30 A.M. when the Pope went to get some food at an all-night diner.

So, the scorecard for forty-plus hours of stakeout: a pair of functional alcoholics on a weekend bender.

Though why wasn't Balaguer going to work at the factory? Could he have Sunday *and* Monday off?

Murizzi checked his watch, wrote down in a little logbook the exact time the meandering drinking buddy made his departure, and then decided to give the surveillance another chunk of unrelieved boredom before driving back into the city for the meeting Shel had asked for that past Saturday.

* * *

billie Sunday looked down at her to-do list. That aggravating man and the child were in all day yesterday, but did they do anything other than fuss over that gangster's case?

They did not. Like two cameras zooming in on one part of the picture, they ignored all the rest.

What Billie's list contained: Notice of Appeal in an armed robbery; Notice of Deposition in a divorce case that Billie knew Shel was looking forward to about as much as visiting the dentist; Motion in Limine to exclude "prior bad acts" evidence for a career bar brawler; Brief in Support of same; three affidavits in assorted cases; more motions regarding crime-scene photographs, a psychiatric expert, a request for attorney fees, a—

No. Stop. You know what the priorities are, and there's no sense fuming over them, especially since Shel and Mairead will be back sometime soon for a strategy meeting after their court hearing.

So Billie took a red Flair pen and wrote the order in which she should do the tasks based on importance and deadlines, cranked a new form into her old IBM Selectric III, and began typing away on the first of the thirteen documents to be done by sundown in order for the Law Offices of Sheldon A. Gold to function for another day without a malpractice suit being threatened or brought against it.

19

As Mairead O'Clare climbed back up the sidewalk on Milk Street from the courthouse, she felt her ankle protest and her stomach grumble. "We going to stop for lunch?"

Shel Gold shook his head. "No. Given the time, the Pope ought to be at the office pretty soon. We can order in pizza for everyone."

Mairead shifted hands on the "traveling file cabinet" of the sample case, now containing papers from the new indictment as well. "I still can't believe it. Trial next *week?*"

"I thought a judge who'd been on our side when she practiced but denied bail from the bench might buy it."

"Shel?"

"Yes?"

"I was thinking more your even making the request. How can we possibly be ready?"

The two of them stepped off the curb and slalomed around a sports car stuck in the bumper-to-bumper traffic that clogged downtown Boston from seven in the morning till ten at night, every weekday. "First of all," said Shel, "the prosecution has the burden of initially offering evidence *and* of ultimately persuading the jury beyond a reasonable doubt. I don't believe they've got the juice to carry that second burden, and I think Seagraves knows it."

"Granted he seemed rocked, but then, so was I. Why did you leak what Billie found out at Stover-Trent, though?"

"Calculated risk. I knew that Ben wasn't jailing well, so I figured that maybe the 'civil claim' would nudge the judge."

"Yeah, but it didn't seem to affect O'Brien's ruling, and now Seagraves will get the details, thanks to his motion for reciprocal discovery."

Mairead noticed Shel smiling contentedly. "What?"

He said, "The Commonwealth's motion was for 'any and all documents' we have, right?"

"So?"

"So, I didn't ask Billie to write down what Lurlene Inch told her about the sexual-harassment claim. Did you?"

"Of course not." *You don't see it, young lady.* "Wait a minute. We don't *have* any documents to turn over."

Affecting a bad British accent, Shel said, "By George, I think she's got it."

Mairead wasn't about to concede anything expressly, but she had to admit that her boss could be pretty cute sometimes, including his now reaching for the sample case at roughly the halfway point of their walk back to the office.

from behind his desk, Sheldon A. Gold watched Pontifico Murizzi bite into a slice of pepperoni and mushroom from one open, square box before the investigator said, "Great pizza. Regina's, right?"

Billie Sunday had opted for the sausage and onion. "Man's a connoisseur, no question. You could do that with wine, we'd all be rich."

"Do me a favor, okay?" said Mairead. "Nobody mention wine for a while."

She laid a slice from both pies on her plate, then sat next to Billie in front of the desk, Murizzi choosing to stand, as always, against the big bank safe.

"Okay," said Shel around a mouthful of the pepperoni and mushroom. "We have a hanging this time, not a hit-and-run, and there's a good chance that Judge Maynard will let Seagraves offer crime-scene and autopsy photos again, especially given the short trial date. So, it's not enough to have the jury think it could have been an accident not involving our client. We need to show them at least one credible, alternative killer. Candidates?"

Murizzi said, "When I was on Homicide, we always liked ex-husbands. Rigoberto is an asshole with a nicely documented record of spouse abuse involving the victim here, and he's probably smart enough to pull off the hanging at her house, maybe with one of his drinking buds as helper. But I don't see a current motive for the guy. He might have killed her out of sexual jealousy, if he'd known about Troy Gallup during the sequestered trial, only I don't think he could have. And besides, once Berto kills her, he can't harass her anymore, and talking with him I didn't get any vibes that he was other than amused about what happened to the woman."

Amused, thought Shel, and shuddered inside.

"Plus," the Pope finishing his slice and wiping his hands with a napkin, "I've been sitting on Berto since Saturday P.M., outside his place up in Lynn. The guy seems about as active as a snail, maybe because of the *cerveza*."

"The what?" said Shel.

Mairead spoke through teeth closed around her pizza. "Spanish for 'beer.'"

Every day, a learning experience. "Still, he's an ex-spouse and prone to violence, so let's keep him on our list. Anybody else?"

Billie said, "More an 'anything else.' Ever since I talked with that Lurlene at the insurance agency, I've been asking myself: If Conchita Balaguer got paid off for the harassment claim without ever having to file it, why would she be calling an attorney afterward?"

Being so worried about his initial assumption that the cash deposit might have been a bribe from Big Ben's camp, Shel thought Billie had a pretty good question. "You come up with an answer?"

"One," she said. "That maybe after some time in the court system as a juror, talking with the others about things legal, she got it into her head that ten thousand wasn't exactly as much as a lawyer might get for her."

"And so," said Mairead in a following tone, "Balaguer calls me to maybe take the case on and sweeten the deal?"

Shel didn't buy it. "Two problems with that. The woman worked in an insurance agency. Why wouldn't she think that a payment she deposited would be a settlement of 'all claims'?"

The Pope said, "Stover told me that the 'clericals' like Balaguer didn't actually investigate or process any of the insureds' claims. She just would have entered them in a computer, with the actual legwork sent out to a claims adjuster."

Shel thought about it. "Still, wouldn't Stover-Trent have insisted on a general release before giving Balaguer *any* money?"

Murizzi shook his head. "Shel, they paid the woman off in cash. Maybe they figured like Billie: We get all formal, she's going to ask for more."

"Point taken," said Shel. "But why doesn't Balaguer go to a lawyer right away, when the harassment happened?"

Billie said, "She was a minority, and maybe she didn't have a lot of trust in the formal system, especially when even the court from her divorce case couldn't seem to keep the ex off her back."

Mairead chimed in. "And during her jury service, Balaguer talked with Hildy Crowell, former investigator of such matters, who told her to get a lawyer."

Shel nodded himself now. "And so Balaguer calls after seeing you in action at the trial."

Murizzi said, "It fits. And Stover or Trent could have killed the woman if they got wind she was going to welsh on their deal with her by seeing a lawyer."

"Okay, add them to the list."

"One thing, though," from the Pope. "Do we know for sure *which* boss at Stover-Trent supposedly did the harassing?"

Billie said, "Lurlene told me it was Norris Stover."

"Part of what I mean." Murizzi took another slice of pizza. "Everything about this 'sex claim' hinges on that woman, and I'm not sure how far to trust her."

Shel said, "Well, is there any other evidence of the harassment?"

Mairead cleared her throat. "I've never seen Stover or Trent, but we know Conchita Balaguer went for Troy Gallup in a big way, and he's kind of a buffed version of Seagraves."

The Pope began eating again. "Our prosecutor?"

Mairead started on her second piece, too. "Down to the cleft in his chin."

Murizzi stopped with the pizza halfway back to his mouth. "Trevor Trent at the insurance agency looks kind of like Seagraves, too."

Billie said, "But Lurlene told me it was Stover, not Trent."

The Pope nodded. "Which brings me back to us relying on her, I think."

Shel figured they were going in a circle now. "Regardless, we have to use Lurlene Inch to explode the bribe theory, and that should remove any shred of motive on Ben Friedman's part to kill Balaguer."

Three nods as the people on the other side of his desk chewed.

Shel said, "What about the 'obese inspector' as a candidate?"

Mairead helped herself to a third slice, clearly not wanting to be the one following up on juror Hildy Crowell.

The Pope said, "I talked with Jorie Tully about that, probably just as she was leaving to serve the warrant at Friedman's house. Our Hildy had a brush with sexual harassment herself, but as the bad guy, and it wouldn't surprise me if, Crowell being a lesbian, Balaguer got hit on from that side as well, with maybe a little dust-up over it resulting in what we saw at the crime scene in Rozzie."

Shel watched Mairead as Murizzi talked. The young lawyer seemed genuinely relieved that the Pope had taken the laboring oar on the sexual-orientation issue, then a little troubled by the reminder of what she'd witnessed at the Balaguer house in Roslindale.

However, Mairead said, "Crowell struck me as devious—and angry—enough to kill somebody, even by hanging."

Billie looked up from her pad. "Yeah, but strong enough to do it herself, without any help?"

Mairead paused. "No. Given the obesity, I don't see it."

"All right," Shel mentally closing the book on Crowell, "any of the other jurors then?"

Mairead set down her new slice, now half-gone. "Ralph Bobransky, the hardware guy, was pissed at Balaguer over the romantic rejection. I think he'd be capable of it, both attitude- and strength-wise."

The Pope said, "They sell a lot of rope in hardware stores."

Motive, means, and hope for opportunity. "Another solid candidate. Good work."

Mairead straightened her shoulders—at the compliment, Shel thought—and he felt a little twitch in his heart.

He said, "Anybody further from among the jurors?"

Mairead used her fingers to tick off names. "On the strength issue, scratch Lorraine Fanton, the saxophone player, and Phil Quinn, the elderly man from Southie. Also Josephine Arria, the nice lady from the flat of Beacon Hill, and probably Ruth Kee as well."

Shel was confused. "Why only a 'probably' on Kee?"

"Well, she's physically smallish, but she does have a twin sister."

"As accomplice, you mean?"

"Yes, but I think she's a scratch on the motive front as well. Kee seemed to despise Balaguer, but from a moral, not emotional, standpoint, and I don't see what the owner of a restaurant would or could gain from killing a worker in an insurance agency."

Shel agreed. "What about the lover boy?"

"Strength galore," said Mairead. "And while Troy Gallup

checked into his health club at five thirty-seven that Monday afternoon, allegedly for an hour-and-a-half workout, there's no official record of when he left it. And, by his own admission, the place was crowded around that time, so he probably wouldn't be missed."

Means and opportunity. "What about motive?"

"Nothing, Shel. To put it the way Gallup might, he jumped her, humped her, and dumped her. I don't think this guy would 'bother' to kill a woman who was just another notch on his bedpost."

Shel tried to put his next sentence gently. "But he did have an affair with the woman, which suggests some passion, and passion can lead to violence. So maybe we should help our next jury see him as a candidate, too."

A small frown from Mairead, but a small nod as well. "I think that does it on the former jurors, then. At least the ones who would talk with me."

Shel said, "We were lucky you persuaded so many of them to cooperate, and even Hildy Crowell proved useful on her 'see a lawyer' advice." He looked over at Billie, then up at Murizzi. "Any other favorites?"

"More a long shot," offered the Pope. "You said the Russian father went berserk after the verdict, and then two days later, he comes in here fists first. If he was still that mad at you when he should have cooled off some, how would he have felt only a couple hours after the 'not guilty' about a juror he thought Friedman had bought?"

Billie said, "Did that poor soul even *know* about the ten thousand dollars?"

Murizzi seemed to relent. "Good point."

Mairead came to life again. "On the other hand, Balaguer was shooting looks at me throughout the closing arguments. Seagraves confronted me with that, so he saw her doing it. Probably the Vukonovs did as well."

Shel tried to remember what he felt when the father attacked him out in the reception area. Mostly pity.

Admit it, though: You weren't looking for anything else.

"Okay, Vadim Vukonov is on our list, too. I'll call Gallina Ekarevskaya, see if she'll let something drop."

"Fat chance," said Mairead, with something else behind her words as well, though Shel couldn't decide what.

Billie said, "Anyway, I count six candidates. Rigoberto Balaguer, Norris Stover, Trevor Trent, Ralph Bobransky, Troy Gallup, and Vadim Vukonov. You going to 'nominate' any of them for special treatment?"

Shel Gold shook his head. "The way I see it, we nominate them all, and let the 'voters' decide."

well, said the Pope to himself, armed with fresh Mountain Dew, at least the pizza was worth the drive.

Murizzi sat again in his Explorer on Rigoberto Balaguer's block in Lynn, but in a different parking place and with a *Sports Illustrated* as face cover should he need it. The Pope thought the session at Shel's office had gone pretty well. Mairead really had done a nice job on the jurors, and that Billie was sharper than a lot of the lawyers—and even cops—he'd ever dealt with. Also, in all the back-and-forth, Murizzi felt pretty good that his minor tidbits were viewed as contributions and not throwaways.

So, back to the stakeout, and maybe you get lucky.

He'd just unscrewed the top from another Mountain Dew when a car pulled up in front of Balaguer's house. The driver seemed to be wondering if a too-small space was really big enough, but then gave up without trying and glided nose first into a limo-sized one two doors down. The Pope watched the single occupant turn the act of getting out into a derricking operation. And then he wished he'd spent a little more time at Friedman's trial eyeballing the jury box.

Because from the way the plus-*plus*-sized female waddled up the sidewalk and seemed to have to take a breath before using the path to the front entrance, she sure looked a fuck of a lot like the way Mairead had described one Hildy Crowell.

"Motive, but not enough physical strength." Only now

the "inspector" was making a house call on the deceased's shitbird of an ex-husband, who Crowell could have told about the bed-bouncing between ex-wife and Troy Gallup as soon as the judge released the jury that Monday afternoon.

Feeling a good deal more useful again, Pontifico Murizzi picked up his cell phone.

20

"Matthew?" said Billie Sunday, knocking softly on the door to her middle son's bedroom. She'd been a little worried coming into the house, not because it was noisy, and not because it was silent, either. It was because the music she heard coming quietly from Matthew's room wasn't hip-hop. In fact, she thought it might be Mozart or Beethoven, one of those.

"Matthew?" repeated his mother, knocking a bit louder.

"Yeah, come in."

She opened the door, saw him stretched out on the bed, but in a Red Sox T-shirt and Celtics basketball shorts, a book that looked like part of the encyclopedia set Robert Senior had bought at a yard sale maybe three weeks before... before his accident. "Everything okay?"

"Sure," turning a page in the book, but not looking up.

The thirteen-year-old's bruises from the fight at school were now nearly a memory. The beauty of youth, things healing so quickly.

At least, physical things.

His mother said, "Can I sit down?"

"Guess so."

Billie settled slowly onto the side of his bed, angling herself so as to be able to see the section of the encyclopedia book he was reading.

Or at least staring at.

"Never knew you were so interested in Zaire."

Just his shrug.

Billie said, "There a reason why you're studying a country I couldn't find on a map of the world?"

"Yeah."

If he wanted his teeth pulled out, she could play dentist. "And that would be?"

Matthew closed the book. Not suddenly, more slowly, even thoughtfully. "You know those three dudes dissed Rondell?"

"The three white boys we went to Mr. Hightower over?"

"Yeah. Well, the one actually doing the dissing, he had some issues with Rondell, turns out."

Billie edged a little closer to her son on the bed. "What kind of issues?"

"Turns out Rondell ain't—"

Billie let the slang pass.

"—this genius music philosopher, teaching me the where and what-for of hip-hop. Turns out he been hanging around the stores and the gigs he could get into so's he could score some sh . . . drugs."

Billie made the "What did I tell you?" stay down in her throat even if she choked on it, mainly because she wanted the answer to a much more important question. "How did you find this out?"

"White dude who did the dissing come up to me this morning in the yard, saying he could see from my threads I was into the music, like Rondell. Said him and his 'buds' were getting tired of Rondell skimming them off on some deliveries and blowing them off on others. Said maybe if I was connected to the hip-hop 'scene,' then maybe I could be a 'new and improved' Rondell, getting a bigger slice if I was more reliable on my deliveries."

Billie shook her head. "Rondell acted as the go-between for drugs between his hip-hop friends and the white boys who started the fight."

"Yeah, but it wasn't like, racist, Momma. More 'racial,' on account of a white dude'd have a hard time, cozy up close enough to a real gangsta-niggah—sorry, that's what even Rondell called himself—to get trusted with the deliveries."

"What Rondell call*ed* himself?"

Matthew's voice turned funny. "When I went to him, ask him to tell me the white dude full of bull on all this. Only Rondell, he say..."

Billie noticed tears in her son's eyes for the first time in she couldn't remember how long.

Matthew swiped at his face with the back of one hand. "Rondell say, 'You one stupid, momma-whipped niggah, you didn't know that be what I been doing, last few months up here, last few years down in Liberty City.'"

Which Billie remembered as the African-American neighborhood of Miami where all the rioting was maybe a decade before. "What did you do then?"

"I punched his lights out for him, but just one, wham to the chin," a short crossing motion of Matthew's fist, all bone on it and behind it, the boy not yet filling out, "and then when he was on the ground, I told him to stay the... hell away from me." Now her middle son looked straight up into his mother's eyes, the tears brimming out of both of his own. "He played me for a fool, Momma. You had him down from Jump Street, but he made me think I was his best friend, and all the while he just playing me along, like I was some kind of camouflage clothes for all the shit—sorry, but the unbelievable *shit*—he was pulling on everybody, especially me."

Billie wanted to reach out, hug the boy to her breast, but felt he'd have to make the first move for both of them to feel right about it. And move he did, rolling his body along the comforter like he was putting out a fire on himself before burying his face in her thigh and crying in great, gulping sobs of anger, shame, and...

Yes, embarrassment, too. That his mother could be so right and he could be so wrong, even at the grown-up age of thirteen.

* * *

through the passenger side of the Explorer's windshield, Mairead O'Clare looked at the spiffy though older three-story building somewhere in Charlestown before saying, "And she went into that house?"

"Into that doorway, anyway," Pontifico Murizzi said, waving his hand toward it. "I asked a couple of neighbors. A woman named Hilda or Heidi supposedly has the condo on the second floor."

"Supposedly?"

"Seems the woman doesn't mix much. Guy down the block thought it might be because she was pushing three hundred pounds."

Young lady, be certain you understand the situation as comprehensively as possible. "But you weren't sure the woman you followed from Rigoberto Balaguer's is Hildy Crowell?"

"Like I said before. All I'm sure of is that the obese specimen I saw go into Rigoberto's, stay for an hour, and then leave is the same woman I tailed here and watched go into that three-decker."

Mairead tried to decide what to do. She'd already called Shel on her cellular, but either he wasn't home or he wasn't answering.

The Pope rapped his knuckles twice on the dashboard, but more excited than impatient, Mairead thought. Then he said, "So, how do you want to play this?"

"Well, if it's somehow *not* Hildy Crowell—"

"Now *that's* what I call giving somebody the benefit of the doubt."

"—then we'd still want to know who it was visiting Rigoberto Balaguer, right?"

"My thoughts exactly." Murizzi opened the driver's-side door and hopped out.

Mairead followed suit and caught up to him at the building entrance. The buttons were identified only by numbers 1, 2, 3, with a little speaker. "Pope, I don't see any last names here."

"Believe it or not, that was the first thing I checked."

His sarcasm is warranted, young lady. "So, we'll have to get the woman to open up for us?"

"Not so hard," said Murizzi. "She's never heard my voice, right?"

"Right."

"And the neighbors said second floor, so . . ."

Mairead watched the Pope press the door button marked 2. Within ten seconds, a voice came back, "Who is it?"

Murizzi mouthed the word "Her?" to Mairead, but she wasn't sure, so she just waggled her hand, palm down. The Pope seemed to accept that.

"Hello? Who is it?"

"Sorry," said Murizzi. "Federal Express. I got this package for you."

A pause. "What name's on it?"

"That's the screwy thing, tell you the truth. They're not supposed to accept these down at the counter without a name, but this one's got just this address, the apartment number, and some kind of agency name for the sender, scribbled in caps that don't make no sense to me."

"God, I'm just getting into the tub. Leave it downstairs."

"No can do, lady. Your secret pals sent it 'Signature Required.'"

"So, I have to get dressed and—"

"Look, I got a schedule, you know? If this thing's important to you, tell you what. Buzz me in and I'll come on up. I can hand the thing to you, and—"

"Can't you just slip it under my door, and then I'll—"

"No can do that either, lady. Thing's like two inches thick."

"Damnit. All right, let me put on a robe and I'll meet you at the door up here."

"Okay, only let's go, huh? I got a couple kids I'd like to kiss good night."

The door made a bumblebee noise, and they were into the building. As they climbed the stairs, the Pope leading, Mairead thought she'd really not have wanted him after her when he was still on the Homicide Unit.

At the second landing, Murizzi knocked and the door opened about four inches, just enough to see two eyes and the middle of a broad, fleshy face.

Mairead peered around the edge of the door and said, "Hi, Hildy. I think you want to talk with us."

shel Gold was already sitting in one of the leather chair arrangements in the Plaza Bar, a glass of Australian Shiraz on his table when Gallina Ekarevskaya came in the door, spoke a few words to the hostess, then saw who she was looking for and came striding over. Her outfit today, Shel was pleased to notice, consisted of a peach dress that fell to the knee, with two-inch heels and a scarf that made her look both successful and confident.

Just what you need in an opponent.

As Ekarevskaya arrived, he stood and shook her offered hand.

She looked up at the ceiling and said, "I should sue gangsters more often."

Shel followed her eyes up, taking in the magnificently wrought room that could have been in the Taj Mahal. "When I first started doing divorces, which I don't like very much, I used to ask a new client to meet me here for a first conference."

Ekarevskaya lowered herself into the adjoining chair like a ballet dancer taking a bow. "You mean your first meeting ever would be in a bar?"

"Not any bar, Gallina. This particular one. In the late afternoon, the only people in it are guests of the hotel—the Copley Plaza then, the Fairmount Copley now—so we had relative privacy, but just enough people that I didn't think the client would break down yelling or crying."

"Smart of you, Sheldon."

"Plus, they took one look at the decor of this place, and I figured I could name my retainer, them thinking I'd expect that kind of money to maintain my lifestyle."

"While in fact, you were being certain that if you accepted a type of case you did not enjoy, as least you would be well compensated for it."

"And in advance."

"Well," said Ekarevskaya, telling the approaching waitress to just bring her whatever Shel was having, "I, unfortunately, have *not* been paid in advance by the poor Vukonovs."

"I'm surprised."

A skeptical look. "That I have not been paid?"

"No, that you'd order red wine without knowing what it is instead of some designer vodka."

"Ah, Americans," Ekarevskaya moving the hem of her dress perhaps an inch higher with one beautifully manicured finger. "You always believe yourselves to be without prejudice. 'All men are created equal,' 'It's a free country.' When in fact, you—like the rest of us—have your biases."

Shel waited until the waitress served the wine to Ekarevskaya before saying, "Meaning not all Russian immigrants drink vodka."

"Or even *like* it. And all Russian men who come to America are not 'new mafia' looking for illegal opportunities, and all Russian women are not—how do you say it, mail-order brides?"

"Yes. Only now, I read that the 'catalogs' are more sophisticated."

"True." A little chill seemed to seep into Ekarevskaya's eye as she sipped her wine. "Now American men can ogle Internet sites depicting Russian women dressed to please. Or to tease. Toward 'luring' the men to come to Russian cities for 'tours,' to walk into a reserved bar or restaurant full of attractive young women and have their 'pick.' But the only reason the men are there is because they chafe at the rights that American women insist upon, and the only reason the Russian women are there is to get themselves a decent meal and perhaps a ticket out of a depressed society where half their own men are alcoholics with a life expectancy of less than sixty years."

"Tell you the truth, Gallina," Shel said, now playing

with his glass rather than drinking his wine, "I'm more interested in a Russian couple."

"My clients."

"Yes. There a reason why they decided to spring the trap on Ben Friedman out at Logan?"

"My decision, not theirs, as I told you it would be. I wanted no problems with initiating the lawsuit, and you kept conveniently forgetting to ask your client for authority to accept service of process on his behalf."

"Fair enough. But why were they in the courtroom this morning for his new arraignment?"

"Because it is a public hearing, and they wished to be."

"And why weren't you with them?"

"Because I did not wish to be."

Shel had given a lot of thought to phrasing his next gambit. "It won't surprise you to hear that we've been trying out a number of other candidates as Conchita Balaguer's killer."

"Sheldon, you can audition them to sing and dance if you like. But I believe Mr. James Seagraves will now finally get his conviction."

"My associates seem to think that your side would run a strong campaign."

"Run a . . . ? You seriously consider the Vukonovs killers of that juror?"

"The husband at least."

"Because Vadim is a butcher by profession, and strong of physique and stomach?"

"And because he erupted in the courtroom and later came after me in my office."

"Vadim believed his family had been deprived of justice. He was distraught."

Shel leaned forward, not liking at all the way he'd have to phrase a different sentence. "Distraught is one thing, Gallina. But the way both the husband and the wife overplayed their parts in that trial . . . ?"

Now the chill turned to frost. "Remember an earlier time

in your own life, Sheldon. Call them 'the father and the mother,' and perhaps you would see them through different eyes."

Shel fought the arc of grief that seared him still over Richie and Natalie.

"And besides," said Ekarevskaya, "there was also the element of fear. The Vukonovs believed a notorious gangster had killed their son, which would make even native-born Americans fearful, would it not? And then, when Mr. Friedman was found not guilty, it made them think of all the corruption they had left Russia to avoid. But now it is the same in this, their adopted country."

"And so Vadim comes after me."

"For which I already have apologized, despite the fact that Vadim himself admitted you were too strong for him."

"Which he couldn't know until after he attacked the lawyer who got the gangster off, just as the husband might have avenged his family against a juror paying unusual attention to my associate during the trial."

"I saw Ms. Balaguer staring at your table. I imagine everyone in that courtroom did. But what is the Vukonovs' motive, Sheldon? Even after the not-guilty verdict in the murder trial regarding their son, they still have a dream case civilly against your client."

"But did your clients know that? And why did you wait so long to have him served?"

Ekarevskaya gathered her handbag with a flourish. "One question cannot be answered, and the other I already have." She rose. "Your tab, I believe. But excellent wine, despite the context."

Then, as at the Kinsale Pub, Sheldon A. Gold watched Gallina Ekarevskaya in her peach dress stride away from his table and toward the door.

Admit it: The woman knows how to make an exit, too.

pontifico Murizzi thought Hildy Crowell's place pretty much captured his first impressions of her.

The furniture in the condo's living room was kind of plushy, overstuffed like the human calzone sitting on the couch. He and Mairead each took a matching chair, so they formed a triangle of conversation.

Not that the flow was exactly going Crowell's way.

"I could call the police," she said.

The Pope opened both hands like the old-country priest who'd presided over his mom's parish. "You could've done that without letting us in, Hildy."

Murizzi sensed his using her first name—and probably even nickname at that—rankled, so he decided to play out "bad cop," hoping his partner would pick up on "good cop."

"Hildy," from Mairead, the softer tone she used making it not even sound like the same word, "you know we have to talk, so let's try to get it over with, okay?"

"Talk about what?"

The Pope said, "Your house call on one Rigoberto Balaguer."

"Who is . . . Oh, is that Conchita's ex-husband?"

Murizzi felt like gagging, this one was so transparent. "Hildy, let's cut to the car chase. You got bounced from your last job for playing touchy-feely in the little girls' room."

"You fucking bastard. Where do you—"

"But, thanks to your furtive mind there, you land on your feet in another investigative job, this time backstopping the shitbirds who slip through the abuse net."

Nothing this time.

Mairead said, "Really, it's better to talk this out."

The Pope let Irish finish, then even let Crowell stew a bit before continuing. "Here's what I'm guessing, Hildy. I'm guessing you somehow caught Rigoberto on his stalking the ex-wife. I'm guessing you turned him on that, saying you've got a choice, Berto: Work with me, or spend the next couple of years with the guys in the exercise yard at Cedar Junction playing pin the donkey in the tail."

"Typical macho hetero shit."

Murizzi squelched a laugh, because he didn't think it'd be in character at the moment.

Mairead said, "Hildy, we know somebody killed Conchita Balaguer by hanging. We don't think you could have done it alone, then we see you with her cloying ex-spouse. We bring this out in court, what does it do to whatever operation you're using him to help you with?"

"Better question," said the Pope. "What does it do to what's left of your career?"

"You can't introduce any of that in court, and you know it."

Murizzi folded his arms and leaned back into the chair, sensing now that he held a pat hand. "Actually, we were thinking more the newspapers, Hildy."

The Pope had been through the next minute more times than he could count. The "wheels within wheels" debate inside a moke's head, trying to figure which was the frying pan and which was the fire, not appreciating yet that they were all fires unless the interrogator was willing to put them out, no further questions asked.

Crowell said, "Over half of all Americans are overweight, and seventeen percent are obese, did you know that?"

"Hildy?" from Mairead.

"Nursery school children prefer pictures of kids their age who are crippled or disfigured to . . . fat ones."

"Hildy," said Murizzi. "You're not exactly answering in the context of the question here. Now, do we go to the media, or do you level with us?"

"All right." Crowell sashed the robe a little tighter around her, which the Pope didn't think was possible, given what the fabric had to cover. "I'd had video surveillance on a pay phone not far from where Mr. Balaguer worked, because local phone logs showed some calls from it to his ex-wife. I got him on tape."

A dead stop. Murizzi wanted to signal Mairead not to prompt the woman, but his partner did just right, sitting quietly, looking expectant, even encouraging with just the slightest of nods.

Crowell seemed to register the nod, because she did the

same, kind of like one person yawning after another. "I offered him a deal: Cooperate or do time."

"Cooperate with what?" asked Mairead.

A little more reluctance from Crowell, but the Pope was pleased Irish still held off pressing her.

"Mr. Balaguer is in a therapy group, six men who meet once a week as part of their court-ordered probation. All are chronic, and in three cases, rather 'proud' offenders. Mr. Balaguer was to cooperate in finding out over drinks or other one-on-ones what each did in the real world but *didn't* reveal during group."

Murizzi said, "You flipped Berto into being a snitch."

Now Crowell raised her voice. "I 'recruited' him into helping me protect other victims of abuse."

"But," said Mairead, "how in the world did you arrange to be on the same jury as his ex-wife?"

"I didn't. Pure coincidence."

The Pope's bullshit meter jumped off the scale. "No sale, Hildy."

"Honest to God. I get my yellow notice, and I go in that day. I didn't even know Chita's last *name* when we first started talking before being impaneled."

Murizzi still wasn't buying. "But then you just happen to kind of mentor her, right?"

"Wrong, asshole." Crowell turned back to Mairead, which to the Pope meant that "good cop/bad cop" was firing on all cylinders. "Chita came to me with what she said was a 'problem.' I figured it'd be about her ex-husband, so I braced myself. Turns out it was just about... well, not *just* about, in terms of importance, but this sexual harassment thing at the insurance agency."

Murizzi had to smile at that one. Hildy, the investigator of such things, gets bounced for such thing, then sees such thing as minimal because it doesn't affect her new, central interest of spousal abuse. Fucking hypocritical—

"Hildy," said Mairead, "did Ms. Balaguer tell you who was harassing her there?"

"No. Just 'this person at work.'"

"Male or female?"

"She didn't say, didn't even use pronouns."

Irish shook her head. "That's pretty hard to swallow."

"But it's the truth! Look, I admit that Chita and me getting called the same day for jury duty and sitting on the same trial is sort of incredible—"

"Try fucking incredible," put in the Pope.

"—but I told you about her and her problem at work, didn't I? Why would I do that if I'd killed her? Or had Berto help me?"

Murizzi noticed that Crowell used the guy's own nickname for the first time and wondered if Mairead picked up on it, too.

Then Irish said, "Hildy, now you're even calling him by 'Berto' instead of 'Mr. Balaguer.' And you could have told him after you jurors were released about his ex-wife having a rollicking affair while sequestered. How do you think that will look, whether in a courtroom or on a front page?"

"Or for that matter," said Murizzi, "on an indictment of you for 'accessory before'?"

"Look, you people, please?" Hildy Crowell clamped her eyes shut, to the Pope kind of like a kid who knows she's about to cry but is trying not to until she's alone. "I admit Mr. Balaguer is working with me, I admit I counseled his wife on the jury—though I don't see any conflict about that. I even admit that"—Crowell looked at only Mairead now—"that I found her very attractive, all right? But I swear I didn't kill her, or even help kill her. I just didn't!"

"Actually, Hildy," said the Pope, wanting to close on a high note, "we still kind of like your Berto there for that one."

billie Sunday fluffed up the two extra pillows she kept on her bed, then punched them into the shape she wanted. The kids always made fun of her when one of them would be up before she was and poked a head inside the room, see her lying there hugging them. What Billie never told any of her boys, though, is that it was something she'd started in the first few weeks after Robert Senior had been killed, something to get her through the long, empty, eyes-wide-open nights, when the specters of what loomed ahead as a single mother of three seemed to all rush into her head at once and spin, like clothes in a washing machine. The pillows amounted to a habit Billie had never tried to break, though, because they reminded her of lying with her husband, him holding her tight and saying everything would work out in the "by-and-by."

Which is what he always used to chase away those bogeymen of the sleeping hours. Robert Senior said, "by-and-by," and it meant you had all the time you needed for God to square things away, whether it had something to do with their household finances or the health of a son, or getting shot at in the wrong part of the world while on duty protecting somebody else's family.

Which in turn reminded Billie of Matthew, and their talk earlier that evening. The talk and the cry. When he was William's age, she might have taken him to bed with her instead of the pillows, to rock him and soothe him until his breath started getting more regular, and the muscles in his little arms would twitch, like a puppy dreaming of chasing a kitten. She could never fall asleep before one of her boys when he had a scary thing to deal with, but now Billie was pretty sure Matthew's fever over Rondell had broken, and better, clearer times were ahead for her middle son.

And so, running her nails over the extra pillows a little, she said goodnight to Robert Senior and slowly felt her own breathing get more regular until she couldn't have sworn whether she was asleep or awake.

mairead had just noticed how closely the new Fleet Center for Celtics and Bruins games abutted the ramps for Interstate 93 and Storrow Drive when the Pope said, "You did a great job back there, Irish."

She turned to Murizzi, who changed lanes toward an exit that would take the Explorer more directly to her apartment building on Beacon Hill. "That's how you spent a lot of your time in the police department?"

"Not when I was wearing a uniform, but on Homicide? Yeah, only even then, it was mostly paperwork, not tag-team interrogation like we just pulled."

"You enjoyed it, though, didn't you?"

"More or less. The Mutt-and-Jeff is a—"

"The what?"

"Mutt-and-Jeff, the routine we played on Crowell. Me the hard-charger, you the shoulder to cry on."

Mairead turned back to the windshield. "I thought it was kind of cruel."

"Cruel how?"

"Under false pretenses, we pushed our way into her home—"

"She knew who we really were before she let us in."

"Let me finish, okay?"

"Okay," said the Pope, quietly.

Young lady, don't take the anger you feel at yourself out on another.

Mairead tried to modulate her voice, if not her emotion. "We corner the woman in her living room, when she's not even really dressed, and then we badger her like two wolves after a deer, each of us attacking from a different direction."

"Kind of like two lawyers asking questions in a courtroom, you mean?"

Mairead could feel the grin on Murizzi's face without having to see it. "Big difference, Pope: There the witness has the judge as referee if the game gets too rough."

"Too rough? Okay, you told me some orphanage stories back at that jazz club, right? Let me tell you a couple of station ones."

Mairead didn't reply.

"When I first put on the blue, you had your grass-eaters and your meat-eaters, just like the skels, and, frankly, just like you lawyers. The grass-eaters played by the book: If they collared the guy righteous, they processed him through and let the system take its course. Not many heroes, but a lot of good cops were grass-eaters, and the streets were safer for it."

Mairead noticed Murizzi shift in the driver's seat, seeming to slow for a yellow light intentionally, as though to prolong their time together in the truck. "Your meat-eaters, now, without their uniforms on, they were tough to distinguish from the mob guys. At best, these cops slapped the skels around. At worst, they'd throw down a knife if they'd used their guns without the dead guy being in arm's reach of them."

"Pope, that's horrible."

"Toss in unconstitutional, maybe even inhuman. But it was reality, Irish. Closer on to what Hildy Crowell supposedly 'inspects,' if we got the sense that some hubbie or boyfriend was beating the wife or girlfriend on a regular basis, a couple, three of us would pay the guy a house call ourselves, drag him out into the backyard so the neighbors could hang out their windows like they were fucking skyboxes. Then we'd kick the shit out of the guy, usually to the body or with rolled-up *Boston Globes*, not leave much visible. And all the while one of us would be educating him, saying, "Now, Dino—or Leroy, or Timmy—this isn't how you fucking treat a woman, right?"

Mairead could feel the revulsion roll inside her like a wave of nausea. "That . . . is . . . barbaric."

"With hindsight, maybe yeah. But it worked."

"What do you mean, it worked?"

"The guy would stop beating on the woman involved."

"Or maybe he just beat on her hard enough to persuade her never to file another complaint against him."

"Possible, but I doubt it."

"Because . . . ?"

"Some neighbor who saw the backyard boxing lesson—usually somebody with a gripe against the abuser—would have blown the whistle on the guy."

"It's still barbaric to vigilante somebody like that."

"First, we weren't 'vigilantes,' we were cops. Second, the good citizens knew that, and they appreciated what our efforts tried to do for their neighborhood."

Mairead just shook her head before saying, "Another question?"

Murizzi turned onto Charles Street. "Shoot."

"How come the Homicide Unit didn't focus on Conchita Balaguer's ex-husband from the outset?"

The Pope checked his rearview mirror. "They probably did, in the sense that when you called it in, I'm sure nine-one-one had somebody running the computer for spouses and exes, restraining orders or warrants. Only thing is, when Jorie Tully—probably with your brother-at-the-bar Seagraves breathing down her neck—realized who we had hanging from that beam, she turned to Ben Friedman, whose alibi smells worse than Rigoberto's for the time period in question."

"So the detectives focus on one person, just like that?"

"No, not always, and hey, maybe not even here. I mean, Jorie did scoop you on most of the jurors as possible witnesses, right?"

"Right."

"And they didn't exactly slap Friedman in irons the morning after you found Balaguer dead. But you got to understand something, Irish."

"Which is?"

"Every investigation, high-profile like this juror homicide or a small-potatoes B and E in municipal court, starts out like a dragnet—not the TV show, but the 'open mind.' Who did this to our citizen? But at some point along the way, maybe even with nobody on the squad realizing it happened, the investigation shifts, from the 'who did it' to a 'he did it' thing. After that, an innocent suspect better be battening down his fucking hatches, because he's gonna have some competent pit bull like Jorie or Artie Chin—even yours truly till a few years back—chomping on his ass. And cops like us—meat-eaters when we have to be—never give up."

Mairead noticed they were arriving at her building. "You're not the man you used to be, Pope."

She could see the confusion—even some hurt—in his face.

Pontifico Murizzi said, "What?"

"Don't worry," Mairead O'Clare said, getting out of the passenger side and preparing her left ankle for the inevitable drop from the high running board to the ground. "It was a compliment."

21

A week later, on Monday morning, Pontifico Murizzi sat in the gallery of Suffolk Superior's courtroom number 10 again, thinking, You should have made book on this one.

It had been a busy seven days since Mairead and he had gotten Hildy Crowell to open up in her condo about Rigoberto Balaguer. The Pope spent most of his time hand-carrying packets of papers for Shel and Mairead that Billie Sunday was turning out like a printing press. Defendant's List of Potential Witnesses, Motion to Sequester Commonwealth Witnesses, and about a dozen Motions in Limine—which Murizzi always thought was a screwy way to name something, since some of the motions clearly asked for evidence to come in, not just stay out or be "limited," like the expression implied. And then, the last part of the week, him serving subpoenas to appear at trial.

Assuming, that is, we're ever going to *have* a fucking trial.

You couldn't blame the judge. The Pope didn't know if the Honorable Keith Maynard had been assigned this case because he'd sat on the last one involving Big Ben Friedman, but it seemed a good idea, since the guy was already familiar with all the players. Only problem, try to get a jury that didn't already know nearly as much as the judge about Friedman and the killings.

"I don't think I could be objective, Your Honor, based on

what I remember about the defendant from that horrible case of the little boy who . . ."

"Didn't recollect who the man was till I got a look at him, which was when I knew he'd . . ."

"All I can think of, Your Honor, is what happened to one of the jurors from his first . . ."

And so on.

As Judge Maynard asked the court officer to call for another three panels of jurors to be brought into the session, Murizzi noticed Shel beckon his client to lean in close for a confab. At first, Friedman seemed kind of surprised, but then he listened more and started to nod, adding a couple of remarks himself with his hand closed into a fist.

Which the Pope didn't think was overall the *best* light for the fucking mobster to put on himself.

Then Shel Gold stood slowly. "Your Honor, the defense would like to make a suggestion."

Judge Maynard looked down hard at the defense attorney, then spoke in that deep bass voice of his. "Mr. Gold, I understand from Judge O'Brien that you moved for an *ultra* speedy trial in this case yourself. I think a request for change of venue would be a little late now."

"I agree, Your Honor. What the defendant would like to do is *waive* his right to a trial by jury and proceed before you alone."

"What?" said Seagraves, rising from his own chair, jaw as distended as Murizzi's own.

Then, as Seagraves sputtered about the "loose cannon" tactics displayed by the defense, the Pope began to nod, even grin.

"Counselor," said Maynard to the prosecutor, "I'm not aware of any provision in our constitution, statutes, or court rules that provides the Commonwealth with a right to trial by jury in a criminal case if the defendant decides to forego one. Are you?"

"Not at present, Your Honor, but—"

"Would you like a few hours to brief and then argue to me on it this afternoon?"

Murizzi watched Seagraves fume for about five seconds before saying, "No, Your Honor."

"Very well, then," from the bench. "I'd like you and Mr. Gold to spend those hours instead generating an Agreed Statement of Facts for me to work from. It would be helpful for that to be on my desk by one P.M. so that we can resume at two. Anything else?"

Shel said, "Not at this time," while Seagraves seemed to trust himself only to shake his head.

"golden Boy, I hope you know what the fuck you're doing here."

Shel found himself agreeing with his client's sentiment. The older attorney and Mairead O'Clare sat on mismatched chairs outside the courthouse's "lockup" on the fifteenth floor. Behind the reinforced screening over a picture window in the white cinder-block wall, Ben Friedman perched awkwardly on a fixed chrome stool. The stool yanked Shel back to the malt shop he and his—

Ben Friedman's shackles rattled like a tambourine. "Okay, Golden Boy, I know I already agreed to this, but give me again why you thought it was such a brainstorm to ditch a jury here."

Shel noticed Mairead growing more intense as well. Admit it: Even she thinks you're nuts.

"Well, Ben, I was weighing two factors. First, it might take us a full week to get an 'untainted' jury of fourteen seated in that box."

Big Ben said, "'Untainted' meaning morons who don't read the papers or even watch the news on TV."

"Pretty much. And with you sitting in jail the whole time, getting more and more frustrated even during the courtroom hours, which wouldn't have improved the impression you'd be making on the jurors who did get selected."

"Okay, okay. With you so far, but why go with just the judge, especially since he heard the first trumped-up shit against me?"

"A couple of reasons on that, too. Once we got an untainted jury impaneled, the first thing Seagraves would do is take advantage of a Motion in Limine that Judge Maynard allowed last week, that the Commonwealth could introduce evidence of the first trial involving the Vukonov boy to establish your apparent motive for killing Conchita Balaguer, a juror from that case."

"Yeah, but she voted *for* me back then, like the other jurors told your Wild Irish Rose here."

Shel could feel some steam coming off Mairead. "Yes, Ben. But the prosecution's theory of this current case is that you bribed Balaguer to support you in the first case and then killed her because she was demanding more money to keep quiet about it."

"Which I already *told* you I didn't do."

Mairead said, "But with that nearly ten-thousand-dollar deposit she made, and the looks she gave us during the trial and my finding her body, the prosecution can 'prove' you did, in the sense of offering credible evidence on that theory, even if it isn't 'true.'"

"Christ, what a fucking system for the most powerful country on the face of God's earth." Ben rubbed his own face with the palms of his hands, the chains jingling some more. "All right, so you were worried that we'd shovel sand against the tide for a week to get an 'untainted' gang of morons, then Seagraves would taint them anyway."

"Now build on it," said Shel. "There might be some jurors who'd claim to be untainted, but really wanted to avenge what they might believe was an unjust verdict from the Vukonov case."

Shel watched his friend mull that over. "What, that I'm like fucking O.J., with his wife and the waiter?"

"Or just that they believe where there's smoke there's fire, and find you guilty on general principles."

"Golden Boy, Golden Boy. You should have stayed with prizefighting. At least there we could *tell* you when the fix was in. But still, why is judge-only a *better* bet?"

"Again, several reasons. One, Maynard is familiar with

the overall facts of both incidents. Two, the Commonwealth's case against you is circumstantial, just like the hit-and-run charge. And three, I think we have pretty credible evidence ourselves that the ten thousand had nothing to do with a bribe, but rather was merely a settlement of Balaguer's potential claim against her employer for sexual harassment by one of her bosses."

"Putting a knife in the heart of Seagraves's 'motive' for me."

"Right. Plus, when no jury's present, trial judges like Agreed Statements of Facts, which should make the trial shorter and your waiting time in jail end sooner. Also, the impact of any conflict—should one of my people appear as a witness—is lessened when there are no jurors having to decide who to believe. And some questionable evidence comes in when there's no jury because judges are comfortable they can limit in their own minds a piece of evidence to just the 'proper' issues better than untrained laypeople. That should help us on some of the 'candidate painting' we need to do toward showing other believable suspects in Balaguer's killing."

Shel watched Big Ben nodding, but more emphatically than he had in the courtroom. Mairead the same, which pleased her boss even more. Then Shel got a surprise.

Big Ben turned to Mairead and said, "I want to pay you a compliment, and a little more."

"I'm sorry?" Mairead said, looking to Shel as though she was genuinely confused.

"You two are working for me, and I don't have the nice turns of phrase like Golden Boy, here, account of I went through the school of hard knocks, and he went to Harvard."

Mairead's eyes grew wide as she turned to Shel. "You went to . . . Harvard?"

"Just for law school," he replied, not wanting to step on whatever concession he sensed Big Ben was about to make.

The gangster went on. "But that don't mean I'm not grateful, Irish Rose, for what all you've done for me. I really didn't clip that little Russian kid, and you've done a helluva job coming up with the kinds of facts that might let me walk on this juror thing, too. So, I just wanted you to know, you're to me like family now, with all the bennies that carries with it. And I want to thank you for helping a dinosaur like me maybe beat a rap he don't deserve." Ben snorted a little, like a sniffle if you listened closely enough. "Okay, end of speech."

Shel Gold wondered if Mairead, even blushing as she was, realized how hard it had been for his old friend to admit that he needed, and appreciated, the professional help of a woman half his age.

sitting at the defense table in courtroom number 10—and still in something of a daze after that bizarre conference with Benjamin Friedman in the lockup—Mairead O'Clare had been pleased at least that her ankle no longer ached. But she couldn't believe Shel hadn't mentioned, in the four months they'd been working together, that he was a graduate of Harvard Law School.

I mean, every other attorney from there I've ever met manages to work it into the first couple of sentences.

Maybe, young lady, you've just never met anyone quite like Mr. Gold.

Judge Keith Maynard said, "Given the Agreed Statement of Facts, for which I thank counsel on the record, I don't see the need for either side to present an opening, but Mr. Seagraves, you may if you wish."

"No thank you, Your Honor."

"Mr. Gold?"

"Not at this time, Your Honor."

"Very well, then. The Commonwealth's first witness, please?"

"We call Detective Marjorie Tully."

Mairead turned toward the rear of the courtroom as Tully was hailed through its now open doors. Which caused the young lawyer to note that, with the exception of the Pope and the Vukonov parents, there was no one else in the gallery she recognized, because anybody who might testify had been "sequestered," now in the sense of being excluded from the courtroom.

Tully took the chair on the witness stand, and Seagraves led her through an abbreviated version of her time on Homicide. However, Mairead kept drifting back to what Friedman, again sitting next to her at the defense table, had told her: "You're to me like family now."

Probably just an expression, young lady.

Yeah, but consider the source, thought the young woman raised with no family.

Mairead snapped out of it when she heard her name being recited in open court.

Seagraves said, "...O'Clare, who, as stipulated in Agreed Statement of Facts Number Three, found Ms. Balaguer's body the night the decedent deposited nearly ten thousand dollars into her—that is, Ms. Balaguer's own—checking account."

Mairead took notes on the rest of Detective Tully's testimony, but it was pretty consistent with what anyone could have predicted: crime-scene information, the local-log telephone call made from Conchita Balaguer's house to the Law Offices of Sheldon A. Gold that evening, and Mairead's trip by cab to the house thereafter.

"Thank you, Your Honor," said Seagraves. "No further questions."

"Mr. Gold?"

Mairead watched Shel stand and move to a spot directly in front of the witness stand, not needing to drop back farther here to be sure all witnesses could be heard by even the last juror in the box.

He said, "Detective Tully, did you uncover any reason to believe that Ms. O'Clare was involved in the actual death of Ms. Balaguer?"

Mairead caught her breath: kind of a bombshell as lead-off question.

Tully leaned forward a little. "The telephone company's

local log shows only a call being made from the decedent's house to your law firm, where Ms. O'Clare works."

"I see. And when you questioned Ms. O'Clare about that call, what did she tell you?"

"Objection, Your Honor," from Seagraves. "Hearsay."

Mairead expected the judge to ask Shel to argue why it wasn't hearsay or fell into some exception to the hearsay rule, but Maynard merely said, "There's no jury here. I'll allow the question."

Mairead could feel Friedman swell a bit beside her at hearing his "Golden Boy's" prediction come true, and she correctly predicted herself that as soon as the judge was looking away from the defense table, their client would give her an elbow in the ribs to punctuate his pleasure.

Patience, young lady. As the gentleman explained, he knows he's a little . . . unpolished.

Yeah, well, he does it again, and I'll polish one of his—

Tully said, "Ms. Balaguer supposedly told Ms. O'Clare that she wanted a lawyer regarding a 'substantial' sum of money."

"Anything else?"

"That Ms. Balaguer told Ms. O'Clare that the decedent had been impressed by what she'd seen Ms. O'Clare do as an attorney during the Vukonov trial."

"Now, according to the medical examiner's report, and our Agreed Fact Number Seventeen, Ms. Balaguer's time of death has been estimated forensically to be between four P.M. and seven P.M. that night, correct?"

"Yes."

"And your investigation also established that Ms. O'Clare was either in my offices with our receptionist as witness, or in that cab, with the driver as witness, from three P.M. to seven-thirty P.M. on that day?"

"Yes."

"In other words, Ms. O'Clare's participation in Ms. Balaguer's death would be physically impossible."

"Yes," said Tully, quickly adding, "but that doesn't mean she couldn't have been connected to it."

Shel seemed to welcome the hedge. "As if that deposited cash had been part of a scheme to . . . bribe Ms. Balaguer in some way?"

Mairead noticed Seagraves hunching forward in his chair, like he wanted to object, but restraining himself.

Tully said, "Exactly."

"Tell me, Detective," Shel said, now shambling slowly across the courtroom. "Have you been able to identify the source of that money?"

Mairead tried to take notes as casually as possible, but was dying to know whether the police had—

"No."

"But," said Shel, "in your experience, most bribes are paid in cash?"

A small ticking up of Tully's mouth at the corners. "That's standard operating procedure."

"And is it also 'standard operating procedure' for such cash to then be deposited in a record-keeping bank?"

"Objection," Seagraves said, now rising. "Detective Tully has been established as an expert on homicide investigation, not bribe analysis."

The judge shook his head. "Oh, I think she just qualified herself on that ground. But, in any case, I'll take judicial notice of the unlikelihood that a person bribed in connection with a jury-tampering effort would deposit the proceeds in a formal bank account."

Mairead intuited that it was time for Shel to shut up, and, turning to the judge with a "Thank you, Your Honor," he did.

22

From his seat in the gallery, Pontifico Murizzi tried to decide whether he liked watching a judge-only trial more than a jury one.

First off, you didn't have all those annoying side-bar conferences, where the attorneys and the stenographer picked up and moved over to the side of the bench farther from the jury in order to hash out something the laypeople in the box weren't supposed to hear. The Pope felt for the jurors on those occasions: pretty fucking boring, and kind of insulting, too, when you thought about it. Like kids are old enough at eighteen to die for their country, but not to order a couple of beers at the corner tavern. The jurors' version: You can decide whether this dirtbag goes to prison, but only on the information that we insiders think you ought to have.

On the other hand, there wasn't quite the—what's the word for it? "Atmosphere," probably. That sense in a jury trial of the cross between a theater production and a one-ring circus, the air so thick with tension and anticipation that you could almost taste it on your tongue. Maybe because, without the ordinary citizens sitting in the box as "audience," you didn't have the same sense of the insiders playing "roles" for them. A jury-waived scenario, the only people in the courtroom—aside from the witness, granted—were "us," kind of the way Murizzi imagined the cast party after a play would be, the few non-insiders tolerated as "guests" but not treated like "audience" anymore.

Or maybe, more simply the way his mother would put it, The things you think when you've got nothing else to do, Pontifico.

On the whole, the Pope gave Jorie Tully a B-plus for her effort. She was a little cocky, which wouldn't have played so well to a jury, and then Shel scored some good points on the bank-deposit thing.

The assistant medical examiner, testifying now on direct by Seagraves, was the same guy from the Vukonov trial. The prosecutor did a solid step-by-step through the routine: time of death (a simple rereading of that Agreed Fact), cause of death (asphyxiation—"which would have been slow and painful, over the course of as much as five minutes, as the victim would have kicked and struggled, choking"). The ME gilded the lily with some crime-scene and autopsy photos toward establishing "extreme atrocity and cruelty," which (along with "deliberate premeditation") was a way in Massachusetts to prove murder in the first degree.

Murizzi handicapped Seagraves as hitting the atrocity side hard because the guy wasn't so sure of the premeditation evidence he had. The Pope also figured that Shel wasn't objecting because there was no jury to have its "passions unreasonably fanned by inflammatory descriptions," as Murizzi had heard a judge in one of his own cases comment in the past.

But then the Pope got a surprise: When Seagraves finished with a "Thank you. Pass the witness," it was Irish, not Shel, who stood to cross-examine.

"Now, sir," said Mairead, "could one person have managed to hang Ms. Balaguer in the manner you've described?"

"Possibly, but I'd say it was more likely two people."

"And what did your autopsy findings list Ms. Balaguer's weight to be?"

"Uh, I'm not . . . May I review my notes?"

"Certainly."

Murizzi liked that. The Agreed Statement of Facts apparently lulled the assistant ME into thinking this would be a milk run, and so he hadn't really done his homework.

"Uh, here we are. Ms. Balaguer weighed one hundred eighteen pounds."

"So, a fairly strong person, acting alone, could have committed the physical act of hanging her from that beam?"

As the ME paused, the Pope crossed his arms. Mairead couldn't see him, but he liked also how she could control what had to be pretty rough flashbacks for her to the way the vic had looked in that rec room the night Irish found her.

"Sir?"

"I'd say a *very* strong person could have, yes."

Mairead now turned her back on the witness stand. "You testified also at the trial of Benjamin Friedman for the death of Yuri Vukonov, did you not?"

"I did."

"Were there any such 'very strong persons' in the courtroom at that time?"

"Objection," from Seagraves, as even Murizzi wondered why Mairead was apparently eyeballing the poor couple who'd lost their son to that hit-and-run driver, whoever he was.

"Ground?" from the judge as Mairead turned back to the bench.

Seagraves actually pointed. "The witness is a pathologist, not a . . . personal trainer."

The Pope watched the judge turn toward Mairead now. "Counselor?"

"Your Honor, the assistant medical examiner already has offered his opinion that only a 'very strong person' could have physically hanged Ms. Balaguer from that beam. I'm simply trying to gauge what he means by his definition."

"I'll allow it," said Maynard.

"Well," from the witness, "yes, I believe there were."

"Several of the jurors?" Mairead said, now looking at the empty box.

"Perhaps."

"Such as the foreman, Ralph Bobransky, who, as Agreed Fact Number Thirty-nine provides, owns and works in a hardware store?"

Seagraves was about to rise as the ME said, "I don't recall him, specifically."

"Or Troy Gallup, who, as Agreed Fact Number Forty-two provides, is six-foot one-inch tall and very muscular?"

"Your Honor," said Seagraves wearily, "how can the witness be expected to remember one juror among four*teen* seated in just one of the many trials he has testified—"

"Counselor, *I* remember him," replied Maynard, and Murizzi could see Seagraves visibly deflate.

Now Mairead turned away from the bench again, and the Pope began to fear she was about to gild the lily herself.

"Aside from the members of the jury, were there any other people with the kind of strength you believe would be required?"

"Yes," too confidently from the ME.

"Who?" said Mairead.

Now the witness did the pointing. "The defendant, Benjamin Friedman."

Murizzi thought, Irish, you asked for that one.

However, Mairead actually grinned before saying, "Or Mr. Vadim Vukonov?"

This time, even the Pope turned right to face the couple. If looks could kill, Mairead, old Vadim there would put you lying faceup on the defense table, a rosary laced between your fingers. But why are you goading the guy?

Seagraves's voice rang loud and righteously. "Your Honor, this is an outrage! To allow—"

Maynard said, "Counselor, if you have an objection, state it."

Mairead turned back to the bench. "Your Honor, I withdraw the question, and I have no more at this time."

* * *

shel wanted to ask Mairead why she had stared at the Vukonovs during cross, when there was no jury needing cues to get her implications, and when the judge could easily have taken offense himself at her focusing on a mother and father still in mourning for their child.

But instead Shel watched Seagraves, who'd just called Ralph Bobransky to the stand. After the preliminaries of the tall, gangly man serving on the first jury were established from the Agreed Facts, the prosecutor turned toward Big Ben at Shel's left.

"Now, Mr. Bobransky, could you summarize the jury deliberations on the case of *Commonwealth versus Friedman* for the murder of Yuri Vukonov?"

"Yes." The witness tilted his head oddly, almost as if he still were blind. "Since I was the foreman, I thought it made sense to take a 'straw poll' right away, to see where we all stood."

Shel could see Keith Maynard wince. Though probably long since disabused of any real belief that jurors followed instructions, the judge still couldn't enjoy hearing exactly how they'd strayed in a case before him.

Seagraves said, "And where did the jury stand?"

"Our first-blush vote was eight for guilty, four not."

"I see. And was the decedent, Ms. Balaguer, one of those four?"

"Yes. The others were Troy Gallup, Phil Quinn, and Lorraine Fanton."

"Can you describe what happened during the deliberations thereafter?"

"Well, like I said before, eight of us were for guilty to start with, but then Troy and Chita began to—"

"Ms. Balaguer?"

"Sorry?" from Bobransky, a different tilt to his head.

"When you say 'Chita,' you mean—"

"Oh, sorry. Ms. Balaguer, yes. Troy Gallup and *Con-*

chita Balaguer started to argue vehemently that a man like Benjamin Friedman wouldn't have killed the little boy. Or had him killed."

Shel heard crying again from the gallery—Mrs. Vukonova, from the direction of it—and Mairead turned to look, with a funny expression on her face. Shel was about to tell her to stop doing that, but fortunately didn't have to, as Judge Maynard, after glancing briefly toward the sound of the crying himself, had returned to the witness.

"So," said Seagraves, "Ms. Balaguer was one of the defendant's principal advocates?"

"Yes. She was zealous on it, that Mr. Friedman just *had* to be innocent."

"And what did you think, Mr. Bobransky?"

"I thought she was laying it on rather thick. I mean, after all, I later read in the newspapers—once we got unsequestered—that he was a . . . gangster."

Shel sensed his friend bristling at that one, but couldn't see a good reason to object when Judge Maynard—who certainly knew of Ben's "activities"—would have long ago come to his own conclusion on the issue.

"Thank you," said Seagraves. "No further questions."

Shel stood now. "Mr. Bobransky, you said that three jurors *other* than Ms. Balaguer also voted not guilty in the straw poll, correct?"

"Correct."

"And therefore they did so before Mr. Gallup and Ms. Balaguer began advocating for Mr. Friedman's innocence?"

The head tilted again. "Well, yes. Of course."

"And by the end of your deliberations, the entire jury in that earlier case voted not guilty, correct?"

"Unanimously," some fidgeting in the chair. "I was foreman, so it was my responsibility to make sure of that count."

"So, Mr. Gallup and Ms. Balaguer persuaded you as well?"

"That's how I voted. Finally."

Delivered with a frown, which suited Shel just fine. "Now, you've testified that those two jurors were a team in arguing for Ben Friedman."

"Like we've just been talking about."

"Were they a 'team' in any other way?"

"Objection," from Seagraves. "Relevance?"

"Mr. Gold?" said Maynard.

Shel moved a step toward the bench. "Your Honor, obviously someone murdered Ms. Balaguer. I'm merely establishing the possible motive of an alternative suspect."

Maynard pursed his lips, and for a moment Shel was afraid that—

"I'll allow the question. The witness may answer."

"Well, yes. It was obvious."

"What was obvious, Mr. Bobransky?"

"That Troy and Chita—Ms. Balaguer—were, ah, having a romance."

"They were sleeping together?"

"Objection, Your Honor. How can the witness possibly know such a thing?"

Shel thought Seagraves was being kind of shortsighted, as Gallup himself would have to admit to it, but said, "Withdraw the question. Mr. Bobransky, did Ms. Balaguer and Mr. Gallup have adjoining rooms?"

A new angle to the head. "After the first night, yes. Of the trial, I mean. They switched around so they could have a door opening between them."

Shel found himself in the unusual position of sensing someone besides himself cringing, in this case the judge. "Now, Mr. Bobransky, was theirs the only 'romantic relationship' that occurred during the trial?"

Shel heard Maynard clear his throat, but if it was a cue, Seagraves didn't act on it.

"As far as I know, yes."

"Did you ever harbor any desire for Ms. Balaguer yourself?"

"Your Honor," said the rising prosecutor.

The judge looked down. "Mr. Gold, even without a jury present, is this really necessary?"

"I'm afraid it is, Your Honor. And I have a sound basis for asking the question."

"Very well. Witness to answer."

Bobransky looked up to the bench. "You want me to say exactly what?"

Maynard fixed him with what Shel would have called baleful eyes. "Exactly the truth, sir."

The witness turned back to Shel. "Yes, certainly I thought she was attractive."

"And you approached her?"

"I chatted her up." Head tilt. "You would have, too."

Shel bore in. "And what was her reaction to your approach?"

"Chita was hot for Troy, as anybody could see, so I accepted it."

"But despite Ms. Balaguer seeming to favor Mr. Gallup, you still approached her anyway?"

Bobransky flared. "Why not? I was blind for twenty years, mister, and I figured, maybe she's giving it away, what's to lose?"

There was a moment of pure silence in the courtroom. Shel used it to move toward the clerk. "Your Honor, may I show the witness Commonwealth Number One, in evidence?"

"You may."

The clerk gave Shel the section of rope, half an inch in diameter, which he carried over to the stand. "Mr. Bobransky, we've stipulated that this is a piece of the rope used to kill Ms. Balaguer. May I hand it to you?"

"All right."

Shel transferred the two-foot section as though it were a sleeping snake. "Can you identify this?"

Shel heard a rustling behind him. From the direction and distance, Seagraves, trying to decide whether or not to stand again.

Bobransky handled the rope deftly, running a thumb over some of the fibers at one cut end. "Sure, I can identify it."

Another moment of dead silence. "Please do so, sir."

"It's braided, nylon-core, sash cord. Pretty standard stock."

"You sell it in your hardware store, then?"

"Of course I—hey, what are you saying?"

"Thank you, Mr. Bobransky. No further—"

"You goddamned shyster, what are—"

Maynard's voice was like a peal of thunder. "Mr. Bobransky, that's enough! Anything more, and I'll hold you in contempt of this court."

Shel turned from Ralph Bobransky, but now, like Mairead earlier, he found it hard not to notice Tanya Vukonova, crying softly and apparently sincerely into her handkerchief.

mairead sat watching Shel watching her in an empty courtroom down the hall from Judge Maynard's session. They'd just returned from seeing Ben Friedman in the lockup on floor fifteen, the gangster's main theme having been, "Golden Boy, you and your Wild Irish Rose here reamed that fucker Seagraves a new asshole, *big* time."

Still shaking off that memory, Mairead said, "What?"

Shel replied, "You went a little too far with the medical examiner."

A sting, and Mairead fought not to overreact. "How so?"

"You could have gotten him to admit to 'very strong persons' without including Ben."

"Maybe, but there was 'no jury present,'" intentionally mimicking Judge Keith Maynard's cadence.

"Two thoughts on that," and her boss came forward in his chair. "First, you don't want to get sloppy in a jury-waived trial, only to carry over bad habits to one where jurors are evaluating you. And, through you, your client."

Concede, young lady. "Sorry."

"Second point: There *is* a jury in that courtroom,

Mairead. It just happens to be made up of only one person in a black robe, but as a result, we can't risk offending him."

Now Mairead couldn't hide her reaction, especially since she felt an implication of somehow displaying racism. "How did I offend him?"

"I said '*risk* offending him,' like when you stared at the Vukonovs during your examination on the 'very strong person' string, and turned and stared again at them when the mother began crying. Nobody likes a bully, or someone who seems to trade on the misfortunes of others, including hurting those others for no justifiable reason."

Mairead knew the man across the table from her had lost his own son, so she tried to make allowances for what might be a blind spot for him. "Shel, that's not what I was doing."

"Doesn't matter, if that's the way it could have appeared to the one 'juror' that really counts."

You'd lost this argument before it even began, young lady. "Okay, you're right," said Mairead, deciding as a result to keep a nagging suspicion to herself.

23

Shel scratched Moshe behind the ear over his good eye. The cat, curled on Shel's lap in the La-Z-Boy, often awakened his owner, still reclined at three or four in the morning, by some subtle licking. The cat's sandpaper tongue against his hand would rouse him gently.

Like the kiss of a loved one.

Shel felt a shiver, Moshe stirring just a little under the book that rested on the cat's shoulders, the creature never seeming to mind this imposition. That's what Shel did on a trial night when there was nothing pressing toward the next day. Read.

There was a time when he'd listen to music—instrumental only, not voices like he'd have to face the next morning. But after Richie . . . after Richie, symphonic music seemed the only thing that would calm Natalie, at least a bit, and as a result listening to it himself and alone was like tearing his heart out all over again. So he turned to books, generally ones on history, including biographies.

He knew that Billie Sunday tried to spend the time with her kids, kind of refresh herself for carrying the weight of the office stuff the next day when Shel and Mairead would be on trial till late afternoon. He didn't know what his new associate did, and, truth be told, he often didn't want to think about what the Pope might be doing to while away the hours.

Sometimes, when Shel was disappointed in a book, he

would watch cable TV, the Discovery Channel, or the History one. He tended to stay away from *Law & Order* on A&E, though: The prosecution won too many of its cases to be inspirational for him.

Shel returned to the book he'd begun several nights before. It dealt with the so-called "Cathar heresy" in France during the thirteenth century. The official church of Rome, through a nobleman named Simon de Montfort, slaughtered entire villages of the formerly faithful whose only sins, as far as Shel could tell, were recognizing the inherent equality of women and renouncing material wealth for interfering with the spirituality of religion. Nevertheless, the book credited de Montfort with developing many methods of torture—from burning at the stake to blinding and mutilating a hundred men save one, who was left with a single eye to lead a macabre conga line of heretics through the villages as an object lesson to the rest. Those practices were refined during the later Spanish Inquisition, and some were still used even by the Nazis, including the requirement that Jews wear a yellow emblem stitched to their coats, so as to identify them publicly.

Shel closed the book, causing Moshe to stir a little more, and then reached for the TV remote.

There have to be happier things to be reminded of.

schlumped into her one big easy chair in the studio apartment on Beacon Hill, Mairead channel-surfed, wondering what Shel did on trial nights.

She remembered from their first case together what he believed in doing while awaiting a verdict, at least when a high-roller client like Big Ben Friedman wasn't taking the team out to an expensive lunch. Shel would randomly read legal volumes, looking for bits of information when he knew he couldn't work conscientiously on another real case. Personally, that made little sense to Mairead.

As if this channel-skimming is vastly different, young lady.

Mairead smiled outwardly to hear inwardly Sister Bernadette's voice use the "Valley Girl" prefix "as if," even though in context it wasn't, really. But after a long day of trial, and what promised to be a longer one the next, all Mairead wanted to do was *not* concentrate the way she'd have to while onstage before that "single juror." And channel-surfing the cable offerings filled a "short attention span" interlude just right.

At least until Mairead O'Clare found the third period of a tied game in hockey's Stanley Cup play-offs.

Setting down the remote, she settled deeper into the armchair.

sitting on the fantail of his houseboat, Pontifico Murizzi used one of those "waitron" professional corkscrews to lever open a nice bottle of Montepulciano d'Abruzzo. The evening breeze coming onshore at the marina was cool enough to rule out a white, and besides, the Pope always searched for reasons to drink red, which he thought of as "real" wine, much the way his father used to pronounce it so at the beginning of any family gathering, regardless of the food served.

And then Jocko had favored reds, too.

Okay, how long you gonna beat yourself up over something you couldn't control and can't reverse?

Making the best of a sad, if not exactly bad, situation, Murizzi rationed an ounce or so of the wine into his glass, swirled it vigorously, then heaved the contents overboard. After which he poured another four ounces toward actual drinking.

Just like Jocko had shown him.

The Pope glanced at the next slip, still empty. But not for long, what with Memorial Day coming up in a matter of weeks. And then the "real" summer, as far as boaters were concerned, beginning after that. Pretty soon the harbor would be full of weekend warriors, the year-rounders hunkering down on their boats like Murizzi's uncle Piero, staying shuttered inside his retirement cottage on Cape Cod, air-conditioning and boob tube going full blast, preferring to leave the beaches—and even more, the roads—to the infestation of tourists that swarmed over the peninsula like locusts with SUVs. The Pope knew Piero wasn't even particularly pleased with his nephew owning an Explorer, kind of like embracing the enemy, you know?

Murizzi stole another glance at the empty slip, then took a sip of wine, letting the tannin and alcohol burn down his throat, taking the chill off the night air. He figured to allow himself two glasses, no more.

Just in case you have to be "on deck" in a different sense for Shel and Mairead in the morning.

24

As ADA James Seagraves called Troy Gallup to the stand on Tuesday morning, Shel Gold wondered why.

Both prosecution and defense had listed "lover boy," and a number of the other jurors, as potential witnesses in the pretrial documents exchanged with each other. However, Gallup didn't seem a source that could much help the Commonwealth's version of what supposedly happened.

"Now, sir," said Seagraves, "it has come out in previous testimony that the decedent, Ms. Conchita Balaguer, and you had a relationship during Mr. Friedman's first trial."

"Kind of."

Seagraves seemed to tighten his tone. "You and she slept together, did you not?"

"Yeah, only Chita didn't get a whole lot of sleep, if you know what I mean."

Shel was relieved that Gallup was the only one in the courtroom who laughed out loud, though he felt Big Ben swallow one.

Seagraves bore in. "You and she were intimate?"

Gallup now seemed confused, and Shel began to appreciate why Mairead thought him a total jerk. However, the older attorney couldn't see any reason to object to the leading nature of Seagraves's questions, as Gallup wasn't doing any damage yet.

"You mean," said the witness, "did we do the dirty deed? I thought I already—"

"Mr. Gallup, you and Ms. Balaguer made love to each other, correct?"

"Of course we did. She was sizing me up from the first time she laid . . . eyes on me."

This time only a leer from Gallup, directed toward Mairead, but when Shel looked up at Keith Maynard, the judge's eyes were squinched shut.

"During deliberations," said Seagraves, "Ms. Balaguer was an advocate for Mr. Friedman, correct?"

"She jumped on my bandwagon, yeah."

Seagraves paused, and Shel could sense his dilemma: Do I ask a "why-type" question of this macho schmuck?

The prosecutor said, "And what was your view of her reason?"

"Simple. She wanted to back me up against the eight other jurors who voted guilty in Ralph Bobransky's straw poll. As a way to keep me . . . 'intimate.'"

Shel snuck another peek at Maynard. This time the judge seemed very relieved that the defense had decided to go jury-waived so a new batch of ordinary citizens wouldn't be debased by what members of a prior jury might have done.

"So, you didn't think Ms. Balaguer *genuinely* believed in the innocence of Mr. Friedman?"

Shel rose, speaking almost apologetically. "Your Honor, I've forborne objecting so far, but—"

"Yes, Mr. Seagraves," from the bench. "I think you've led your own witness quite far enough down whatever path you're pursuing."

"Sorry, Your Honor," said the prosecutor, to Shel more as a way of blowing off exasperation than really apologizing. "Mr. Gallup, what, if anything, was the reaction of the other jurors to your and Ms. Balaguer's arguments?"

"They bought them. In the end, nobody could really see why this rich guy—even if he was a gangster—would risk killing a kid when a simple bat to the kneecap of his father should have done the trick."

Shel heard crying from the Vukonovs' area of the gallery, but softly again, not like the theatrical effort at the first trial.

Even Seagraves seemed appalled by Gallup's callous attitude. "Sir, it has been established that Ms. Balaguer deposited nearly ten thousand dollars in cash into her bank account within hours of being discharged from jury duty on the day of her death."

"Yeah, so I've been told."

"By whom?"

"Mairead there," accompanied by another leer.

"Your Honor, may the record indicate the witness is referring to Ms. O'Clare, cocounsel for the defendant?"

"So noted," said Maynard.

Seagraves moved closer to the stand. "Prior to Ms. O'-Clare's speaking with you, did Ms. Balaguer ever mention such money?"

"Kind of. Chita said she was going to get a chunk of it once our trial was over."

Seagraves looked meaningfully toward the defense table, then said in a very even voice, "Pass the witness."

As Mairead stood to inquire, Shel noticed Gallup's eyes stray to her legs and stay there.

She said, "You mentioned 'a chunk of' money, but never specified the amount."

"Right. Chita never told me. I didn't know until—"

"Mr. Gallup, did Ms. Balaguer ever tell you anything about the source of this windfall?"

"No."

"Did you form an opinion about this money nevertheless?"

"Sure."

"And what was that opinion?"

"Objection, Your Honor," Seagraves said, rising. "Without information, even a lay opinion is without basis."

Maynard nodded, but said, "No, I'll allow the witness's impression to come in. You may answer the question."

"My impression?" A shrug. "I thought Chita was dangling this 'chunk' of money as bait, try to keep me interested in her after we weren't sequestered anymore."

"Did Ms. Balaguer ever tell you anything else about her life?"

"Objection, Your Honor," Seagraves said, rising again. "Clearly hearsay."

Shel watched the judge look to Mairead. "Ms. O'Clare?"

"Your Honor, the prosecution established that Mr. Gallup and the decedent were 'intimate,' and then opened the door to topics discussed during their . . . pillow talk. For the sake of completeness, the defense would like to know what else they might have discussed that's material to this case."

Seagraves jumped in. "The completeness doctrine is just an issue of timing, Your Honor, not a separate hearsay exception. Ms. O'Clare still must identify some independent reason why any further discussions would be admissible under the Commonwealth's rules of evidence."

Maynard considered that for a moment, then said, "No, Counselor. I'll allow it. If parts of their intimate exchanges were material, perhaps others are as well, and there's no jury here to be misled by them if they are not."

Shel began to think he should go "judge-only" more often.

Mairead turned back to the witness stand. "Mr. Gallup, any other discussions between you and Ms. Balaguer?"

"Sure," a leering smile now. "You want a play-by-play, or—"

Judge Maynard spoke frostily. "Begin with an enumeration of the topics discussed, please."

Gallup looked up at the bench. "Topics? Okay, Chita and I talked about how being sequestered really sucks unless you've got a little something on the side, like we did. And she went on and on about her ex-husband."

"And what did Ms. Balaguer say, specifically?"

"That the guy was . . ." This time, the witness just glanced up at the judge, who was writing something down, "... a real asshole," Gallup said, leering at Mairead even more.

Ordinarily, Shel might have been glad that *some*body in the courtroom was enjoying himself, but lover boy seemed to be an exception to most rules, hearsay and otherwise.

"Again," said Mairead. "Specific examples?"

"Oh, he beat on her while they were married, she got a restraining order against him, he kept hounding or stalking her, like, with phone calls, threats. The whole spectrum of assholedom."

"Mr. Gallup, did any other juror appear interested in Ms. Balaguer romantically?"

"Well, I don't think he was planning a wedding, but yeah. Ralph Bobransky had the hots for her, too. You know, 'eyeing little girls with bad intent'?"

Shel Gold vaguely remembered that line from a rock song more of his generation than Troy Gallup's, but for once in his life he was grateful that titles and artists never stuck with him.

the Pope sat in his favorite spot in the gallery, where you could see all the players without the attorneys at the two tables inside the bar enclosure blocking anybody out.

Had to hand it to Mairead. Shel you expect to be pretty smooth in the courtroom, all the years he's had and smart to boot. But this Irish seems to have found her place in the world, and woe be unto the sonuvabitch who tries to take her on when she's ready.

The Pope was also liking this jury-waived format better every hour. The judge ran the case less like a lawyer and more like a lieutenant. A kind of "let's get all the facts, maybe even stumble over the truth somewhere along the line." A helluva lot better than the usual game of patty-cake to see which side had invested in the better thespian, played out in front of twelve or so ignoramuses who probably cared more about Red Sox tickets or a home-cooked meal—or getting "a little something on the side," like that shitbird Gallup.

Aside from the usual pensioners and oddball court fanatics hanging around any juicy murder trial, the Pope was a little surprised at the lack of media. Granted a lot of what would be heard might be a rehash of what went on during the first trial, he always thought television especially thrived on that sense of "we already know what's going to happen, so we can package it for max sensationalism in advance." Shit, you'd think even just the sleazy bedtime stories between Balaguer and Gallup would have justified a camera at least, if no on-air studs.

Then again, he was kind of glad for the poor immigrants on the other side of the aisle. Fucking mother looked like she was gonna have a nervous breakdown, even worse than in the first trial, tell the truth, because now she was more—what, sincere? Whereas last time out, she was kind of theatrical about it, the high-school actress doing a bad death scene.

The Pope also noticed that while the father was always with her in the courtroom, the albino security guy from around the butcher shop never showed. Which was probably a smart play on their part: If they thought Friedman was gonna retaliate at this stage, probably be more likely against the shop and not the wife or husband running it.

Which made Pontificio Murizzi think about Balaguer's ex, the snitch Rigoberto, and Berto's fat spymaster, Hildy Crowell.

"they haven't laid a glove on us, have they, Golden Boy?"

From their side of the lockup screen, Mairead watched her boss shrug modestly. "No knockdowns, I'd say, but Seagraves has scored some points."

Ben Friedman waved that off with both hands. Necessarily, since they were manacled together again. "And I have to repeat myself with you, Irish Rose."

She said, "Mairead would be fine," admitting to herself that the gangster's nickname for her rankled while the Pope's simple "Irish" did not.

Friedman continued. "Thanks to my lifelong friend here, I haven't had to be in many courtrooms. But you're holding your own and then some, even with being so young and those funny-looking hands."

If I bite my tongue any harder, I'll squirt blood at this—

"And I meant what I said that other time in here, too. You're a member of the family now, so if you ever need any kind of favor, or even if you don't think you do but I see something, you're—"

"Ben," said Shel quickly, "not to interrupt, but we have only a few more minutes before court will resume, and looking over the Commonwealth's witness list, I don't think they'll be very much longer, so we need to be ready with our witnesses."

Friedman seemed shocked. "You think we'll need them at all? Isn't there some kind of motion where you knock that sanctimonious fucker Seagraves out of the box without having to put on any show yourself?"

"Yes. But given the 'ultra-speedy' trial we requested, and the fact that no jurors are being inconvenienced by sitting in the courtroom for more days of trial, I think the judge may let the Commonwealth survive any motion I might make on the prosecution's evidence."

"So, this is where the no-jury thing comes back to bite us?"

"In a sense. And Judge Maynard probably will also let Seagraves call some supplemental witnesses if the prosecution gets surprised by anything we've done."

Mairead watched their client smile and thought of those bad *Jaws* sequels, when they focused so much on the shark that all you saw was teeth without soul.

He said, "Like you're gonna surprise them with that girl from the insurance agency on my 'bribe,' right?"

"That's what we're hoping."

Now Mairead saw the smile freeze on Big Ben Friedman's face. "You better do more than fucking 'hope,' Golden Boy. You better land a genuine haymaker somewhere along this fucking line to nowhere."

25

Seagraves rose from his chair. "Your Honor, the Commonwealth would like to call a witness not on the list previously provided to the defense."

Shel thought, Well, you saw this coming.

As he stood himself, Shel was aware of Mairead looking up at him with something approaching awe, Big Ben's face a little less complimentary.

"Your Honor," said Shel, "the name of this witness?"

Seagraves said, "Edsel Crow."

Shel was surprised by the choice, but didn't see how it affected his argument. "Your Honor, surely the prosecutor could have anticipated Mr. Crow's necessity last week, before—"

Shel cut off abruptly, because he saw Maynard's right hand go up in a "stop" sign.

"Counselor," began the judge, "I'm sure a lot of things could have been 'anticipated,' but we've all been burdened by a *very* speedy trial here, so in my discretion I will allow Mr. Seagraves leeway."

"Yes, Your Honor," said Shel, figuring from Maynard's tone that the ADA could probably pull at least another, and maybe a third, such move and still get away with it.

There was a different atmosphere as soon as the rear door of the courtroom opened and Edsel Crow began to walk down the aisle. A chilling, Shel would have called it. As though a predator had just entered the sheep pen.

After Crow was sworn and took the stand, Seagraves said, "You are employed by the defendant, Benjamin Friedman?"

"Yes."

"And you were subpoenaed by the Commonwealth to appear at trial here today?"

"Yes."

"And would you have attended if you had *not* been summoned?"

"Maybe, maybe not."

Shel found his hand trembling a little, the way it had when he'd stood outside Ben's door after getting past the no-necks at the gate. This man can scare you even without a gun in his hand, and even in an environment where he doesn't have the strategic edge.

Seagraves turned to the bench. "Your Honor, given Mr. Crow's responses, request permission to treat him as a hostile witness?"

"Granted," said Maynard, the only one other than Crow with the hint of a smile on his lips.

"Now, sir," Seagraves said, turning back to the stand, "Ms. Conchita Balaguer, a juror in your employer's first trial, was killed two weeks ago, just hours after the verdict in that case."

"So I heard."

"Who was in the Friedman house that afternoon into evening?"

Shel waited while Crow reeled off Tiffany Bomberg leaving for Florida and Dario Calcagni just . . . leaving.

"And what was Mr. Calcagni's destination?"

"He said he was going up to see his mother in Maine."

"Your Honor, Agreed Statement Number Sixty-one specifies that, in fact, Mr. Calcagni went to Florida instead."

"So noted, Counselor."

"Now, Mr. Crow—"

"Do you always kick things off by saying 'now' before a question?"

As Crow's words died in the courtroom, a little part of Seagraves's reasoning began to seep into Shel's awareness.

"I beg your pardon?" from the prosecutor.

Shel thought about that response, too. Not "I ask the questions here." Seagraves wants Crow to come out of his shell in a way the man didn't in the earlier trial.

The sniper said, "I mean, it's a waste of everybody's time, you say the word 'now' when of course it's 'now,' it can't *be* any other time than 'now.'"

Maynard stepped in. "Sir, you will confine yourself to the questions put to you."

Crow looked up, the judge not smiling anymore. "Your party."

Seagraves seemed to swell with confidence. "With both Ms. Bomberg and Mr. Calcagni gone from the house on that Monday afternoon, where were you?"

"Out back of it."

"Doing what?"

"Sitting on station."

"On station?"

"In the treehouse, with my Barrett."

"Your . . . ?"

"Rifle. A Barrett Eighty-two Ay-One, fifty-caliber, laser-scoped. With a Browning machine-gun round, the muzzle velocity's three thousand feet per second, and the effective range is seventy-five hundred yards."

"A 'sniper' rifle, then?"

"That's my job, just like in Desert Storm."

"The Persian Gulf War?"

"Yeah," said Crow. "That one."

"And what were your more current duties toward Mr. Friedman?"

"Protect him. And his."

"His family?"

"And friends."

"But—Your Honor, Agreed Statement Number Fifty-six—I thought there were two guards at the gate to Mr. Friedman's home?"

"They can't stop everything."

"But you can."

"So far."

"Mr. Crow, how many people have you killed?"

Shel expected the "twenty confirmed kills" testimony from the first trial. Instead, Crow said, "Even God's lost count."

Great, thought the lawyer. Terrific. The guy thinks he's Jack Nicholson in *A Few Good Men.*

"And you're an expert, I take it, at surveillance of targets?"

"Identification of targets, acquisition of targets..."

"When the police began surveilling Mr. Friedman's house, you were aware of that, weren't you?"

Shel felt a nudge at his shoulder, Mairead passing a note along the table to him. From the handwriting, Ben's. It read, *My Injun's doing a great job, but what's Seagraves driving at?*

Shel ignored the note.

Finally, Crow took a moment to answer. "I spotted the stakeout, yes."

"And when was this?"

"Tuesday, the morning after your juror was killed. It wasn't hard, two plainclothes guys sitting in a brown sedan on the street, when the neighborhood has driveways three cars wide."

"And what did you do about it?"

"Told Mr. Friedman."

"That his house was being watched."

"Yes."

"And then, shortly before the authorities appeared to serve the search warrant, you helped Mr. Friedman be smuggled *past* that surveillance in the back of a...pool van."

"Yes."

"Did you tell your guards at the driveway gate about that?"

"No, they didn't know."

"I see," from Seagraves. "Tell me, Mr. Crow, did you spot any surveillance of Mr. Friedman's house that Monday afternoon or evening?"

"You mean the night before, when your juror got hanged?"

"That's what I mean."

"No, I didn't."

"But if there were any, as an expert on surveillance spotting, you would have, correct?"

"If they were there, yes, I would have made them."

"So, it's possible, isn't it, that you and Mr. Friedman could have left the house sometime after, say, four P.M. on that Monday evening, perhaps both of you smuggled out by a vehicle not noticed by the nonexistent surveillance, and under the *un*informed noses of your own security guards?"

Shel could see Crow's eyes turn not so much color as texture, a metallic glaze coming over them as the man realized the trap Seagraves had set for him.

Edsel Crow said, "It's possible, but nothing like that happened anytime that night."

"Thank you, sir," Seagraves said, making his way back to the prosecution table. "Pass the witness, Your Honor."

from his perch in the gallery, Pontifico Murizzi watched Shel Gold rise to cross-examine Edsel Crow. The Pope thought, You lie down with dogs, Shel...

"Mr. Crow, during Desert Storm, could you describe your actual duties?"

"Like I said before, I was a sniper."

"You shot enemy soldiers at some distance."

"Mostly."

Murizzi saw the expression on Shel's face and thought, Don't ask this whack-job another question, not one.

But Shel, after a moment, said, "Meaning, some of them were more... close-up?"

"Right."

"Enemy soldiers who threatened our troops?"

"Mostly."

Shel, Shel. What did I fucking tell you?

"And all of these kills were with firearms."

Crow stopped. It felt to the Pope like he was back with his buddy Tony at that state agency computer, waiting for some kind of electronic information to get pulled up from a data bank.

Then the witness said, "All but two were by rifle."

Shel, you're past the point of no return here.

"And, Mr. Crow, what weapon did you use on those two individuals?"

"Knife. Couple of sand nig—"

Oh, nice touch, thought Murizzi. "Sand niggers." Just the expression to win over our judge.

Crow coughed. "A couple of Iraqi militia sat down near me, and I didn't want to wreck my chances of taking out some of their brass that I'd zeroed a minute or two before."

"So," said Shel, "you used a knife for the sake of silence."

"That, and to catch the expression on their faces, the look in the eyes when they knew I was the last thing they'd ever see. You don't get much chance for that, being a sniper, because while you can watch their faces explode, they don't show that last, slow blink."

The Pope had been with a lot of crazy fucking people in a lot closer quarters than the airy courtroom, but all of a sudden he felt about as fucking cold as he could remember since being a kid in a snowstorm.

"No further questions," said Shel, looking a little queasy to Murizzi's eye.

"Your Honor, a few questions on redirect?" said Seagraves.

"Certainly," said Judge Maynard, sounding shaken, too. "But after this witness, I think we'll take our lunch break."

Seagraves went straight to the stand. "Mr. Crow, were you trained to kill with any other weapons?"

"Sure. Pistols, crossbows, even garrotes."

"Explain that last, please?"

"You come up behind somebody—a guard, maybe just a sentry walking the perimeter—and you flip a cord or wire around his neck, then turn and pull him up on your shoulder, choke him out."

"Like hanging someone by rope."

"Not exactly. You wouldn't be able to see the guy's face, his eyes—like I said before—if you garroted him."

"But you would be able to see that light of life flickering out if you hanged the person, perhaps from an overhead beam, and then stood by to . . . watch?"

Edsel Crow, maybe finally appreciating how much damage he was doing to his boss by strutting his Rambo shit, just said, almost solemnly, "Yes."

well, *young lady, this certainly isn't Locke-Ober's.*

Mairead couldn't have agreed more. The three of them—Shel having asked the Pope to come, too—were crammed in the rearmost booth in a small sandwich shop off Congress Street, a few blocks from the courthouse. Shel sat on one bench, while Mairead shared the other with Murizzi.

The Pope said to Shel, "Crow nearly sank you there."

Mairead watched her boss give his full-body shrug. "Could have been worse."

"Yeah." Murizzi shifted his butt, Mairead feeling the tingle in her thigh. "He could have taken out a piece and shot a couple people from the witness stand."

Shel squeezed his eyes shut.

Mairead asked the question she'd held back till then. "How could Crow *do* that to his own boss?"

Shel waited until the waitress came over, took their orders, and began yelling them at the guy wearing a hair net behind the counter. "I'm sure he thought he was helping Ben."

"Okay," said Mairead, "that you're going to have to explain to me, Shel."

A nod. "Seagraves was clever. He left Crow off his witness list, probably because what Crow could testify to really went more to pretrial issues like bail, or at most Ben's 'fleeing the jurisdiction' on the issue of consciousness of guilt."

"With you so far."

"But then, betting—and rightly—on Judge Maynard's willingness to allow someone *not* on the list to testify, Seagraves calls Crow, somebody who's used to having an enemy in a position where he can kind of 'spar' with the opponent."

Mairead said, "I still don't get it."

The Pope nudged elbows with her. "Like Crow was playing a mind game with somebody he was going to shoot."

The way you might try to psyche out another hockey player, shift after shift, toward gaining an advantage.

"Now I get it."

Shel smiled sadly. "Only in the courtroom, Crow is a flyweight to the prosecutor as heavyweight."

"But wouldn't Crow realize he was actually *hurting* Friedman by all that posturing?"

Murizzi said, "The guy probably thought just the opposite. Crow's job is to defend his boss against people who are after the man. So, by flexing his muscles—his credentials as a killer—on the stand, to him it'd be like he was warning Seagraves off Friedman."

Mairead shook her head. "Some 'credentials.' Now what?"

Shel sighed. "The Commonwealth will probably rest, unless Seagraves has another rabbit in his hat. And I think Maynard will deny my motion for a required finding of not guilty."

"Which means we start our case?"

Shel smiled again, but not sadly. "I think it'd be a good idea."

"With one of the jurors?"

"No. Maybe you can convince me otherwise, but after

Mr. Crow's . . . performance, I think we should lead with our best counterpunch."

Mairead almost said "Being?" before she noticed the Pope smiling, too.

Murizzi looked at her boss. "She'll be there, if I have to carry her across the threshold."

As the waitress brought their meals, Mairead O'Clare said, "Lurlene Inch."

26

billie Sunday stopped eating the salad she'd picked up for lunch and set the remainder beside her typewriter on the reception desk.

You're enjoying the greens, but best to finish them later.

At which point, Billie realized that the simple meal was the first one she'd really been able to swallow for a while without a knot in her stomach over something. But now Matthew had split with Rondell, and Robert Junior was looking into colleges and tutoring up with some of his classmates for the PSAT. William, of course, was still a worrier, but that was the boy's nature, and not much could be done about that. Except to love him for who and what he was.

Something Billie couldn't say for the stack of hen-scratched sheets from a legal pad that Shel and Mairead had left for her to churn out on the old Selectric III.

"Well," said Billie Sunday, out loud but to nobody except herself, "it's only paperwork, and that can't kill you."

"mr. Gold," said Judge Keith Maynard, "I'm going to deny your motion."

Shel's prediction during lunch on the required finding of not guilty had come true.

Maynard adjusted his glasses. "Does the defense plan to call any witnesses?"

"Yes, Your Honor. Ms. Lurlene Inch, please?"

Shel heard a couple of quiet giggles from the gallery regulars over the name of the receptionist at Stover-Trent.

After Inch took the stand and set down her handbag, Shel drew out enough background on the insurance agency and her connection with it to be able to ask, "Did Conchita Balaguer ever speak with you about her former husband?"

"Yessir, she surely did."

"And what did she tell you?"

"Objection," said Seagraves. "Hearsay."

"Mr. Gold?"

"Your Honor, as provided in Agreed Fact Number Fourteen and the accompanying attachment, Ms. Balaguer had sought and received a restraining order against her former husband, Rigoberto. I'm now offering Ms. Balaguer's out-of-court statements not to prove their truth, but just to show they were made in order to reflect her state of mind concerning her former husband."

"Mr. Seagraves?"

"Just because the fact is 'agreed' doesn't make it admissible, Your Honor. In addition, the decedent's statements would have to be *believed* to show her state of mind, and her state of mind regarding her former husband is not a material issue in the case against Mr. Friedman for murdering Ms. Balaguer himself."

Maynard paused a moment, then said, "Sustained."

Sublimate it: He's ruled for you on most everything else.

"Ms. Inch," Shel said, now shifting to a different spot in front of the witness stand, "did Ms. Balaguer receive telephone calls at work?"

"Yessir. One of Chita's—I'm sorry." Inch looked up at the judge. "Your Honor, am I supposed to call her by 'Ms. Balaguer,' too?"

"That's not necessary," said Maynard, smiling benevolently.

"Thank you. That'll make things a lot easier for me. I'm kind of nervous." After a little laugh that even Shel would have called "engaging," she came back to him. "Chita's job was to take calls I'd refer to her from our *in*sureds about claims they might have?"

Shel felt as though Inch had asked *him* a question. "How about personal calls?"

"Well, we're not supposed to do any personal business on company time, but, yessir, Chita would get that kind of call now and then, like all of us."

"And did any of these calls seem to upset her?"

"Yessir, they surely did. Brought her to tears, even?"

"And do you know who these calls were from?"

"Objection," said Seagraves again. "The only way the witness could possibly know that would be from a hearsay statement by the decedent."

"But that's just not so," blurted Inch, who then said, "Excuse me, Your Honor."

Shel waited a moment, ostensibly to allow Judge Maynard to speak but also sensing something from the woman he couldn't quite put a finger—

"That's all right, Ms. Inch," from the bench. "Please, tell us what you were going to say."

"Just that I got so I could recognize his voice?"

"Whose voice?" asked Shel.

"Rigoberto's," Inch carefully enunciating each syllable of that name, as though she really, *really* wanted to get everything just right. And then it hit Shel.

She's setting you up. Inch is playing the perfect witness for the judge to set you up.

And admit it: You can't think why.

Needing her testimony, Shel nevertheless plunged ahead. "Ms. Balaguer's former husband?"

"Right. He'd call all the time, sometimes three, four times a day?"

"Your Honor," said Seagraves in a weary voice.

"No," replied Maynard. "I'll allow it."

Shel thought, He's not even bothering to say, "There's no jury here" anymore.

"Ms. Inch," Shel said, now feeling as though he were treading on eggshells, but more because of the witness than his opponent. "What was Ms. Balaguer's reaction to these calls from her former husband?"

A puzzled frown that was too cute for words. "Well, like I told you—sorry, Your Honor—like I '*tes*tified' before, she was real upset, crying and all?"

"And what would you do?"

"Well, I'd try to comfort her, naturally."

Shel felt like a heel, and Maynard shot him a glance that said he deserved to. The bacon, lettuce, and tomato sandwich from lunch stirred a little in Shel's stomach.

"What I meant was, did you continue to put such calls through to Ms. Balaguer?"

"Oh, sorry. No sir, I began telling him he couldn't speak with her no—anymore." A brave smile now. "He'd get mad, and then he'd call again, trying to change his voice? But I stood up to him."

Maynard actually beamed at the woman, and Shel's BLT flopped like a fish behind his belt buckle.

Can't quit now, though. "Ms. Inch, during the time you worked with Ms. Balaguer, did you ever see bruises or other wounds on her?"

"Objection. Leading the witness."

"I agree, Mr. Seagraves, but I'll allow it. However, Mr. Gold, a little more care in the phrasing of your questions, please?"

"Sorry, Your Honor. Ms. Inch?"

"Yessir. She'd come to the office with sunglasses on cloudy days, with long sleeves on real hot ones. And I did see the bruising, like somebody was beating on her?"

Seagraves started to rise, but Shel watched Maynard just wave him back down.

Okay, now for the counterpunch. "Ms. Inch, were there any problems Ms. Balaguer had *on* the job?"

The puzzled frown again, and more unsteadiness in Shel's stomach.

He added, "Regarding a potential claim she might have had?"

Deeper puzzlement on the face of the short woman in

front of him. "Claim? You mean like for *in*surance?"

"No, Ms. Inch. Having to do with her employment at Stover-Trent."

"I'm sorry, sir. I just don't get what you mean?"

Now the BLT hopped on a roller coaster. "Did Ms. Balaguer ever make a claim against one of her bosses at the agency?"

"Objection, Your Honor. He's still leading his own witness."

"Your Honor," said Shel, "I'm just trying to refresh her recollection."

"One more question along this line, then. Ms. Inch, you may answer."

"Your Honor," the small face looking earnestly up at the bench, "I surely would if I could just figure out what Mr. Gold's trying to ask me."

"Ms. Inch," said Shel, hitting the Emergency Stop on that roller coaster without much success. "Did Ms. Balaguer ever claim that one of her bosses at the agency sexually harassed her?"

Lurlene Inch literally reeled back from his words. "Of course not!"

Admit it: You're croaked. "Do you recall telling a Ms. Billie Sunday of my office that Stover-Trent paid ten thousand dollars in cash to Ms. Balaguer on the afternoon she returned from jury—"

"Your Honor!" Seagraves slapped the palm of his hand on the prosecution table so hard that Shel could feel the vibration, even through the carpet. "Regardless of whether a jury's present, that question is totally inappropriate. He's impeaching his own wit—"

"I'm just trying to refresh her recollection, but even if I weren't, it's a prior inconsistent statement, and—"

"Enough! From both of you." Now Maynard turned to the witness stand, speaking softly, encouragingly as though to a shy child. "Ms. Inch, do you have any knowledge whatsoever of this alleged claim Ms. Balaguer is supposed to have had against Stover-Trent or one of its principals?"

"Your Honor, I'm real, *real* sorry, but I don't have any idea what Mr. Gold's talking about, or why he'd say these terrible things about the two fine gentlemen I work for."

Judge Maynard turned back from her to Shel. "I trust—Mr. Gold, I hope and pray—you had a good-faith reason for that line of questioning, because I certainly don't see it."

"Your Honor," began Shel.

"Silence." After ensuring he'd have just that, Maynard continued. "If there were a jury here, I might even entertain a motion from Mr. Seagraves for a mistrial, together with costs borne by the defense for the Commonwealth's having to retrace its steps. However, since I'm sitting as both ruler on law *and* decider of fact, that won't be necessary. And, given that I have other matters I can attend to for the balance of the afternoon, I suggest we recess now for the day. Tomorrow morning, Mr. Gold, you can resume your case as you see fit. The witness is excused, and we are adjourned."

Sheldon A. Gold noted that as Lurlene Inch stepped down off the stand, she was even smart enough not to smile at him as she walked by and down the aisle toward the doors.

a few minutes later, at the defense table in the now-empty courtroom, Mairead tried to do for Shel what she knew he'd try to do for her. "Talk about being sandbagged."

From the first row of the gallery, Pontifico Murizzi said, "Hey, no sweat. We can get Billie over here first thing in the A.M."

Blinking, Shel looked at him. "To do what, exactly?"

Mairead answered instead. "To rebut what Lurlene just did to us."

Shel turned to her, but kindly, she thought.

Rather like the judge with that young woman on the stand.

"Mairead, I call Billie as a witness, and what's Seagraves going to do?"

"Object, probably. Hearsay again."

"Hearsay *on* hearsay: I'd be offering Billie's testimony on what Lurlene Inch told her out of court about what Inch says Stover or Trent said in giving Conchita Balaguer ten thousand dollars."

"Okay," Mairead said, straining to remember the right reasoning path from her Evidence course back at New England School of Law, "but what Stover or Trent said in giving Balaguer the money would be res gestae, right? Something that explains the act of handing over the cash."

"Yes," said Shel, "but it gets worse. I'd still have to account for the level of hearsay that's Billie's testimony on what Inch told her."

"But that's a prior inconsistent statement, right?"

"Right. And as such, I could use it to impeach even my own witness if that person—here, Inch—admitted to the statement. Since she denied it, the rules of evidence probably let me offer the statement by extrinsic evidence—here, Billie—the source of the ten thousand being a material issue in the case."

"That," said the Pope, "is what I suggested, right? Billie comes over tomorrow morning."

Mairead saw Shel almost smile. "But, even if the judge allows her to testify, you both saw how Maynard bought into Inch's act up there."

Murizzi nodded toward the bench. "Lurlene just about charmed the robe off the guy."

"So," Mairead said, following all too well now, "if Billie testifies to 'tis, and Lurlene to 'tain't, the judge as decider of fact goes with their receptionist over ours."

Shel's turn to nod. "Especially since, when Billie heard the information, she was in effect acting as a spy from the defense camp."

"In a case," said the Pope, "where the question is, Did our gangster-defendant hang a juror who voted not guilty for him because of a bribe when she tried later to up the ante via blackmail."

Mairead shook her head. "But, Shel, you can't just leave things the way they are. I mean, Inch's testimony is like a dead horse lying on the floor, stinking up the place."

Mairead noticed Murizzi smiling, maybe because her comment sounded like one he'd make.

The Pope said, "Okay, I've got another suggestion."

Shel's eyebrows went up. "Which is?"

"We get to the . . . 'Nub' of the matter."

"Huh?" from Mairead, before she realized it was a "duh"-type question.

"Norris Stover," said Murizzi, "or 'Nub' for short. I serve a subpoena on the guy, and his partner, Trevor Trent, and you lead off with one of them tomorrow."

Shel pursed his lips. "And you somehow think either will give us more than Lurlene Inch did today?"

"Shel, I don't know. But, like Irish said, we've got to do something."

Mairead nodded, and when her boss said he'd rather go up to the fifteenth floor and take the heat from their client alone, she decided to wait at the defense table until he and the Pope were both gone.

Then she opened the big sample case and began sifting through the papers from the first Ben Friedman trial, looking for whatever *wasn't* there.

27

"Hello, Mr. Murizzi," said Lurlene Inch, as though it was the most natural fucking thing in the world to see him coming through the door of Stover-Trent a third time, the first being when he met her, the second being when he served a subpoena on her.

"Where's your boss?"

"Which one would—"

"Nubby would be ducky," said the Pope, in a flat, even voice.

"I'll see if Mr. Stover is available?" Lurlene picked up the telephone at her reception desk, but still gave him her sex-ray look. "Yessir, Mr. Murizzi is here to see you?... I'll tell him."

"Mr. Stover just won't be able to make time for you this afternoon. But maybe if—"

"You have any idea what the penalty is for perjury in a capital case?"

Lurlene smiled without showing any of her tiny teeth. "I believe it's... 'state prison for life or any term of years'?"

Christ, she's read the statute. We all underestimated this one, me worse than anybody. "You come clean now, tell the truth about—"

"About what, Mr. Murizzi?" The same innocent, just-trying-my-level-best expression on her face. "I can't help what your spy thought she heard me say. But cross my heart, I don't know where Chita could have gotten that ten thousand dollars."

The Pope moved up to Lurlene's desk, put his palms on the top of it, and then zoom-lensed his eyes to within six inches of hers. "I'm gonna see you in the slam, little missy. And the other inmates there are gonna eat you up."

Not even a blink. "I don't think so, Mr. Murizzi. Especially if all the guards turn out to be as cute as you are?"

The Pope turned from her and strode toward the closed door to Norris Stover's office.

From behind him, he heard Lurlene's voice say, "I'm calling the police now."

Murizzi didn't give her the satisfaction of a reply.

When he got to the door, a part of him was hoping it was locked, but the knob turned smoothly in his hand. Swinging the door open, the Pope caught a frozen tableau of Norris Stover behind his desk, Trevor Trent twisting around from the client chair in front of it.

"Two for the price of one," Murizzi said, leaving the door open.

Trent, the closer of the pair, rose first, squaring himself, at nicely over six feet, maybe four jacket sizes larger than the Pope. "Pontifico, I distinctly heard Nub tell Lurlene we were not available for you."

"I decided not to take no for an answer."

Stover now rose as well, circling around his desk. "Get out, or I'll have Lurlene call the police."

"She's a step ahead of you on that one, Nubby." Murizzi didn't reach for the documents in his back pocket as yet, figuring the open door would give him plenty of advance warning. "Now, which of you 'best and brightest' told her to lie on the stand?"

Trent folded his arms, almost bored. "We don't know what you're talking about."

"Better to have said, '*I* don't know,' Trev. Sounds a little more credible, and preserves deniability for your sorry ass when Shel Gold brings all three of you in for the next round."

"Next round of what, Pontifico, perjury?" Trent kept his arms folded, but leaned his thighs against his partner's desk, rocking a bit. "You really think a district attorney who wins a conviction against a career criminal like 'Big Ben' Friedman—based on Lurlene's exploding your theory of how Chita got her ten thousand dollars—is then going to prosecute his star witness for lying under oath?"

Give the dickhead credit, he's slick enough. "The money had to come from someplace."

"Why not ask Chita's bank, then? That's where she deposited it."

These guys somehow had the cash on hand, maybe from skimming premiums. Stashed in a safe-deposit box, or under their fucking mattresses. But it wasn't going to be traceable, Murizzi'd bet his pension on that.

Stover said, "Last chance to get out before we have you arrested."

The Pope said, "Your partner here's always been the star, am I right, Nubby? You took forearm shivers to the face mask pulling for his option passes so he could get the press and impress the girls while you were still wiggling loose teeth and scraping snot and mud out of your nose. Well, now's your chance to square accounts, one fell swoop. Roll on him about this now, and there's maybe a chance you and Lurlene can stay out of the can."

"Murizzi," said Trent now, unfazed as ever. "You cannot prove that ridiculous fable about one of us sexually harassing Chita, and you cannot prove that we were the source of the money she deposited that day. And, even if you could," glancing toward his partner, "do you *really* believe that a friendship going back twenty-five years to an Ivy League institution would founder on the allegations of an overweight black mole you planted in our midst?"

The Pope looked from one to the other, then heard the front door to the agency open behind him. Taking out the two separate but nearly identical papers from his back pocket, he said, "Maybe I can't prove it, but Shel Gold has a knack for showing pompous turds like you wrong about most things."

Trent huffed out an affected sigh. "We had an expression back at Dartmouth that rather captured the way Nub and I feel right now."

"I'll bite," said the Pope, moving forward and extending the subpoenas.

"Fuck you," chanted both the assholes in unison as the Pope served them without resistance before hearing a whiskey-soaked male voice over his shoulder say, "All right, everybody just hold it right there."

billie Sunday could tell something was weighing heavy on Shel as he came back into the office suite so early in the afternoon, but she thought it might be better to broach it indirectly. "Where's Mairead?"

"Off on a frolic of her own."

"Say what?"

The aggravating man shrugged out of his suit jacket as he shuffled toward his office. "Old expression in personal injury cases. If an employee injured somebody, and the somebody sued the employer, the defense would be that the employee was 'off on a frolic of his own,' meaning something that the employer shouldn't be responsible for."

"Shel?"

"Yes."

"You all right in the head?"

"Bad day." He stopped, then turned back to her. "An hour ago, Lurlene Inch testified that she didn't know how Conchita Balaguer got that ten thousand dollars."

Billie wanted to say something, then decided to let Shel finish first.

He shook his head. "When I confronted her with what she told you, she denied ever discussing sexual harassment or a settlement thereof."

"She's lying," Billie's initial assessment of the woman at

Stover-Trent storming back with an "I told you so" look on its face.

"I know she is, but the damage is done."

"Well, let's undo it, then. Put me on the stand tomorrow."

A nod. "I'm considering it. Before I do, though, a couple of questions now?"

"Ask them."

"You were going through a rough patch with Matthew, right?"

"Right."

"Could that have . . . distracted you in any way?"

Billie tried to keep the emotion she was really feeling out of her voice. "No."

"You're sure of what Lurlene Inch told you about the claim and the cash?"

"Absolutely."

"Then I may call you, unless something else shakes loose."

"Like what?"

"The Pope is serving subpoenas on Stover and Trent both, but his real mission is to try to drive a wedge between them."

"Get the one to turn on the other."

"Exactly. If that's successful, I may not need you. If it isn't . . ."

"It'll be my word against their three."

"And so I have to be sure what ammunition I've really got."

Billie thought back to something Robert Senior would have said. "Locked and loaded, Shel."

"Thanks, Billie. And I'm sorry it's come to this."

"Couldn't be helped."

As Shel went into his office, Billie turned back to her Selectric III. Not so much to type as to buy some time, let the bile in her throat go back down before it triggered tears.

Tears over what Shel's little talk implied. Oh, Billie knew what her boss felt he had to do: Be sure how one of your witnesses was going to answer before you asked a question on the stand. That was only good lawyer sense.

Problem is, Billie Sunday felt more than a bit hurt that, after she'd already told Shel what she'd heard at Stover-Trent, her boss still thought he had to go through the routine he'd use on a witness off the street with a woman who'd worked for him lo these fifteen years.

"mademoiselle, you have the number address you want?"

Mairead O'Clare sat in the rear seat of the taxi, the black driver—even without turning his head—speaking very clear English with what sounded like a French accent.

"One-eight-seven."

"Mercí."

As she debated fastening her seat beat, it still bothered Mairead that Tanya Vukonova seemed more sincerely upset over testimony in the Balaguer trial than when she more theatrically gushed her grief in the first trial involving her own son's death. Shel, because of his own tragedies, had kind of a blind spot about that, but still, it was something that should be checked out.

Which Mairead had spent a quiet two hours in the empty courtroom number 10 doing. Recalling the end of the first Friedman trial, when the verdict was announced and Vadim Vukonov went ballistic. Trying to attack their client, making a mess of the defense table, and even throwing and kicking a sheaf of papers down the aisle as he was forcibly escorted from the courtroom.

Which in turn meant that sheaf—whatever it was—had to be missing from their files. But after searching for the "negative needle in the haystack," Mairead couldn't remember anything having been in the file pre-verdict that wasn't there now.

Until she began cataloging all the papers Shel and she hadn't generated themselves. Police incident reports, autopsy results, motions from the prosecutor.

Juror questionnaires from the court system?

No, they had to be returned to—wait a minute. What about my notes on them?

Mairead went through the file quickly, then twice more slowly. Her notes had been stapled into a "sheaf," and they were gone. She began to connect the dots.

Vadim Vukonov believes he's been cheated by a corrupted system, thanks to Conchita Balaguer seeming to play visual "footsie" with the defense table from the jury box. The grieving and frustrated father grabs a sheaf of papers containing the jurors' names and neighborhoods. And Detective Jorie Tully told Mairead that night at Balaguer's house that the dead woman was reachable via Directory Assistance, including a residential address to... visit.

However, Mairead also knew the rules of professional conduct for attorneys prohibited contacting the Vukonovs personally once they were represented by counsel, here Gallina Ekarevskaya. A "stakeout," like the police did on Big Ben Friedman's house, therefore made more sense. But the Pope—the most capable surveillance person—had already been stuck with sitting on Rigoberto Balaguer for several days, and besides Shel had sent the private investigator off to serve emergency subpoenas on Stover and Trent for the following morning of court, when Billie herself might also have to testify.

Which leaves you, young lady.

Mairead had stopped at her apartment first, changing from court clothes to jeans, running shoes—the ankle still feeling recovered—and a baseball cap to mask some of what she knew to be her eye-catching hair. Mairead also wore a long-sleeved T-shirt to cover most of the hemangioma and a softball glove to hide even more, the other hand in her pocket. On a whim, she picked up an old aluminum bat buried in the back of her closet. Mairead figured that, with all the college students in Brighton, one more waiting forlornly for her ride to the game wouldn't make her stand out very much across from the butcher shop.

"Mademoiselle?"

Mairead shook her head. "Yes?"

The driver was glancing repeatedly into the rearview mirror. "Is there a reason why someone should be following us to your baseball match?"

Shit. "Not a good one. Are you sure?"

"I grew up in Haiti," the voice said, lilting upward on the second syllable. "Believe me when I tell you I know about people following others."

Mairead decided not to turn and look, as that might tip the tail that they were alerted. "Can you describe who it is?"

"A man, I think," a glance into the mirror. "But the sunlight shines just wrong on his windshield."

"Can you lose him?"

Now the head twisted around, only a few snaggled teeth left in the mouth of the now clearly older man. "As I tell you, I grew up in Haiti, and evading followers is one thing we learn very early and very well."

Mairead thought her driver did a fine job of slowing for two yellow lights before jumping the third and making a left turn onto a southbound street diagonally away from her stated destination. Three more turns on residential blocks, and the cabbie backed into an alley to wait and watch the traffic go by its mouth.

After a few minutes, he said, "I have not seen your admirer."

"Thanks. Can you take me to the address now?"

"Directly."

After the cab dropped her off a block away from the butcher shop, Mairead did a little concentric-square scouting of the area. Far fewer college-looking kids than she would have guessed. More people wearing clothes that looked foreign-made, the tailoring noticeably different. More older women, too, speaking what she guessed to be Russian or similar languages, many of the small shops having unreadable signs in Cyrillic lettering under their English ones.

You may not blend in quite as perfectly as you thought, young lady.

Mairead went back to the butcher shop's block, then waited for two older men to leave a bench and walk toward a café. She took the bench, lounging with her arms draped over the back slats, both to look relaxedly bored and to shield the hemangioma on her non-gloved hand.

Mairead watched the ebb and flow of the shop's customers, many standing around on the sidewalk to talk. Tanya Vukonova exited once, helping a very elderly woman carry a small package a block to an apartment building before returning to the shop's doorway. Surprisingly, Vukonova then scanned the street, like she was looking for somebody.

Or, young lady, as though she was making sure the coast was clear.

Mairead nodded, keeping the peak of her ball cap as low as possible to shield her face yet still allow her to monitor Vukonova's movements.

Then the mother just went back into the shop.

Now, what was that all about?

Mairead might have spent a good long time wondering had she not caught in her peripheral vision two people walking out from the alley behind the store. Frankly, without seeing Mrs. Vukonova escort the elderly woman just minutes before, Mairead might not have recognized the grieving mother's gait.

Especially when it seemed to quicken as Tanya Vukonova walked hand-in-hand with the bearish man beside her who was unmistakable, even though Mairead could see only the back of Vadim Vukonov's head.

Choose, young lady: the shop or its owners.

Mairead grabbed her bat, stood up from the bench, and began to follow them.

28

After Shel Gold listened to Pontifico Murizzi's account of serving Stover and Trent, the lawyer stayed seated at his desk, saying, "We're lucky you weren't arrested for trespass."

"One of the uniforms remembered me from the old days."

Shel clasped his hands together on the ancient blotter in front of him. "So you figure these people will stonewall it all the way?"

"Sounds like. Nub and Trev made a point of telling me again how far they went back, and we've got about as much chance of breaking Lurlene as the Watergate scandal did G. Gordon Liddy."

"Tell me about it." Shel searched for a ray of sunshine. "Will the two insurance moguls at least come across as jerks to a judge?"

"They're Ivy Leaguers, Shel—no offense meant."

"None taken."

"If I were you, I'd be weighing what the three of us talked about in that empty courtroom a couple hours ago. You've got two middle-aged, white-collar white guys and Lurlene—the fucking apple of Judge Maynard's eye—against one middle-aged, single mother of three, black like His Honor but a defense employee who infiltrated an apparently legit business."

Shel couldn't dispute the blunt pessimism. "At least Keith Maynard is a pretty straight shooter."

"For a judge, anyway. But it's still three against one, with no paper trail backing up our version of the ten thousand."

Admit it: The man's right, and it's just a question of where His Honor hears the lie coming from.

Although, at that moment, Shel Gold thought a better question might be: What's Mairead up to?

the Vukonovs stopped at a small house near a park and climbed the stoop. From her constant half-a-block-away, Mairead stopped to undo and retie her shoelaces. The door of the house was opened by a slight, blond man—no, virtually platinum—with a small boy, identical hair. Vadim Vukonov tousled the boy's hair, and Tanya bent down to give him a big hug. Then the four of them went back down the stoop, a soccer ball cradled between the platinum man's elbow and hip.

At the sidewalk, they turned and headed for the park.

Mairead trailed after them, passing through a parking area ringed by tall and large-crowned poplar trees. What looked like a pickup soccer game was in progress on the left about fifty yards into the expanse of grass, and the platinum man even waved to some of the participants. However, the foursome continued deeper into the open green space, finally stopping near a small stand of hemlocks that provided an irregular shield from the baseball diamond beyond it.

Two softball teams wearing contrasting jerseys and billed caps warmed up with infield drills and fungoes. Over the foreign-language shouts from the competing—and much closer—soccer game, Mairead got an occasional "Atta boy," or "Way to peg it home." To maintain her cover, she began walking toward the diamond, keeping the soccer field to her left, and the foursome to her right and in front.

Vadim Vukonov and the platinum man began kicking

the soccer ball back and forth, quickly getting fancy at it. Then they began to include the boy, making a triangle of the game while Tanya Vukonova sat near one of the evergreens and called out encouragement in what Mairead assumed to be Russian. Drawing somewhat closer to the three playing foot-catch, she could see the men—especially Platinum—were more talented, but the boy, around nine, was much quicker, almost hyperactive in moving for the ball.

Mairead stopped to try her shoelace routine again. All four were snapping off quick phrases in Russian, the boy babbling excitedly. Even the Vukonovs, who in the courtroom had never exhibited anything but grief—staged or sincere—were beaming, this interlude with the other man and probably his son maybe providing a little break from their own private hell over Yuri.

And suddenly, Mairead felt very, very ashamed. Never having had parents herself, she realized that, during the trial, she'd not really empathized with the Vukonovs over losing a child.

Which is understandable, young lady. You saw these poor people as a threat to your client, whom they mistakenly believed had killed their son.

Yeah, but it doesn't make me feel any better now, spying on them during the one time they might feel normal again.

Mairead began to angle away from the foursome now, more toward the soccer game, figuring to continue on toward the baseball diamond, then just circle around and leave the park altogether. As she drew even with the boy, who had rotated position in the game to be closest to her, she noticed how truly silvery his hair and even his eyebrows were. Like a little old man, or even somebody who dyed—

Mairead stopped short, maybe fifty feet from the boy. Jesus Mary. Could that be it?

Horrible, young lady. Even just to contemplate.

But only one way to be sure.

* * *

billie Sunday watched that spooky Pontifico Murizzi walk out the suite door after saying good-bye to her. Then she felt more than heard Shel behind her.

Without turning, she said, "So, when do I testify?"

"Tomorrow morning, unless Mairead's come up with a better idea."

"And just what is she supposed to be working on during this 'frolic of her own'?" said Billie Sunday.

mairead waited until the boy turned with his back to her, preparing to kick the soccer ball. As soon as it left his foot, she cried out, "Yuri!"

"Dah?" said the boy, spinning toward her with a bright smile that disappeared as soon as Vadim Vukonov roared behind him. Mairead looked from the resurrected boy to his father and the platinum man, both now sprinting toward her, fury in their expressions.

Safety in numbers, young lady.

Mairead turned and ran herself toward the nearest crowd, the soccer game.

She was about to yell for help when, behind her, a deep voice filled with laughter and Russian words began yelling instead.

The closest soccer players turned first, then laughed also and began to run after their own ball, which had been passed upfield and away from Mairead.

"Help! These men are after me!"

The last player chasing the ball also turned briefly, but at some more joking Russian from behind her, he just laughed again and waved before joining the chase in his own game.

Mr. Vukonov has them convinced you're just playing tag or some other—

Mairead veered, slinging off her glove but keeping the

bat as a weapon. If needed. After all, she was well conditioned from hockey and jogging, so unless one of these guys was a track star...

Mairead twisted her head around once, Platinum gaining on her. Vadim Vukonov was running a surprisingly strong third, his wife clutching Yuri and receding into the background.

Which is when Mairead felt her right big toe stub itself into an irregularity of sod that gave only grudgingly. She flew forward, sprawling onto the grass and losing her grip on the bat as she impacted the ground. Scrambling back to her feet, she thanked God her left ankle still felt fine and grabbed for her bat. Whirling around, Mairead saw Platinum just ten feet away, Vukonov hard behind him.

And both now had knives in their hands.

For all Mr. Vukonov's strength as a butcher, young lady, the other may be the one to mind.

Platinum faked a thrust, then jumped back with the agility of a leopard when Mairead swung her bat. As Vukonov arrived, chest heaving, Platinum grinned malevolently, growling something in Russian to him. Vukonov's eyes blazed as he answered.

Mairead tried to bluff her way into command. "Give it up, Mr. Vukonov. You and your friend don't have a chance of getting away with this."

"You think..." Vukonov said, gasping for breath in ragged gulps, "I give up...now? Just because you..."

"I've seen Yuri. He's alive. Your plan is finished."

"Not finished...Just almost...complete, eh?" Then one word in Russian to his friend, maybe the man's name.

Platinum nodded once and grinned some more. Then he began to circle around Mairead, both hands below his waist, the one holding the knife back nearer his hip, the other hand flat and palm down but extended, as though hoping to parry a swing of the bat.

Platinum looked awfully professional.

He'll come in from below, young lady, because the hu-

man body is well armored from above. So don't use your bat as in softball: Use it more like a bayonet, to ward off the blade, perhaps jab the man in the face or solar plexus.

Except the aluminum bat was shorter than a rifle, and, worse, Mairead could feel Vukonov begin to circle around her from the other side.

You can't let either of them get behind you.

Mairead kept backing up, trying to keep both men in sight. But it was two cats against one mouse, and she had nothing but open field everywhere and therefore no way to protect herself against attack from the rear.

Then Platinum suddenly lunged for her. She parried the open hand away, but as she went to jab him, he slid, like a runner stealing second base. Though soccer hadn't been her favorite sport, she recognized the tackle technique, getting her front foot just out of the way but having her back foot knocked out from under her.

And she went down, hard on her back, the wind whooshing out of her lungs.

She managed to lever up on an elbow as Platinum, now standing straight, disdainfully kicked her bat a good ten feet from Mairead's other hand. He muttered something in Russian to Vukonov, who pressed his foot hard onto Mairead's other wrist, pinning it painfully to the ground. And now both men were grinning.

"My friend says you are like . . . a lamb before the butcher," the blade of Vukonov's knife glinting as the May sun began to set.

Mairead refused to show fear. "A butcher all right. Who'd kill some other parents' child for money."

She had the feeling that Vukonov's next words in Russian were a translation of hers. Then the big man bent at the waist, and a smell came off him. The blood of a thousand dead animals.

Vukonov said, "I would kill you slowly and enjoy it, but here . . . in the public park, quick is more better."

Mairead refused to shut her eyes. If this was—

What in the world?

I see it, too, young lady.

She'd spotted the aberration in her peripheral vision. A blurry red dot that wavered on the forehead of Platinum. Then suddenly, his head just . . . exploded out behind him, his body arching to the rear like a decapitated high jumper going backward over the bar. A second later, a sound like a sharp clap of hands came from those tall poplar trees near the entrance to the park.

Mairead watched Vadim Vukonov straighten back up, glancc at his friend's body in disbelief, and then turn toward the sound. She saw another blurry dot, this one tripping up the bridge of his nose, and then a shower of black hair and yellow chips, gray jelly and red mist filled the air above her as another clap echoed in the distance. Vukonov's big body, arching liked Platinum's, now collapsed, the torso falling past Mairead, the inert, heavy legs pinning hers to the ground as his foot had her wrist.

Registering the rainbow of colors staining her clothes, Mairead also could hear, much closer, the wailing of a woman and the crying of a child.

29

Sitting in a conference room at the Suffolk County District Attorney's Office in One Bulfinch Place, Shel Gold was finding it hard to believe. Partly because there were so many people crowded into the ten-by-twenty space, but mostly because of the nightmare it conjured up for him.

This is what it would have been like if the police had ever figured out who took Richie from Natalie's carriage in that mall.

At the head of the table, and apparently in charge, was James Seagraves, Shel at the opposite end. In between on one side was a video camera, angled so as to catch Seagraves and the two Russian women, Tanya Vukonova and her lawyer, Gallina Ekarevskaya. Mairead O'Clare sat on Shel's left, a male lawyer from Worcester County next to her. The Pope stood behind Shel, and Detective Jorie Tully stood behind Seagraves. Absently, Shel wondered whether everybody who'd ever worked in the Homicide Unit preferred not to sit.

He also was relieved that Seagraves had excused young Yuri from all this.

The prosecutor checked with the video operator, who gave a mute thumbs-up. Then Seagraves said, "Ms. Ekarevskaya?"

"In exchange for the sentencing recommendation we have discussed with you, my client wishes to disclose fully to the authorities exactly what has occurred these last months."

Shel expected Seagraves to ask a follow-up question, but he didn't. Instead, the man just said, "Proceed."

Ekarevskaya turned to her client, laid a hand gently on the woman's forearm, and said, "Tell them what happened, Tanya."

Vukonova nodded, already tearing up. "My husband is part of mafia in our town near Moscow. He and I come to this country because Vadim is told of great opportunity here to make money. First, you work inside the law, and then outside it. But when we open the butcher shop, we do not do so well. Then, in February, other men from Russia tell us that a customer—Mr. Friedman—is a very rich gangster here. Vadim and his friend Artyom decide they maybe can . . . take some of Mr. Friedman's money."

Vukonova said something in Russian to Ekarevskaya, who produced a handkerchief for her.

Even so, Seagraves said, "I'm sorry, but no more communications in anything but English, please."

Ekarevskaya shot daggers at him, which somewhat relieved Shel of what he himself had been afraid Seagraves hadn't asked at the beginning of the videotaped session.

Vukonova sniffled into the hankie, then went on. "Vadim and Artyom go in Artyom's car many miles away—to a small town in the county of Worcester—and there they watch for . . . a boy who looks like my Yuri. Then they steal him and hold for two days, so the boy's parents will not—"

Again to the hankie, and Shel found himself choking up as well, though not for Tanya Vukonova.

The male lawyer next to Mairead spoke for the first time since the introduction. "You kidnapped my clients' son to substitute for your own as a victim?"

"*Dah*—yes. I am sorry, but yes. Vadim and Artyom think by waiting some days, the boy's parents will not see any connection between the two things. Then Vadim tells our Yuri he must hide from some bad people. My husband takes the other boy, and Artyom knocks him out, so he is... asleep. Then Artyom... he borrows a different car, and... runs over the boy behind our shop. Vadim makes me... makes me take the boy in my arms and tell the police when they come that it is my Yuri. Then we say about Mr. Friedman making the threats to us three days before."

Seagraves held up his hand. "Why didn't you just identify the driver as Mr. Friedman, or one of his men?"

"We did not know—" Vukonova shot one word in Russian to Ekarevskaya, who answered, "Alibi," before the prosecutor could object.

Vukonova said, "Yes, we did not know if Mr. Friedman or his men would have the alibi for the time of the... accident, so we are not sure about the driver. Or the car."

"A better question," from the lawyer for the dead boy's family, "would be how the police department and prosecutor's office could have not discovered this from the start?"

Silently, Shel agreed with him.

Seagraves said, "Detective Tully?"

"There were no fingerprints of your clients' son on file." She nibbled at her lower lip. "I admit Homicide didn't know that then, but I've checked since. The FBI's data banks did have the usual information about height, weight, hair color, and so on. And his photos were everywhere, including the National Center for Missing and Exploited Children's website. But our decedent's skull was crushed, so photos—even dental records—wouldn't have helped. Mrs. Vukonova here identified the body we found in that alley as her son's, saying she'd seen him struck on his bicycle by the car. When the first uniforms arrived, she was... cradling the corpse in her arms." Even Tully, Shel noticed, had to take a breath on that one. "There was no question of an incorrect identification in our minds."

The male lawyer closed his eyes and shook his head, Shel feeling beyond him to the parents the man represented.

Seagraves moved on. "So, Mr. Friedman is indicted, and you expect a guilty verdict, allowing you to sue more easily civilly and get a large judgment—or settlement—from him."

Vukonova looked to Ekarevskaya, who nodded. Her client nodded back to Seagraves.

"But then," continued the prosecutor, "the first trial ends in acquittal, so your husband . . . ?"

"Vadim is mad more than I ever see him before. He says to me, 'That Jew gangster corrupts the juror who is always staring at his table.' Vadim attacks Mr. Friedman in the courtroom, but comes away with some jury information, out in the hall. In this rage, Vadim and Artyom take rope that day and go to her house. They come back, and drink vodka all night. They . . . celebrate, like it is a holiday. But, to make the story seem better, Vadim attacks Mr. Gold in his office, to play the sad and angry father."

Admit it: You were so close to the man's apparent situation, you didn't spot the act.

Vukonova dropped her chin to her chest. "Vadim and Artyom think Mr. Friedman will be blamed for the juror, and they are correct. On the television, we see he will come back from Florida for second trial, and then they believe that we should begin lawsuit against him, so we tell our lawyer, Gallina, to start."

Shel noticed Ekarevskaya glancing toward him. You can reveal my lie or not, she seemed to convey. Shel engaged her eyes, then barely shook his head in the negative.

Vukonova appeared to miss their exchange. "So, the second trial begins, and we still play our roles, like to see the Jew gangster again in your court. But we are not really a part of this, so Vadim thinks it is safe for us now to see Yuri, who is changed in his haircut and color and stays with Artyom in his house. Yuri wants very much to go outside, play like other boys, so we do that. At first, just in the yard behind Artyom's house. But the yard is so small, Yuri says to his father, 'Can we go to the park?' And we all do, once, twice, with no problems. But when we go today, this lawyer with the strange hands . . ."

Shel felt Mairead stiffen a little, but not say a word.

"... she calls out my Yuri's name, and Vadim now knows all is loss to us if she escapes. So my husband and Artyom go after her. I am afraid they will kill her, too, but then... then..."

Vukonova began to sob, uncontrollably to Shel's mind, though Seagraves let her go a full thirty seconds before finally saying, "Maybe we should suspend for a while."

"One question first?" said Shel, sensing Mairead almost jump beside him.

He spoke to Seagraves, but watched Ekarevskaya from the corner of his eye. When she nodded, Shel spoke again.

"Ms. Vukonova, did your attorney, Ms. Ekarevskaya, know *anything* about what your husband and his friend were planning or had done?"

"No!" Vukonova now clutching the hankie in her fist like something she herself was trying to crush. "Oh, no. Vadim does not trust lawyers here. He is afraid our Gallina will not help us, maybe tell police on us, even."

Shel nodded, watching Gallina Ekarevskaya blink twice, but otherwise show nothing.

pontifico Murizzi waited outside the conference room, having pried from Jorie Tully that both Big Ben Friedman and Edsel Crow were being brought to the DA's office for their unconditional release. Mairead came out of the room next.

Murizzi said to her, "You okay?"

"Better than a few hours ago."

"That's a healthy enough answer." Then he heard a door and glanced in that direction. "Here comes Al Capone and Baby Face Nelson."

The Pope noticed Mairead straighten up a little, like—despite what she'd just been through—she didn't want to show even client-criminals any weakness.

When Friedman got close enough, he said, "I got to thank you again, my Golden Boy's Wild Irish Rose."

"It's still Mairead."

Friedman shook his head, rubbing his wrists where Murizzi figured the recent shackles probably still chafed. "It's good to be tough, but when you're not tough enough, it's even better to have family around you."

"Family," said Mairead, tonelessly.

Edsel Crow inclined his head a degree toward his boss. "Mr. Friedman told me to treat you like family. With him in the slam, and Ms. Bomberg and Mr. Calcagni in Florida, I didn't have anybody else to protect." Then Crow grinned. "Lucky for you I stuck with it after that cabbie of yours lost me. I don't spot your ball cap and bat walking into that park, I'd never have been up a tree in time to ace those Russians before they filleted you."

The Pope thought back to Crow's attitude on the witness stand. The guy talks freely only about stuff he enjoys, like killing people.

But then Mairead surprised Murizzi. "You're right, Mr. Crow. I won't say it doesn't bother me, but I have to thank you. Both of you. And I do."

And then Irish walked away without another word, which struck Pontifico Murizzi as a genuine touch of class.

mairead went straight home to the Beacon Hill apartment, but the prospect of sitting in a little room, even if it was her own nest, didn't have much appeal. In fact, being inside, period, seemed almost unbearable.

Well, young lady, you can always go for a jog.

Her toe still hurt from stubbing it in the park, and she didn't want to stress out her finally pain-free ankle either. So instead Mairead put on a T-shirt and clean jeans over sandals that would let her foot move without much restriction. Then, getting an idea, she pulled a cotton sweater from its drawer in her bureau.

The closer Mairead got to the waterfront, the cooler the air became, making her glad she'd brought the sweater. As she reached the seafood restaurant beside Pontifico Murizzi's marina, she looked carefully toward his dock first, to make sure he didn't have...company. But then Mairead noticed that she could see the back deck of his boat pretty clearly, and that's when she realized that the big sailboat Jocko seemed to live on was gone.

I wonder, young lady.

Mairead went into the restaurant and talked with the barmaid, who said, "The Pope? Sure, I know him." Then Mairead made the request, adding a tip of ten dollars to the tab.

Wrapping her sweater around the bottle of red wine as the barmaid requested, Mairead went back outside and down the pedestrian ramp to the floating dock. She walked along it, making sure that Murizzi's boat wasn't making any funny movements that might mean he was... entertaining.

At the Pope's stern, Mairead said, "Hey, permission to come aboard?"

The sliding glass door opened, the Pope in T-shirt and shorts himself. Mairead remembered him once telling her he never got cold, so she didn't mind suggesting he come out on deck.

"What's in your sweater?" he said, moving past the two resin chairs and the matching table to where she stood on the dock, his eyes looking a little sad, Mairead thought.

She slipped the bottle out. "I thought maybe we could sit on the deck, share some more wine."

The Pope didn't say anything for a minute. "Not too chilly for you?"

Mairead held up her sweater, wiggling it a bit.

Another pause. *Or maybe hesitation, young lady*?

"Okay," he finally said. "I'll be right back."

As she climbed over the gunwale, the Pope disappeared into the cabin. He reemerged with two glasses and a fancy corkscrew. When Mairead handed him the bottle, Murizzi looked at the label and said, "Maybe you learned something in law school after all."

The cork was popped, and the Pope poured a little wine

into each glass, then swished the liquid before pitching it overboard.

He said, "Something I learned." Murizzi poured again, then angled his fuller glass toward the empty slip next door. "From Jocko."

"But where's his sailboat?"

The Pope smiled, but Mairead thought his eyes couldn't help his lips bring it off. "Plying the deep blue sea. Mediterranean, he said."

She nodded once, and then, as they sat down, made a decision. "Last time we drank wine together, I told you about me and the orphanage."

"I remember," said Murizzi, "though I'm kind of surprised you do."

Implying, young lady, that you were a bit deep in your cups.

Mairead decided not to let that stop her. "So, what's good for the goose . . . ?"

The Pope just looked at her.

She said, "What I mean is, was it tough for you, being a cop and gay?"

His expression changed radically, and for just a second, Mairead wasn't sure if he was going to reply, throw his wine in her face, or toss her overboard like the first ounce.

Then Pontifico Murizzi said, "Tell you the truth, Irish, it was a lot tougher being Italian and gay."

At which point, Mairead O'Clare thought they both sensed that it was okay to laugh for real.

Terry Devane is the pseudonym of an attorney and award-winning novelist who lives in Boston. Learn more about the author and the books at www.terrydevane.com.